MARY DAHEIM

THE ALPINE RECLUSE

An Emma Lord Mystery

Look for these exciting Emma Lord mysteries by Mary Daheim:

THE ALPINE ADVOCATE
THE ALPINE BETRAYAL
THE ALPINE CHRISTMAS
THE ALPINE DECOY
THE ALPINE ESCAPE
THE ALPINE FURY
THE ALPINE GAMBLE
THE ALPINE HERO
THE ALPINE ICON
THE ALPINE JOURNEY
THE ALPINE KINDRED
THE ALPINE LEGACY
THE ALPINE MENACE
THE ALPINE NEMESIS
THE ALPINE OBITUARY
THE ALPINE PURSUIT
THE ALPINE QUILT
THE ALPINE SCANDAL

Ballantine / Del Rey /
Presidio Press /
One World

ISBN 978-0-345-46815-4

U.S.A. $6.99 CANADA $8.99

S EAN

Praise for Mary Daheim
and *The Alpine Recluse*

"Daheim is back with another entertaining entry in her long-running Alpine series. . . . [*The Alpine Recluse*] winningly depicts life in a small town in Washington's Cascade Mountains."
—Booklist

"This is an excellent cozy mystery. It has all the ingredients to make it a success. . . . You will want to go back and read the other 'Alpine' books by Mary Daheim."
—Mysteries Galore

"Mary Daheim writes with wit, wisdom, and a big heart. I love her books."
—CAROLYN HART

"Eccentric and interesting characters, a thoughtfully drawn puzzle, and wonderful local color explain why the Emma Lord series is so popular with cozy mystery readers."
—Internet Writing Journal

"Highly recommended . . . Daheim readers will be awarded with great multigenerational characters to pull you into the story and make you realize what good mystery writing is all about."
—I Love a Mystery

"*The Alpine Recluse* is a fabulous Emma Lord journalistic police procedural tale. The story line is action-packed. . . . Fans of the series will appreciate Mary Daheim's hot thriller."
—HARRIET KLAUSNER

"Daheim's series about murder and mayhem in a small town might make you look at your neighbors a little differently. Always entertaining."
—Crime by Collins

By Mary Daheim

THE ALPINE ADVOCATE
THE ALPINE BETRAYAL
THE ALPINE CHRISTMAS
THE ALPINE DECOY
THE ALPINE ESCAPE
THE ALPINE FURY
THE ALPINE GAMBLE
THE ALPINE HERO
THE ALPINE ICON
THE ALPINE JOURNEY
THE ALPINE KINDRED
THE ALPINE LEGACY
THE ALPINE MENACE
THE ALPINE NEMESIS
THE ALPINE OBITUARY
THE ALPINE PURSUIT
THE ALPINE QUILT
THE ALPINE RECLUSE
THE ALPINE SCANDAL

THE
ALPINE
RECLUSE

An Emma Lord Mystery

MARY DAHEIM

BALLANTINE BOOKS • NEW YORK

2007 Ballantine Books Mass Market Edition

Copyright © 2006 by Mary Daheim
Excerpt from *The Alpine Scandal* copyright © 2007 by Mary Daheim

Published in the United States by Ballantine Books, an imprint of The Random House Publishing Group, a division of Random House, Inc., New York.

BALLANTINE and colophon are registered trademarks of Random House, Inc.

This book contains an excerpt from the forthcoming book *The Alpine Scandal* by Mary Daheim. This excerpt has been set for this edition only and may not reflect the final content of the forthcoming edition.

Originally published in hardcover in the United States by Ballantine Books, an imprint of The Random House Publishing Group, a division of Random House, Inc., in 2006.

ISBN 978-0-345-46815-4

Cover illustration: Peter Thorpe

Printed in the United States of America

www.ballantinebooks.com

OPM   9   8   7   6   5   4   3   2   1

For Maureen Moran—in gratitude for over twenty-five years of professional and personal support. You are my valued friend and ally, an unfailing source of humor, intellect, and compassion.

Chapter One

IF I WANTED to be hot," I said to Leo Walsh, "I'd go to hell in a handcart. There's no reason why it should be ninety-four degrees in Alpine, even in August."

Leo gave me his off-center grin. "You could always take a couple of weeks off and visit Adam in Alaska. I'll bet it's not ninety-four at St. Mary's Igloo."

"I'll bet it isn't, either," I grumbled from across the desk in the cubbyhole that was my office but felt more like a pizza oven even at eleven in the morning. To think I was sorry for my son, Adam, when his first assignment as a priest sent him up to the Frozen North. Now I envy him. "When will it ever rain? Everything is tinder-dry, Leo. It's a wonder the woods don't explode."

"They did," my ad manager said in his usual wry manner. "Or haven't you been checking the AP wire this morning?"

"I have," I retorted. "I mean *all* the woods, not the ones burning up in eastern Washington and other parts of the West. Grass fires, too. Not to mention that water and power rates are going to skyrocket because we haven't had enough rain, let alone snow."

"Why don't you write an editorial taking a tough stand against hot weather?" Leo inquired reasonably. "Maybe you can change it."

I glared at him. "That's not funny. Nothing's funny in this heat."

"Come on, Emma," Leo said, no longer smiling. "At least western Washington's not humid like the Midwest or the eastern seaboard. Dry heat's not as bad. I worked on a newspaper in Palm Desert where it was over a hundred and twenty degrees for a week."

"No wonder you drank," I snarled. "Besides, people from southern California deserve to be hot. Native Pacific Northwesterners like me don't."

Leo took no offense at my remark. We'd known each other too long and too well not to be able to speak candidly. He merely sighed. His well-worn face showed the ravages of his former bouts with the bottle. In my heat-crazed state, I decided that he'd also spent too much time in the sun. "Mad dogs and Californians . . . ," I muttered.

"Quit bitching and just look at the ad layout," Leo finally said, tapping the Grocery Basket's mock-up on my desk. "Jake O'Toole went over it with a fine-toothed thesaurus. What gets into that guy, wanting to use all those big words that half the time aren't what he really means?"

"Heat," I said. "He's a native, too."

"Knock it off," Leo retorted, temporarily forgetting that I was the boss. "Jake's been doing it forever when he talks, but he started in with the grocery ads back in April. *Unsullied* for fresh tomatoes? *Temperate* for tender pork chops? *Unskeletal* for boneless chicken breasts? I'm not even sure *unskeletal* is a word."

At last, I scanned the layout. "You're right. It's stupid. Jake should stop trying to show off, especially when he doesn't know what he's talking about. It might be a midlife crisis. Maybe I'll talk to Betsy. His wife's a sensible woman."

"Go for it," Leo urged, standing up. "I'm changing this damned thing." He cocked his head. "With your approval, of course."

"Of course." Leo knew he didn't need my approval, which, I suppose, was why he occasionally forgot that I was *The Alpine Advocate*'s editor and publisher. He did an excellent job, about fifty rungs above the lugubrious and lazy Ed Bronsky, a leftover ad manager from Marius Vandeventer's ownership.

"Lugubrious," I said, and managed a smile.

"Huh?" Layout in hand, Leo turned around to look back at me.

"The header for the grocery ad is 'Lazy Days of Summer.' It's a wonder Jake didn't ask you to put in *lugubrious*."

Leo grinned again. "He did—sort of. Only, he wanted to use *lubricious*."

I nodded. "He would."

"Would what?" Vida Runkel inquired. Leo made way for her semimajestic passage into my cubbyhole, then left. "Oh, goodness, it's even warmer in here than it is in the newsroom! Why didn't Kip put a vent in this low ceiling when he repaired the roof after the big storm?"

I remembered the punishing rain and windstorm of eighteen months ago with nostalgia. "Because I'm an idiot," I told my House & Home editor.

Vida, who was wearing a sleeveless red and white print dress that resembled a bedspread, eased her imposing body into one of the two visitor chairs. "Would what?" she repeated.

I recounted Leo's misadventures with Jake O'Toole.

Vida shook her head. The unruly gray curls were already damp around the edges. "Jake hasn't been himself lately," she declared. "It's much more than his pretentious—if often inaccurate—language. He and Betsy have stopped fighting in public."

"Really?" I was surprised. The O'Tooles, who had been married forever, were famous for bickering in front of other people. But in fact, they were a devoted couple who used their often heated exchanges as a sort of love-making. "Do you think they're having problems?" Vida would know. She knew everything that went on in Alpine.

She gave me a quizzical look from behind her big-framed glasses. "I don't really think so. It has more to do with the store. Staff, I'd guess. Jake's had to fire at least two of his courtesy clerks in the past month. High school students, you know, and quite irresponsible. And of course there's always Buzzy."

Buzzy was Jake's younger brother who had had a somewhat checkered career until he finally went to work for the Grocery Basket as the produce manager. "What's wrong with Buzzy now?" I asked.

"Now?" Vida pursed her lips. "I honestly don't know. It might be trouble at home with Laura. The only thing I've heard for certain is that Buzzy had a row with their peach supplier, and that he ordered Ugli fruit, which no one in Alpine would dream of eating because it's so . . . ugly. It all rotted in the bins. I was tempted to mention it in my column, but I didn't want to hurt the O'Tooles' feelings."

I was dubious. Vida didn't usually worry about hurting other people's feelings, being extremely outspoken in her criticism of fellow Alpiners. The O'Tooles, however, were big advertisers, buying a two-page color insert to compete with the regionally produced ads of their archrival, Safeway.

"Which reminds me," Vida went on, "have you a 'Scene' item? I only need two more for this week's edition."

I tried to put my heat-hazed brain to work. "Scene Around Town" was Vida's popular front-page column featuring snippets of local happenings, involving usually nonnewsworthy events such as Dutch Bamberg's lawn mower accidentally executing a hapless frog, Edna Mae Dalrymple discovering fudge smudges on a cookbook that had been returned to the local library, or Darla Puckett's zany adventures at the Home Depot's faucet fixtures section in Monroe.

"Rip Ridley's growing a beard," I finally said. "I saw him at the Alpine Mall yesterday."

Vida gaped at me. "Impossible! The high school would never allow a faculty member to have facial hair. Except," she added more softly, "for Effie Trews, but she can't help it."

"School hasn't started," I pointed out. "Rip swears he won't shave until the football team wins its first game this season."

"Oh, dear." Vida sighed. "He could end up looking like Santa Claus. Principal Freeman will make the coach shave before school starts. Which reminds me—I saw Old Nick Saturday morning. Imagine!"

For a moment, I was puzzled. "Old Nick?" Then, before Vida could respond, I remembered. "You mean that hermit who lives someplace near Sawyer Creek?"

"*Some* place," Vida said wryly. "No one has ever been certain. I don't think he's been seen in town for several years. Frankly, I thought he was dead."

Hermits weren't uncommon in the forests of western Washington. Most were harmless, though some could be dangerous. They'd fled civilization for various reasons, like monks going off to the desert. A few would show up in town a couple of times a year to buy, beg, or steal supplies. But Old Nick was rarely seen. Indeed, in all of my thirteen years of Alpine residence, I'd never sighted him.

"I'll put him in 'Scene,' " Vida declared. "That should fill up the column. Unless something more gossip-worthy comes up between now and tomorrow's deadline."

My eyes had strayed into the newsroom. "Something just came in," I groaned. "Ed Bronsky."

"Oh, dear!" Vida exclaimed. "We're trapped."

"You're not," I whispered as Ed rumbled toward my office. "Go, or else there won't be enough air in here for the three of us to breathe."

"Plenty of hot air," Vida murmured, hurriedly getting out of the chair. "Why, Ed! What a surprise! I was just leaving. So was Emma."

Bless Vida. "Bad timing," I said, forcing a smile. "Is there something you'd like to drop off, Ed?" *Like about a hundred pounds of excess weight?*

"Hey, hey, hey," Ed enthused, "it's more than a news brief. It's front-page stuff. You'd better hold up, Vida. You won't want to miss this."

Vida frowned at her watch. "I'm afraid I'll have to. I'm already running late for my eleven-thirty appointment. Emma can fill me in later." With a pitying glance in my direction, Vida exited my office in her splayfooted manner.

Ed plopped down in the chair next to the one that Vida had vacated. He was wearing a yellow tank top and khaki shorts, a most unflattering look. But the only thing that would have covered Ed's rotund form was a Quonset hut.

"Who's reporting on tonight's county commissioners' meeting?" he asked, removing a folder from his leather briefcase.

"Scott Chamoud," I replied, referring to my only news reporter. "He always does."

Ed shook his head. "You'd better do it, Emma. Huge news." He placed the folder on my desk and tapped it three times. "I'm going for a county bond issue."

"You're what?"

He shoved the folder at me, knocking some other papers off my desk. "It's all there. I'm asking the commissioners to put a bond issue for my Mr. Pig Museum on the November ballot."

I tried not to show my astonishment at Ed's gall. For

several months, he'd been talking about building a museum in honor of his self-published autobiography. "Aren't you a little late?" I asked, instead of what I was really thinking, which was *Aren't you out of your mind?*

Ed shook his balding head. "Check the state laws." He tapped the folder again. "It's all in there. It's a bond issue, not an initiative. I've done my homework." For a brief moment, a shadow of doubt crossed Ed's face. "I mean, if I missed a beat someplace, we could hold a special election next March."

Reluctantly, I opened the folder. It contained several pages of what looked like printouts from the Internet. A quick flip showed that Ed had made some notes, along with leaving various types of food stains, including a couple of watermelon seeds.

"Why?" It was a stupid question, but it was a stupid idea.

Ed looked affronted. "You don't think I'd be crazy enough to put up my own money for this, do you? My proposal can help turn Alpine into a destination place, like Disneyland."

Or the Arctic Circle. "You're serious."

Ed nodded vigorously, his three chins wagging. "You bet. I outlined the whole thing to you months ago."

"Yes." Heaven help me from having to hear him repeat his outrageous ideas.

"So," Ed continued, "since Mr. Pig will be a theme park that benefits everybody in Skykomish County, it should be up to the citizens to help pay for it. Right?"

The fortune that Ed had inherited from an aunt in the Midwest wasn't a bottomless pit. I realized that he probably couldn't afford to build any kind of viable attraction with his own money. On the other hand, Ed's original concept hadn't sounded viable—or plausible.

Ed seemed to read at least part of my mind. "I'm doing away with some of the hokey stuff. It's going to be mainly the Hog Wild rides and Family Farm Fun, just like Iowa."

It was useless to point out to Ed that he'd never lived in Iowa—though his late aunt might have been a resident. It was also pointless to remind him that his autobiography—originally entitled *Mr. Ed*—had nothing to do with pigs or farms or anything other than Ed's actual boring life in Skykomish County. A vanity press had helped him self-publish the book, and somehow, through the wonder of Japanese cartoon animation, the Bronksy family had been turned into pigs as a TV series. For one brief season, *Mr. Pig* had pranced across television screens in Japan. Fortunately, the program had sunk somewhere off the coast of Honshu.

I pretended to study a page of Ed's proposal. "Is this on the commissioners' agenda?" I asked.

Ed nodded again. "Darned tootin'. I just came away from brunch with George Engebretsen."

Brunch to Ed didn't preclude breakfast and lunch. He'd never met a meal he didn't like. "What did George say?" I inquired. "Did he think the other two commissioners would go for floating a bond issue?"

Ed winked. "They know who's got clout around here. George's up for reelection this year."

"Yes." I marveled that any of the three commissioners would seek reelection. They were all old and virtually senile. They were also usually unopposed. Being a SkyCo commissioner was a little like being elected pope: It appeared to be a lifetime job.

"So you'll be there tonight," Ed said flatly.

"Leave it to me," I said, handing the folder back to Ed.

Ed made a clicking sound with his tongue. "Gotcha. See you tonight."

I smiled.

Ed would not see me. If I had to spend a hot night, it

wasn't going to be at the county courthouse. I much preferred my little log cabin on the side of Tonga Ridge, where a cooling breeze sometimes wafted through the evergreens at the edge of my backyard.

But that was before things really started heating up in Alpine.

"Thee and me and a dog named Spree," said the voice on my answering machine at home that evening. "How about coming down for the weekend? There's a good concert at the pier."

As I turned on all the fans in the house, opened the front and back doors and several windows, I considered Rolf Fisher's offer. He hadn't mentioned concert specifics. Who doing what when? *Where* was easy; summer concerts were held on Elliott Bay's Piers 62 and 63, not far from the Pike Place Market. I changed into a shapeless cotton shift, poured Pepsi over ice, and nibbled on baby carrots pulled from the Overholt farm's rich black dirt. Rolf was probably in transit from his job at the Associated Press bureau to his condo on Seattle's Queen Anne Hill. Even though he hadn't mentioned who was performing, spending a summer evening on the water might offer a cooling effect. But it also meant looking into the setting sun while being packed in with a crowd of other sweating Puget Sounders.

Still, I'd be with Rolf. That was worth consideration. We weren't in love yet; we were still at the being-in-lust stage. And because we lived eighty-five miles apart, we'd been together less than a dozen times since our first real date the previous November.

I decided to wait until after seven to return Rolf's call. In the summer, he often worked late, helping to fill in for vacationing colleagues. Unlike some of the younger bureau staffers, Rolf didn't have to go home to a family, only to his aging mutt named Spree.

But Rolf didn't answer when I dialed his number at seven-thirty. I didn't leave a message; I'd try again closer to nine o'clock. I could have called him on his cell phone, but I didn't want to bother him if he was at work. Nor did I want to seem like a besotted teenager, tracking him down, checking his whereabouts, fretting over what he was doing and who he was doing it with.

When the phone rang an hour later, I thought it might be him. But it was Vida, and she sounded annoyed.

"I may have a hole on my page," she said crossly. "Dot and Durwood Parker aren't home."

It took me a moment to recall why the Parkers' absence was noteworthy. Or why they were newsworthy. "Oh," I finally said. "They've been on an Alaskan cruise, right?"

"The Inland Passage," Vida responded. "They got back yesterday. I swore I'd never write another Alaska cruise feature, but this was different because they ran aground. You'd think Durwood was steering the ship."

Durwood Parker was a retired pharmacist and the worst driver who'd ever lived in Alpine. Indeed, Sheriff Milo Dodge had yanked Durwood's license years ago.

"What time was your interview?" I inquired.

"Six-thirty," Vida replied. "I was invited to supper. Dot was making a Chinese chicken salad. I ran the recipe a year or so ago. It's actually quite good."

"I assume you drove to their house," I said.

"Of course. Everything was closed up, except for a window or two. Their car was gone. Naturally, Dot would've driven. But there was no note, and there's certainly not enough wind to blow anything away. So airless these days. I waited for over fifteen minutes." Vida paused for breath. "I've telephoned twice since then, but they don't answer. I'm also tempted to call the hospital to see if something happened. The Parkers aren't spring chickens, you know."

I knew. Durwood and Dot must be close to eighty. "Did you try calling their daughter?"

"Yes, I phoned Cookie a few minutes ago, but her line was busy," Vida replied. "I refuse to pay seventy-five cents to have the phone company ring me back when the line is free. That's a terrible gyp."

"Maybe they're getting forgetful," I said. "You've got until deadline tomorrow afternoon to do the interview."

"But not with Chinese chicken salad," Vida pointed out. "Dot wouldn't bother making an elaborate lunch."

That, I figured, was a sacrifice my House & Home editor would have to make in order to fill her page. I rang off, then placed another call to Rolf. Still no answer. Maybe there was breaking news in the city. I wondered how Scott was doing with the county commissioners' meeting. The old farts droned on for hours. My unfortunate reporter probably wouldn't escape until after ten. I was certain that Scott was sitting in the stuffy meeting room at the courthouse, longing to be back in the embrace of his fiancée, Tamara Rostova. They were planning an October wedding, and making noises about eventually moving away from Alpine. I dreaded the thought of finding someone to fill Scott's place. The list of competent journalists who were willing to work for a small weekly paying small wages was short.

By eleven o'clock I still hadn't reached Rolf. Maybe he'd gone out to dinner after work. Maybe he was still manning the AP desk. Maybe he'd found another woman. Feeling faintly sorry for myself, I got ready for bed.

My bedroom is small, but not airless at night. When my son visited in June the weather had already turned unusually warm. Before his priestly duties sent him to a remote Alaskan village, his mechanical aptitude was only a notch better than my own, which consists of sometimes operating an electric can opener. For Adam, necessity had been the mother not only of invention, but application. He had installed fans in both bedroom windows. The whirring noise bothered me the first two nights, but I got used to it. Again, I blessed my son for making my summer nights bearable.

Still, I lay awake for a while, wondering what had happened to Rolf. I suppose it was the sound of the fan that kept me from hearing the distant wail of fire engines. Usually, I'm alert to any emergency calls, as they signal news in Alpine. But it was only when the sirens multiplied and grew near my house that I sat up in bed.

I looked out the half-opened window. An orange glow filled the sky. Blinking several times, I focused and saw sparks not more than a hundred yards away. Out of the corner of my eye I caught the sight of flashing lights as the emergency vehicles hurtled along Fir Street. Only a few seconds passed before the sirens stopped. I judged that the fire was no more than a block away.

Hurriedly, I got out of bed and threw a bathrobe over my short summer pajamas. Instead of slippers, I put on sandals. By the time I reached the street, my next-door neighbors, Val and Viv Marsden, were already outside. So were several others, all cautiously moving toward the conflagration.

"We were just getting ready for bed," Viv Marsden said breathlessly. "It must be the new house in the cul-de-sac. You know—where Tim and Tiffany Rafferty live."

I knew all too well. Tim and Tiffany had been married for less than a year. They'd bought the vacant lot at the end of Fifth Street a few months before their wedding. Six months later they moved into the finished three-bedroom house that had been built by Dick Bourgette, a local contractor.

If it had seemed hot during the day, the temperature soared as we edged closer to the burning house. The firefighters were already plying their hoses. The Marsdens and I couldn't get any farther than a few yards from the corner.

I peered around through the smoke, which was beginning to sting my eyes. Other neighbors were outside, too, but I couldn't recognize them. Sparks were flying, and the crackle of the flames was deafening. Two loud explosions assaulted my ears, like back-to-back bombs. I heard glass shatter, too. The windows had blown out.

"Holy Christ!" Val cried in a ragged voice. "It's a damned inferno!"

It certainly was. The night air smelled not only of smoke, but other, more repugnant odors: chemicals, plastics, fabric, food—everything that was used to make life livable.

I winced as I heard timbers break and crumble inside the Rafferty house. "Do you see Tim and Tiffany?" I asked Viv.

"I can't see anything." She coughed. "This is awful." She turned to Val. "Let's go back. Maybe we should use our own hoses. If the fire spreads to the trees, our house could be in danger, too."

"You're right," Val said. "Let's go."

I didn't blame Viv and Val. Only one other house was between their property and the cul-de-sac, a small rental that had stood vacant for over a year. Maybe I should follow the Marsdens' lead. The evergreens and the wild berry bushes and the rest of the undergrowth could burst into flames at any moment. The only saving grace was that Dick Bourgette had cleared a swath of ground for a garden that had yet to be landscaped.

While I was putting a tissue over my nose and mouth, the sheriff pulled up in his Grand Cherokee and the medics arrived from the opposite direction. Milo Dodge awkwardly got out of his vehicle, looking as if he'd thrown his clothes up in the air and run under them.

"Anyone inside?" I heard him shout to the firefighters.

The answer was lost in the din and the smoke. From across the street, I could hear Edith Holmgren calling frantically to her various cats. My not-so-congenial neighbors to the west, LaVerne and Doyle Nelson, were ambling down the street with one of their obnoxious teenagers.

I stood rooted to the dirt track that passed for a sidewalk in my part of Alpine. There was something so primeval about fire. Even though my eyes hurt and my breathing was impaired, I couldn't stop staring at the flames, licking ever upward above the roof.

Or what was left of it. I heard more sounds of crashing timbers. Despite the firefighters' best efforts, the house was doomed. I knew that the main concern now was to contain the blaze. I also knew that I should be taking photographs.

Incredibly, a familiar—and welcome—voice was speaking in my ear. I turned to look up into Scott Chamoud's handsome face.

"I followed the sirens," he said. "I didn't get out of that damned commissioners' meeting until almost eleven."

He had his camera. Without waiting for me to respond, he began to prowl around, looking for a good—and safe—angle. I'd started to cough and sneeze. The heat was still intense, although it appeared that the fire was burning down and the smoke was turning white instead of black. Having used up the single tissue I'd tucked into my bathrobe pocket, I wiped at my eyes with my sleeve.

Scott kept shooting film. Milo was still across the cul-de-sac, talking to the medics. Walking out into the street and between the various emergency vehicles, I approached the sheriff. He didn't see me until I poked him in the upper arm.

"Where are Tim and Tiffany?" I inquired.

He glanced at me impatiently. "How the hell do I know?"

I realized he couldn't know. A sickening feeling overcame me. What if the fire had started while Tim and Tiffany were sleeping? They might have been overcome by smoke inhalation. They might be dead.

As the night's tragic events unfolded, it turned out that I was only half-right.

Chapter Two

I STAYED NEARBY, keeping watch with Scott. The sheriff looked angry and helpless, shifting his tall frame from one foot to the other, occasionally exchanging a word with Del Amundson, one of the medics, or Deputy Sam Heppner, who had shown up in his regulation uniform. Sam, I figured, was on night duty, and probably had been patrolling Highway 2 or some of the side roads in Skykomish County.

Waving my hand in front of my face in a hopeless attempt to dispel some of the heat and smoke, I tried to figure out where the flames seemed most concentrated in the house. It was impossible. Virtually all of the wooden structure was burning except for one wall to the east. Ironically, I could see a brick chimney that apparently had been part of a fireplace. On a hot August night, that wouldn't have been the place where the blaze would have started.

"No sign of Tim or Tiff?" Scott asked, echoing my own thoughts.

I shook my head. We both had to raise our voices to make ourselves heard over the crackling cacophony of the fire. "Maybe they weren't home."

Scott didn't speak for a moment, standing motionless with his camera at the ready. For the moment, there was too much smoke for picture-taking. "Tiffany's working," he said suddenly. "I saw her at the Grocery Basket on my way to the meeting. I had to pick up a couple of things Tamara forgot this afternoon after she finished teaching at the college. Tiff checked me out, and was griping about her back."

I suddenly remembered that Tiffany was pregnant. The news had appeared in Vida's "Scene" column a month ago, mentioning that the baby was due in December.

"I wonder if she knows," I said, grimacing. "Doesn't the evening shift work until the store closes at midnight?"

Scott looked at his watch, which had hands that glowed in the dark. "It's getting close to that now. God, I hope somebody tells her before she gets home."

"Maybe Tim went to the store to give her the bad news," I said hopefully.

The flames were dying down, though the heat was still fierce. More people had gathered in the area between Fifth and Fir streets, including a half-dozen cars. I spotted Milo's new deputy, Doe Jameson, directing traffic. Doe had been hired only a month earlier after the sheriff had squeezed enough out of his budget to accommodate some much-needed extra manpower. Or, in this case, womanpower. Doe was a solidly built twenty-seven-year-old part Native American from Seattle who preferred small towns to big cities because she liked to fish and hunt. Scott had written a feature story on her for the *Advocate,* and informed me that she was tough but fair. At present, she was ordering the gawkers to move on.

In fact, Doe was moving in our direction. "Ms. Lord," she called, "Scott. Are you done here?"

"Done?" I responded. "As in, 'to a crisp'?" I immediately regretted the smart-ass remark. "We want to find out about Tim and Tiffany. Where are they?"

"No idea," Doe replied. "Somebody said Mrs. Rafferty was on the evening shift at the Grocery Basket. Tim may be tending bar at the Venison Inn or working at the radio station. You can't put anything in the paper tonight anyway, right?"

As uncomfortable as I felt, my journalistic instincts compelled me to stay put. But it was Scott who intervened.

"I'd like to get a couple of shots of the firefighters after they've gotten everything under control," he explained. "They're mostly volunteers, you know. Showing how hard they work is a way to reward them. Gritty, grimy, all worn out, but willing to serve."

Doe Jameson must have been the only woman in Alpine who wasn't susceptible to Scott's considerable charms. She narrowed her dark eyes at him and frowned. "Can't you just write that in the story?"

Scott tried his dazzling smile. "One picture's worth a thousand words."

"Ohhh . . ." Doe shrugged. "Just keep out of the way." She turned around as a couple riding a motorcycle roared up to the intersection. "Damn! Bikers! That's all we need!"

Sam Heppner was already confronting the bikers, who appeared to be harmless, ordinary Alpiners. I recognized them when they removed their helmets. Jerry and Mary Beth Hedstrom ran Mountain View Gardens, the local nursery, and had bought a Harley when they both turned forty-five in April.

Milo had stopped Doe, apparently giving her some instructions. She nodded once, moved quickly to the squad car, and drove away. The sheriff headed in our direction.

"I sent her to meet up with Tiffany," Milo said, looking grim. "Sam says she's still at the Grocery Basket. I don't know where Tim is. He's not at the Venison Inn or

KSKY. Fleetwood's out of town, and Rey Fernandez is in charge."

The reference to my archrival, Spencer Fleetwood, made me realize that I hadn't seen the radio station owner at the current scene of breaking news. That was unusual. As a rule, he was always on the spot, ready to gloat over beating me on a story.

"Maybe Tim's already with Tiffany," I said, looking beyond Milo to what was now the smoldering wreckage of the Rafferty house. There was still smoke, still embers, still parts of the frame, and a section of roof that dangled like a ragged black blanket.

The sheriff didn't comment. I coughed and sneezed several times, resorting again to my sleeve. *Dignity* had never been my middle name. Scott was moving in on a couple of the firefighters, aiming for a close-up. Milo didn't stop him. Instead, he looked down at me and scowled.

"You got any coffee?" he asked.

"I can make some," I said. "Are you going to leave the scene?"

"For a couple of minutes," the sheriff replied. "I have to take a leak."

"Come on." I made a vague motion for him to follow me. Having been lovers as well as friends, there was no state of disarray in which Milo hadn't seen me. But we'd shared more than physical intimacy over the years. We'd suffered our personal tragedies and disappointments— along with our professional confrontations with evil. The sheriff and I trudged back to my house like two old warriors, comrades in arms, weary veterans of murder and mayhem, carrying our personal and professional wounds like battle scars.

The first thing I did when we got back to the house was to grab a bunch of tissues, try to clear my respiratory passages, and put some drops in my eyes. After blowing my nose and blinking several times, I faced the kitchen counter. I always prepare the coffeemaker at night, not only to save time in the morning, but because I tend to be in a bit of a fog until I've been up for at least a half hour. Before I could turn on the switch, Milo returned from the bathroom, opened the cupboard door, and was gazing at my liquor stock.

"Maybe I'll just have a short shot of Scotch," he said, reaching for a bottle of Ballantine's. "What about you?"

I hesitated. "About a half-inch of bourbon," I finally replied, getting glasses out of another cupboard. "Pepsi might keep me awake. Coffee certainly would."

We moved out into the living room, where Milo flopped into his favorite easy chair and I sat down on the sofa. "Do the firefighters have any idea what started the blaze?" I inquired.

"Not yet." Milo took a deep sip of his drink before lighting a cigarette. I opened the drawer in the end table and procured an ashtray I kept for him. For me, too, upon that rare occasion when I relapsed into my old cigarette habit. "They didn't smoke," Milo said, gazing at the match he held in his big hand. "At least, not this stuff."

I'd known Tim Rafferty for years, back when he was a college dropout who'd tried to find himself by tending bar in various local watering holes. He and Tiffany—whose maiden name was Eriks—had been a couple forever, finally making it legal after moving in together about three years ago. I'd figured at the time that Tiffany wanted to start a family before her biological clock started ticking down. Tim was well over thirty; I guessed she was a couple of years younger. When Tim wasn't slinging drinks, he worked part-time as a DJ on KSKY. He also did some E-trading on the Internet. Tiffany had held a series of jobs, the most recent being her stint with the Grocery Basket. Somehow, they made ends meet, though Tim was no genius, and I'd always considered Tiffany something of an airhead.

But that didn't mean I wasn't worried about them. "I hope they're okay," I said.

The sheriff grunted, not an encouraging response.

I'd taken my watch off before I went to bed. The digital clock on my DVD player informed me that it was 12:17 A.M. "Tiffany and Tim can stay with her folks," I remarked. "Or Beth, Tim's sister. She still lives in the family home."

Milo still didn't say anything. Beth Rafferty was one of our 911 operators, but she didn't usually work nights. A divorcée who'd taken back her maiden name, Beth had lived at home with her ailing mother. Recently, the senior Mrs. Rafferty—who suffered from Alzheimer's disease—had been placed in the local nursing home. She had gotten to the point where Beth didn't dare leave her mother alone. It was the usual tragic story wrought by the disease: unable to recognize her nearest and dearest, leaving food cooking on the stove until it burned away, going outside and forgetting how to get back into the house—if she could remember that she had a house. Beth and Tim's father, Liam, had been dead for a couple of years.

"What's going on with the boyfriend?" the sheriff asked, seemingly from out of nowhere.

The question caught me off guard. My log cabin smelled of smoke from the fire and seemed oppressive. Maybe my brain was smoky, too. "Boyfriend?" I said stupidly.

"Right." Milo's expression didn't change. "Rolf."

Rolf and Milo had met only once. The occasion had been my first date with Rolf, an evening spoiled by a break-in at my house. Since that time, the sheriff hadn't really quizzed me about the relationship.

I shrugged. "We don't get to see much of each other. It's one step above an online romance."

"He seems like an okay guy," Milo noted casually. Too casually? I could never be quite sure with Milo.

"I think so." The truth was, I found Rolf difficult to read. He was a great kidder. I was never sure when he was teasing or when he was being serious. Maybe that was part of the attraction.

Milo's cell phone rang. He dug it out of his shirt pocket and answered.

"Shit," he said after listening for a moment. "You sure? Okay, I'll be right there."

The sheriff downed the rest of his drink, put out his cigarette, and stood up. "That was Sam. He said they found a body in the rubble." Milo grimaced. "Tiffany's okay. It must be Tim. Goddamn it."

I felt sick, physically and emotionally. The weather, the fire, the smoke—and now this. It was the summer from Hell. I'd seen Hell before me tonight, consuming Tim Rafferty. I slouched on the sofa in a stupor, staring at the front door that Milo had slammed behind him.

Finally, I gulped down the rest of my drink and sat up straight. The digital clock read 12:38 A.M. Only a few minutes had passed since Milo had received the disastrous news.

News. If I'd still been working the city beat on the Portland *Oregonian* as I'd done for years before buying the *Advocate,* I would have been back at the fire scene, interviewing Sam Heppner and Tiffany Rafferty or on my way to the morgue in the hospital basement or at the sheriff's office consulting with Milo. But I was in Alpine, and the newspaper wouldn't go to press until tomorrow night. Maybe that was my excuse for staying in my little log house, even if the odor of death and destruction filled its muggy air. Maybe I was losing my edge. My mind might be next.

I was being ridiculous. I was upset, hot, and tired. And I missed Ben. My brother had spent over six months in Alpine, filling in for St. Mildred's pastor, Dennis Kelly. Father Den had returned April 1 from his sabbatical, but Ben had stayed for two weeks so that he and Adam and I could spend a few days in Vancouver, British Columbia. We'd had a wonderful time—right up until I had to say goodbye to both of them at Sea-Tac airport's check-in curb. Adam had gone back to Alaska. Ben had headed for Milwaukee to fill in for yet another priest who was taking a six-month leave, an old buddy from their seminary days. My brother's intention had been to return to his work in the home missions, but because of the clergy shortage, he was willing to bail out a friend who needed a break. The half year Ben and I'd spent together had been wonderful. It was the first time in over thirty years that we'd lived in the same place at the same time for more than a couple of weeks. The previous occasion had occurred when Adam was born. Because his father, Tom Cavanaugh, was married to somebody else, I'd gone to stay with Ben at his mission parish on the Mississippi Delta. The final trimester of my pregnancy had been a bittersweet three months for both of us.

I tried to stop thinking. If I didn't go to bed, I'd be worthless the next day. After another five minutes, I emptied Milo's ashtray, put our dirty glasses in the dishwasher, turned out the lights, and headed into the bedroom. Even the window fan system couldn't dispel the odor of acrid smoke.

As if I needed a reminder of what had happened that night.

*   *   *

"I should have been there," Vida declared the moment she stepped into the newsroom. "When I heard those sirens, why on earth did I assume it was just another grass fire?"

I offered her a weak smile. "Because we've had several already?"

She shook her head, which was covered with an enormous orange straw hat. "I should have known. There were so many sirens, though admittedly, they weren't that close to my house. Poor Tim. Of course, he always was rather foolish."

I was standing by the coffeemaker, where Ginny Erlandson, our office manager, was placing sweet rolls from the Upper Crust Bakery on a tray. "I sort of liked Tim," Ginny said. "We were in high school together. He was kind of a show-off, though. But he wasn't stuck-up like some of the other kids."

Vida shrugged. "Smoking in bed, no doubt. And drinking. It's that combination that starts fires. Do you want me to talk to Tiffany?"

I considered the suggestion. My initial reaction was to have Scott interview the Widow Rafferty—when Tiffany was up to it. But I knew Vida was bursting with curiosity. Maybe she could use her coaxing soft-soap manner. It might be better to have a woman handle the story, given that Tiffany was pregnant.

"Yes," I said, "but she may not be ready to talk to outsiders. She's lucky if she doesn't miscarry."

Vida quickly counted on her fingers. "Four months along. She should be all right. I'll talk to Cookie Eriks. Or perhaps Dot Parker. She *is* her grandmother, after all, and I still have to interview the Parkers about their Alaska trip."

I'd forgotten the Parker-Eriks-Rafferty connection. Even after so many years in Alpine, I still had trouble unraveling all the family ties. "Okay," I said. "I'll do the main story, and have Scott handle whatever sidebars we need. You'll write the obituary, of course."

"Of course," Vida agreed.

Scott appeared from the back shop, where he'd been conferring with Kip MacDuff, our production manager. "I should have hung around longer last night," he asserted with a scowl. "I left right after you did, so I missed it when they found Tim's body."

"Don't feel guilty," I said. In fact, I hadn't driven by what was left of the Rafferty house that morning. It would have taken me only a block out of my usual way down Fourth Street, but I'd doggedly kept to my routine. Seeing the smoking rubble would have been a bad way to start the day. "I wasn't there, either. Besides, we wouldn't run pictures of . . . Tim's remains."

Scott nodded. "I know. But I could have gotten a shot of the firefighters standing over the place where they found the poor guy. A silhouette, maybe, with their outlines against the sky."

I smiled appreciatively at Scott. He was an adequate writer, but it was his photographic skills that made him so valuable. His artistic talent was inherent, of course, and his technical expertise was growing. The better he got, the more readily he'd be able to market his skills to a wider world.

I didn't want to think about that. Besides, I had work to do. I took a mug of coffee and a sweet roll into my office to start the day. But before I sat down at my desk, I called out to Scott.

"What about the county commissioners? Was there any big news last night?"

Scott set his own mug of coffee down next to his computer screen and came to the doorway. "They're still arguing over whether the county or the city has jurisdiction out by the fish hatchery. The new bridge over Burl Creek that everybody wants may be inside the city after all, if the Peabodys can ever figure out where their property line ends. Right now, they think it's in the middle of their chicken coop."

"Anything else?"

"The usual—potholes in the ski lodge road, potential flooding on the Skykomish River, that illegal dump site off Highway 187." His expression turned puckish. "And Ed."

I sighed. "I was afraid of that. Did he present his bond issue proposal?"

"Oh, yeah." Scott shook his head. "That's why the meeting ran on so long. Ed had charts and diagrams and even clips from that Japanese TV series, *Mr. Pig*. Leonard Hollenberg—he's getting really senile—thought Ed was promoting some kind of 4-H thing. Leonard couldn't figure it out, because hardly anybody around here raises pigs, but he thought it'd be a good idea."

"What? A bond issue? More pig farms? Japanese cartoons?"

"More pigs, I guess," Scott replied with a grin. "Leonard said he really enjoyed a nice ham on Sundays. Hams don't taste like they used to. He insisted that his complaint be put into the record."

"Was it?"

Scott shook his head. "George Engebretsen voted nay to Leonard Hollenberg's yea, and Alfred Cobb was asleep. As usual."

"So what happened to Ed's proposal?"

"They tabled it."

"Ooooh—good grief!" Vida, who—naturally—had been eavesdropping, yanked off her glasses and began rubbing her eyes in that furious and infuriating gesture that indicated extreme disgust. "Such a trio of ninnies! It's a wonder they ever accomplish anything! Not," she added, putting her glasses back on, "that I don't think Ed is out of his mind."

I had to put my own mind on our deadline. I'd already written my weekly editorial, a less-than-sterling piece about the need for arterial stop signs at the intersection of Spruce Street, Foothill Road, and Highway 187—or, as it was better known, the Icicle Creek Road. The high school's main entrance faced Foothill Road, and in the past three years teenagers driving their cars out of the student parking lot had caused a rash of accidents. Fortunately, no one had been killed or seriously injured, but it was only a matter of time. I'd hoped that the stop signs would be installed before classes started after Labor Day, but Mayor Fuzzy Baugh was dragging his feet. Progress came slowly to Alpine—if at all.

I had the basics for the fire story, so I began writing the first few paragraphs. Any gaps could be filled in later after I heard from Milo.

The phone rang about ten minutes later. I guessed it was the sheriff—but it wasn't.

"Are you dead?" Rolf Fisher asked. "If so, where do I send flowers? And is it proper to wear my yarmulke to a Catholic funeral?"

"I've never seen you wear it yet," I replied. "You aren't Orthodox, are you?"

"I'm very unorthodox, as you should know by now," Rolf responded, "but that doesn't mean I'm not religious in my own way. Can you come down this weekend? I'll show you my yarmulke if you show me your rosary."

"I tried to call you last night," I said. "You didn't answer."

"That's because some moron hit a utility pole with his SUV," Rolf said. "My home phone's still not working. You didn't answer my question."

"Oh." I paused to double-check my calendar, though I don't know why. I knew it was empty. "When's the concert? Friday or Saturday?"

"Saturday," he answered. "But come Friday anyway. We can go someplace really grand for dinner. There are a clutch of new restaurants I haven't tried. In fact, there are even more old ones I've never been to. I don't get out much."

I smiled into the receiver. I could picture Rolf, lounging in his chair at his desk, looking dark and lean and alarmingly attractive. "I hate driving in Friday-night traffic," I said. "But maybe I can make the sacrifice. At least your condo is air-conditioned."

"We'll heat it up in any event," he responded. "Oh, darn the world and all its worries! Here comes breaking news out of yet another place I can't pronounce. I'll talk to you before Friday." Rolf rang off.

However earth-shaking the big news might be in Seattle, it wouldn't get into the *Advocate*—unless it had a local connection. While we subscribed to the AP wire service, we used its material only if there was a Skykomish County angle. Sometimes, when we needed to fill space, it was a stretch. A logging story, an environmental piece, state and national parks—all could somehow be tied in to our readers' interests if we could get a local comment. Otherwise, SkyCo residents got their news from the outside world via TV, radio, the Internet, and the daily newspapers. The *Advocate*'s audience cared more about one of Grace Grundle's cats getting lost in Old Mill Park than a man-eating tiger on the prowl in Calcutta.

"I'm fighting an uphill battle," Vida announced from the doorway. "I may be losing. I wonder if I should."

It was unlike Vida to surrender on any issue. "What is it?" I asked.

"It's Elsie Overholt at the Alpine retirement home." Vida paused, sticking a couple of loose hairpins into her scattered gray curls. "She's pestering me again about writing that column."

"You mean the old-timers' thing?"

Vida nodded. "Elsie's ninety-five if she's a day, and I must admit, she has all her faculties. Or at least as many as she ever had. I suppose it's not the worst idea I've ever heard, especially as people in general live longer."

Elsie, whose family owned a farm run by her grandson Ellsworth, had contacted Vida earlier in the year about writing a column that would appeal to the older generation. Vida had rejected the suggestion, insisting that there wasn't room on her page. That was true enough, but we could squeeze it in elsewhere if we had to, and Elsie had recently stepped up her campaign to become a regular *Advocate* contributor. For free, of course.

"We might find room on the editorial page," I said. My weekly piece filled less than two columns. Letters to the editor took up another column or so, depending on who wanted to nail me to the wall. The rest of the page featured whichever spokesperson had the time to put together an article about the community college, the public schools, the park service, the timber industry, the local churches, or any other general-interest topic.

Vida looked resigned. "Well. I suppose I'll have to call Elsie back and tell her we'll try it. When we have space."

I nodded. "It might work out. Can she write?"

Vida shrugged. "She taught in grade school eons ago. She must be at least literate."

"Okay." I saw Milo coming into the newsroom. "Go ahead. Here comes the sheriff."

Vida moved only enough to let Milo enter my office. If he had something to say that was worth delivering in person, it must be important. My House & Home editor wouldn't miss it for the world.

I looked up at Milo with an inquisitive expression. He didn't sit, but stood looming over my desk, his long face grim.

"Doc Dewey had to ship Tim's corpse over to the

medical examiner in Everett early this morning," Milo said in a tired voice. "Doc couldn't handle the autopsy on . . . what was left. For once, the Snohomish County MEs weren't real busy, so we didn't have to wait in line." He stopped, removed his regulation hat, and ran a hand through his graying sandy hair. I sensed that he was stalling, that he hated to say what was going to come next. But he forged ahead. "Tim died before the fire started."

Milo stopped again. Vida, who was standing just behind him, looked impatient. "Well?" she said.

The sheriff kept his eyes fixed on me. "Cause of death was a blow to the head. It looks like we may be talking about a homicide."

Chapter Three

EVEN VIDA WAS shaken by Milo's bombshell. "Does Tiffany know?" she asked in astonishment.

Milo shrugged. "That's up to Doc Dewey. He's got her at the hospital, making sure the baby's okay. Her folks are there, too. I'll tell Beth when I go back to headquarters. She's tough. She came to work despite Tim's death. She said it'd be too hard to find a sub on short notice."

"Very brave." Vida glanced at her wristwatch. "I have an appointment with Dot and Durwood at eleven. Goodness, it's a quarter to now. I wonder if they're home. I must call." She dashed out to her desk.

I wished Milo would stop looming. "How was Tim killed?" I asked.

"Blunt instrument," the sheriff replied. "The ME's findings aren't complete. He may not know—if he *can* know—what it was until later today."

I frowned. "Robbery?"

"Could be. Classic setup. The house is dark, burglar figures nobody's home. Maybe somebody who knew the Raffertys and their schedule breaks in, Tim wakes up, they get into it, and Tim gets his skull smashed in." Milo fiddled with the collar of his regulation tan shirt. I noticed that he was already beginning to sweat under his arms. It was supposed to hit ninety by afternoon.

"Where was the body found?"

"In the bedroom," the sheriff replied. "This is going to be hard to reconstruct with so much of the house burned. We're calling in somebody from the state to help figure out how the fire was started. Assuming it was done to cover up the murder."

"I suppose," I said grimly, "that Fleetwood will have this on the noon news."

"I haven't told him," Milo said. "I don't know if he's back in town. He was taking a long weekend."

I shook my head. "It won't matter. KSKY will still beat us. I should be used to it. You'll have to make a formal announcement today. It's going to be all over town in an hour anyway. A murder might get buried in the second section of the *Seattle Times* or *P-I,* but it's the biggest story of the year in a town like Alpine."

Milo was backing out of my office. "Aren't you being kind of crass?"

"Yes." I had the grace to look sheepish. "But it's the curse of the weekly newspaper. Hell, it's the curse of the dailies, too. Everything is broadcast as soon as it happens these days. No wonder print journalism is dying."

Milo lifted a hand in a semiwave. "Bitching doesn't help. See you."

"Let me know when you find out anything new," I called after him.

The sheriff kept going. As he closed the newsroom door, Vida hung up the phone. "Dot and Durwood are terribly upset. I'm going to their house right away. The Alaskan cruise story will have to be put on hold, I suppose."

As Vida left, Scott came in. "I just saw Dodge outside. Was Tim really murdered?"

"That's what the medical examiner says." I got up from my chair and met Scott halfway. "I need a coffee refill. I also need some ventilation in that damned cubbyhole. It's beginning to feel like a sauna again."

"You should drink more water," Scott commented in a detached voice. He was looking worried. "Who'd want to kill Rafferty?"

I paused with my hand on the coffeemaker. "How well did you know him?"

Scott considered the question. "Not very well. But once in a while I'd meet Tammy at the Venison Inn for a drink after work. She tends to be late." His grin was apologetic, maybe for her tardiness, maybe for confessing that his beloved had a flaw. "Sometimes I'd sit at the bar until she got there. Then I'd talk to Tim if he wasn't real busy."

"Did he ever say anything of interest?"

Scott shook his head. "We'd talk sports, mostly. Sometimes he'd get off on his E-trading and try to convince me it was a good way to make money. I always told him I didn't have any spare cash to invest. Tammy didn't, either." Again, Scott looked apologetic. "No offense, but you know—journalism and teaching don't make people rich."

I smiled reassuringly. "Nobody knows that better than I do," I said, although I figured that Tamara Rostova probably made almost half again as much money in her job at the community college as Scott did working for me. "When was the last time you talked to Tim?"

Scott grimaced. "It's been a couple of weeks. Maybe closer to a month. Tammy and I haven't hung out much at the Venison Inn lately. During summer quarter, she usually gets done with work a couple of hours before I do. Besides, she's knee-deep in wedding plans. I didn't realize how complicated all that stuff is. And expensive." He was looking worried again.

I nodded. "Can her parents afford to help?"

"Pretty much," Scott said. "Her dad's a structural engineer. He works for a big firm in Seattle. Her mom teaches the violin. But they aren't rich, either."

*Richer than anybody working for a newspaper or a
community college.*

"Did Tim want you to invest money through him?" I
asked, pouring out half a cup of coffee.

"We never got that far," Scott replied. "I had the impression he mostly gave advice. But I'm not really sure.
He claimed to be good at it."

"But he still worked part-time tending bar and on
KSKY," I pointed out. "While Tiffany checked out customers at the Grocery Basket."

"Right." Scott grinned. "But they're having a kid. I
mean—well, that's what maybe they were saving up for
before . . . last night. *If* they were saving." My reporter
looked vague. I guessed he didn't know much about saving money. He had no reason to, I reminded myself, and
felt guilty.

Guilty. Who was guilty of crushing Tim Rafferty's
skull? Milo's burglary theory might be correct. Or was it
too obvious? The sheriff lacked imagination; I had too
much of it. But who would want to kill Tim? He had his
faults, but he seemed like a basically harmless, even in-
significant, individual.

I went back into my stuffy little office and rewrote the
lead for the fire story. I wouldn't be able to finish it or fill
in the gaps until I learned more from Milo.

But I could talk to Beth Rafferty. I wondered if she
was still manning the 911 calls in her cubicle at the sheriff's office. I knew her slightly. She seemed like a much
more stable personality than her younger brother. A few
minutes later, Deputy Dustin Fong was ushering me
down the hallway that led to Beth's inner sanctum.

"Sheriff Dodge told her a few minutes ago," Dustin
said in his customary sympathetic manner. "She was
upset, but refused to go home until after her shift's over.
I don't know how she does it."

"Is she busy this morning?" I asked just before Dustin opened the door for me.

"Not very," Dustin replied. "A couple of highway calls—breakdowns on the pass. A kid who fell in the river, but his folks got him out before anything serious happened. Tourists, I think."

Beth Rafferty was sitting at her console, looking as if she was in a daze. "Emma." She spoke my name without looking at me.

I felt inadequate. "I don't know what to say."

Keeping her headset in place, Beth moved her intelligent hazel eyes to my face. "I know. It's so terrible . . ." She shook her head and bit her lip. "It must have been that nut."

I didn't know what she was talking about. "What nut?"

Beth sighed heavily. "What's his name? Old something-or-other. The recluse who's been hanging around that vacant house by the cul-de-sac."

"Old Nick?" I said. There was nowhere for a visitor to sit in the cubicle, so I perched on the edge of Beth's desk. "Have you seen him?"

"No," Beth replied, "but Tiff did. Twice. The first time was at night. He scared her half to death."

The vacant rental was only two doors down from my own house. But my log cabin was set back from the street, a good twenty yards deeper than the other homes facing Fir. My view of the area was also blocked by the trees and bushes that grew around the cul-de-sac.

"I've never seen Old Nick," I said. "Do you think he's dangerous?"

Beth glanced at her console. "We've gotten a couple of calls about him in the past few weeks. He's been sighted off Fir Street, toward First Hill."

"But did he do anything except prowl around?"

Beth made a face. "To be honest, no. One call was

from Grace Grundle. You know how she is—always so afraid somebody's going to hurt one of her cats. The other was from a teenage girl who was babysitting. We sent one of the deputies—Dwight Gould, I think—to check out the place, but the nut—Old Nick?—was gone by the time Dwight got there."

"Milo knows that Old Nick has been hanging out by your brother's house?"

Beth nodded. "I told him when I found out that Tim had been—" She clenched her fists and clamped her lips shut.

"They'll check it out," I said to ease the awkward moment. "How's Tiffany?"

Maybe I imagined it, but Beth's expression changed ever so slightly. She seemed to freeze, as if the mention of her sister-in-law's name annoyed her.

"Tiff's okay," Beth said tersely.

"And the baby?"

"Fine." Beth picked up her bottled water and took a sip. The sheriff's headquarters wasn't air-conditioned, but a huge fan had been installed behind Beth's chair. "Her folks are taking her to their place as soon as Doc signs the release form."

"I've never known the Eriks family very well," I said. "They live in the Icicle Creek development, right?"

Beth nodded again. "A couple of blocks from where Dodge lives. Wayne and Cookie Eriks are on the edge of the development, near Railroad Avenue."

The less attractive homes in the neighborhood were closer to the railroad and farther from the golf course. Not that any of the houses were upscale. The development was strictly middle-class modest.

The console lit up. Beth's "911" was calmly professional. "Please speak more slowly," she said after a pause. "How old? Three months? Turn the baby upside down. . . . Yes, do it now. . . . Hold him firmly. . . .

Good. . . . No, I wouldn't try to give him vitamins anymore, either. . . . It wouldn't hurt to check with Dr. Sung. You're sure that Emerson is all right? . . . Yes, I hear him crying. He sounds angry. That's what I'd expect. . . . Of course. You're welcome." She shook her head and spoke to me. "Another kidlet who hates liquid vitamins. They refuse to swallow, then choke and start turning blue. Mom panics. She can't imagine that an infant could have such definite dislikes and opinions."

"Or be so ornery," I said with a little smile. "They're born with personality traits. My son was always strong-minded, especially when it was something he didn't like. I swear he had his first tantrum when he was a day old."

Beth looked wistful. "I've never had kids. When I give advice like I did just now, it's because of my emergency training. If I can, I try to resolve crises before anybody else has to be summoned."

"You deserve a hero medal," I said.

She turned grim. "I wish I could've been one last night for Tim."

"Do you know who called in the fire?"

"I was off duty, of course," Beth replied, "but Evan Singer was here. He told me it was Edna Mae Dalrymple. She was up late reading a book they'd just gotten in at the library. She wanted to finish it in one sitting because there were several patrons waiting to read it."

Edna Mae was Alpine's head librarian. She lived on the corner of Fifth and Fir, across from the Rafferty house. Perhaps she'd been in the group of onlookers on the other side of the street. Edna Mae is a nervous, rather timid creature, but conscientious. I'd mention her name in my story.

"Are you staying on all day?" I inquired.

"I might as well," Beth said wearily. "There's nothing much I can do until Tim's body is sent back to Driggers Funeral Home. Evan fills in some evenings, but he's got

plenty on his plate managing the Whistling Marmot
Movie Theatre. I'll see my mother at the nursing home
after work. Frankly, she won't understand. Half the time
she doesn't know who I am. Her personality's changed,
too. The irony is that *I* hardly recognize *her*. Or at least
not as the person who was my mother."

"Did Tim visit her often?"

"No." She held her head with one hand and looked
away. "He said there wasn't any point. That's not true,
really. A couple of times, I took her there to dinner. Mom
had no idea where she was or who she was with. I might
as well have taken her to Old Mill Park." Beth's voice
broke. "Damn it, Emma, I wish Tim and I'd been closer
these past couple of years. I feel as if I've lost my entire
family."

I was aware that there'd been friction between
brother and sister, dating back to their father's death. It
was a sore subject—and not just with Beth, but in a different, horrible way—with me. I didn't want to think
about that now. Nor, I was sure, did Beth.

But she had to. "You'll soon have a new niece or
nephew," I said, trying to find a bright spot.

Beth, whose eyes glittered with unshed tears, gave me
a cynical look. "I doubt that I'll see much of the baby.
Tiffany isn't exactly the sensitive, thoughtful type."

The console's light went on again. Beth composed
herself immediately. I hesitated. The call could mean
news. But I sensed that Beth wanted to return to her professional world of woe and stop thinking about her
own. I didn't blame her. With a little wave, I left.

Vida was hungry. She returned to the office just in
time to catch me going out the front door on my way to
the Burger Barn. "I'll go with you," she declared. "The
Parkers didn't serve so much as a cookie, let alone a Chinese chicken salad."

"So how are they otherwise?" I asked as we crossed Front Street under a bright, hot sun.

"Upset, but managing," Vida replied. She pointed to one of the concrete planters where petunias, lobelias, and alyssums were drooping sadly. "Honestly, can't Fuzzy Baugh see to it that these flowers get watered in this weather? He is the most useless creature we've ever had for a mayor."

Fuzzy was the only mayor I'd known since I arrived in Alpine. He was a good politician, oozing native Southern charm. But his administrative skills were lacking. Still, he was better than the county commissioners. At least Mayor Baugh wasn't senile.

It was almost twelve-thirty, the Burger Barn's busiest time. Vida and I had to wait five minutes before we were seated in a booth. Ordinarily, Vida would've insisted on one that was by a window, but because her hunger seemed even stronger than her curiosity, she sacrificed a view of passersby.

"Well now," she said after we'd given our order to a plump blond waitress named Courtney, who immediately brought our beverages. "That's better. I can speak freely. Did you realize that Maud Dodd and her grandchildren were standing behind us? Maud is such a gossip!"

"Really."

"Yes," Vida said, her eyes darting around the area at the other customers. "Of course, she's known Dot and Durwood for years, too. I wouldn't want to mention them where she might overhear."

"Naturally." I waited while Vida laced her iced tea with sugar.

"The Parkers had only gotten the news about the cause of Tim's death a few minutes before I got there," Vida explained. "At first, Durwood just sat there in his recliner, not speaking. Dot was in tears. I did my best to comfort them, but you can imagine the shock."

"They were fond of their grandson-in-law?"

"I shouldn't go so far as to say *that*," Vida responded, her gray eyes ever watchful. "They're fond of Tiffany. Frankly, I always thought they favored Laura over Charlotte."

"Huh?"

Vida waved a hand. "Cookie Parker Eriks is actually named Charlotte. They've called her Cookie forever. Laura is their older daughter. She married Demetrius—Deeky—Kristopolous, some distant relative of the Doukas family. Laura and Deeky live in Bremerton. They have two grown children, somewhat older than Tiffany. Frankly, LaLa and Cookie have never gotten along."

"LaLa?"

"Laura. That's her nickname."

"Ah." I think I understood the family tree, but I hoped Vida wouldn't make me take a quiz after lunch. I had, however, lost the main thread of our conversation. "So . . . ?"

Vida quickly saw my confusion. "My point is that Dot and Durwood not only favored LaLa over Cookie, but LaLa's children over Tiffany. Personally, I suspect that if LaLa's children had been raised in Alpine and not over on the Kitsap Peninsula in Bremerton, Dot and Durwood would have discovered that they were no better than Tiffany. All those sailors, you know. In Bremerton."

Bremerton was a naval shipyard, but I still didn't quite understand what Vida was trying to say. "LaLa's children are both girls?"

Vida shook her head. "No. She and Deeky have one of each. I'm not saying that their children got into serious trouble. I'm sure I would've heard about *that*. I merely mean that their grandparents always saw them when they were on their best behavior. Of course, Bremerton is by far a larger town than Alpine. So much more temptation."

"I see," I said, and thought that at least I got the gist of Vida's meaning. "Was Tiffany a wild teenager? The first time I met her, I think she was out of high school."

Vida gazed up at the ceiling where tired fans did their best to dispel the hot and greasy air. "Yes. Tiffany would've been twenty, twenty-one back then. That was just a year or two before she started dating Tim. My, they were together for a long time, even if they didn't marry until recently." She paused as Courtney brought us our meals. I'd ordered my usual burger basket; Vida had requested the chicken version. She ate two fries before she spoke again. "As I recall, Tiffany wasn't a troublesome teen. She dated a number of boys and was a cheerleader at the high school. Tim was probably a senior when she was a freshman. He was on the football and baseball teams, though he wasn't one of our outstanding athletes."

I managed not to smile. To my knowledge, Alpine hadn't turned out anyone with great athletic ability in the past fifty years.

"Tim went to Western Washington University in Bellingham for a year or two, but dropped out," Vida continued, adding more salt to her fries. "He never had goals. He isn't—pardon me—*wasn't* stupid, simply average and unmotivated. Tiffany strikes me as quite empty-headed."

"Yes," I agreed. "She's vapid."

Vida munched on her chicken and nodded. "Apt. Cookie and LaLa are both reasonably intelligent, I suppose, but to be fair, Durwood was a very good pharmacist even if he is a terrible driver, and Dot kept the books when they owned the drugstore. Perhaps the brains just petered out over time."

"Tiffany is an only child?" I remarked. "I thought there was a brother."

"There was," Vida replied. "Ringo. He died in a rafting accident on the Snake River several years ago." She peered at me closely. "Don't you remember? It was after you moved here."

I pushed at my memory. "Yes, I do now. But I hadn't been here long, and I didn't know the Raffertys. What was his real first name?"

"Ringo." Vida picked up an onion ring that she'd ordered on the side. "Cookie was a big fan of the Beatles." Lest she think I was about to criticize the plethora of family nicknames, Vida narrowed her eyes at me. "Gus Eriks—Tiffany's other grandfather, now deceased—had a sister-in-law who loved the Ink Spots."

"And?" I waited for Vida to gobble up her onion ring.

"She called their son Ink Spot. Inky, for short." She bit off another piece of chicken and bun. "I don't think she realized that the Ink Spots were black. That was before television."

"Oh," I said.

"Anyway," Vida went on after she finished chewing, "after I'd been there a few minutes, the Parkers settled down."

That was more than I could do after the laborious—and weird—family tree I'd just been climbing. "I assume they can't guess how the fire started."

"Certainly not," Vida retorted. "Dick Bourgette doesn't build shoddy homes. Dot and Durwood knew of no complaints about faulty wiring or chimney flaws or anything of the sort. The fire must have been set deliberately, as I'm sure Milo would agree."

We both paused to wave at Stella Magruder, who was hurrying past to the pickup counter. No doubt she was taking lunch back to her beauty parlor down the street. I'd scheduled a Thursday appointment with her to cut my shrublike brown hair. "Did they mention Old Nick?" I inquired of Vida.

She looked owlish. "No. What about him?"

I related my conversation with Beth Rafferty. Vida was intrigued. "I had no idea Nick was lurking around that vacant house off the cul-de-sac. How could you not have known, Emma?"

I shrugged. "It's not on my usual route. I take Fourth, not Fifth, or go over to Alpine Way in the opposite direction."

"Hmm." She turned thoughtful. "Milo will have to hunt him down. I can't imagine why Old Nick has shown up in town after so many years."

"What do you know about him?" I asked with another wave for Stella, who was still hurrying but now held two white paper bags bearing the eatery's red barn logo.

"Let me think." Vida ate more fries before continuing. "Goodness, it must be close to thirty years ago. I didn't actually see him, but Harvey Adcock told me that this disreputable-looking creature had come into his store and bought an axe and a hammer and—I forget what else. He had a long gray beard and barely spoke. And he paid for everything in change. At first, Harvey thought he was crippled because he walked with such difficulty. But it turned out he was carrying all those coins in the pockets of his overalls."

"When did you see him?"

"Much later—a year or more," Vida replied. "He was going through the bins in back of the Grocery Basket. I saw him once or twice after that, always foraging. And then he simply disappeared. It's probably been over ten years since the last sighting. What's odd is that he never seemed to stay in town for more than a few hours. I can't imagine him holing up in a vacant house."

"He may be sick," I suggested.

"Perhaps."

I finished my burger. "Say, why did the Parkers stand you up last night for the interview? Did they forget?"

Vida suddenly looked uneasy. Her gaze, which had never ceased scouring the restaurant to keep tabs on the other customers, now became fixed on her almost empty plate. "That was rather odd. Dot apologized, but she didn't explain."

"Maybe she was embarrassed. Because they did forget," I added.

Vida looked me in the eye. "I don't think so. I can't help but wonder if they aren't hiding something."

I made a face. "Like what?"

She sighed. "That's what bothers me."

Vida looked more than bothered. She looked worried.

Her reaction made me worry, too.

Chapter Four

I DIDN'T KNOW the Parkers nearly as well as Vida did.
Durwood had retired and sold the pharmacy shortly
before I moved to Alpine. Except for Durwood's ghastly
driving record, they were highly respectable—and among
the few to whom Vida granted grudging approval. If the
Parkers had evaded the question of their whereabouts
the previous evening, Vida and I could only surmise that
they had to attend to personal problems.

"Family matters," she guessed. "But what? Really,
Dot and Durwood are decent people. I'd hate to think—"
She stopped, shaking her head.

"Think what?" I asked, glancing at my bill.

"I don't know," Vida admitted. She opened her coin
purse, where she kept bills as well as change. "Cookie
and Wayne Eriks are a trifle old for midlife crises. Still,
you can never be sure. Tim and Tiffany are—were—
technically newlyweds, though that doesn't really count
since they lived together for so long." She counted out
seventy-five cents for a tip. "Goodness, I'd like to know
why Tim was killed."

I had put a dollar on the table. "You don't care for
Milo's burglary theory?"

Vida squinted at me through her big glasses. "It does
sound glib, doesn't it?"

"Maybe," I allowed. And then I did something I
rarely do in front of Vida. "Damn!" I swore.

"Emma!" Vida had been sliding out of the booth. She stopped abruptly on the edge, steadying herself by gripping the Formica-topped table. "Are you hurt?"

"Sorry," I said, looking around to see if anyone nearby had noticed my mild oath. Thankfully, no stares had been turned in our direction. "It just occurred to me. Tim's death is being treated by Milo—and for all I know, the rest of the deputies—as if his loss is of no consequence. Granted, he wasn't one of our more outstanding citizens, but I don't like it. He was a human being, about to become a father, and now he's dead, and has left Tiffany to raise their child alone. It isn't right that his murder should be relegated into a cut-and-dried burglary gone wrong."

Vida slipped back into her original place. "You're right. It's not fair to the Parkers, either. We can't let Milo slough this off. They deserve better. They *are* Alpiners, after all."

We returned to the office, determined to make sure that Tim Rafferty didn't become an unsolved mystery.

By three o'clock, I was growing anxious to finish my lead story. Scott's fire photos were outstanding. Thanks to Kip's high-tech expertise, we could use color with good resolution. I decided to run the most dramatic picture four columns and six inches deep on the front page. Scott had captured the brilliant orange flames and flying sparks against the dark backdrop of the trees that climbed up Tonga Ridge. We'd put two other pictures, including the close-up of the firefighters, inside on page four. Vida had cropped Tim and Tiffany's wedding photo to show only the groom. The head shot would go on the vital statistics page. It was the only obituary in this week's edition.

"That's really sad," Ginny said, looking at Tim's photo.

"He's just about my age, and now he's dead. It's kind of scary, isn't it?"

Kip nodded solemnly. "He's just a few years older than I am. He'll never get to see his kid. What did I hear on TV a while ago? Nobody's guaranteed tomorrow."

Ginny shivered. "It makes you think."

"Ah," Leo sighed, stubbing out his cigarette in a ceramic ashtray he'd swiped from the Flamingo in Las Vegas, "mortality. Even the Young must face it. Consider the rest of us, every day a step closer to the grave."

"Stop that!" Ginny glared at him. "You're creepy!"

My ad manager cocked his head to one side. "Truthful. Realistic. Down-to-earth. Or under it, if you will."

In agitation, Ginny ran her fingers through her curly red hair. "I'm just thinking of Tiffany. I don't know how she's going to raise a baby by herself. She's so . . . helpless."

"She'll have support," Vida put in. "She has parents and grandparents."

"Women can manage as a single parent," I asserted. "I did."

"That's different," Ginny said, her plain face very serious. "You had a college degree; you were smart. You weren't like Tiffany."

My own expression was ironic. "I think that's a compliment."

My office manager flushed. "It is—I guess. But Tiffany is—" She stopped and clapped a hand over her mouth. "Gosh, I'd better pull Tim's classified ad. Or should I?"

In addition to her other duties, Ginny handled our classified section. "What ad?" I asked, feeling stupid.

"The one he's been running for months," she replied. "The baseball stuff."

Leo handed me a copy of the previous week's *Advocate*. "Here. It's under 'Hobbies and Toys.' "

Admittedly, I rarely read our classifieds. They were the purview of Ginny, and by extension, Leo. Only a half-dozen ads were listed under HOBBIES & TOYS. It was easy to pick out Tim's:

> MLB All-Star baseball
> memorabilia; autographed,
> authentic, mint condition.

An e-mail address and Tim's phone number were included. "Tim's been running that?" I asked.

Ginny nodded. "For a long time. Maybe since last winter."

"He's got some cool stuff," Kip said. "One time at the Venison Inn I saw an autographed Ken Griffey Jr. baseball from his days as a Mariner. It was in a case. Tim said he could get five hundred dollars for it."

"Where'd he get this memorabilia?" I asked.

Scott, who had just hung up the phone, came around from behind his desk. "He's been collecting for years. Tim told me once he had an autographed baseball card showing Griffey when he played in the minors in Bellingham. Tim got it when he was going to Western Washington up there. I don't know how much he bragged, but he swore he had items signed by Alex Rodriguez and Randy Johnson when they were Mariners. Other guys, too, and not just the M's. I think he bought some of it on eBay."

Being a baseball fan, I was impressed. "Did he ever sell any of the stuff around here?"

Scott and Kip both nodded. "Some of the baseball cards, anyway," Kip said. "He had a ton of those. Kids especially bought them because they didn't cost a lot. You know—unless it's a rookie card of a future Hall of Fame player or autographed by some other big name, the cards aren't worth that much."

Leo was looking bemused. "No Honus Wagner, huh?"

"Honus Wagner?" Vida repeated. "Didn't he work in the mill during the 1920s?"

Leo chuckled. "No, Duchess," he said, using the nickname that Vida loathed. "The only wood he worked with was his bat. He played in the first part of the last century, and his card—that's singular, and therefore it's unique—is worth I don't know how many hundreds of thousands of dollars."

"Oh, good heavens!" Vida exclaimed. "That's ridiculous! Such a fuss over athletes! I've never understood it."

Leo shrugged. "It's big business. Don't tell me Roger has never collected sports items?"

The reference to Vida's spoiled-rotten grandson softened her features. "Well now—I don't think so. But then Roger doesn't tell his Grams *everything*. Of course, he's in college now and has little time for hobbies."

Roger was fumbling and stumbling his way through Skykomish Community College, where he dropped classes the same way that I'd always presumed he dropped his dirty underwear. His intention was to major in drama, which, I supposed, was better than majoring in crime. Frankly, I'd always figured Roger's biggest talent was for getting into trouble.

"Gosh," I said, wanting to keep the topic off of Roger, "Tim's memorabilia must have been burned up in the fire. I assume he kept it in the house."

Nobody seemed to know, but Kip and Scott guessed that was probably true. I wished I'd known about Tim's collection. It was my own fault for being ignorant. I, of all, people, should check out our classifieds on a regular basis. I might have been able to replace a couple of Adam's treasured baseball items that had been stolen during last year's break-in at my house. The fact that Tim was a Mariners' fan only added to my crusade to make sure he didn't become just another statistic. I always rooted for the underdog. So did Tim, or he wouldn't have cared about Seattle's baseball team.

An hour later, Milo called me. "I heard from the ME in Everett," he said. "I figured you'd want to know the results. The paper comes out tomorrow, right?"

After all these years, the sheriff still seemed vague about the *Advocate*'s deadlines. Sometimes I thought he was putting me on, though he certainly wasn't the only Alpiner who didn't understand that the actual production of the newspaper took more than ten minutes.

"What did the ME say?" I asked.

"It was a tough one," Milo began. "It seems Tim was killed by a blow to the head. There was enough left of his skull to detect what the ME is pretty sure are wood splinters. He figures it could have been a baseball bat."

"So," Milo said, "Rafferty had a big sports collection? I didn't know that."

I could hardly criticize the sheriff for not reading the *Advocate*'s classified section when I seldom checked it out myself. I proofread everything in the paper but the ads. That was up to Leo and Ginny.

"Maybe that's why he was killed," I suggested. "The burglar theory works better now that we know he may have had something worth stealing." If nothing else, my agreement with the sheriff's theory might goad him into finding a genuine suspect.

"Yeah, maybe." As usual, Milo wasn't one to jump to conclusions. "It'd mean that the thief had to take some time. Break in, get caught by Tim, bust his skull, get the goods out of the house—and set the fire to cover his tracks."

"It's possible," I remarked. "You *are* considering alternatives, though?"

"Like what?"

"Like—" I stopped. Milo hated it when I tried to help

him do his job. I couldn't blame him—I certainly wouldn't want him trying to do mine—but it seemed that he was accepting the easy, if plausible, explanation. "Never mind. Can I say that you suspect robbery as a motive?"

"Not yet," Milo replied. "It's too soon. Possible homicide, possible arson, ongoing investigation. Keep it vague. You know the drill."

I sighed. "Okay. Have the state's arson experts arrived yet?"

"They got into town a couple of hours ago," Milo replied.

I refrained from snapping at him. "Are they at the site?" I asked, jumping up to look out into the newsroom in an effort to locate Scott.

"They were there when I left half an hour ago," the sheriff said.

It was a quarter after four. I spotted Scott coming in from the back shop. We had time for him to get a photo and a quick interview. Not that the investigators would know or tell him anything, but at least we'd have their arrival in the paper. I'd already told Scott that I wanted him to follow up every scrap of information in the Rafferty case.

There was no point in badgering Milo further. I'd mention Old Nick's presence later, when he didn't already have a full plate and I wasn't facing a deadline. Scott could handle the sidebar on the arson angle. I'd just hung up the phone when Vida returned, presumably from talking to Tiffany.

"Well?" I said to her after I'd sent Scott on his way. "How's the widow doing?"

"Tiffany's a mess," Vida responded, looking more disgusted than sympathetic. "All she can talk about is what's going to happen to her and the baby."

"That's understandable," I said. "You know how women are when they're pregnant. It's all about the child they're carrying. The rest of the world isn't very important."

Vida scowled at me. "Goodness! Was I like that with my three girls?" She paused, apparently thinking back to her own childbearing days. "I can't imagine being so wrapped up in myself, especially not after the first birth. Of course, you only had one."

"I've seen it in other women," I countered. "In Tiffany's case, it's not as if she has a wide range of interests."

"Perhaps." Vida sat down at her desk. She never took notes, and it was obvious that she was anxious to write her story. It wouldn't take long. Her two-fingered typing was faster than most people's properly trained efforts. "This will be brief," she asserted. "What can I say except that she's upset and concerned for the baby and their future?"

"What about her parents, Cookie and Wayne?"

Vida harrumphed. "It's 'poor Tiffany' this, 'poor Tiffany' that. They're not stupid, but they haven't got any *sense*. No wonder Tiffany's such an addlepate. By the way, the funeral's set for Friday, Faith Lutheran. Not that I ever heard about Tim and Tiffany attending services there. I can't think why Reverend Nielsen allows it."

I left Vida to her work—and her indignation. Tim and Tiffany had been married at the ski lodge by a justice of the peace from Monroe. Even though it had been March, there was still snow on the ground, and somebody had played "Winter Wonderland" on the guitar for the recessional. Tiffany had insisted that the guests call the JP "Parson Brown," even though it was a woman and her last name was Shovelburt.

By five-fifteen, the paper was ready to be sent to Kip in the back shop for his expert final prepublication. At five-sixteen, Spencer Fleetwood strolled into my office.

"Met your deadline?" he asked in his casual manner.

"Why aren't you at KSKY? Aren't you a little short-handed?"

Spence looked chagrined, and I immediately felt callous. "I'm sorry. Really. Have a seat."

He shook his head. "I thought you might like to have a drink after work."

Despite the professional and personal accommodations Spencer Fleetwood and I had made over the years, I remained wary of the man. The newspaper and the radio station had done some co-op ads together. The two of us occasionally went out to dinner and had once spent a weekend together—with separate hotel rooms—in Seattle. We had much in common. Yet I still perceived him first and foremost as a rival, and found his superficial arrogance annoying, even though I'd learned that he was as vulnerable as the rest of us.

"Well . . ." I stared at my computer monitor, which was waiting to be turned off. Spence was a source when it came to Tim Rafferty. Getting out another edition of the *Advocate* was always a small triumph worth celebrating. "Okay," I finally said.

"Not the Venison Inn," Spence said as I turned off the computer. "Half of Alpine will be there, toasting Tim."

"You're right," I agreed. Our choices were limited. "Where then?"

"How about Katzenjammers in Leavenworth?"

I gaped at Spence. "Are you kidding? That's a long drive over the pass."

"Forty minutes tops," he replied, "less on a Tuesday night. Not so much traffic and the weather is perfect."

"Speak for yourself," I grumbled. "I'm not dressed for anything fancy."

"It's not that fancy," he insisted. "We can eat dinner on the patio and watch the sun go down. It'll be cooler." Spence surveyed me from head to toe. "Besides, you look fine. Good, in fact. I hear you're in love."

I was wearing black cotton slacks and a lime green tank top. I'd gotten the separates at a Nordstrom end-of-summer sale the previous year. I was presentable, perhaps. But, I told Spence, "I'm not in love. I'm seeing someone, though."

He laughed. "I know, I know. Rolf Fisher from the AP. You think we don't take the wire service, too?"

I looked askance. "You make it sound as if Rolf sent out a statewide bulletin."

"Media gossip," Spence said. "Alpine isn't the only place that has a rumor mill."

Driving over the summit to Leavenworth wasn't the worst idea I'd heard lately. I hadn't been out of town in over a month. Besides, Spence and I wouldn't have to worry about eavesdroppers. I told him we could leave as soon as I made one last check with Kip in the back shop to let him know where I'd be in case of any late-breaking news.

"I can still scoop you," Spence called after me. "Rey Fernandez is working the evening shift."

I didn't respond.

Once Spence turned his BMW onto Highway 2, we were driving with our backs to the bright sun. He was right about traffic; it was relatively sparse, except for the omnipresent trucks that crossed Stevens Pass from eastern and central Washington. The state's apple orchards lay beyond Leavenworth, but the main harvest would come later, in September and October. Only the Gala apples were about to be picked, and Vida had already been searching her voluminous files for pie and sauce recipes—none of which she could make successfully even if she were forced at gunpoint. Fortunately, most of our readers didn't realize that our House & Home editor was a terrible cook.

Apples had come to mind because Spence and I had both contacted the Washington State Apple Commission for some co-op advertising to run in September. Consequently, as we climbed to the summit of Stevens Pass, we talked of business and not of Tim Rafferty. Spence also remarked that Vida's weekly radio program had garnered the biggest audience in the station's history.

"I did some informal polling," he said as we passed the main entrance to the now-deserted ski area. "Over fifty percent of all SkyCo households tune in *Vida's Cupboard* every Wednesday. It's amazing."

"She *is* amazing," I said, and meant it. The previous year, Vida had faced a traumatic personal crisis that might have destroyed a lesser being. But scandal had been avoided. She had rebounded with her energy intact and her head held high. My admiration for her had grown even more. And while the cause was a taboo subject—even between us—I'd let her know of my great esteem for her dignity and character.

"The crazy thing is," Spence said as we began to descend the eastern slope of the Cascades, where only scant patches of snow remained at the highest altitudes, "Vida never has any real *news*. She simply talks about this and that, and then does her weekly interview."

"She knows she has to save news for the *Advocate*," I reminded Spence. "That was our bargain when I found out she'd signed on to do the program."

"I know," he agreed, "but still, it's astonishing how much listeners love to hear her gab about Janet Driggers's new hairdo or Cal Vickers's compost heap."

"It's like her 'Scene Around Town' column," I said, noticing two bicyclists who were huffing and puffing up Highway 2 with backpacks bowing them down. "Names make news. It's not the news, it's the names. Everybody knows everybody else in Alpine—and the county."

Spence nodded. "That's so true. But even after several years running a small-town radio station, I'm still amazed.

By the way," he added as we began to follow the We-natchee River into Leavenworth, "have you ever been to Katzenjammers?"

"No," I replied, my gaze turned toward the river on my right. "I like the name." More than that, I liked the fact that Spence hadn't chosen one of the restaurants where Tom and I had eaten during the course of a wonderful weekend in Leavenworth. Memories could still be painful—though, with time, also comforting. "The river's low," I noted. "The last few summers have been so dry." Weather was always a safe topic.

Spence took my cue as if we were doing a radio interview. "Bad for agriculture, winter sports, and hydroelectric power. I don't mind sunshine, but I understand why people around here pray for rain."

Our conversation stayed in neutral until we reached Leavenworth, a town that had been built to look as if it had sprung from the Bavarian Alps. Virtually every building on the main byways was built to resemble the old, colorful chalets of a German village. It was kitsch, but it had charm. I liked it.

We turned off the highway and ended up two blocks from the main drag, where we parked in front of an antiques shop. It was exactly six o'clock. Spence led me down a flight of stairs. I glimpsed the main dining room with its whitewashed walls and wooden beams. Our request for the patio was granted.

"Tim Rafferty." Spence spoke the dead man's name in a more constrained manner than his mellow radio voice. We'd ordered cocktails and were sitting under a big blue umbrella facing a rockery garden. It was still very warm, but not as insufferable as my tin-roofed office.

"Yes," I said. "Have you any idea why anyone would want to kill Tim?"

Spence's brown eyes glinted. "Only me, when he wouldn't show up for a stint at the station."

"Was he irresponsible?" It wouldn't have surprised me. Some of Tim's actions in the past had reeked of immaturity.

"Oh . . ." Spence seemed to be considering his words as carefully as if he'd been on the air. He'd turned away slightly. I waited, studying the distinctive profile that always reminded me of a hawk or some other bird of prey. "Not entirely. He enjoyed being a so-called radio personality. But in the past couple of months, he was a no-show three times. He had excuses, always something to do with Tiffany and her pregnancy. But it was damned annoying because he never called to let me know he wasn't coming. This last time—it was Thursday night, before I left town for the weekend—I threatened to fire him if he did it again."

The fact that Spence hadn't canned Tim was another symbol of our common bond. Only the rawest—or most desperate—of broadcasters would want to work in a small venue like Alpine.

"I gather you didn't believe Tim," I said. "His excuses, I mean."

Spence shrugged. "From what I can tell about Tiffany, she'd make a medical crisis out of indigestion. That part might be true. But I still blame Tim for not advising me that he wouldn't come to work."

Our drinks arrived, a martini for Spence, bourbon and water for me. So far, only another half-dozen customers were on the patio. I didn't recognize any of them.

"Did Tim complain about Tiffany?"

Again, Spence was cautious with his answer. "Not exactly. He joked about being married. I got the impression that he would've been just as happy to keep the status quo. But she wanted a baby, and I suppose he was pressured into making their relationship legal. The Erikses and the Parkers probably insisted."

"But the Raffertys seemed happy?"

"I've no idea," Spence replied, putting his expensive sunglasses back on. He was facing west, and the sun was beginning to settle down behind the mountains. "I hardly ever saw them together. Did you?"

A pair of chipmunks frolicked in the rockery. The air smelled forest-fresh, tinged only with the scent of spices from the restaurant kitchen. I couldn't help it. My mind traveled back to that weekend with Tom. There had been snow everywhere. Leavenworth was decked out for Christmas. It had been a magic time, full of love and laughter.

"What's wrong?" Spence asked, looking curious.

"Nothing," I lied. "I was just trying to remember how Tim and Tiffany acted when they were together. Somehow," I went on, speaking just a little too fast, "I always seemed to encounter them in some kind of crisis. She was the clingy type. But he seemed willing to protect her."

"That probably enhanced his masculinity," Spence said. "He acted cocky, but I felt his self-esteem was fairly low."

"With good reason," I murmured. "I have noticed lately that Tiffany seemed sullen. Of course, when I've seen her she's been at the Grocery Basket on her feet, working. I chalked it up to her being pregnant and feeling miserable."

Spence ate the olive in his drink and looked thoughtful. "I wonder if I should tell Dodge about the crank callers."

"What crank callers?"

He shrugged, though I thought he seemed a bit reluctant and didn't answer right away. I waited in silence, noting that—as always—he was impeccably dressed, wearing a Ralph Lauren short-sleeved tan shirt with cream-colored linen fatigues. His wardrobe wasn't extensive, but what he owned was quality. I often wondered how he afforded it. Maybe he was a prudent shopper. Then again, he'd never had children.

"The usual," Spence finally replied, signaling for our server to bring another round. "Probably the same nuts who write you unprintable letters. There's one, though, who's called several times this past month. I don't recognize him. Neither did Rey or my engineer, Craig. In fact, it sounds as if this guy is disguising his voice. I'll admit, the calls have been more personal, not the usual rants about the music or the advertisers or the news."

"What does he say?"

"I took one of the calls," Spence said, lighting one of his exotic black cigarettes. He offered me one, but I declined. They were too strong. "Tim's never been around when the calls have come in. Anyway, this creep said that if Tim didn't get off the air and tend to business—whatever that means—he'd break his face. Rey took the last call over the weekend while I was gone. The guy told him that Tim was a nasty SOB who ought to get run over by a logging truck."

I was surprised. "That's strong stuff. My critics only want to run me out of town."

Spence nodded. "Exactly. This guy sounds as if he may have a grudge. When I asked Tim about it, he just laughed it off. He said it was probably some drunk he'd refused to serve at the Venison Inn."

That was possible. I frowned at Spence. "Do you agree?"

Finishing his first martini, Spence leaned forward in the patio chair. "No. Not now, after what's happened to Tim. I suppose that's why I'd better talk to the sheriff."

But Spence had talked to me first. On a previous occasion, he'd held out on Milo—with disastrous results. I assumed Spence didn't want to repeat that mistake. I was his guinea pig. No doubt that was the real reason for taking me to dinner out of town.

At least I hoped so.

We dined on veal and crab cakes. We talked almost exclusively about Tim. Spence knew about the sports memorabilia, but had never seen any of the items. He was also aware that Tim did some E-trading, but had rejected his employee's financial advice.

"I've got my own portfolio," Spence had informed me. "It's modest, but it's solid."

Not wanting to drive the westerly route until dusk, we took our time, lingering over cheesecake and coffee. Spence had decided to hire another part-timer from the college. Rey Fernandez would have his two-year degree in December. He'd done an admirable job, but had returned to college in his late twenties and was anxious to move on. Like Scott, Rey had skills that were marketable beyond Alpine.

"I'll see Dodge first thing in the morning," Spence said as he pulled into the parking space next to my Honda Accord in front of the *Advocate* building.

"You should," I urged him. "Maybe somebody got some bad investment advice from Tim."

"That's always a possibility."

I thanked Spence for his good idea to get us out of town. There were no awkward good-nights with us. Somehow the spark of attraction hadn't struck either of us. A woman was in his life somewhere; I sensed that, and figured she lived out of town, though probably not in Seattle. I'd deduced her existence because Spence's weekend absences had increased in recent months. I could have asked him about her, but I didn't. I don't know why. Maybe I respected his discretion. Maybe she was married.

It was dark by the time we returned, but a light was

on in the back shop. After Spence drove away, I went inside to see if Kip was almost finished putting the paper together.

My production manager was working on the front—and final—page. "It turned out tight," he said. "I had to run Scott's arson investigation sidebar next to the main story instead of inside. That meant the jump from your story almost didn't fit on page three."

"How come? The sidebar shouldn't have taken up more than an inch or two. There wasn't any real news."

Kip brushed at the auburn goatee he'd been growing since spring. "There was news after you left. Scott called it in around eight. I tried to reach you on your cell, but you were out of range."

The mountains had interfered. I'd been on the wrong side of the Cascades. "What happened?"

Kip turned off the optical character scanner. "It was an easy fire to figure out. Maybe—just maybe—it wasn't planned. But whoever set it just poured gasoline around the house and lit a match. An amateur, according to the investigators."

An amateur arsonist, I thought. But a deadly killer. Kip and I stared at each other in dismay.

Chapter Five

I CALLED SCOTT when I got home around nine-thirty. First, I congratulated him on getting the latest information into the paper. Then I asked if there was anything I should know that he hadn't included.

"Speculation on Floyd's part," he replied, referring to Robert Floyd, who had led the state's arson team. "Like where the gasoline came from, whether it was on-site, or whoever brought it along."

"In other words," I interpreted, "was it premeditated."

"Right. I talked to Dodge, but he wouldn't say anything at this point."

"That sounds like our cautious sheriff," I remarked. "I'm sorry I wasn't around to take the call. I owe you."

"Hey—it's part of the job," Scott replied.

He was right. But in the background, I heard Tamara shout, "Bonus, bonus, bonus!"

In her dreams.

Wednesdays were always comparatively slow, especially in the morning before readers started to call and complain about the latest edition. Thus, I decided to pay a condolence call on Tiffany. Maybe she had some inkling of why her husband had been killed.

But first, I checked in with Milo. He actually had some information.

"Cal Vickers told me Tim always kept a gallon of gas in his garage," the sheriff said. "Tim used to be the kind of dink who could never figure out that 'E' meant empty. I ought to know; a few years ago we had to tow his ass from Highway 2 back to Alpine a couple of times. That's why I checked with Cal at the Texaco station first thing this morning. Tim had gotten a lot better about filling up, but he still kept an extra gallon on hand, just in case."

"Is that printable?" I inquired.

"You mean for next week?"

I made a face into the receiver. "No, I was thinking about running around town and handwriting the information on all the copies of the *Advocate*."

"Funny, Emma." But the sheriff didn't sound amused. "Use it if you want to," he said, "but don't say it's for sure. By the way, Beth Rafferty told me that recluse, Old Nick, has been seen around the area lately."

Not having mentioned the hermit to Milo earlier, I feigned ignorance. "Any further sign of Old Nick?"

"Nope. Somebody's been hanging out at that vacant house by the cul-de-sac, though," Milo said. "We're trying to find the owner."

I reflected on the occupants over the years. As I recalled, they were nondescript—a couple of college students, maybe; an older man who'd lost an arm, possibly working in the woods; a couple who'd kept a rusted-out pickup in the front yard. "Nobody ever stayed there very long. It's always been a rental, hasn't it?"

"They don't know anything about it at Doukas Realty." Milo paused to speak to someone, but I couldn't hear what he said. "Toni Andreas just brought me some fresh coffee. It tasted weird first thing this morning."

The sheriff's coffee always tasted weird. I refused to drink it when I visited his headquarters. "So the owners don't live around here?" I asked.

"Talk to Vida," Milo suggested. "See if she knows. If anybody does, it'd be her."

Vida, however, was surprisingly uninformed. "Dear me," she fussed, "I don't recall. Many of those houses on the south side of Fir Street were built by one of the Gustavsons in the forties, after the war. Except yours, of course."

My log cabin had been built as a summer retreat by a family from Everett. "Between Alpine Way and Fifth, most of them look alike," I noted. "They're all two- or three-bedroom bungalows."

Vida was resting her chin on her hands and concentrating. "As you know, the ground becomes very steep and rocky behind your house. That's why Fir is the last east-west through street. I don't think that part of town was ever a tract owned by one individual. The records at the courthouse should show who bought the property and put up the house. I could swear it's been there since I was a girl."

Vida wasn't sensitive about her age, though she rarely mentioned it. Maybe we avoided the topic because I was afraid she could be considering retirement, and she might—wrongly—think that I felt she'd earned the right to quit working. I knew she was over seventy, if not by much. But the *Advocate* without Vida was inconceivable. Nor could I imagine her ever surrendering her job.

"So you think the house might have been built before War World Two?" I said tactfully.

"Yes. Once the ski lodge was opened, there was quite a bit of construction in town, despite the Depression." Vida frowned. "Really, you have no idea how often I've chastised myself for not paying more attention to my surroundings when I was young."

I couldn't envision a time when Vida hadn't exercised her rampant curiosity. I figured that right after her birth, she'd interrogated every other infant in the nursery, and that when she was two days old, she'd known their history going back three generations. I could picture her crawling into their cribs, ordering them to stop crying and identify their parents, grandparents, and siblings. Naturally, she would have worn a funny baby hat, possibly with a feather in it.

"I'll check it out this morning," Vida vowed. "It may take a while. The county clerks in SkyCo have always been incompetent. It's even possible that a lien was put on the house and that it doesn't belong to anyone."

She left a few minutes later. I waited until ten o'clock to telephone the Erikses' residence and find out if I could visit Tiffany. Cookie Eriks answered in her whiny voice. Tiffany was still asleep. Could I wait until closer to noon? Or better yet, stop by around four? The family had a one o'clock appointment to meet with Al Driggers at the funeral home.

I opted for the earlier time. Tiffany might be an emotional wreck after a session at the undertaker's.

Vida was still gone when I left at eleven-thirty. It took only five minutes to drive to the Erikses' home in the Icicle Creek development. The house was a typical tract structure, a split-level with minimal landscaping and in need of a new roof. Wayne Eriks was employed by the Public Utility District; Cookie occasionally worked in retail, usually during the Christmas season.

A camper was pulled off to one side of the front yard. I parked on the edge of the street, by a row of mail and newspaper boxes. The *Advocate* hadn't yet been delivered, and probably wouldn't be for another hour. Even during the summer when our teenage in-town carriers were out of school, they couldn't seem to get going until after noon.

Cookie Eriks answered the door. She was a thin, drawn woman with only a passing resemblance to either of her Parker parents. "Emma," she said, making a nervous motion with one hand. "Come in. Tiffany's in the shower."

"How's she feeling?" I inquired as she led me up an uncarpeted flight of stairs to the living room.

"Poor girl," Cookie sighed. "She's exhausted. Imagine, losing everything! I don't know how she stands it."

"It's terrible," I declared, sitting down on a sofa that had been covered in blue corduroy. "Tiffany and Tim had been together for so long."

Cookie was still standing, shaking her head and wringing her hands in front of a Roman brick fireplace that was filled with trash. "All her furniture, all her clothes, all her wedding presents! It's a blessing, really, that she hasn't had any baby showers. The first one is in October."

Words seldom failed me, but they did then. I reminded myself to make allowances for Cookie, who could still be in a state of shock. She had, after all, lost a son in a rafting accident. If Tiffany had been at home Monday night, she might have lost her daughter and grandchild, as well.

"She can stay with us as long as she wants to," Cookie went on, beginning to pace around the living room. "We have three bedrooms. Though we've turned one into a den." She paused and cleared her throat. Maybe the den had once been Ringo's room. "Tiffany's old bed is where it always was, but when she moved in with Tim a while ago, she took everything else. That's all gone, too."

The poor woman seemed wound up like a spring toy. Vida had complained about self-absorption on Tiffany's part. It must run in the family. My heart went out to Beth Rafferty, who was now left alone with a helpless mother.

"Was there insurance?" I asked in a mild voice.

"What?" Cookie jumped as if I'd poked her with a sharp stick. "Insurance? I don't think so. Tim didn't expect to die young."

"I meant for the house," I said.

"Oh!" Cookie put a hand to her long graying blond hair, which was more or less held in place with a big silver clip. "Yes, I think so. Tiffany thought so. We'll have to check. Wayne can do that, maybe. He went to work today. They needed him at the PUD."

More than he was needed at home? But I was being unfair; I was trying to help, not hinder. "You can call Bernie Shaw," I pointed out. "He handles most of the homeowners insurance in Alpine."

Cookie nodded in a jerky fashion. "Yes. Yes. He probably has ours. I let Wayne take care of all those business and money things. Tim handled all of theirs."

I couldn't figure out how Durwood and Dot Parker had raised such a nincompoop. Cookie was in her fifties, a baby boomer whose peers had fought for women's rights. But maybe they never marched as far as Alpine. It wasn't the first time I'd met a local female in her age group who seemed helplessly dependent. Apparently Tiffany had followed in her mother's timorous footsteps. I'd never had the choice of letting a man take over or even share the burden of running a household. My independence had been a necessity.

I decided to change the course of the conversation. "So Doc Dewey told Tiffany that she and the baby are doing fine?"

Cookie nodded again, not quite so jerkily. "I don't know how Doc can be so sure, though. Dr. Sung is Tiffany's regular doctor. He's young, he knows all the latest methods. Doc's old-fashioned, almost as stodgy as his father was."

Cedric Dewey—Old Doc, as he was known—had been a wonderful family practitioner, still making house calls until his death a few years after I moved to Alpine. At that time, it was his son, Gerald, who was considered the modern medicine man. Over a decade later, Elvis

Sung was a newcomer and a member of the younger generation. The comparisons were inevitable, as was the criticism: The older folks didn't feel that Dr. Sung knew them as well as Gerald Dewey did—just as young Doc was said to lack his father's personal touch.

"Besides," Cookie went on, "Doc gave Tiffany something to help her sleep. Imagine! Everybody these days knows that pregnant women shouldn't take medicine except vitamins. Anything else can harm the baby. No alcohol, either. My dad says it's all nonsense, but what would you expect, him being a pharmacist and all. It cuts into the drug companies' profits."

I remembered being eight months pregnant, sitting with Ben in tin shacks on the Mississippi Delta, listening to amazingly talented black blues players, and drinking whatever was available at the homely little bars. Those evenings were the best of a bad time, and Adam hadn't seemed to suffer from the outings. But what did I know? Maybe I was just stupid. Or lucky.

"Did Tiffany take what Doc prescribed?" I asked.

"No!" Cookie was shocked. "She knew better. But of course she hardly slept a wink. Oh! Here she comes now. How are you, honey?"

Tiffany Eriks Rafferty wandered into the living room, wearing a green cotton bathrobe that would have been two sizes too small for her even if she hadn't begun to show. I assumed the robe belonged to Cookie. Tiffany wasn't a large person, but she was well proportioned, unlike her skinny, shapeless mother.

Tiffany didn't look at me. "I'm thirsty. Is there any more apple juice?"

Cookie's face expressed alarm. "Oh, dear! I'm not sure. I'll go see." She left the room, leaving me alone with her daughter.

Tiffany finally gazed in my direction. "I have to lie down on the sofa, Emma. Can you move?"

"Sure," I said, getting up and going over to an armchair near the fireplace. "I'm so sorry about what's happened. Let me know if there's anything I can do to help."

Tiffany collapsed onto the sofa. She was barefoot, and her right arm dangled toward the floor. "What can you do? It's all too awful."

"Yes," I agreed, but felt obligated to assure Tiffany that she wasn't the only person who had to navigate rough waters. "As you know, I raised a child by myself. After I did that, his father was killed years later, before we could be married. In fact, Tom died in my arms, murdered just as Tim was."

A faint spark lit in Tiffany's eyes. "Are you saying I should have been there when Tim died? Is everything my fault?"

"Of course not," I said firmly. "I'm trying to tell you that many other people have suffered tremendous losses. Look around you. It's hard to find anyone who hasn't suffered. It's part of life."

"I guess." Tiffany looked unconvinced. She seemed to be sulking. For a woman in her early thirties, she struck me as incredibly immature. But she'd led a sheltered life. In many ways, growing up in a small town is difficult enough. But after the death of her brother, I guessed that her parents had been overly protective. Then, upon coming of age, she'd fallen in love with Tim, who took over where her parents had left off. One of his virtues was that he'd always seemed concerned for her welfare.

"I realize you lost your brother, too," I said, making my voice gentle. "How old were you then?"

Tiffany scowled at me as if I were Torquemada, leading the Inquisition. "Seventeen. Ringo was four years older. Why do you want to know? I wasn't there when it happened."

Her defensiveness was becoming a leitmotif, like the

ominous Fate chords in *Carmen*. "I know," I said, although I didn't remember the story very well. I made a mental note to check it out in our back issues. "I imagine the two of you were close."

Tiffany held up one hand and stared at it, as if she were deciding on whether or not to get a manicure. "He was my big brother. Sometimes they're okay, sometimes they're a pain."

"That's true," I allowed. Ben was older than I was by almost the same number of years. When we were growing up, he'd always treated me with a superior air. It was his due, of course. Sometimes he still pulled rank. And sometimes his attitude maddened me.

Cookie returned with a yellow plastic tumbler. "I couldn't find any more apple juice, hon. Is orange okay?"

Tiffany made a face. "Orange juice gives me heartburn. I'll just have some bottled water."

"Oh, I'm sorry, I forgot! I'll get the water. If I can find it." Cookie retreated to the kitchen.

I had several questions I wanted to ask Tiffany, specifically about the circumstances of Tim's death. But her self-absorption and her suspicious manner stymied me. Nor did I want to upset her. People showed their pain in different ways. I couldn't get a good read on Tiffany Eriks Rafferty.

I stood up. "I should be going. I understand you have an appointment this afternoon. I don't want to keep you."

Tiffany glanced across the room at a clock with hands and numbers on a wood slab decorated with a painting of an idyllic farm scene. "I've got plenty of time to get ready." She looked at both hands. "I should do my nails, though. They get ruined using the cash register so much."

"Yes." I couldn't think of what else to say. I made my way out before Cookie returned with the bottled water.

* * *

It was after noon, and I was hungry. But instead of heading for a restaurant, I drove to the Grocery Basket. I could pick up something from the deli and, with luck, talk to Jake O'Toole. If I got even luckier, Betsy O'Toole might be there. She would not only be more candid, but wouldn't abuse the English language the way her husband did.

The store was busy. I saw Buzzy, Jake's brother, in the produce section, unloading ears of corn into a bin. Jake was talking to a man wearing a Budweiser jacket and holding a clipboard. If Betsy was around, she'd be in the office. Katie Freeman, the high school principal's daughter, had just finished checking out Bertha Tolberg, who had purchased a half-dozen bags of groceries. The Tolbergs raised chickens on their farm, so I assumed Bertha wasn't buying eggs.

With a nod to Bertha, I approached Katie, a tall, fair-haired teenager who wore transparent braces. "Is Betsy in the store?" I inquired.

"Oh, hi, Ms. Lord." Katie's smile was self-conscious. "Yes, she's working on invoices. Should I page her?"

"No, I'll surprise her," I replied. I needed privacy. "Thanks, Katie."

The O'Tooles' office was only slightly bigger than my own cubbyhole and even more jammed with materials. I knocked first, then opened the door as I heard Betsy respond.

"Emma," she said in a pleasantly surprised voice. "To what do I owe this honor? Or did we sell you a bad ham?"

I shook my head. "I've come to grill *you*, not your meat."

Betsy smiled. "I'm not sure what's worse." She pushed her chair back a few inches from the desk and removed her glasses. "Let me guess—it's about Tiffany and Tim, right? Have a seat—if you can find one."

The only other chair in the little room was piled high with folders. "May I?"

"You can toss them in the Dumpster for all I care," Betsy said. "Jake's overorganized. I drive him nuts because I'm not." She waved a hand at her surroundings. "He saves every scrap of paper and files it away for God-only-knows-what. Then he gets ticked off at me because I don't keep everything in here neat. I tell him I keep our house tidy, why should I have to be the cleaning lady at the store? Men!" She shook her head.

I set the files on the floor next to a Campbell Soup carton that was filled with yet more folders. "I just came from calling on Tiffany and her mother," I said. "Have you gotten to know Tiffany very well since she started working here?"

Betsy shook her head again. Maybe she was showing off her recent foil job, which had turned her shoulder-length hair into leonine streaks of brown and gold. "It's hard to communicate with fog. Talking to Tiffany is like talking to a phantom. Honestly, the poor girl isn't very bright."

"But she could handle her job?"

"Once she caught on," Betsy said. "It took a while to train her. Katie Freeman is half her age, and she learned in about an hour. But the real problem with Tiffany is her attitude. She's rude with customers, especially the older ones who get a little fuddled. A week ago, she practically had Grace Grundle in tears." Betsy hung her head. "I shouldn't be talking about Tiffany like this, especially after what's happened. But frankly, Jake and I would have fired her if she hadn't been pregnant, and we knew she'd be quitting in a few months. We hoped she wouldn't want to come back to work. Now that Tim's dead, I suppose we're stuck with her."

Betsy was more than candid; she was downright blunt. But that was her style. She'd honed it over the years with the public wrangling she practiced with her husband. After the visit with Tiffany and Cookie, I found Betsy's attitude refreshing.

"Do you think that pregnancy caused her irritability?" I asked.

"Maybe. But Tiffany never has been the cheerful type." Betsy sighed. "I suppose you're trying to figure out if she was having problems at home with Tim."

Having had people wonder about the status of her own marriage over the years, it was natural for Betsy to assume that any outward display of discontent would indicate relationship problems. "Well," I said, not entirely sure what I was trying to find out, "I was thinking more along the line of money trouble. Tiffany must have had to work. Obviously, she isn't cut out for a career."

"She sure isn't," Betsy agreed. "She has no ambition, and she's lazy. But they bought that property by you and they built that house. Tim's jobs never paid very well, though I understand he did some of that E-trading on the Internet."

"He also had a baseball memorabilia collection," I pointed out.

"Oh, that's right." Betsy paused as the phone rang. "I'd better take that. I'm expecting a call from our produce people. They're mad because we've been buying so much local stuff this summer."

The call, however, was from Ryan O'Toole, their oldest son. Betsy made it quick. "The big black suitcase is in the basement behind the furnace. Don't touch the rest of the luggage. The red ones are strictly for your dad and me. And take out the garbage."

She set the receiver down in its cradle. "Ryan's off to WAZZU. They start early because of the semester system. He leaves for Pullman tomorrow. Would you believe he's a sophomore already?" Once more, she shook her head. But before I could say anything, she snapped her fingers. "That's right! Ryan bought some baseball stuff from Tim a couple of years ago. He saved his money from working as a box boy here and got some autographed cards. Only four or five, but they cost him fifty dollars. I thought it was a gyp, but then I'm not a baseball fan. Jake and I like hockey."

No doubt the fighting part, I thought. "Then Tim did sell some of his collection," I remarked before confessing that I'd never noticed his ad in the *Advocate*.

Betsy shrugged. "So what if you can't keep track of every detail? That's what a staff's for. You think I know every item we stock in the store? I don't. For one thing, Jake's always changing brands or trying something new."

"So you think Tim and Tiffany got along okay?" I said.

Betsy considered the question. "Oh, shoot, Emma, how do you ever really know?" She winked. "Take Jake and me, for instance."

I smiled. "You're right. I suppose I'm trying to judge Tiffany's sense of loss. She seems so wrapped up in herself. And the baby, I think."

"That's Tiffany," Betsy said. "She and Tim lived in a very tight little world."

"No friends?"

"She doesn't mention them," Betsy replied. "Oh— yes, there was another girl she talked about, somebody she'd gone to high school with, but who'd moved to Snohomish. What is her name?" Betsy frowned. "The family was here only for a couple of years. I think the dad worked for the fish and game department. Wylie or Wilder or Willard. Something like that. Does it matter?"

"Not really. I just wondered." I got to my feet. "I didn't recall ever seeing them hang out as a couple with their peer group. Tim apparently chatted it up with customers at the Venison Inn."

"That was his job," Betsy pointed out. "That's how you stay in business. Jake and I ought to know. And now that Tiffany's a widow with a baby on the way, she'd better learn that lesson fast."

"So predictable," Vida declared after I told her about my visit to the Erikses' home. "That's exactly how I'd expect Tiffany to behave. Sulky. Selfish. And Cookie takes the wrong approach. Can you imagine me babying my daughters like that?"

Of course I couldn't, though she'd certainly spoiled her grandson, Roger. Maybe she'd saved up all her spoiling for him, as grandparents often do. But I was more interested in what Vida had found out at the courthouse—if anything.

She had succeeded. Vida never took notes, keeping every detail in her remarkable brain. "The vacant house was built in 1931, right about the time the ski lodge opened. It belonged to a ski instructor, in fact. His name was Ole Knutson. He lived there for three years until he moved on. He was a bachelor at the time, I gather, and rootless."

In Vida's biased lexicon, that translated as not being enchanted with Alpine. "Ole sold the house?" I asked as I unwrapped the bagel, lox, cream cheese, and dill pickle I'd bought at the Grocery Basket's deli.

"Yes, to a couple named Hornby." She sat down in one of my visitor's chairs and removed her hat, a net confection covered with daisies. "They lived there until the war, when he went into the service and she moved away to be closer to her family. The house sat vacant for a year or so, and then she—Marcella Hornby—sold it. I couldn't help but wonder if her husband was killed in battle."

"That's possible," I said. Certainly that would give him an excuse in Vida's mind for not returning to Alpine.

"A man from Monroe—Russell Byers, aptly named, as it turns out—purchased the house from Mrs. Hornby in 1943. Apparently, he owned several houses from here to Snohomish and rented them out, mainly to mill workers. He died in 1968 in a nursing home in Everett."

I swallowed a bite of pickle and gazed quizzically at Vida. "How did you find out these details just from records of sale?"

"I happened to run into Dolph Terrill at the courthouse," Vida replied, looking smug. "Dolph is much older than I am and he has to use a walker, but his mind is still sharp. Or at least his memory for the past is good. I must admit, after we spoke, I saw him go into the women's restroom. I don't think he sees too well."

"That depends on what he wanted to see," I remarked.

"Now, now," said Vida. "Anyway, he recalled that Mr. Byers left everything to his son who lived in Everett. The son—his first name was Clinton—rented the house to a series of tenants, but wasn't much of a landlord. Dolph told me that he didn't think Clint Byers ever bothered to visit Alpine. Imagine!"

"So the place went to pot?"

"In more ways than one," Vida said darkly. "The last tenants were hippies. That was back in the early eighties. Apparently, Clint Byers died or simply faded from the picture. He didn't keep up the property taxes, and the city put a lien on the place. Fuzzy Baugh became mayor not long after that, and has never done anything about the house. It's just sat there, except for the occasional squatters."

"Like Old Nick," I noted.

"Yes." She shot me a look that smacked of reproach.

"I can't believe you haven't seen him—or anything else suspicious—going on a mere block from your home."

I felt defensive. "I explained, I don't take that route to work or to church or much of anywhere else. Furthermore, both the vacant house and the Rafferty place are set back from the street. You know we don't have sidewalks on Fir. Every time they propose Local Improvement District funding to build them, the idea gets shot down."

Vida's expression didn't change. Clearly, she believed I was oblivious to my surroundings. I couldn't say out loud that I wasn't the type to take evening walks so I could peer into my neighbors' windows when they didn't pull the drapes. Vida did it all the time, which was another reason she didn't like summer or daylight saving time. People didn't turn on their lights until after dark.

"Anyway," I continued when Vida didn't honor me with a response, "Milo's checking on Old Nick's whereabouts. I plan to see him after lunch." For emphasis, I bit off another chunk of bagel.

"Bagels," Vida muttered. "I've never understood them."

I ignored the comment. Vida occasionally ran a contemporary recipe she received in the mail, but she usually resorted to her basic old-fashioned cooking file. Tuna noodle casserole with a cornflake crust and Jell-O mold in the shape of a fish were about as exotic as she got. The strange part was that readers seldom complained.

I kept my word and walked down Front Street to the sheriff's office shortly after one o'clock. Milo wasn't in. Toni Andreas informed me that he'd taken a late lunch.

Toni managed to retain her receptionist's job only because over the years Sam Heppner had exhibited the patience of a saint. The deputy had taken the trouble to guide her like a teacher with a special-needs student. Long before she ever got the job, Toni had dated my son, who found her pretty and sweet but dim. She was also the person responsible for the sheriff's loathsome coffee. As I leaned against the curving mahogany counter, she didn't look up from her console. "Dodge said he'd be back around two," she mumbled.

Doe Jameson was nearby, flipping through a stack of reports. "Can I help you?" she inquired in her brisk manner.

I hesitated. Doe was quick to notice my reluctance to query her. "Sheriff Dodge is keeping me in the loop on the Rafferty homicide," she assured me.

"Oh, of course." I smiled, probably looking a bit silly. "Any progress?"

Doe's sharp dark eyes studied me. "In what way?"

"In any way," I retorted, unaccustomed to anything but a certain amount of deference from the sheriff's employees. "Specifically, I was wondering if he'd found any sign of Old Nick at that vacant house next to Tim's."

"Other than that somebody's been occupying it?" Doe shook her head. "No. What's with these recluses anyway? If I believed half of what Jack Mullins says— which I've learned not to—I'd figure that the woods are full of them."

I shrugged. "It's not uncommon. You must have heard about people who want to disappear, cut themselves off from society, live off the land."

"Oh, sure." Doe waved a hand. "I understand all that. I'm half Muckleshoot; I know the lure of becoming one with the earth. But SkyCo seems to have more than its share. And I'm not talking about the perps running meth labs, either. That's different."

My smile became more genuine. "Maybe it's because we're so isolated. There was no road into Alpine until 1930. Fewer than four thousand people live in Alpine, with not quite half that many in the rest of the county. Unlike in a city, the sighting of a peculiar stranger is a real event. When one of these hermits shows up, everybody talks about it. That's one of the things you'll get used to after you've lived here awhile."

Doe considered my words. "I suppose. It *is* different. I wanted to live away from traffic and be closer to the outdoors. But I guess everything has its downside."

I wasn't sure what she meant. "You're referring to . . ." I wanted to be tactful in front of Toni, who was answering the phone, and Deputy Bill Blatt, who had just emerged from the jail area. "To the excitement that an unusual occurrence causes?"

Doe stared at me as if I were some kind of garrulous relic. "No. I'm saying that just because some nonconformist shows up on the scene everybody jumps to the conclusion that he must have murdered Tim Rafferty. What's wrong with not marching in lockstep with the rest of society? Anybody in this town could have bashed Tim's head in with a baseball bat."

Before I could agree, Toni Andreas yanked off her headset, burst into tears, and ran out the front door.

Chapter Six

W<small>HAT'S THAT ALL</small> about?" Bill Blatt asked in his mild way after Toni had dashed out the front door. He went over to the console and picked up the headset she'd abandoned in her distress. "Hello? Hello?" Removing the device from his ear, he set it down. "Nobody there. Did the call upset her? I don't get it."

"Toni's acted weird for the last few days," Doe declared, disgusted.

I looked outside. Toni had disappeared, but she couldn't have gone far. "Excuse me," I said, and left.

I turned in every direction, but Toni was nowhere in sight—not across Front Street by the Burger Barn or the Clemans Building, not down by the post office on my right or the *Advocate* on my left. But Parker's Pharmacy was situated on the other side of Third Street, between my office and Milo's headquarters. It seemed the most likely place that Toni could have gone in such a short time.

I found her in the cosmetics aisle. She had her back to me and wasn't studying the displays, but stood hunched over as if she was still crying.

Several customers were in the store, including two at the dispensary window in the back, but no one else was in the cosmetics section. I approached Toni in the same cautious way I try to get close to a deer that has wandered into my backyard.

I whispered her name as soon as I got within three feet. She stiffened, then turned slowly to look at me.

"Emma? Go away."

I shook my head. "I can't leave you when you're so miserable. What's wrong?" I saw Otis Poole, the Baptist minister, on the other side of the aisle in the corn plaster section. "Come on, let's go outside." Gently, I took Toni's hand.

She didn't resist. We were halfway to the entrance when Tara Wesley came toward us. She and her husband, Garth, had bought the drugstore from the Parkers almost fifteen years ago.

"Hi, Emma, Toni," Tara said in a cheerful voice. "How—" She stopped, noticing Toni's pitiful state. "What's wrong? Are you ill? Did you hurt herself?"

"Toni's just upset," I said, keeping hold of her hand. "She needs some air. See you later."

Luckily, Tara didn't try to detain us. She was probably relieved that a display hadn't fallen on Toni and left the Wesleys liable for damages.

"Do you want to walk down to my office and tell me what's wrong?" I asked when we got outside.

Toni shielded her teary eyes from the midday sun. "No."

"You need to talk to somebody," I said kindly, steering Toni away from the pharmacy. Front Street's sidewalks weren't busy, no doubt due to the hot weather. The only passerby was a teenager on a skateboard. The hobby shop was next to the drugstore, and the Sears catalog pickup was around the corner on Third. An alcove was located next to the main entrance, where customers could collect large items. We rounded the corner while I kept speaking. "Take a few minutes to pull yourself together," I said. "Do you want to go across the street to the Burger Barn and get some coffee?"

Toni shook her head. I honored her wishes and led her

in the opposite direction. A moment later, we were inside the alcove at Sears and out of the sun.

"I'm okay," she asserted, wiping at her eyes with a
finger. "It's just stress."

"Are you due for a vacation?" I asked.

Toni nodded. "I was supposed to take the first week
of September, but I put it off."

"How come?"

Toni sighed and sniffed. "My plans didn't work out. I
thought I'd wait until things were . . . more settled."

"You've got more than one week's vacation, don't
you? Have you taken any this year?"

"I get three," Toni replied, looking beyond me to the
street where a tow truck was driving by. "I took a week
at Easter to visit my cousin in Oregon."

"Aren't your parents retired in Arizona?"

Toni nodded. "It's too hot to go there in the summer,
even with AC. Maybe I'll go for Thanksgiving and take
the other week at Christmas." She spoke slowly, as if she
were figuring it out as she went along.

"That sounds nice," I said.

Toni shrugged and wiped at her eyes again. "I did that
a couple of years ago. Christmas, I mean. It doesn't seem
right to have Christmas with all that sunshine and desert."

I understood. During the years that Ben had spent at
the Native American mission in Tuba City, Arizona,
he'd griped about the lack of atmosphere. Luckily, he'd
been able to spend a few Christmas holidays with me in
Alpine.

"Do your folks ever come back to Alpine?" I couldn't
remember Vida writing about any visits from the An-
dreases. Toni's parents had still lived in Alpine when I
first moved to town, but they left a couple of years later.

"No," she replied. "That is, my mom came once.
After the divorce."

"Oh. I didn't realize your parents divorced."

Toni, whose dark complexion had been deepened by the sun, bowed her head. "They moved into one of those retirement communities in Chandler. They ended up swapping."

"Swapping?" I must have looked surprised. "You mean—swapping mates?"

She nodded sadly. "They've been too embarrassed to visit here. My mom came only because I had appendicitis a couple of years ago. But Dad and her and the other two all get along real well."

The former Mrs. Andreas must have somehow sneaked into town under Vida's radar. My House & Home editor would have a conniption fit when she found out she'd missed this juicy piece of news. "Your parents and their new spouses are friendly?"

"Oh, really tight. They golf and play tennis and party together. I suppose it's kind of nice." She stiffened suddenly. "I'd better go. Here comes Janet Driggers."

Before I could delay her, Toni hurried past me and crossed Third in the middle of the street. I looked in the direction of Front where the wife of the funeral director was marching briskly toward me.

"Well?" Janet said in her direct manner. "What was that all about? I watched from my desk at Sky Travel. I'm working for the living instead of the dead today."

Full of energy and bawdy speech, Janet not only helped Al at the funeral parlor, but had a part-time job with Sky Travel. As she put it, "I'm always sending somebody someplace, but some of them never come back."

"Stress," I said tactfully. "Toni needs a vacation."

"She already booked one and then canceled," Janet retorted. "She was going to Hawaii in September. Now she's lost most of her airline deposit. I never did think she was very smart."

"She's not," I agreed, "but she tries hard."

Janet looked disgusted. "I figure Lover Boy dumped her. I hope he pays her back for the money she lost."

"Who is it?" I asked, realizing that job stress wasn't the only pressure Toni was under. "I remember hearing that she was serious about some guy a while back."

"That was then, this is now," Janet declared, removing her sunglasses and brushing her dark red hair off of her perspiring forehead. "I forget who he was, but it was short-term. And she never gave this new one a name. I assumed he was from out of town. She's always been one for a traveling salesman. You know, 'Did you hear the one about the sheriff's receptionist and the et cetera?' The last guy I saw her with sold tools. That seemed to fit, if you know what I mean." Janet gave me her patented leer.

"Interesting," I said. "She never mentioned her love life to me."

"You never mention yours," Janet said in reproach, "and I hear you have one. What's he like in the sack?"

"We've never done it in a sack," I deadpanned.

"Try it," Janet said. "Did I ever tell you about the time Al brought a body bag home from the—"

"Stop!" I held up my hands, but laughed. "I've got to go back to work."

"And I have to collect the blender I ordered from Sears," Janet said. "It's supposed to mix amazing aphrodisiacs. See you." She breezed off toward the catalog pickup's main entrance.

When I returned to the office, Ginny handed me several messages. At first glance I could see that most of them were from our usual cranks who had taken their first look at this week's *Advocate*. Ginny had made a two-words notation regarding Grace Grundle's call— "pyromaniac loose?" Fuzzy Baugh wanted to make an official statement, assuring his constituents that he was making every effort to prevent fires of any kind. He didn't mention stopping people from smashing each other over the head with a baseball bat. Averill Fairbanks, our resident UFO spotter, had seen a spacecraft shaped like a pumpkin hovering over First Hill Monday night, spewing seeds that turned into flames.

The only call I returned was from Rolf Fisher.

"You people lead dangerous lives up in your mountain aerie," he said drolly. "I didn't see the homicide-arson story until about an hour ago when we picked it up here. Did you know this Rafferty?"

I related my casual acquaintance with Tim and his wife, as well as my proximity to the crime scene.

"On-the-spot reporting," Rolf remarked. "I'm impressed."

"No, you're not."

"That's true. But still, it was a little too close for comfort, right? The woods must be tinder-dry."

"We were lucky it didn't spread," I replied. "There was no wind that night."

"So are we still on for this weekend?" he asked, which I knew was the real reason for his call.

"I hope so." I meant it. I wanted very much to be with Rolf.

"Good. But," he added, "if this thing heats up—excuse the expression—I won't hold it against you if you're chin-deep in breaking news."

And Rolf meant that. Like Tom, he was a journalist who understood that the story came first. "Milo thinks it's a bungled burglary." I explained about Tim's baseball collection, which hadn't appeared in the story picked up by the AP.

"Do you agree?" Rolf asked.

"It's the obvious explanation," I admitted. "But our sheriff goes by the book. He'll work that angle until something proves him wrong."

"You being that something," Rolf noted. "And you *are* something. Maybe I should come up to Alpine if you can't get out of town. We could do some deep, penetrating research together."

I giggled before I noticed Ed Bronsky lumbering toward my cubbyhole. He was wearing a tank top and floral-patterned shorts. His fat, hairy legs and arms reminded me of an overfed gorilla. Vida let out a squawk. Fortunately, she stopped Ed in his tracks just before he crossed my threshold.

"I should go," I said into the receiver. "I'm about to be invaded by a tank wearing a tank."

"Could that be your former ad manager, Ed Bronchitis or whatever his name is? You're lucky he's not contagious."

"Lucky guess," I said. "I'll call you tonight or tomorrow."

I hung up just as Ed managed to get away from Vida's reprimands for his unseemly attire.

"Really, Ed," she was saying, "there's altogether too much flesh when you're almost in the altogether. It's truly obscene."

"You'll put it in 'Scene'?" Ed asked, looking confused. "If you do, mention my proposed bond issue."

"I will *not* mention any such thing," Vida declared. "I don't use unsightly items in my column. It's intended to inform readers, not frighten them to death. We are, after all, a family newspaper."

"I've got a family," Ed growled, thumping into my office. "Dang, Emma, Vida's on the peck today. Is it the weather?"

"Partly," I said, trying to avoid the expanse of stomach between Ed's tank top and the shorts. "Sit down." Ordinarily, I wouldn't have encouraged him to take a seat but I was desperate. The less I could see of him, the better.

"I'm disappointed in you," Ed asserted. "I didn't think I'd have to remind you what your editorial should've been this week."

I looked blankly at Ed. "Oh?"

"As for that reporter of yours, what's with him?" Ed leaned forward, chins a-wagging. "He hardly mentioned that those stupid county commissioners tabled my proposal. I mean, he gave it one sentence at the very end of the story."

"That's because nothing happened, Ed." I shrugged. "You handed your information over to the commissioners. You know perfectly well they have to study it in detail. Authorizing a bond issue or a levy to be put before the voters is a serious matter."

Ed looked aghast. "Study? Detail? Those old duffers can't concentrate for more than two minutes before they nod off."

I couldn't argue that point. But I said nothing as I watched Ed's round face light up. "That's it! I'll run for county commissioner! That's the real problem; nobody ever opposes them except Crazy Eights Neffel or one of the Dithers sisters' horses."

Ed was right about that, too. Crazy Eights, our local loony, had filed several times for election to the office. Four years ago, the Dithers sisters had put their Tennessee walker, Andrew Jackson, on the ballot. The horse had gotten over two hundred votes, ten times the amount that Crazy Eights had ever received.

"Go for it," I said. Why not? Even Ed couldn't be any worse than what we already had. He'd be self-serving, of course, but at least he wasn't in his dotage. "You considered running for mayor a while ago. The fact is, the county commissioners have more clout around here than Fuzzy Baugh. That is, they do when they use it."

Clumsily, Ed got out of the chair. "I'm going to file right away. I haven't missed the deadline, have I?"

I grimaced. "I think the state deadline is the last week of July. But you can always run as a write-in candidate. You'll have to check with the courthouse."

"I'm on my way. Oof!" Ed tripped over the other visitor's chair. "This is news, Emma!" he shouted as he waddled rapidly out of the office. "Huge news!"

"Yes," I said. "Huge."

As soon as Ed was out the door, Vida stomped into my office. "Are you out of your mind? Did I hear you encourage Ed to run for public office? I'm stupefied!"

"Consider the alternative," I pointed out. "George Engebretsen is up for reelection. Frankly, he's the least daffy of the commissioners, but not by much. It's not unlikely that one of the other two will die in office. Isn't it time we got somebody new—even Ed?—in the jobs?"

Vida held her head. "Have we sunk so low?"

"Yes," I asserted. "Face it—before the commissioners weren't all gaga, it took six years to start building the new bridge over Icicle Creek. Two of the three were against opening the community college, but they had to give in to the state on that one. They have absolutely no vision of the future, because they're living in the past. Besides," I added slyly, "if Ed runs, he's bound to annoy enough people to goad some competent potential candidates to declare themselves."

"A good point," Vida conceded. She looked thoughtful. "Yes, I can see that might happen. Do you suppose Ed will give the news to Spencer Fleetwood today?"

"Drat. I didn't think of that. It wouldn't have done any good to swear Ed to secrecy," I went on. "He can't keep his mouth shut."

Vida crossed her arms over her jutting bosom. "It puts me in a bind. My radio program airs tonight. If Spencer carries Ed's candidacy on the news at six, I don't know whether I should mention it when *Vida's Cupboard* comes on at seven."

"Well . . . Ed's a former *Advocate* employee," I pointed out. "It would give the paper a mention."

"Yes." Vida nodded once. "Yes, it would. But down the line, I'll have to interview him." She shuddered. "So off-putting. But needs must."

Vida's phone rang. She hurried back to her desk just as Milo entered the newsroom.

"I hear Toni had a meltdown this afternoon," he said, putting a big booted foot on the visitor's chair Ed had recently vacated. "What was that all about? Doe told me you chased after her."

"Stress," I replied. "Or so Toni informed me. Are you working her too hard?"

"No more than usual," Milo answered, tugging at the sweat-stained collar of his regulation shirt. "Damn, it's hot. Anyway, Toni's load's lighter these days. When she was the only woman on the staff, sometimes she had to help with female perps. Now that Doe's aboard, Toni can skip that part. She never liked doing it."

"So she should have less stress," I remarked.

"Yeah, right." Milo made a face. "The problem is, she doesn't like Doe. Toni thinks she's too pushy."

"Doe is fairly aggressive," I said.

"Hell, yes. That's one reason I hired her." Milo looked pleased with himself. "You know how I had to pare the budget to get somebody new. I think I got us a winner."

"Doe seems very competent," I agreed. "So what's with Toni?"

Milo shrugged. "I thought maybe she told you."

"Stress," I repeated adamantly. "She didn't explain." Hesitating, I wondered if I should pass on what Janet had said. I wouldn't print hearsay in the paper, and generally I didn't pass it along in private.

"What?" Milo asked.

I hedged. "I suppose you can always blame a man."

"What man?"

"How would I know?" The sheriff was beginning to irk me. "You're the one who works with her. Surely—being a detective as part of your job—you know who she's dating."

"She never talks about her love life. Almost never," Milo added.

"Maybe she talks about it to Doe," I said.

"I doubt it. Like I told you, Toni isn't chummy with Doe."

"Who does she hang out with then?"

Milo frowned. "Heather Bardeen. Heather Bavich, I mean, since she got married. Mandy Gustavson. Mags Patricelli—I forget her married name."

I didn't remember it offhand, either. Mags was the daughter of Pete Patricelli, who owned a pizza parlor. Heather Bardeen Bavich worked for her father, Henry, at the ski lodge, and was also the niece of Buck Bardeen, Vida's longtime male friend. I recognized Mandy as one of the many Gustavsons in town who were somehow related to Vida. Mandy had always been employed as a waitress, most recently at the Venison Inn. Trying to keep everyone straight was no easy task, not even after thirteen years in Alpine. The best way was to put them into two categories: those who were connected to Vida, and those who weren't.

"Didn't Mags move to Sultan after she got married?" I inquired.

"Could be." He nodded in Vida's direction. She was still talking on the phone. "Ask her about Mags."

"You ask. You're the one who has to work with Toni."

Milo waved a hand in dismissal. "Toni'll get over it. She was pretty upset about Rafferty's death. I guess it's the younger generation facing up to their own mortality."

I recalled Ginny and Kip's reactions. "Yes. Especially

when they grew up with someone who's died. That, and hitting the thirty-year milestone."

The sheriff removed his foot from the chair. "I didn't come here just to shoot the breeze about Toni. I talked to Wayne Eriks this afternoon. I'd interviewed him earlier to find out if he knew of any reason why someone would want to murder his son-in-law. He didn't, but today when I ran into him while he was working on a pole by the old water tower, he remembered seeing Nick the recluse the other night."

"Where?" I noticed that Vida had hung up the phone and was leaning in our direction.

"By the high school football field, across the street from the other side of the cul-de-sac."

"Ah." I saw Vida, halfway out of her chair. "Which night?" I asked.

"Sunday, just before dark," Milo replied. He raised his voice slightly. "That's Sunday, Vida, the night before Tim died."

"Do you think I'm deaf?" she snapped.

"But nobody's seen him since?" I inquired.

"Nope." Milo started backing away from my desk. "We were pretty sure he'd been at the vacant house in the last few days, though. We could tell from the leftovers. All kinds of leftovers." He made a disgusted face.

I saw Vida wince. Getting out of my chair, I came around to where Milo was standing. "Do you think Old Nick has gone back into the woods?"

"I wouldn't be surprised," he said. "Even if he wasn't involved, the fire and the sirens and the emergency personnel would've scared him off. His kind doesn't like that sort of commotion. That's why they're hermits."

"But," Vida put in, now on her feet, but remaining by her desk, "he may have seen something or someone. You really must try to find him."

Milo had turned around to face Vida. "We're talking

about a guy who doesn't want to be found. That's not going to be easy."

"Boy Scouts," Vida said. "Girl Scouts. All sorts of teenagers who are at loose ends this summer. Let them help."

The sheriff shook his head as he loped through the newsroom. "Too risky. Any kind of accident, and we get the pants sued off of us. Not to mention that Old Nick may be armed and dangerous. He doesn't want visitors. See you."

The sheriff left.

"That's ridiculous!" Vida declared. "Milo doesn't have enough manpower to find Old Nick, and the forest rangers are all overworked these days, what with visitors at the parks and the danger of forest fires and everything else that goes along with summer. I've a good mind to—"

She broke off, a spark gleaming in her gray eyes. I had come out into the middle of the newsroom to listen to her rant. "To do what?" I asked.

"You'll see." She snatched up the phone and dialed from memory. Alpine has only one prefix, but I swear she's memorized over half the numbers in the county. "Todd? Is Todd Wilson there?"

Todd is the PUD manager. I waited.

"Todd? Yes, this is Vida Runkel. Is there some way I can reach Wayne Eriks in the field?"

I waited some more.

"Very well. Have him call me at the paper when he gets in. Please tell him it's urgent. You have my number, of course. Thank you."

"Why do you want to talk to Wayne Eriks?" I asked after she hung up.

"To get his description of Old Nick," Vida replied brusquely. "It would appear that Wayne may be the last person to see Old Nick in recent weeks."

"So?"

"You'll see." Vida looked smug.

I knew it was pointless to press her. "Maybe Wayne *wasn't* the last person to see him around here," I said.

She was quick to catch my meaning. "Yes." Her face had turned solemn. "That person could be Tim Rafferty. That's why I think Old Nick should be found as soon as possible."

Chapter Seven

WAYNE ERIKS SHOWED up shortly before five o'clock. "I thought I might as well stop by instead of call," he said to Vida. "My final job today was out on the Burl Creek Road, so you were on the way back to the PUD office down the street."

"Excellent," Vida said, beaming at Wayne as if he were a long-lost friend. "Do sit."

I didn't recall ever having officially met Wayne Eriks, though I'd seen him around town for years. "Hi," I said, offering my hand. "I'm Emma Lord. I was at your house this morning, but I missed you."

Wayne's grip was strong. He was a man of medium height, but with broad shoulders and the hint of a paunch. His fair skin was peeling from sunburn, and I noticed he was wearing a long-sleeved cotton work shirt to protect himself from further damage. For those who worked outdoors, long, hot summers were especially difficult. I was suddenly grateful for my stuffy little cubbyhole. At least I had shade.

"I know who you are," he said with a gap-toothed smile. "I mean, everybody does."

"It's part of being a publisher," I said in a self-deprecating manner. "I'm very sorry about Tim. It's brave of you to go back on the job so soon after the tragedy."

Wayne shrugged. "Keeps my mind off of it. Besides, we've had a bunch of problems. Everybody's running their fans and even air conditioners, if they've got 'em. That causes outages. Not to mention the morons who let their trees and vines grow into the poles and blow the transformers."

"I know," I said. "We had one catch fire on our street last summer." It was the fault of my evil neighbors, who had allowed a morning glory to wend its way up the pole outside of their house.

Wayne had sat down by Vida's desk. "I remember that. It was in August, just about a year to the day."

Having joined the conversation, I decided it was my turn to eavesdrop. Leo had left for the day, so I perched on his desk. Vida didn't look very pleased, but began to interrogate Wayne.

"Now tell me about seeing Old Nick Sunday night," she said.

Wayne seemed puzzled. "I already told Dodge."

"Yes, of course." Vida gave Wayne her toothy Cheshire cat smile. "But I'm doing my radio program tonight, and I thought I might give a description of Old Nick while I'm on the air. You must admit, his presence in that vacant house next door to your daughter and Tim is highly suspicious."

"You bet it is," Wayne declared. "Damned scary, too." He didn't seem to notice Vida's brief look of disapproval at his language. "Wish I'd known he'd been hiding out around there. I would've run him off. You can never guess what a nut like that is going to do."

"So," Vida said, "you think he may have been responsible for what happened to your son-in-law?"

"Wouldn't surprise me," Wayne said, coughing and blowing his nose loudly into a wrinkled handkerchief. "This Nick must be crazy. He may have gone into the wrong house. I mean, it was dark. I'm guessing his brain's scrambled, so he goes into Tiffany's place instead

of that dump next door. He wakes up Tim, panics—
well, you know the rest." Wayne sighed heavily.

"Yes," Vida said softly, "it could have happened that
way. Now, tell me about seeing him Sunday night by the
football field."

"Right." Wayne sat back in the chair, clasping hands
that still wore work gloves. "I'd gone up to First Hill to
check out a problem we'd been having. It was my day
off, but I wanted to make sure everything was okay at
the box on Disappointment Avenue. It was getting dark
when I got done, but it was still hot, so I decided to take
Fir down Fifth." He chuckled self-consciously. "I was
going to get a cold one at Mugs Ahoy before I went
home."

"So you turned the corner on Fir at Fifth and saw Old
Nick?" Vida prompted.

"That's right." Wayne nodded as he cleared his
throat. "He was sort of leaning against the cyclone fence
that goes around the field. I mean, it's the track part
down at that end, where they do the hurdles and long
jump and that stuff. I noticed, because I've seen kids
hanging out there at night, smoking dope. But this was
no kid. It was a guy with a long gray beard and long hair
and really ratty-looking clothes. Grubby jacket, torn
pants—the whole bit. I slowed down, and he got real agitated, like he wanted to climb the fence. I didn't recognize him. I figured he was some bum from off one of the
freight trains. But you wrote about the hermit being seen
around town, so then I thought afterwards I should tell
Dodge."

"You didn't approach him?" Vida queried.

"Couldn't see the point." Wayne raised his gloved
hands in a helpless gesture. "Those kind of rummies
might do anything. I mean, their brains are all screwed
up. I just kept driving."

"How close were you to him?" Vida asked.

"Oh . . ." Wayne gazed around the newsroom. "From here to the main door. Twenty feet, maybe more."

Vida pressed on. "Can you describe his clothing?"

"Ragged. Old jacket and baggy pants, shirt, some kind of boots."

"Colors?"

Wayne shook his head. "I couldn't tell in the dark. He looked dirty, though. What you'd expect."

"Height? Weight?"

"Average, maybe closer to six feet." Wayne paused. "No way to guess what he weighed with all those baggy clothes. I'd say he wasn't fat, though."

Vida was relentless. "How long was the hair and beard? Did he wear anything on his head?"

Wayne put one hand in the middle of his chest and the other a few inches down his back. "Gray, scraggly. He wasn't wearing a hat or cap. I'm pretty sure of that, though it was hard to tell. I mean, if he had a bandana or something, I couldn't see from where I was in the car."

Vida blinked two or three times at Wayne, almost as if she were memorizing his own features. "Very well. I think that's all. You've been of great assistance."

"Sure." Wayne got up and blew his nose again. It sounded like a duck call. "Glad to help," he said amiably. "I'd like to see that Old Nick nailed."

I slid off of Leo's desk and spoke for the first time since the interview started. "You think the recluse did it?"

"It'd figure, wouldn't it?" Wayne responded. "Either he was robbing the place, or like I mentioned, he made a mistake and went into the wrong house. He's got to be crazy."

Old Nick probably was unbalanced. But as Doe had

pointed out, that didn't automatically make him a killer. I kept my thoughts to myself, however.

Wayne left. Vida immediately began to gather her belongings. "I must dash," she said without looking at me. "I've less than two hours to finalize my radio program."

I knew that Vida didn't need more than five minutes to produce her show, and that included a phone call to whichever local luminary she was interviewing in the final segment. She carried everything around in her head, the same way she approached writing for the paper. I was also aware that she had preferred I wasn't on hand when she talked to Wayne Eriks. My suspicions grew. But it was pointless to confront her. Instead, I applied the needle.

"By the way," I said over my shoulder, "did you know that Toni Andreas's parents divorced?"

"Yes," Vida replied tersely. "My nephew Billy told me."

I couldn't hide my surprise. "You knew?"

Now Vida turned her gimlet eye on me. "I found out only an hour ago. I happened to run into Billy on the street. He told me what happened with Toni today. You never mentioned it."

I went on the defensive. "I've been busy. You were out most of the afternoon."

"Not all of it," Vida snapped. "I hold Billy at fault, too. He should have informed me about the Andreas divorce when it happened. I scolded him severely."

Now it was my turn to suffer Vida's wrath. As for Bill Blatt, the poor guy was expected to keep his aunt up to speed on everything that went on at the sheriff's office. Despite his best efforts to be professionally discreet, Vida could eventually wheedle just about anything out of him.

"Billy insisted he forgot," Vida went on. "That's possible, perhaps. Men are so poor at paying attention, particularly when it comes to personal relationships in the workplace." She picked up her straw handbag and took a step toward the door. "I don't suppose you'd care to tell me what caused Toni's emotional breakdown."

"I don't know," I admitted. "She wouldn't say. Toni simply blamed it on stress."

"Stress!" Vida spoke the word as if it were obscene. "Such an excuse for lack of self-discipline! I've always believed that Toni is a ninny!"

I didn't utter a peep as Vida stomped out. She'd be even more annoyed when—and if—I told her what Janet Driggers had said about the possibility of Toni having suffered a romantic disaster.

Five minutes later I was heading out through the newsroom on my way home when Leo came through the door.

"I thought you'd gone for the day," I said in surprise.

"I had," Leo replied with an aggrieved expression. "But I stopped in at Harvey's Hardware to buy another fan, and he'd given me the wrong information for his ad in this week's paper. He's selling some new kind of house paint that's an acrylic and he mistakenly identified it as latex-based. The whole point is that the makers claim acrylic lasts longer or some damned thing than the latex. Harvey's afraid the vendor will sue him or cancel the line, so I've got to put together a radio spot for tonight on KSKY."

"Hey," I said, annoyed. "Since when do you do ad copy for Fleetwood? Isn't it bad enough that Vida's got a show on the station?"

Leo made a face. "I'm doing it *for* Vida's show, because it's got such good ratings. But I'm doing it because I don't want Spence to make it sound like it was our mistake and not Harvey's. On the other hand, the ad can't make Harvey out to sound like an idiot. It's all of thirty

seconds long. Do you trust me or do you trust Fleetwood?"

"You," I admitted. "It sounds tricky."

Leo had sat down and was already writing on a
notepad. "Not for the clever likes of me. Hold on."

I sat on the edge of Vida's desk and kept my mouth
shut.

"Okay," Leo said after about two minutes had
passed. "How's this? 'Harvey's Hardware is proud to
announce that its new line of Paragon AAA house paints
has gone beyond latex to a new acrylic coating that will
withstand even the roughest and toughest of Alpine
weather. Sun or snow, wind or rain—Paragon provides
protection for you and your mountainside home that
will last for years to come. So drop by and ask your old
friend Harvey Adcock for the latest in all kinds of
paint—interior, exterior, enamel, glossy, latex—and the
new acrylic from Paragon. Remember, Harvey works
hard for all your household wares.' " Leo took a deep
breath. "Think Spence can handle that?"

"It lets Harvey and us off the hook," I said, "but why
not let Vida read it?"

Leo nodded once. "Good idea. I'll e-mail it to KSKY
right now. Harvey already had a spot later in the
evening, but I'll tell Spence to cancel that one. It was for
more window fans, but he's almost out."

I stood up, ready to leave. But Leo held up a hand.
"This'll only take a minute. Want to go to the Venison
Inn for a drink?"

I didn't have anything better to do—as long as I was
home in time for *Vida's Cupboard.* "Sure," I said. "I'll
meet you there."

Leo nodded again. "Good. Order me a Miller Lite."
He began to enter the ad copy on his computer.

I walked out into the late afternoon sun, taking my
time to pass the dry cleaners and reach the Venison Inn.

At almost three thousand feet above sea level, the air isn't particularly thin, and on this semihumid August day, it felt oppressive. One of the few renovations I liked at the inn was the air-conditioning that had been installed when the owners remodeled. It had seemed like a luxury, but the past couple of summers had proved its worth. I felt slightly rejuvenated as I entered the bar.

"Hot enough for you?" Oren Rhodes asked as he came over to the small table where I'd sat down.

I narrowed my eyes at him. "The next person who asks that is going to get hurt."

Oren chuckled, displaying a fairly recent second chin. "It's hotter than Dutch love, as my granny used to say. She wasn't Dutch, though. She was Swiss."

I wasn't interested in Oren's heredity. But it dawned on me that he could answer some questions about Tim. On a Wednesday at five-thirty, the bar was just beginning to fill up. A clutch of workmen sat at the bar, regulars who worked in the woods and the warehouses and the mill. Logging, however, had been curtailed because of the tinder-dry conditions. I recognized a couple of the loggers. No doubt they were griping about the stoppage. The rest of the drinkers were probably complaining about the hardships caused by the weather, too. A bar is always a good place to bitch.

"I'm waiting for Leo," I said, giving Oren a friendly smile. "I'll have a screwdriver and Leo wants a Miller Lite. That'll save you a trip." I grew somber. "You must be shorthanded with Tim gone."

"Thanks, Emma. Yeah, Tim helped out fairly often. Though he hadn't put in the hours lately like he used to. I'm teaching Mandy Gustavson to tend bar. Damned shame about Tim." Oren shook his balding head.

"Yes," I agreed. "It's awful. It doesn't seem right that a young couple with a baby on the way should have a tragedy strike like that."

"It's a rough world out there," Oren remarked, his gaze going past me. Maybe he was seeing that world, which isolated small-townsfolk often try to ignore.

"It is rough," I said, still perfectly agreeable. "This should have been the happiest time of their lives."

Oren's eyes turned back to me. "Oh—well, yes, I guess so. Even with Tim not feeling good."

I was surprised. "He was sick?"

"Not seriously sick," Oren said quickly. "But he'd had a lot of complaints lately, especially for a young guy. That's why he hadn't worked so much." Oren glanced at the bar where someone had called his name. "Excuse me, Emma. I'll get your order."

Leo arrived as soon as Oren left me. "No drinks?" my ad manager said. "How can you get drunk if you're not drinking?"

I laughed halfheartedly.

"What's wrong?" Leo asked, sitting down. "Do you still think I may fall off the wagon and have to crawl to work on my hands and knees?"

"No, no," I replied. After a decade I believed that Leo's battle of the bottle was over. He had never been a true alcoholic, but the type who drank too much in order to cope with that rough world out there. In all the years I'd known him, he'd never taken more than two drinks at a time. A ruined marriage and an almost equally bankrupt career had sobered him up. "I was thinking about Tim Rafferty. Oren mentioned he missed work lately. Spence told me the same thing. I wonder why."

Leo cocked his head at me. "Are you sleuthing?"

I sighed. "I suppose I am. Everybody's jumping to the conclusion that Tim was killed by a burglar or that recluse, Old Nick. It seems too pat."

"It also seems reasonable," Leo pointed out. "What makes you think otherwise?"

"My contrary nature," I retorted. "And I don't like easy answers. Most of all, I hate it when someone like Tim is treated like a nobody. He *was* somebody. Maybe I feel guilty because I always dismissed him—and Tiffany, too—as unimportant. That's not right, it's not fair."

"Emma Lord, Champion of the Underdog." Leo smiled. "I'm not kidding. You championed me when I was down and out."

It was true. I'd met Leo by accident when I was visiting in Port Angeles. He was suicidal, up from California, but definitely down and almost out. Tom, who had been his former employer, had recommended him. Ed had just come into his inheritance from an aunt in the Midwest, and I needed an ad manager, but I'd had my doubts about Leo. On the other hand, anything had to be better than Ed, with his distressing aptitude for *not* selling ads. Leo had more than justified Tom's advice.

Oren returned with our drinks. "Hey there, Leo. Is it hot enough—" The bartender stopped and laughed in embarrassment. "Never mind. Shall I run a tab?"

Leo shook his head. "This is just a pit stop. We're on the pay-as-you-go plan." He pulled a ten out of his wallet.

"You can't afford to treat me," I said as Oren took the bill and went off to the bar to get change.

"It makes me feel like a big spender," Leo said. "So what are you thinking? Tim just didn't like to work or he was making enough money so he didn't have to?"

"Why not say so?" I responded, declining Leo's offer of a cigarette. "I gather Tim liked to brag. I'm wondering if he really was sick. Sometimes, I'm told, men whose wives or girlfriends are expecting don't like mommy and baby getting all the attention. Maybe he was feigning illness. Or maybe he really was ailing, but it was psychosomatic."

Leo licked beer foam off of his upper lip. "Tim's always seemed to be the dominant one in that lash-up. Tiffany's the clingy type."

"Yes," I said. "She seems semihelpless. Tim's always been very protective. But that doesn't mean he couldn't be jealous of the baby. It happens."

"Oh, I kind of remember that with our kids," Leo said with a shake of his head. "Especially Katie, the first one. Liza couldn't talk or think about anything else. She read every expectant mother and baby book that was in print. Old Dad is bound to feel left out. Our work is done, and suddenly we're in the background." He wore his wry off-center grin. "Maybe Tim fell off his mountain bike to get some sympathy."

"He had a fall?" I said in surprise. "When was that?"

Leo and I both looked up and waved at Skunk and Trout Nordby, who owned the local GM dealership. "About a month ago," Leo responded. "Right after the Fourth of July, I think. I should have given it to the Duchess for 'Scene,' but I forgot. Don't tell her."

"I won't," I said. "I'm already in trouble for one of my omissions. Was Tim badly hurt?"

Leo shook his head. "Just banged up. I think he was kind of klutzy by nature."

"Oh. I was wondering if he was too debilitated to defend himself against whoever killed him."

"Doubtful," Leo responded. "I don't think he even went to the doctor."

I was halfway through my drink. It was going on six. The bar was filling up. It looked as if many Alpiners were seeking air-conditioned sanctuary.

"Do you want to eat here?" Leo asked.

I considered the suggestion. "Sure. I wouldn't dream of turning on the stove. Just as long as I get home in time for *Vida's Cupboard*."

"Me, too," Leo said. "Let's order now." He signaled to Oren.

Our conversation changed after we'd perused the menus. Leo requested the pork sandwich; I chose the crab Louie. It was a pleasant hour, and I was back in my stuffy log cabin by a quarter to seven.

After opening both doors and raising the windows as far as the screens would permit, I started to turn on my laptop computer. Before I could hit the START command, I rethought my open-house policy. Maybe there *was* a burglar loose in the neighborhood. Maybe it was an arsonist. Maybe Old Nick was still hanging around, just a few yards away from my home.

Swearing silently, I got up from the sofa and closed both the front and the kitchen doors. Security wasn't usually a consideration in Alpine. But I'd had one break-in already during the last year. I didn't feel like being a victim again.

By the time I returned to the living room, it was almost seven. I switched on the radio, poured a Pepsi over ice, and sat back down on the couch. Spence—or whoever was at the studio's controls—was playing some of the golden oldies that always led into Vida's show. The music seemed appropriate.

The sound of a creaking door announced Vida's entrance after the hour turn.

"Good evening from *Vida's Cupboard* to everyone in Alpine and the rest of Skykomish County," she began in her slightly strident voice. "We've had another hot day here in our beautiful part of the world, but not to worry—it's a mere month until autumn begins and we can welcome the rain."

Only in the Puget Sound basin would the promise of less sun and more rain be good news. Like the indigenous trees and plants, natives in particular need their roots watered. Vida went on to talk about garden care and summer suppers.

"Lloyd and Jean Campbell are hosting an ice cream social Sunday for family and visiting friends from Fargo, North Dakota. Lloyd is going to make the ice cream himself with his special blackberry recipe. The berries are in season right now, ripe for picking all around Burl Creek, Second Hill, and the areas west of the fish hatchery. Just be careful that the bears aren't feeding, too. You all remember what happened last year to Scooter Hutchins when he didn't leave that Mama Bear alone. Scooter, by the way, is looking much better now that he's finished a series of operations on his nose, which were done by a very skilled Seattle cosmetic surgeon."

Vida reminded her listeners that they could read all about the Campbells' gala in next week's *Alpine Advocate*. She did not give the name of Scooter's surgeon, although it would have been helpful just in case some other local decided to go one-on-one with Mama Bear this year. But she cautioned that berries and bears were not a safe combination during August.

Vida continued with her chatty tidbits until the commercial break. Leo got his way about the Harvey's Hardware ad; Vida read it live, and with much enthusiasm.

"I know," Vida intoned, beginning the final segment of her broadcast, "that I promised Delphine Corson would visit us this evening to give some fascinating tips on late summer floral arrangements. But due to recent events in town, I've asked Delphine if she can postpone offering her wonderful ideas until next Wednesday. Thank you, Delphine, and all your helpers at Posies Unlimited. We anxiously await your colorful advice."

There was a very brief pause. I leaned closer to the radio. Vida continued. "Due to the tragic events surrounding the death of Tim Rafferty, a popular fixture on KSKY-AM, I'm enlisting the help of all Alpiners to investigate leads in the unfortunate homicide and arson case. Our hearts and prayers go out to the Rafferty, Eriks, and Parker families at this time. Of course, we know how hard Sheriff Milo Dodge and his able deputies are working to solve this heinous crime. However, we also know that the sheriff's office has limited personnel."

I frowned. Was Vida treading on Milo's toes?

"One of the potential witnesses is a recluse known to many of you as Old Nick," she went on. "It appears that he has been living in the vacant house on Fir Street near Fifth, next to the cul-de-sac where the Rafferty tragedy occurred. First, let me give you an eyewitness description of Old Nick, who was last seen Sunday night."

I noticed that Vida didn't identify Wayne Eriks by name. Perhaps she didn't want to make him a target in case Old Nick really was on a rampage. As she described the recluse, she spoke slowly, having urged her listeners to take notes.

"It is very likely," she said, "that Old Nick has returned to the woods. During the summer we have many able, strong young bodies with free time. One of our fine college students is organizing a search party to help find Old Nick in order to assist the sheriff's department in its investigation. Dear listeners, let me introduce my grandson, Roger Hibbert, who will lead this crime-solving crusade."

I almost fell off the sofa. What was Vida thinking of? I was aghast, appalled, amazed, and anything but happy.

"Roger," Vida was saying, "can you tell us about your plan?"

There was a pause. Vida must have provided notes. Roger was probably trying to read them. *If* he could read.

"Tomorrow morning at ten o'clock we'll meet by the picnic tables at Old Mill Park," Roger said in a voice that had grown surprisingly mature since I'd last spoken with him. "Anyone between the ages of eighteen and twenty-one is invited to join us in our search for Old Nick. We'll have trail maps available. Snacks will be on hand before we start because we want to be well nourished. Please bring a bottle of water and wear sturdy walking shoes."

He read the announcement well. I had to admit that when Roger had made his acting debut in an ill-fated amateur production a year and a half ago, he'd shown hints of acting talent.

"Thank you so much, Roger," Vida said in a voice bursting with pride. "Now can you tell us how you decided to head this vital search?"

Another pause. Roger must be gathering his wits. They could be anywhere.

"That *is*," Vida interjected, "how you came up with this idea *on your own*?"

"Oh—well, yeah, right." I thought I heard a gulp from Roger. "It seems like, well, you know, like older people these days think kids don't have any responsibility. So, well, like I figured I could show them—the older people—that we do. Have responsibility, like. So I thought we could help. Plus, I think being a detective is really cool."

"Ah." I could practically see Vida beaming. "You've had some experience," she continued, "being a detective, haven't you, Roger?"

"Yeah. A while ago I lost my retainer. You know, for my teeth. My folks were kind of upset 'cause those retainers cost like a grip of money. So I thought I should find it. I went back over where I'd hung out and what I was doing, and like, you know, retraced all that, and that's how I found the retainer in the Dumpster at the high school. I'd left it in my lunch bag under some Twix wrappers."

"Brilliant!" Vida exclaimed. "A perfect example of sound logic and keen detection!"

Roger, Master of the Obvious. Even I could have figured out that the kid would take off his retainer when he ate, which occurred frequently. But at least he'd saved Amy and Ted Hibbert several hundred dollars.

"So," Vida was stating with enthusiasm, "all of you young people out there listening have a chance to be a detective, too. Remember, ten o'clock tomorrow morning at Old Mill Park. Further instructions will await you. Before I close *Vida's Cupboard* this evening, I'd like to thank Roger once again, as well as KSKY for the opportunity to perform this public service. Good night and a pleasant week to everyone until we take another peek into *Vida's Cupboard*."

The closing of the cabinet's sound effects concluded with a gentle click, presumably keeping Vida's gossip from running amok until next Wednesday. I sat back on the sofa and questioned her wisdom. Not to mention her sanity. Two minutes later, I was sipping Pepsi when the phone rang.

"Did you know about this?" The sheriff was yelling in my ear.

I grimaced. "Of course not. And please don't shout."

"Goddamn it," Milo went on, still bellowing, "she's making me look like a moron! She's putting a bunch of dumb kids at risk! There'll be lawsuits all over the county! What got into her anyway?"

"Honestly, I don't know," I responded. "*Please* stop yelling. I'm as flabbergasted as you are." Although, I realized, I should have known. Vida had certainly behaved suspiciously when Wayne Eriks had come to the office.

"They'll never find him," Milo declared, lowering his voice but still fuming. "I'm going to the park tomorrow

and tell them to disband. I ought to arrest Vida for interfering with the law."

"You wouldn't arrest her."

"I'd sure as hell like to."

"I wouldn't blame you for sending them all home.
That is," I added, "if anybody shows up. Vida didn't
offer a reward."

"Oh, they'll show up." Milo's tone was bitter. "At
least enough of them to cause trouble. If they go off-trail
into the woods, they'll either get shot by some jerk running a meth lab or they'll start a forest fire or they'll get
lost and then we'll have to search for *them*. I'm going to
nip this thing in the bud. In fact, I'm going to drive over
to Vida's house right now and tell her to have Fleetwood
broadcast a retraction. I hold him responsible, too."

The sheriff banged down the phone.

I wondered if I should go to Vida's, too. Maybe I
could ease the conflict between them, which I knew
could grow into a conflagration as dangerous as any forest fire.

I needed a few minutes to think. Vida might not go
straight home. It was likely that she'd given Roger a ride
and would have to drop him off at his parents' home in
The Pines. She might stay for a while, visiting with Amy
and Ted, as well as finalizing her plans with Roger.

Still debating with myself, I turned on my laptop and
checked for e-mail messages. Happily, there was one
from Adam. We e-mailed each other several times a
week because the phone connection between Alpine and
St. Mary's Igloo was so poor. My son's phone line was
on a radio delay, and there were always long pauses between our exchanges. The halting conversations drove
both of us nuts.

"Mom," he began, "got your package with the Starbucks coffee and the thermal socks. Thanks. Can you
send more socks? I already gave mine to a couple of

parishioners who need them more than I do, or will when fall arrives."

But the rest of Adam's message wasn't what I'd expected. I read it three times. Adam continued:

"This may sound weird, and I feel kind of strange telling you about this, but a few months ago I started getting e-mail from Toni Andreas. I guess she got my address from you."

I recalled Toni asking for Adam's address in the early spring. I'd been waiting for Milo at the sheriff's office after work. We'd gotten to talking about Adam's Alaskan assignment, and I'd mentioned that loneliness was one of his biggest problems. Toni apparently remembered their brief dating period with some fondness. She'd asked if it would be okay to e-mail him sometime. I'd told her that was a nice idea, then forgot the incident until now.

"Toni wrote that she was seeing a married man," Adam went on. "She's not Catholic, but she asked for my advice. Face it, I haven't done much marriage counseling, so I advised her to break it off. I didn't go into any religious or moral issues, but said that people were bound to get hurt, including her. She wrote back saying this guy was really unhappy in his marriage and planned to leave, but that his wife was pregnant and he'd have to wait until the baby was born. Then I wrote and told her that was all the more reason to stop seeing him. Furthermore, it sounded like the first in a long line of excuses while stringing her along. The last time I heard from her was about three weeks ago when she said he wasn't going to wait until the baby came, but planned on seeing a lawyer to start divorce proceedings. Meanwhile, she and the guy were going on a trip together. I answered saying she should put the trip off until she had proof that he really was going through with the divorce. I didn't hear back, so I figured I'd pissed her off. Then this afternoon I checked out the *Advocate* online and read about what happened to Tim Rafferty. Scott's story mentioned that Tim had only been married a few months and that Tiffany was expecting a baby. I couldn't help but wonder if Tim might be the guy Toni was seeing. Let me know. I'm worried about her. Love and prayers, Adam."

Chapter Eight

ADAM'S E-MAIL UPSET me. His guess about Toni Andreas seeing Tim Rafferty rang true. It would explain Toni's distress. It also might explain why she'd canceled her vacation plans.

But what did it mean? As I put my glass of Pepsi in the fridge and gathered up my handbag, I reflected on Tiffany's reaction when I'd called on her. She'd shown no overwhelming grief for her husband—only concern for herself and the child she carried. Was this because she was shallow? Or because she was so absorbed in the creation of a new life? Those had been my thoughts at the time. Now I wondered if her sense of loss was dulled by Tim's infidelity and her realization that the marriage was in trouble.

As I drove the four blocks to Vida's house on Tyee Street, the temperature felt like it had dropped several degrees in the last hour. I didn't even have to turn on the Honda's air conditioner. When I turned off of Fifth Street before it dead-ended at the middle school, I saw Milo's Grand Cherokee up ahead, parked next to the curb like a big red warning light.

"Where the hell is she?" he demanded, getting out of his vehicle as he saw me pull up on the other side of the driveway.

"Probably at the Hibberts'," I replied, joining him on

114 Mary Daheim

the sidewalk. "Stop looking at me as if I'm to blame for all this."

Milo, who was dressed in his civvies, scowled. "I don't. But I sure as hell am mad at Vida."

"I'm dismayed, too," I said. "But while we're waiting, let's talk about Toni Andreas."

"We already did," Milo said impatiently. "Why are you so damned curious?"

I hesitated. In confiding in me, Adam had—however well intentioned—betrayed a private matter between himself and Toni. It wasn't as if she'd gone to confession; she'd only asked his advice. But I was still reluctant to say more. And I certainly wasn't going to mention my son's name. Maybe I should shut up and speak directly to Toni.

"Never mind," I said, both relieved and anxious as I saw Vida's Buick approaching. "Here comes your favorite rabble-rouser."

Ignoring our presence, Vida drove all the way into her detached garage toward the back of the house. Ordinarily, I would've expected her to stop as soon as she turned into the driveway and immediately ask what the sheriff and I were doing on her premises. But I figured that she was surprised to see us, had an inkling of why we were there, and needed time to marshal her defense.

There was, however, no vacillation in her purposeful manner as she came in our direction. "Well now," she said, sounding somewhat brittle, "what's this all about?"

Vida was tall, standing over six feet if you counted the crown of her straw hat, but Milo had almost six inches on her. He loomed—or so it seemed to me.

"I'm stopping this harebrained idea of yours right now," the sheriff declared. "If anybody shows up at Old Mill Park tomorrow, I'll be there to hustle their butts right out into Park Street."

THE ALPINE RECLUSE 115

Vida didn't flinch. "Really now. For what reason?" Her voice was calm.

Milo swung an arm in an impatient gesture. "Because it's damned dangerous. You can't take the law into your own hands. You know that."

"Do mind your language, Milo," Vida cautioned. "You're talking nonsense. This is strictly volunteer, no one under eighteen will be allowed to take part, and it's no different than when Boy Scouts or some other youth group is asked to help with a search party. It's done all the time in cities. King County has had a volunteer search-and-rescue group for almost fifty years, and some of them are as young as fourteen. As you know perfectly well, I might add."

"It's not the same," Milo asserted. "Those volunteers have to go through rigorous training. Besides, you didn't consult me. This hermit guy could be dangerous. And then there's the weather. It's bad enough we've got campers and hikers and all these other bozos running around the woods making the fire hazard even worse, but a bunch of irresponsible kids is . . . well, it's just too damned risky."

"Language, language," Vida murmured. "I really think you should thank me. And Roger, of course."

Milo started to say something—no doubt about Roger—but puffed out his cheeks and stopped. I wondered if he was going to explode.

The sheriff exhaled. "What if these kids find Old Nick? How will they apprehend him? Will they be armed?"

"Are you referring to firearms?" Vida asked, indignant.

"Any kind of weapon," Milo responded. "Will they?"

"They don't anticipate violence," Vida said staunchly. The sheriff realized that in a war of words with Vida, he was bound to get shortchanged. "You know the law," he said. "Nobody under twenty-one can carry anything but a shoulder weapon, like a hunting rifle. And if they do carry, they have to have a permit."

"Yes, yes," Vida said testily. "I'm aware of the rules. Are you finished?"

Milo gazed up at the cloudless sky, perhaps envisioning hordes of stampeding youth rampaging through the woods with lighted torches and AK-47s. I looked back at the sheriff, who was obviously still aggravated.

"I won't have it, Vida," he finally said under his breath.

"You can't *not* have it," she asserted. "If you try to stop us, you will violate our constitutional right of assembly. Please don't interfere and make a spectacle of yourself."

Milo looked stumped. I felt sorry for him. I also felt helpless and wondered why I'd come.

Vida apparently wondered, too. For the first time, she looked directly at me. "What do you think, Emma?" she asked pointedly.

"I think," I said slowly, "it's not a good idea. Did you clear it with Spence?"

Vida lifted her chin. "Spencer Fleetwood does not censor my program."

"I'm concerned about liability," I said.

Vida glared at me. "Since when have you been concerned about Spencer Fleetwood?"

"I didn't mean that exactly," I replied, feeling awkward. What I'd implied, of course, was that if Vida had come to me with such a proposal, I would never have given her permission to run it in the *Advocate*. "I merely wondered," I clarified, "if KSKY was helping sponsor the search."

Vida shot me her most disdainful expression. "This

civic undertaking has no sponsor other than Roger— and me, as his grandmother and staunch supporter."

I didn't believe for a second that Roger had come up with the idea. Roger didn't have ideas. Or if he did, he'd suggest that one of the volunteers dress up in a bear suit or upon apprehending Old Nick, his captors should give him a wedgie.

I glanced at Milo. He looked grim, perhaps contemplating defeat. I *thought* Vida had the law on her side, though I didn't approve of her plan. Still, it would hardly be the first time that individuals had gone off searching for a lost loved one in the woods. Many family members or friends had struck out on their own when they felt that official search-and-rescue parties couldn't or wouldn't do enough.

"You've been warned," Milo said sternly. "If anything happens to these kids, SkyCo isn't responsible. And Fleetwood can put *that* on his damned radio station." The sheriff turned on his heel and loped off to his Grand Cherokee.

"My, my," Vida murmured, watching Milo slam the door after getting behind the wheel, "he's certainly being a pill about this." She looked back at me. "As are you."

"I'm sorry, Vida," I said. "I think you're putting these young people at risk, Roger included."

For a fleeting moment, I thought I saw an uncertain expression cross her face. But her words were resolute. "Nonsense. They'll have to keep in parties of three. That's in case there is some sort of accident. One can go for help while the other stays with the injured party. They all have those cell phones these days. Granted, there are areas around here where the phones aren't usable, but they're still a safeguard. We're sure to get some former Boy Scouts who know how to follow a trail, even one that's obscure. And these youngsters have been raised in the forest. They understand the dangers."

She almost had me convinced. But that didn't matter. Vida was unstoppable. "Good luck," I said in a voice that was almost sincere. "Will you be taking pictures or shall I send Scott?"

Vida straightened the yellow streamers on her hat. "Well—I can do it. I can write the story, too. I'm basically an onlooker. This is all Roger's doing. He's very keen on finding Old Nick."

I didn't know what else to say. I tried to smile. "Then you'll be in the office tomorrow until the . . ." I almost said "shindig." ". . . until the event starts at ten?"

"Of course." Vida now looked smug.

"Okay. I'll see you then." With a little wave, I walked back to the Honda.

"Dear Adam," I typed on my laptop after I got home, "I'll get more socks on my lunch hour tomorrow at Alpine Ski. In fact, I'll get a bunch of them in different sizes so that you can hand them out to anyone who needs them. What about gloves? You didn't mention them."

I paused. Was there anything else my son needed for himself or his little band of Alaskan natives? He didn't like to ask, especially for personal items. I remembered when he was in college—various colleges before he finally got his degree. He'd request—even demand—anything, including purchases I couldn't possibly afford and he didn't really need. Almost ten years later, he was incredibly selfless. He had learned the lesson of distinguishing between wants and needs. I'd prayed for him to be able to do that since he was a teenager.

I moved on to his question about Toni Andreas. "I don't know if Toni was seeing Tim. According to my sources—and you know your journalist mother can never reveal them, but it wasn't Vida in case you're guessing—Toni was dating somebody she wouldn't name. She's been very upset since Tim died, and had a meltdown at the sheriff's office today." I went on to explain my role in her flight from behind the desk and to relate what little she'd told me.

"So I don't know what to make of it," I continued. "Please let me know if she contacts you further. I'm worried about her, not to mention that I'm up to my ears in trying to figure out who killed Tim and set the house on fire. Everybody seems to think it was a hermit who has recently been sighted in town and has been hanging out at that vacant old dump next to the cul-de-sac. You may remember the place; it's always been rundown."

I wrote briefly about Vida's call to arms—or legs, at least—adding the part about her confrontation with Milo.

"So it's one thrill after another here in Alpine," I concluded. "By the way, you never told me if you'd learned to use a harpoon yet."

I kept the laptop on for a few minutes. St. Mary's Igloo was two hours behind our Pacific time zone. It was only six-thirty there, and Adam might be home in his tiny cinder-block house.

But there was no immediate response from him, only a couple of e-mail ads from JCPenney and Eddie Bauer. Just before nine, I shut off the laptop.

Sitting on the sofa, staring into space, I wondered about Old Nick. If Vida didn't know anything about him other than that he'd been a recluse for thirty years, nobody else would know, either. Some of the hermits were merely dropouts from society who couldn't cope with the civilized world. Some were crazy, some were running from the law, and occasionally there was someone who simply wanted to see if it was possible to live off the land. I couldn't help but speculate about which category Old Nick fell into. Indeed, he must have left behind someone who would have wanted to know what happened to him. But that somebody—a mother, father, brother, sister, wife, lover—might be dead.

After half an hour, I gave up thinking about Old Nick and turned my mind to Tim and Tiffany Eriks.

I couldn't find any answers there, either.

Leo was already in the office when I arrived a couple of minutes before eight on Thursday morning. He was waiting for the coffeemaker, mug in one hand, unlighted cigarette in the other. Ginny was out front, Kip was out back, and neither Vida nor Scott had come in yet.

"Roger plays John Wayne in *The Searchers*," Leo said with a wry expression. "I can't wait for the sequel, *Lost in Space*."

"You heard the program," I remarked.

Leo nodded as the coffeemaker's red light went on. "Of course. It's required listening for everybody in Alpine, right? I also heard the retraction."

I stared at Leo. "What retraction?"

"From Spence. I stayed tuned to make sure they didn't run that window fan ad for Harvey's Hardware. Along about nine o'clock, Fleetwood himself came on the air and said something to the effect that KSKY was not responsible for the content of individual programs such as *Vida's Cupboard*. But he wished the search party luck."

"Hedging his bets," I murmured.

Leo poured coffee into his mug. "Spence also announced that the Skykomish County sheriff's office didn't endorse Roger's idea, either, and had issued a warning to not take part due to extreme dry weather conditions."

"Oh, my." I couldn't help but smile. "Vida will be— as she'd put it—wild."

"She's late," Leo remarked, glancing at his watch. "It's four minutes after eight. Has she got the bakery run for the day?"

"No," I replied. "It's Scott's turn."

"Hmm." It wasn't like Vida to be tardy. She always arrived precisely at 8:00 A.M. unless she had an early morning assignment. "I suspect she's organizing the rally. I wonder if I shouldn't drop by instead of letting Scott cover the whole affair." I poured myself a cup of coffee. "I'd better check my calendar."

I'd forgotten that I had a hair appointment at eleven. Usually, I try to schedule haircuts for our slow day, Wednesday, but Stella Magruder had been booked when I called last Friday. Still, I had nothing else scheduled until three when I had a phone interview with a state official in Olympia about the proposed Wild Sky Wilderness legislation. Maybe I would go down to Old Mill Park. Maybe I should go in disguise, lest my presence provoke Vida's wrath.

Vida and Scott arrived at the same time five minutes later. Scott had brought elephant ears and maple bars. Vida had brought unshakable cheer.

"Not so warm this morning," she declared, despite the fact that it was already seventy-two, the same as it had been early in the previous day. "You can feel autumn in the air."

"Then how come there's a heat haze along the tree line?" Leo inquired.

"It will dissipate," Vida said with confidence. She had on a different straw hat this morning, bright red with white polka dots on the matching red ribbons. After pouring herself a cup of hot water—her usual pick-me-up when she wasn't drinking tea—she sat down and began sorting through her in-box. And hummed.

Her humming—always off-key and seldom recogniz-

222

able as a song—drove me nuts. It was a signal of self-righteousness on Vida's part as well as a barrier against intrusion or interference. After snatching up a maple bar, I retreated to my cubbyhole.

Milo didn't call. That was ominous, as was Scott's report when he returned from his early morning rounds, which included checking the police log.

"Sam Heppner told me there was nothing new on the Rafferty case," Scott said, leaning against the door frame. "Nothing else, except for the usual traffic violations, a street race on Alpine Way, and a couple of prowler reports. By the way, Toni Andreas is out sick today."

I wasn't surprised. She'd probably worked herself into an emotional tizzy. I'd already informed Scott that he'd be covering the search party gathering. Vida could take some pictures, but the event wasn't suitable for her House & Home page. She might argue, but the line was firmly drawn.

The rally was news to Scott, who, along with Tamara, was in the Alpine minority. They rarely listened to *Vida's Cupboard*. Being young and in love, they probably had better things to do. Scott, in fact, thought Vida—or Roger—had a good idea.

"Why not?" he'd said, both of us keeping our voices down so that Vida couldn't overhear. "Those kids might be doing something a lot crazier or more dangerous than hiking around the woods."

I supposed he had a point.

Scott and I left the office at a quarter to ten. Vida had departed a couple of minutes earlier. My reporter and I walked along Front Street together, but parted company at the sheriff's office. I had just enough time to needle Milo, although I half expected him to have gone to the park, too.

He was, however, in his office, drinking his vile coffee

and flipping through the latest issue of *Combat Handguns*.

"What's new?" I said in a hopeful voice.

The sheriff leaned back in his chair, stretched, and yawned. "Not much."

I didn't sit down, but leaned on the back of Milo's visitor's chair. "Then I guess I won't ask how the investigation's going."

He shook his head slowly. "Nope."

"You *are* investigating, aren't you?"

He shot me a dark look. "Don't be a pain in the ass, Emma."

I shrugged. "Just curious. What's wrong with Toni?"

Milo pulled his chair closer to the desk. "She says she's got a virus. There's one going around, I guess. There always is."

I was dying to tell Milo about the possibility that Toni might have been seeing Tim Rafferty on the sly. But I had no real evidence, still only vague intimations from Adam and Janet. The sheriff despised personal guesswork as much as the professional variety.

"That's too bad," I said. "Maybe that's why she had such a bad day yesterday."

"Probably. Wrong time of the month, I figured."

You would. But I didn't say it out loud. "Are you going to Roger's rally?"

"Hell, no. I'm sending Dwight and Dustin." Milo sipped coffee. "This is better today. Doe made it. Her coffee's not bad."

"I'm going to stroll by for a few minutes," I said, pushing the chair away. "In fact, I'd better go. Keep me posted."

"Right." Milo turned back to his magazine.

I headed out onto Front Street again, noting the barrenness of the mountains I could see from my vantage

point. In the past, the snow hadn't completely melted
from Mount Baldy until after Labor Day. This year, it
had trickled off the slopes by the first week of August.
Global warming be damned, I thought, and walked
briskly past the post office, the Alpine Hotel, and the old
railroad station. I crossed Alpine Way after a short wait
for a couple of trucks rolling into town. At the entrance
to the park, I spotted a big banner with red letters on a
white background:

THE SEARCH IS ON!!!

Halfway through the park, I saw that was indeed the
case. Or at least, the search party was arriving. Some
thirty young people were clustered in the picnic area several yards beyond the statue of town founder Carl Clemans. Scott was moving outside the group, holding his
camera and seeking good angles.

At the center of the group was Roger, with Vida not
far behind him. Having turned eighteen, Roger was now
taller than his grandmother and considerably wider. He
seemed to be in charge, offering sign-up sheets, taking
down information, and checking ID cards. Maybe I'd
underestimated the kid.

Scott saw me and gave a thumbs-up gesture. I didn't
know if he was saying that he approved of the turnout
or that he was taking good pictures. I recognized most
of the crowd, though I could identify only a few by
name. It seemed to me that one day I was admiring an
infant in the aisle of the Grocery Basket, a toddler a
short time later at the Alpine Mall—and the next thing I
knew, the child had turned into a high school student.
Despite the slow pace of a small town, the years had
gone by too fast.

More volunteers were arriving. A handful of parents

were present, as well. I saw Norm Carlson in his Blue Sky Dairy uniform, leaning against one of the empty picnic tables.

"Are your daughters joining in?" I asked after I'd approached Norm.

He nodded. "Both of them. They've been working part-time this summer at the Bourgettes' diner. They decided this'd be their great adventure. Georgia and I hope it's safe."

"Have you ever seen Old Nick?"

Norm shook his head. "He's a myth as far as I'm concerned. Oh, I've noticed a couple of those hermits over the years, but not Nick. In fact, a while back—five, six years, maybe—I found one hanging around the dairy. He was trying to cadge some milk. Harmless, but creepy. The problem is, some of them are badasses, if you'll excuse the expression. I heard about one in King County who killed trespassers. After the guy died, they found him in his cabin with about six skulls lined up on his mantelpiece." Norm shuddered. "Another one had shrunken heads over his bed."

Milo had told me similar stories years ago, gleaned from his law enforcement peers in other counties. Coincidentally, I saw Dwight Gould and Dustin Fong strolling in from the park's south entrance.

Norm saw the deputies, too. "Are they going to break this up?" he asked in what sounded like a hopeful voice.

"They can't," I replied. "This is a public park and these are volunteers. This isn't exactly a first when it comes to search parties in this area."

"Right." Norm looked thoughtful. "Georgia and I told the girls to stick together."

"That's good advice," I said. "I understand they'll go in threes."

"That's smart." He moved away a few paces, toward the group. "Maybe I'll grab a snack. 'Scuse me, Emma."

"Sure." I walked over to a place where I could see what was on the table where Roger was conducting his heroic business. There were plates of cookies, bags of chips, bottled water, and what looked like power bars. Vida had been shopping. Maybe that's why she'd been late to work.

With the help of another beefy boy, Roger climbed up onto the table, megaphone in hand and suede hiking shoes trampling some bags of chips.

"Okay, everybody!" he bellowed, as ear-shattering as ever his grandmother could be. "Listen up! You got the description of this Old Nick dude, right? You got trail maps and the rest of your gear. You all got your assignments, north, south, east and . . ." He stopped briefly, consulting his grandmother. ". . . west."

Roger probably hadn't done well in geography. He was pointing in the wrong directions. Maybe the others didn't know the difference.

"Remember the rules," he went on. "Everybody report back here by six o'clock sharp. Earlier, if you're draggin'. Meanwhile, be careful, and now haul ass!"

I saw Vida flinch, but she didn't reprimand her grandson. Instead, she broke into a wide smile and clapped her hands. Roger got down from the table, joining the other beefy boy and one of our former *Advocate* carriers, Oren and Sunny Rhodes's son, Davin. Roger immediately led his buddies over to a pretty, buxom girl I recognized as a Gustavson. Apparently, he was trying to talk her into making it a foursome. She seemed reluctant.

As the others began to prepare for departure, I moved away. Scott approached me, looking sheepish.

"I interviewed some of the volunteers before you got here," he said. "Including Roger."

I made a face. "Well, you had to interview him. He seems to be running this show, and if you didn't include him in the story, Vida would have your head on a silver platter."

"That's what I figured," Scott replied. "Actually, he did okay."

I shot my reporter a wry look. "He didn't fall off the table." My gaze shifted to Vida, who was engaged in conversation with some of the parents, including her daughter Amy and son-in-law Ted. "Of course, Roger enjoys being the center of attention."

Scott and I decided we might as well head back to the office. It was ten-thirty, and I wanted to check for messages before I went to Stella's Styling Salon for my haircut.

There was nothing pressing in the calls Ginny handed me. Except for Scott, the newsroom was empty. Ginny had also delivered the mail. There was nothing of importance there, either—just the usual boilerplate news releases, filler material, and the notice of the next Washington State Newspaper Association meeting.

I retraced my steps down Front Street, crossing over to the Clemans Building, where Stella had her salon. It was already getting overly warm. I was perspiring by the time I greeted Stella.

"Your hair's so thick it makes you even hotter," she declared, surveying my image in the mirror at her station. "You haven't had it cut since April. What have you got in mind before I bring out the mowing machine?"

I smiled back at Stella, who was always blunt. Her own hair was very short, with gold highlights mingled among a rich brown shade. I had no idea what Stella's real color was. In all the years I'd been going to her salon, she'd changed her hair along with the seasons.

"Short," I said, "like yours, but not quite as short. Tapered on the sides, high on top."

"Your perm's grown out," Stella said after a studious

look at my head. "You have absolutely no curl. Great body, nice color—*but.*"

"But?" I gazed at her mirror image. "You refer to my utter lack of talent for styling my own hair?"

Stella nodded. "You're inept. Take Toni Andreas, for example. I tried to talk her out of letting her hair grow out. It's thick, like yours. But she has some curl. It looks okay. I told her so a while ago when she came in for a facial. Toni knows how to do her hair. Of course she's . . ." Stella paused. "She's a bit younger."

"Like twenty years?" I said dryly.

Stella waggled her head from side to side. "Something like that." She motioned for me to get up so that we could move on to the shampoo sink. "But would you really want to be thirty again? Especially if you're a woman and still single."

"I *am* still single," I pointed out.

Stella positioned me in the chair by the sink. "You're different. No offense, Emma. By that age you'd had a kid, you had your college degree, you had a solid career, you weren't trying to beat your biological clock." She stopped to turn on the water. "Girls these days—even in small towns—wait so long to get married. Oh, I don't blame them," she continued as she began to shampoo my hair. "Richie and I were barely twenty-one when we got married. Those first few years were an awful struggle, especially with babies on the way. But I wouldn't want to be single and thirty now. It's different."

I relaxed under Stella's expert hands. "I gather Toni has complained about her status."

Stella laughed wryly. "Everybody complains to their hairdresser. It's like being a bartender."

"I know," I said. "Occupational hazards."

"You don't complain," Stella said with a touch of reprimand.

"No. I have an entire newspaper in which I can vent."

"But not about your personal problems," Stella pointed out as she rinsed the soap out of my hair.

"I'm not the type to talk about my personal life."

"Rare," Stella said tersely, winding a towel around my head.

We returned to her station. The salon wasn't busy. There was no air-conditioning, only a couple of ceiling fans that Richie Magruder had installed recently.

"I wish," I said, "that I knew what was wrong with Toni. She had an emotional breakdown yesterday. I tried to help, but she wouldn't tell me what was wrong."

"I heard something about that," Stella said. "You actually talked to her?"

I recounted what had happened at the sheriff's office and by the Sears catalog store. "Stress," I said. "That's all she'd tell me. She's out sick today."

"No kidding." Stella's artfully made-up face was stamped with curiosity. "I wonder."

"About what?" I watched my own expression of feigned innocence.

Stella had removed the towel and was beginning to snip. "About the guy who was causing her to be so upset. That is, one minute Toni was happy as a deer with a salt lick, and the next she'd be down in the sawdust hopper. I've only cut her hair once this year—back during the winter, maybe right around New Year's. But she comes in fairly often to have her nails done or get a facial. In fact, the last few months she'd been here pretty often. That's always a sign that romance is in the air."

"And the hair?" I murmured.

Stella laughed. "Funny Emma."

"I'm serious," I asserted. "Women usually don't get their hair cut short if the man in their life likes long tresses. You know what I mean. Hair splayed on the pillow like a fan, running their fingers through—"

"You're right," Stella broke in. "Toni's always had

short hair until this spring. Changing your hairstyle means a big change in your life, one way or the other. You get dumped, you decide to color your hair blue or some damned thing. You find Mr. Right, you let him dictate how you look. Women are like that. You've got a new man in your life, Emma. How does he like your hair?"

"Not falling out in clumps," I retorted. "Actually, he's never said. Would it matter? I can't do anything with it except get a decent cut."

"You *are* a freak," Stella remarked. "Sometimes I worry about you. But then I worry about all my clients. I've been worried about Toni, if you want to know the truth."

Finally. I knew it was only a matter of time before Stella dished the dirt on Toni. She loved doing it, but she always needed coaxing. I supposed that was how she dealt with her conscience.

I asked the obvious question. "How come?"

Stella stopped snipping long enough to see how my hair was shaping up. "I shouldn't say anything," she said in a low voice, "but the last time Toni came in for a manicure about a week ago, Tiffany Eriks—I mean, Tiffany Rafferty—was getting highlights in her hair. You know how it is with those foil jobs; the person is virtually unrecognizable with all those things covering her head. In fact, I'd recommended that Tiffany put off doing it until the baby was born. Sometimes the chemicals don't take when you're pregnant. But Tiffany insisted. She can be stubborn in her own way. So Toni sat down at Debbie's nail station"—Stella nodded toward the front of the shop—"and just before Debbie got started, Tiffany stood up to stretch her back. Toni saw her, and would you believe she got up from the chair and ran out the front door. We haven't heard from her since."

"How odd." I waited for Stella to confide her conclusions.

"Toni had never mentioned the name of whoever she was seeing," Stella continued, as if on cue. "That made us all suspicious. He had to be married, right?"

"He could have been someone from out of town," I said, playing devil's advocate. "Someone nobody in Alpine would know."

"But wouldn't she say so?" Stella responded, now sounding rather excited. Too excited, maybe. She was cutting off quite a bit of my hair. "You know—a drop-dead gorgeous guy from Everett, a big spender from Seattle—*some* kind of identification. Women *have* to talk about the men in their lives. Unless they don't dare."

"Which means the man is married," I noted. "How did Tiffany react?"

"I don't think Tiffany even noticed Toni," Stella replied. "She's pretty self-absorbed."

"So you think that Toni was seeing Tim Rafferty?" I grimaced. "Hey, Stella, I'm beginning to look like a boy."

"What?" Stella frowned at my hair—or what was left of it. "Oh, no, Emma, it's darling. Pixielike, and perfect for this hot weather."

"I'm too old to be a pixie," I informed her.

Stella began to fluff up my hair with her hands. "No, no. Think how easy this is going to be when it comes to maintaining it. Even you can manage with the help of some product. Here, let me show you." Stella reached into a small cupboard next to the mirror. "Bumble and Bumble styling cream. All you do is put about this much on your hands and . . ."

I wasn't paying attention. If Adam's guess, Janet's suggestion, and Stella's deductions were correct, then Toni Andreas had been having an affair with Tim Rafferty.

Toni had canceled her vacation plans. Why? Because Tim couldn't or wouldn't go with her?

Tim, Tiffany, Toni—altogether too many people whose names began with *T*. But *T* also stood for *triangle*.

And triangles of a romantic type often supplied a motive for murder.

Chapter Nine

VIDA WAS TWITTERING away at Ginny when I returned to the office at one o'clock. "Such a fine specimen of youth," she was saying. "I must confess, I've despaired over the younger generation, but when given a chance, they can bravely bear responsibility. And leadership! You should have seen how the other youngsters reacted to Roger!"

"You must be very proud of him," Ginny remarked in her quiet manner.

Vida's sharp gaze shifted as she saw me come into the newsroom. "Naturally," she affirmed. "Who wouldn't be proud of someone who wants to help his or her fellow beings?"

"That's true," Ginny agreed with a quick glance in my direction. She knew that Roger annoyed me, and probably felt as if she was caught in a buzz saw. "I'd better get back to the front desk," Ginny said, and skittered off to sanctuary.

"Any reports yet?" I inquired of Vida, trying to sound neutral.

Vida stared at me over the rims of her big glasses. "What do you mean?"

"I mean," I said, "has any trace of Old Nick been found?"

Vida pointedly looked at her watch. "It's scarcely after one. The searchers have been gone for less than three hours. I'd hardly expect them to have returned with any sort of information by now."

She was right, of course. But I couldn't resist needling Vida. On the other hand, I wanted to consult with her. I tried weaseling my way out of the confrontational state between us.

"I was wondering if Old Nick actually left town," I explained. "That is, he might have gone somewhere else to hide out."

"That would be uncharacteristic of his type," Vida asserted, though her expression softened. "Those hermits always return to their lairs."

"Yes, I suppose they do," I allowed, gingerly approaching her desk. "How do you like my hair?"

"What hair?" Vida asked. "You don't seem to have any."

"That bad, huh?"

"Well now . . ." She pursed her lips. "It *is* very short."

"Stella got carried away," I said.

"Indeed. She also seems to have applied some sort of goo," Vida said, still studying me from all angles. "I won't permit Stella to put anything except a wisp of spray on my hair."

"It'll grow out," I said hopefully. "Don't you want to hear why Stella lost focus?"

"You're serious?"

I nodded. Vida leaned forward. "Do sit," she urged, sounding like her usual self.

I saw no further reason to hold back on what Adam and Janet had told me. Stella's account only confirmed their suspicions. A possible affair between Toni and Tim might be a motive for murder.

"My, my," Vida remarked when I'd finished. "That's most intriguing. Tiffany's reaction makes more sense if Tim had been unfaithful. I almost feel sorry for her. But can you tell Milo all this? You know how he hates tales out of school."

I nodded again. "Maybe I should invite him over to dinner and ply him with strong drink."

Vida was disapproving. "That's a poor idea—for various reasons."

Vida couldn't know but probably suspected that there'd been many occasions in the past when Milo ate dinner at my house—and stayed on for dessert in the bedroom. But those interludes had ended a long time ago. Now Milo and I had settled for being friends. Good friends, I liked to think.

"I don't intend to seduce him," I asserted. "I only want to make him more receptive to the idea that Old Nick shouldn't be the sole suspect."

Vida frowned. "You must admit Nick's presence in the vicinity is highly suspicious. Do you think either Tiffany or Toni would be able to overcome Tim and crush his skull with a baseball bat?"

"A woman could do it if the man was asleep," I pointed out.

"Yes, that's so." Vida considered the concept. "Tiffany's alibi must be checked. She had a dinner break that night, didn't she? It wouldn't take her five minutes to get home. As for Toni, if Tim let her in while Tiffany was at work, he might have gone to sleep after a romantic interlude." Vida ran a hand through her jumble of gray curls. "Goodness, it's quite gruesome to dwell on."

"It puts us on the spot," I said. "Milo doesn't seem aware of what's going on in Toni's life. I'm not sure I want to be the person who suggests that one of his own employees could be a suspect."

Vida nodded absently. "A pity I don't know that new deputy better. Doe, I mean. Still . . ." Vida drummed her short nails on the desk. "There's always Billy."

I agreed. "Your nephew is a very sympathetic kind of guy."

Vida looked troubled. "He's engaged, you know. I don't want Billy having coffee with Toni turned into gossip fodder. Earlene is very nice."

The engagement was news to me. "Earlene?"

"Earlene Engebretsen," Vida replied without her usual bravado. "A niece of George's, the county commissioner. She grew up in Skykomish. Actually, her last name is Farrell. She married a most unfortunate young man from Monroe. They had a baby—Brant is now four, I believe—and then Corey—the husband—walked out on them. Earlene has had no help from Brant's father, and has very gallantly raised the boy by herself. She works at a restaurant in Sultan. I admire her fortitude."

I sensed that Vida secretly disapproved of the match, especially since Bill would be taking on a child who wasn't his own. It was no wonder that she hadn't blared the news on her trumpet.

"A small December wedding is planned," she added, as if she were typing it into an engagement article for her House & Home page.

"Congratulations," I said. "Bill will make a fine step-father."

"Yes, I should think so," Vida allowed. She squinted up at the window above her desk. "I'll put a flea in his ear about Toni," she went on. "Though I still think Old Nick was involved. Certainly he's someone that Milo should talk to. He may have seen or heard something. I'm convinced that Roger's search party isn't in vain."

Vida would want to believe that. I left her then and went into my office. I wasn't sure that Bill Blatt would get Toni to open up. Another woman—Vida, for instance—might elicit what had been going on in Toni's love life. I'd already flunked the course.

Sitting at my desk, I tried to remember the names of

Toni's friends. She might have confided in them. As for Tiffany, according to Betsy O'Toole, the young widow had no special chums.

I wrote down the names Milo had mentioned as Toni's girlfriends. First was Mandy Gustavson. I didn't know her very well, though all the Gustavsons were somehow related to Vida. I listed Mags Patricelli next. Neither Milo nor I could recall her married name. I didn't know her, either, except for occasionally seeing her at church.

But Heather Bardeen Bavich was a possibility. Since her marriage to Trevor, she'd continued to work for her father at the ski lodge. Her husband's job was in Everett. The couple had settled in Monroe, approximately halfway between the two work sites.

Until her marriage, Heather had been the restaurant hostess, usually working in the evenings. But the couple had had a baby in the spring, and when Heather returned to the ski lodge, it was during the day, behind the main desk. I called to ask if she had time for a break.

"I don't take breaks," she said. "I work only six hours a day, so except for getting some lunch in the coffee shop, I don't take extra time."

"That's commendable," I remarked. "I didn't realize your dad was such a slave driver."

"He isn't," Heather replied. "But he *is* my dad."

Heather and Henry Bardeen had a close relationship. Heather's mother had died young, and her father had never remarried. "Do you have time to answer a couple of questions?" I inquired.

"About what?" Heather sounded puzzled.

I didn't blame her. A phone interrogation was going to be awkward. There was no opportunity to work my way into her confidence without wasting time.

I came to the point. "You're a friend of Toni Andreas, right?"

"Yes," Heather replied, sounding surprised. I suspected that wasn't the query she'd expected. "Toni was two years behind me in high school, but we were both in choir. I always felt kind of sorry for her."

Ah. The perfect opening. "Yes, I can see why you would," I said, "which is why I'm calling. I don't know if you've talked to her the last day or so, but . . ." I went on, detailing Toni's distress.

"That's a shame," Heather said when I'd finished. "I haven't talked to her, in fact, not for . . . oh, maybe a month. I don't have much spare time at work or at home these days with the baby and all. Now I feel guilty. Maybe I should call her before I leave this afternoon. You say she's taking a sick day?"

"Yes." I paused. "I hope it's not the job that's upsetting her. She's worked in the sheriff's office for several years. I would think that with the hiring of Doe Jameson, Toni's job would be a little easier."

"Maybe." Now it was Heather's turn to hesitate. "I'm not sure that she likes Doe that much. Maybe Toni enjoyed being the only female on the staff. I don't know." Heather sighed into the receiver. "The sheriff isn't going to fire Toni, is he?"

"Oh, no, nothing like that," I assured Heather. "It's just that Toni always seems to be on such an even keel." As in complacent, almost apathetic. "In fact," I continued, lowering my voice to a more intimate level, "Milo seems oblivious to any problems Toni might be having. You know men. They don't notice mood shifts, or if they do, they always figure it's that time of the month."

Heather laughed in her moderate manner. "Yes, that's the truth. I insist that Trevor and I sit down every week and discuss our relationship. I know he can be sensitive if he really tries."

"That's a good idea," I said, though from my age and perspective, it sounded like a waste of time. Men—and women—will listen, but that doesn't mean they can change. "Maybe," I hinted, "Toni's in love."

Heather was silent for so long that I wondered if we'd been disconnected. Finally, she spoke. "Toni's history with men is poor. That's one reason I don't see her much since I got married. She envied me, especially after I told her I was pregnant. She feels left out."

"That happens with some women," I said. "Then they settle for any man who comes along. It's sad. There are, as my granny used to say, worse things than *not* being married."

"There are?" Heather sounded as if she didn't get it. "Oh! Yes, I see what you mean. That's true. So many husbands are abusers, one way or another. Thank heavens Trevor isn't like that."

I made one last stab at getting something useful out of Heather. "So you think she's settled for someone second-rate? I wasn't aware that she was dating anyone right now."

There was another long pause. "I think she makes poor choices."

I forced a laugh. "I hope not. Years ago, she dated my son, Adam."

Heather laughed, too. "Oh, that was different. I mean, that was a casual thing, if I remember. Adam wasn't in Alpine very long. I'm talking about the last few years, when Toni started to feel desperate. There was a counter-top salesman from Seattle and a truck driver from Wenatchee and a dog handler from the Monroe reformatory. I don't mean he was a convict," she added quickly, "but he trained dogs for prisoners or something like that. Toni seemed to date men who were never around much until—" She stopped. I waited. "Until lately."

"Toni was seeing somebody local?" I asked.

I heard a clatter at her end of the line. "Oh! I spilled

my coffee!" Heather exclaimed in a not-very-convincing voice. "I must go, Emma."

"Wait!" I hadn't slogged this far without getting an answer. "Heather—are you there?"

"Ah . . . yes, but I made such a . . ."

"Was Toni seeing Tim Rafferty?"

"Um . . . maybe. I mean . . . I'm sorry, I have to hang up." The receiver clicked in my ear.

I stared out at Vida, who had been making phone calls the entire time I'd been talking to Heather. I returned to my Wild Sky editorial, but kept one eye on the newsroom. Five minutes later, Vida got off the phone and started toward the restroom. I waited until she came out.

"How," I inquired, "are you related to Mandy Gustavson?"

Vida showed no surprise at the question. "Ernest's sister, Evelyn, is her grandmother. Evelyn married a Gustavson, so that makes her my great-niece-in-law."

Vida's late husband had as many Runkel relatives in town as Vida had Blatts on her side of the family. It was no wonder I could never keep them straight. "Do you know Mandy very well?"

"Of course," Vida replied. "Why?"

I told her about the truncated call to Heather Bavich. "I thought Mandy might confirm it. I only know Mags Patricelli by sight," I added.

"Mags *Dugan* since her marriage," Vida noted. "No, I'm afraid I'm not well acquainted with Mags, either. So you want me to see if Mandy can confirm the story about Toni and Tim? Certainly. I'll take some geranium cuttings to her this evening."

That sounded like as good an excuse as any. I went back into my cubbyhole and dialed Milo's number. He answered on the second ring.

"I think I'll barbecue burgers tonight," I said. "Want to join me?"

"I can't," he replied. "I have a meeting at seven-thirty. Don't you read the *Advocate*?"

I'd forgotten that this week's calendar listed the sheriff as the library's Thursday-night speaker. The public meetings were held each month, and occasionally an out-of-town writer was invited. Usually, however, the highlight was one of our local luminaries. The events seldom contained much news value, so I let Edna Mae Dalrymple, the head librarian, turn in a detailed—though accurate—account.

"Drat," I said. "Oh, come anyway. I'll leave work a half hour early so I can get the barbecue started. You can have a drink, eat, and be at the library by seven-thirty. I'll make homemade French fries."

"What's up with you?" Milo asked in a bemused tone. "I don't think this invitation flew off the top of your head."

Either I have no feminine wiles—and no knack for subterfuge—or the sheriff was occasionally more prescient than I thought. "I want to discuss the Rafferty case with you," I hedged. "I want to do it in a more comfortable setting than our offices or Vida's sidewalk."

"You make good French fries," Milo said, "but you always screw up the barbecue stuff. Get it started early, I'll cook the burgers. See you around five-thirty."

What was left of the afternoon remained quiet. I dutifully quit work at four-thirty, ignoring the thermometer that the dry cleaners had installed outside their building next door to the *Advocate*. It had to be ninety or above. I preferred not knowing.

After pulling into my carport, I decided to go around to the rear of the house and start the grill immediately.

I didn't expect to already have company.

My backyard is mostly grass, sloping uphill to the tree

line, where much of the property is under blessed evergreen shade. Sitting at the edge of the grass under the
cooling branches of fir, cedar, and hemlock were Roger
with his three companions, including the buxom blonde
I'd noticed at Old Mill Park. They were passing a joint
between them and seemed oblivious to my arrival.

I watched for a moment. I hadn't noticed a vehicle
parked in front of my house, but they could have walked
the dozen blocks from the park, even if Alpine Way was
on an incline. Maybe the quartet had camped out all day
behind my log cabin. They couldn't be seen from the
street or by the neighbors.

"Roger!" I shouted. "Have you found him?"

Roger, who had just taken the doobie from Davin
Rhodes, turned slowly in my direction. He just stared.

I walked across the lawn, brown and sparse from lack
of rain. "Have you found Old Nick?" I repeated.

"Not yet," Davin called to me. He looked sheepish.
Maybe my former role as his employer carried some
weight. "We're just chillin'."

After taking a deep drag, Roger dropped the joint,
stood up, and apparently was going to crush it with his
heel.

"Hey!" My tone was sharp. "Bring that thing over
here and I'll hose it down. Do you want to start a forest
fire?"

Roger kept staring at me. But the blonde reached
down and picked up the butt. "I got it," she announced,
coming toward me.

I'd already turned on the hose. "Put it there," I said,
indicating a spot of concrete near the grill. "Thanks." I
doused the half inch of weed, then carelessly sprayed the
hose at the boys. "Oops! Sorry! But that's a good way to
cool off."

Roger jumped, as did Davin and the burly teenager I
didn't recognize. The trio shuffled down the slope.

"We got tired," Roger declared. "It's like *hot*."

"It's like that," I said, trying to ignore the fact that I was sweating like a hog. Glancing back at the place where the little group had been sitting, I noticed something glint in the sun that filtered through the fir branches. "You might as well collect those beer cans while you're at it. I don't want to have to make the sheriff arrest you for littering and trespassing. He'll be here any minute."

Davin's eyes grew round. "Dodge? He's coming *here*?"

"That's bull," Roger said in a petulant voice. He wouldn't look at me, but kept ambling down the grass toward the driveway. The blonde and the burly boy followed him.

Maybe it was the heat that frayed my temper. I'd put my purse down on the concrete. Reaching into it, I pulled out my cell phone and dialed Milo's number. He answered on the second ring.

"Milo," I said in a loud voice, "you'd better be on your way. I've got some perps for you to bust."

"Burglars?" the sheriff said in surprise.

"Trespassers, litterers, underage drinkers, use of an illegal substance. You'd better hurry. I haven't had time to start the grill."

"Jesus," Milo muttered. "You're serious?"

"More or less." I eyed Roger as he turned to listen.

"I'm coming," Milo said. "You'd better have the Scotch ready."

I rang off. "Now," I said pointedly, "do you think I'm kidding?"

Roger again avoided my gaze. He made a flapping motion with his hand. "C'mon, guys, let's book."

Only Davin Rhodes remained as the burly boy and the blond girl hurried after Roger, who was trotting off down the driveway.

"Are you going to report us to the sheriff?" Davin asked anxiously.

"Go pick up those beer cans," I said.

Davin ran back up the slope. I began to cope with the briquettes and the lighter fluid. A moment later, Davin returned with six cans of very cheap beer, all apparently empty.

"Where shall I put them?" he asked, still looking worried.

"The recycling bin's by the back door." I paused. "Thanks, Davin."

"My folks'll kill me if I get busted," Davin said in a miserable voice.

In his five years as an *Advocate* carrier, Davin had been generally reliable. The few times that he had missed work or otherwise screwed up had been because of Roger's shenanigans. Davin was a born follower. Unfortunately, he'd chosen Roger as his leader.

"Let's cut a deal," I said. "You tell me what you kids did today, and I'll keep my mouth shut."

"What we did?" Gavin's cheeks, which had grown pale, now reddened. "Well . . . see, it was like this . . . Roger decided we should be like the command post. We started up Alpine Way, but that was when we ran into Tats."

"Tats?"

Davin nodded. "He's a guy we know from high school. We call him Tats 'cause he's got all these tattoos. His real name is Walter. Anyways, he's older than we are, like twenty-one, 'cause he flunked sixth grade. Twice. We—well, Roger—had Tats get us some beer. So after that, we sort of hung out around town, waiting for reports from the troops in the field. That's what Roger calls them, see. We were starting back to the park when we stopped here. To . . . rest."

I believed most of what Davin told me. I could fill in the gaps for myself. "So has anyone reported good information?"

Davin brightened a bit. "Yeah. We got a bunch of calls. The troops found lots of stuff, like empty chips bags and grocery sacks and pop cans and even a paintbrush."

That sounded like the ordinary leftovers from careless campers and hikers. Except for the paintbrush. Maybe someone had been marking a trail. "But no sightings of Old Nick?"

Davin shook his head. "Not yet."

"Okay." I smiled. "Get going. The sheriff really is on his way."

Davin's expression was still anxious. "You won't rat us out?"

"Don't worry about it. Go."

Davin ran, apparently trying to catch up with the others, who had disappeared down Fir Street.

Five minutes later, Milo arrived just as I was defrosting the hamburger. "Where'd you put the perps?" he inquired before getting ice out of the fridge. "In the closet?"

"I let them off with a stern warning," I said. "That is, I let Davin Rhodes off. The other three fled on foot."

Milo sighed. "Roger."

I nodded. "Along with a busty blonde and some other kid I don't know." Briefly, I recounted my discovery in the backyard.

Milo yawned. "Sounds like Roger. I suppose the whole goofy crew'll meet up in Old Mill Park at six. Bill and Doe are standing by."

I was slicing potatoes in thick strips, the way the sheriff liked them. "No emergency reports from the field? No drink for Emma?"

"Oh. Sorry." Milo put ice into the glass I'd set out and poured a generous measure of Canadian whiskey into it. "Water?"

"Fine."

"No reports," Milo said after he set my drink down on the counter next to the cutting board. "Beth Rafferty says 911 has been pretty quiet today except for some calls from stalled motorists going up the pass. This heat is killing engines and radiators are boiling over."

"It's killing me," I grumbled. The kitchen, which faces west, felt like a steam room. "Let's go outdoors. I *think* I got the grill started."

I'd failed. Milo shot me a look that indicated I was inept when it came to practical matters. I didn't mind. Not only was it true, it made him feel good to be superior once in a while. A big part of our problem as a couple had been that we shared so few interests except for sports. My affection—or maybe he considered it an affectation—for the fine arts had always bored or frustrated him. I understood that he felt he wasn't as well educated or as sophisticated as I was. That was partly a matter of background: I'd been raised in the city, he'd grown up in a small town. As Seattle came of age during my younger years, I'd had more exposure to culture. I could do nothing about our differences.

"We'll be lucky if we eat by seven," he muttered, toiling away with the charcoal.

"If you didn't want your burgers done to a crisp, it wouldn't matter," I pointed out. "Have you heard from Toni?"

"No. Why would I? She's sick."

"Lovesick, maybe," I said, trying to keep my voice light.

Milo stood back from the blaze he'd created. "What?"

"I hear she's been involved in a bad relationship."

"Who hasn't?" Milo watched the fire with steady eyes. The flames began to die down. "Or have you forgotten my divorce?"

"I wasn't here when you got divorced."

"You didn't miss much," Milo muttered. "How are you going to cook the fries on this thing?"

"I don't. I put them in a deep fryer. That way, I don't have to turn on the stove and heat the kitchen up to a hundred and twenty degrees."

"Oh. Well, if you'd been here, you would've met Old Mulehide. I don't think the two of you would've gotten along."

"Old Mulehide" was the nickname Milo had given his ex-wife, Tricia. She'd cheated on him with a high school teacher known as the Snake. Eventually, Mulehide and the Snake had married and moved to Bellevue, taking the three Dodge children with them.

"Maybe," I persisted, "you might ask Toni what's troubling her."

Milo took a swig of his drink. "Hey, I don't get into my staff's personal lives. They're supposed to leave that stuff behind when they close their front door."

"Some people can't do that," I pointed out. "It eats them up inside so they can't perform their jobs."

"Then they need to work it out or find another job," Milo asserted. "One of the reasons I hired Doe Jameson is because she seems so levelheaded. I don't need three females driving me nuts."

I glared at Milo. "Are you counting me as one of them?"

"Huh?" Milo looked up from the cigarette he was lighting. "Hell, no. You don't work for me. I meant Toni and Beth."

"Beth?" I was puzzled. "She always seems to be in control."

"She usually is," Milo said, puffing out more smoke than the grill was managing. "Oh, sure, I know she's upset now after her brother's death, but she was starting to lose it before that. Not like Toni," he went on more slowly. "No big fit-pitching, but she hasn't been herself. Jumpy. On edge. Forgetting stuff. That's not like Beth."

I agreed. "She worked the day after Tim died. That was brave."

Milo studied the coals, which were beginning to glow red. "Beth never takes time off. She'll feel guilty tomorrow when she has to go to Tim's memorial service."

Quickly, I checked my watch—ten to six. We were on schedule, despite Milo's misgivings. "How does she get along with Toni?"

The sheriff shrugged. "They hardly see each other. Beth's back in her dungeon, as she calls it, and Toni's out front. Besides, Beth used to be located in the courthouse until we moved her."

"Maybe," I suggested, "Beth's been worried about Tim."

"Why?"

"Oh—who knows? Money troubles, maybe?"

Milo chuckled. "I get a bang out of you women. You're always trying to figure out what's going on in other people's heads. By the way, yours sure doesn't have much hair. Why'd you do that?"

"I didn't," I said grimly. "Stella did. What's wrong with wondering about other people? Don't you try to get inside the criminal mind?"

"That's different," Milo replied, taking another swallow from his cocktail glass. "That's business. By the way, we've checked on the Raffertys' finances. They've been treading water. I don't think Tim was very good at the Internet trading stuff."

"Did he have insurance?"

"On the house," Milo answered, flipping his cigarette butt onto the grill, "and car insurance. But no life insurance. In your thirties, you still think you're immortal. I never had that problem. In law enforcement, life insurance comes with the job."

"So Tiffany doesn't get anything except for the house, which," I continued, "probably isn't the full replacement value. Did Tim sell much of his sports memorabilia?"

"Nickel-and-dime stuff, I suspect," Milo replied, finishing his drink. "No sizable amounts of money showed up at the bank. There was no sign of a safe at the house, either. I wouldn't think he'd keep valuable stuff just sitting around. If he had any."

I pointed to the sheriff's glass. "Refill?"

He shook his head. "Not tonight. I want to be sharp for this damned library talk. Christ, I don't know how I got myself roped into it."

"Maybe I'll come," I said.

Milo shot me a dirty look. "Don't even think about it."

"Hey," I retorted, "are you afraid of making a fool of yourself in front of me? I make a fool of myself every week when I put out the paper. How many people called you a moron and a jerk this week?"

The sheriff shrugged. "They do it all the time. You can't have my job and not have people think you're dumb as a cedar stump."

I put my hand on his arm. "Well, you're not. Can I come?"

Milo put his big hand over mine. "Oh, hell. Why not?"

"Thanks." I smiled and withdrew my hand. "I'll get the burgers."

"Hey," Milo called after me. "How come Roger and those other kids ended up here?"

I turned around by the open back door. "Because this is as far as they got all day?"

Milo shook his head, but didn't say anything.

I sensed what he was thinking, though. My little log cabin was just a few yards from the vacant house where

Old Nick had been staying. And just beyond it was the charred rubble that had once been home to the Raffertys.

Maybe Roger and his friends weren't as stupid as I thought they were.

Chapter Ten

THE SHERIFF'S THEME was gun safety. He talked about rules, regulations, trigger locks, and pending legislation at the state and local levels. Gun ownership in SkyCo was high. The right to bear arms was an important issue among voters. He'd given virtually the same speech on other occasions, and seemed at ease before his audience of approximately forty concerned citizens. His presentation was, I felt, worthy of at least a couple of inches in the *Advocate*.

A question-and-answer period followed, as it always did when the monthly speaker concluded the formal part of the program. Edna Mae Dalrymple wielded a microphone among the audience members, but couldn't make it work. She fussed with it in her nervous, twittering manner, but finally surrendered. There was really no need. Except for a couple of deaf old codgers at the back, including County Commissioner Alfred Cobb, who didn't care what anybody said, everyone seemed to be able to hear.

Donna Wickstrom, who is Ginny's sister-in-law, was on her feet. Donna's first husband, Art Fremstad, had been a sheriff's deputy who'd died in the line of duty. She had remarried and now ran a small art gallery in the Alpine Building in addition to her day care center.

"I have a question that doesn't pertain to guns," Donna said in her clear, intelligent voice. "I'd like to know what's being done about the Rafferty homicide and fire. If there's an arsonist loose, the public should be informed."

Milo kept his aplomb. "We're taking this as an isolated incident," he replied, speaking far more formally than his usual laconic style. "There's no cause for alarm as far as we can tell."

"Are you saying that the fire was set to cover the murder?" Donna asked.

"That's possible." Milo's expression was stoic.

"Have you any suspects?"

"No one specific."

"Have you any leads?"

"I'm not sure what you mean."

Donna frowned. "I mean—what I *really* mean is that it must be difficult to obtain evidence from a fire scene. Everything was destroyed, wasn't it?"

"Yes."

"Has the volunteer search party turned up any information on the whereabouts of the so-called recluse known as Old Nick?"

"Not to my knowledge, although my deputies are still sifting through their reports."

"Are the volunteers going out again tomorrow?"

"I believe at least some of them will. This is not an official search organization. SkyCo takes no responsibility for their actions."

"Thank you." Donna sat down.

I wondered if she had been deliberately trying to put Milo on the spot. Maybe, after all these years, she harbored resentment against him because Art had been killed while working for the sheriff.

High school coach Rip Ridley asked a different sort of question, something to do with hunting rifles and ammo. My mind drifted.

So did the Q&A session. Alfred Cobb struggled to his

feet to ask why the turkey shoot had been canceled at the Overholt farm. Milo responded that it had ended when the Overholts stopped raising turkeys, which had been about thirty-five years ago. Alfred cupped his hand behind his ear, said, "Eh?" and sat down on Ione Erdahl's lap. Ione let out a yelp. Edna Mae Dalrymple scurried up to the working microphone on the podium, thanked Milo, and announced that the meeting was over. Alfred didn't budge until Coach Ridley bodily picked him up and carried him to the exit.

Several people, mostly men, converged around the sheriff, asking more questions. I gave Milo a thumbs-up sign and started out of the stuffy, ill-ventilated room. By chance, I found myself next to Donna Wickstrom.

"How's the art gallery doing?" I inquired.

"It's a hobby, really," Donna replied. "It's something I always wanted to do. When Lloyd Campbell expanded his appliance store, the couple that owned the original gallery in that building moved it to Sultan. You should stop by to see my setup. I'm only open Friday nights and on the weekend."

"I should," I said as we walked down the hallway that led to a side entrance by the parking lot. "Vida wrote about it when you opened a few years ago, but we might be able to do something new. Do you have any special exhibits?"

"Nothing in particular. Come fall, I plan to hold a holiday crafts fair. Very few people in town buy art for art's sake. Thank God for the summer tourists. Not to mention the skiers in the winter."

"I'll stop in after work tomorrow night," I promised. We'd reached the parking lot. A blessed breeze was blowing off from the mountains. "What time do you open?"

"Five," she replied. "I insist that parents pick up their kids by four-thirty on Fridays. Except for Ginny's, of course. I bring her boys with me and she or Rick collect them at the gallery."

"By the way," I said as I reached my Honda, "I was wondering if you had a theory about the Rafferty murder. You seem to be following it quite closely."

Donna shrugged. "Who wouldn't? It's a terrible thing. And I know what it must be like for Tiffany, losing your husband at so young an age." For a moment, a shadow crossed Donna's pretty face. "I feel for her. I wish I knew her better."

"Don't we all?"

Donna's gaze flickered behind the long, curling lashes. "Yes. I see what you mean. Tiffany is . . . well, not standoffish, but she and Tim always seemed so tight that they didn't have room for outsiders."

"Did you know her at all?" I asked, ignoring Alfred Cobb, who was standing on the edge of the parking lot still demanding that the turkey shoot be resurrected, apparently with or without turkeys.

"No," Donna replied. "I'm a few years older than she is. I only know Tiffany by sight."

"I thought maybe she'd contacted you about day care," I said as one of Alfred's sons and Coach Ridley tried to haul the old coot to a big Chrysler parked in a spot marked for the handicapped.

Donna shook her head. "Maybe Tiffany didn't plan to work after she had the baby. Besides, I don't run the only day care in Alpine."

"No, of course not." I paused. "I take it you didn't know Tim very well, either?"

Donna shook her head again. "He started high school after I graduated. Our paths didn't cross much. I always thought the Raffertys were Catholic, but I see that Tim's services are being held in the Lutheran church."

"The Raffertys—at least the father, Liam—were Irish,

but not Catholic," I pointed out. I knew what Donna, born an Erlandson, meant. Going back a generation or two, Alpine's Irish and Italian Catholics hadn't always mixed well with the predominantly Scandinavian Protestants. "I'm sure the Eriks family wanted Tim buried out of their own church. I don't know Beth Rafferty's religious convictions."

"I do know Beth," Donna said. "She's a nice woman. I feel sorry for her, too. With her mother in such poor shape, Beth has no real family left. Except when the baby comes, of course."

Alfred Cobb was being stuffed into the car in the handicapped spot. Unfortunately, he was put in the driver's seat. His son and Rip Ridley stepped aside. Alfred gunned the engine and shot straight over the curb and across the sidewalk. The Chrysler slammed into the library wall.

"Oh, my God!" Donna cried. "Was that Mr. Cobb?"

"It wasn't Durwood," I murmured.

Donna ran toward the car. Rip and Alfred's son were already there. So were a couple of other people who had barely escaped getting hit by the Chrysler. Fearing that medical help might be needed, I got out my cell phone and dialed 911. I recognized Evan Singer's voice on the line.

"The public library?" Evan echoed. "I'll send an ambulance right away. Is that you, Emma?"

"Yes," I replied, keeping my eye on the activity around the Chrysler and wishing I'd brought a camera. "I can't tell about injuries. Alfred only went about fifteen feet, but he went fast."

"Okay. Is Dodge still there?"

I looked around the parking lot. Milo's Grand Cherokee was parked a few spaces away from the side entrance. In fact, the sheriff was coming out of the building even as I answered Evan's question.

"Yes. I see him. I called you first because I thought Alfred should be treated before he was arrested."

Whatever damage the crash had done to Alfred, it hadn't harmed his lungs. He was swearing his head off as Rip and the younger Cobb—whose name I suddenly recalled was Myron—disentangled him from the air bag.

"Air bag meets Windbag," I muttered as Edna Mae Dalrymple twittered and twitched over to my side. "I don't think Alfred's seriously injured."

"But what about the library?" Edna Mae asked in her birdlike voice. "I can't tell from here. I don't want to get too close in case there's blood. I can't take the sight of blood. Oh, dear! Alfred sounds very upset!"

"I'll check out the building," I said, watching the sheriff approach the damaged car and the cussing Alfred.

The ambulance siren sounded nearby. I couldn't see into the Chrysler. Milo's big form blocked Alfred from sight, if not from sound. Close to the library's outer wall, I could see that the Chrysler's grille was badly mangled and a headlight was broken. The building's brick facade was intact, though undoubtedly marred. The flower bed that bordered the walkway apparently hadn't been crushed, because the front tires never got farther than the concrete.

"A scrub brush should take care of it," I told Edna Mae as I rejoined her by the curb. "The main thing is that no one seems to be badly hurt, including Alfred." Indeed, Alfred was now demanding to know who had moved the goddamned building.

"Thank heavens he's alive!" Edna Mae's small face was still stricken. "I really must go back inside and sit down. This is so terrible! Oh—here comes the ambulance."

"I'll go in with you," I said. "We need to give the EMTs some room to work."

That wasn't precisely true, but I wanted to talk to Edna Mae. I'd forgotten to contact her about the Rafferty disaster.

She led me back into the meeting room, which was now empty except for the custodian who had begun to tidy up. The urns that held coffee and hot water for tea had been unplugged, but were still warm. Edna Mae insisted that I join her in a cup of tea.

"Poor Mr. Cobb," she lamented. "He really shouldn't be driving. He's not only hard of hearing, but doesn't see as well as he used to."

"Yes," I agreed. "That seems to be the case."

She shot me a quick, anxious look. "Do you think he might sue us? I mean, we didn't move the building, of course. But Mr. Cobb *is* a county commissioner."

"He's lucky he doesn't get cited for reckless driving," I replied. "Besides, there were a half-dozen witnesses in the parking lot who saw that it was his own fault for not putting the car in reverse."

"Yes . . . yes, I suppose that's so." Edna Mae plucked at her lower lip. "Goodness, this has been a very nerve-racking week."

She had segued into my line of interrogation. "It certainly has. You were the one who called in the fire, weren't you?"

Edna Mae shuddered. "Oh, I certainly did! I was sitting up late, reading the new Anna Quindlen book. Such an excellent writer, so adept at touching the heart." She smiled softly. "Then I heard this crackling sound. I thought it was fireworks, left over from the Fourth of July. I peeked outside—I always draw the drapes at night, even in the summer—and I could see flames coming from across the street." Edna Mae shuddered again. "I thought it was the Rafferty house, but I couldn't be sure. It was dark by then, you see, and even though the fire cast a glow, it was hard to see with the smoke. So I called 911." She pursed her lips, and the hand that held the paper cup of tea trembled. "If only I'd noticed sooner. Maybe I could have saved Tim."

"I doubt that," I murmured. "It's probable that the fire was started after Tim was already dead."

Edna Mae leaned forward on the folding chair. "But you can't be sure, can you? I feel so guilty!"

"You mustn't," I insisted. "What you can do, though, is to try to remember if you saw anything unusual at the Rafferty house lately. Someone watching it, maybe, or even Old Nick, who was allegedly living in the vacant place next door."

Edna Mae's eyes grew huge. "I've never seen Old Nick. I'm sure I'd know if I had. He's very peculiar-looking, isn't he?"

"He's got a long gray beard and wears ratty old clothes," I said. "You'd notice someone like that in the neighborhood." I hadn't, I reminded myself. Emma, Professional Observer, flunks another test.

"Oh, my, yes, and anyone like that who came into the library. Not," she added, "that we don't get some old and rather odd fellows from time to time. Occasionally, a strange old lady, too. It's very sad. They spend hours, just reading the newspapers, especially in the winter when it's cold."

I nodded. "They're lonely. And maybe they have no heat where they live."

"You'd think there would always be firewood around here," Edna Mae remarked. "It's certainly hot enough now. I was so afraid that the fire at the Raffertys' might jump the street. Everything's so dry. I think summer is a much more dangerous time around here than winter."

"I don't suppose you've seen anyone else around the

Raffertys' house lately," I said in a casual manner. "They seemed to keep to themselves."

Edna Mae looked faintly indignant. "I'm not like some who go around keeping track of their neighbors' every move."

I knew that Vida was first and foremost among those *some,* but I merely nodded.

"Of course," Edna Mae continued, "you have to keep an eye out. For one thing, that cul-de-sac was always a magnet for teenagers before Tim and Tiffany built their house. The high school and college youngsters would go there to party and do heaven-knows-what." She shuddered yet another time, though not so strongly. "And of course, the vacant house was always a problem. Remittance people, that's what I thought. You know—or runaways and such who'd move in. Squatters, too, if you count any of the older ones who lived there."

"Yes," I agreed. "That section of Fir Street's always caused problems."

"It's very close to the high school, too." Edna Mae looked worried. "I do like to keep an eye on the playfield. You never know what's going to happen there at night when it's deserted."

"Not much if it's deserted," I noted.

"What?" Edna Mae stared. "Oh! Yes." She smiled. "You always have your little jokes, Emma. But you know what I mean."

"So you haven't seen anyone out of the ordinary around the Rafferty house?" I repeated, steering Edna Mae back to my original query.

"No." She shook her head. "Just family now and then. Tiffany's parents. Tim's sister, Beth. I believe Beth brought her mother over once right after they moved in. I doubt that poor Mrs. Rafferty knew where she was, though. It's very sad."

The custodian looked as if he was getting impatient

for us to leave him to his business. I wasn't getting very far with my own. "Did you bring your car?" I asked Edna Mae. "If not, I could give you a ride."

"Oh, yes," she replied. "I've been here since nine o'clock this morning. I don't like to walk in hot weather."

"I don't blame you." I stood up. "I should go. I suppose I'd better check to find out if Alfred's okay."

Edna Mae also got to her feet, though she teetered a bit. "I do hope so. He's really quite frail."

I agreed. Moments later, I was back in the parking lot. Milo was still there, along with Coach Ridley and a tow truck driven by Cal Vickers from the Texaco station. I inquired after the county commissioner.

"Alfred wouldn't go in the ambulance," Milo replied, "so Myron took him to the clinic. He looked okay to the EMTs, at least as far as they could tell. The old fart wouldn't let them come near him." The sheriff nodded at the Chrysler, which Cal was studying with professional aplomb. "That's a fairly new car," Milo went on. "It's got some other dents and scrapes. I guess Durwood Parker's got a successor as the worst driver in SkyCo."

"How are the Parkers?" I asked. "I haven't spoken to them since Tim died."

"Dwight Gould went to see them Tuesday afternoon," Milo replied. "Dwight worked in the pharmacy while he was going to high school. He told me they were holding up pretty well. They're tough old birds."

"They're smart, too," I noted, "Durwood's driving record notwithstanding."

Coach Ridley chuckled. "I remember my first season as the Buckers' coach. Sultan was down on our four-yard line, going for the winning TD in the final seconds. Durwood drove his car onto the field and damned near wiped out both teams. Time expired while everybody was running for cover. Durwood claimed he had to work late at the drug store and was only trying to find a parking place."

The sheriff and Cal Vickers laughed, too.

"I don't know how many times I had to tow Durwood's cars," Cal put in. "He was always so good-natured about it all, too. Hell of a guy."

The three men were absorbed in their conversation. They didn't notice me. I went over to the Honda and headed for home.

The library is located on First, between Pine and Cedar streets. As I pulled out of the parking lot, I saw a big truck stalled on the hill, so I took a right instead of a left and drove along Pine. Slowing to a stop before turning right on Fourth, I noticed a figure leaning against the side of the Alpine Building. It was almost dark. My first thought was that whoever it was had staggered out of Mugs Ahoy across the street and couldn't quite manage walking. But then I looked closer.

The man was tall and slightly stooped. Or maybe he seemed that way because he was propped up by the building. His T-shirt and pants were old and ratty. He had a long gray beard.

I was certain that he was Old Nick.

Chapter Eleven

THE SIGHTING OF a man who looked like Old Nick presented a logistical dilemma. There was nowhere to park, except for a loading zone by the tavern across Pine Street. The object of my curiosity lifted his head and looked straight at the Honda. His reaction was the same as if he'd been a deer. He froze for just a second, then turned away and started scampering down the street toward Front.

A car coming uphill had the right-of-way. The driver was going very slowly, not more than ten miles an hour. I had to wait. As the vehicle crossed the intersection, I thought I recognized Darla Puckett. She wasn't the worst driver in SkyCo, but she was the slowest, never going over twenty-five, even on the highway.

As for the man I thought was Old Nick, he was much fleeter of foot than I'd imagined. By the time Darla had passed by, he'd turned the corner on Front. A quartet of teenagers was crossing the main drag, apparently headed for the late show at the Whistling Marmot. I had to wait for them, too. By the time I turned onto Front, Old Nick had disappeared.

"Damn!" I swore under my breath, scanning Front Street. Several people were on the sidewalks, coming or going to the movie theater, the Venison Inn, the video store, the Burger Barn. That section was always busy by Alpine standards, especially on a warm summer night.

I was driving almost as slowly as Darla Puckett, trying to see where Old Nick had gone. If the man was the recluse, it seemed unlikely that he'd gone into any of the business establishments. The only escape route was the narrow alley between the theater and Dutch Bamberg's Videos-to-Go on the corner.

But I didn't see him from the car. He could be hiding in a doorway or even have reached Pine Street. Again, I was amazed at his quickness. Discouraged, I turned up Fifth, looking in every direction when I reached Pine again. The street was now deserted except for a couple who were just coming out of Mugs Ahoy. I kept going, cutting back to Fourth where the middle school blocked the street.

I called Vida as soon as I got home. "I think I saw Old Nick," I said.

"No!" Vida sounded flabbergasted. "Where?"

I recounted my little adventure. "For an old guy, he moves pretty fast," I added.

"You're sure you aren't mistaken? It's dark; it may have been someone else with a beard."

"It wasn't that dark," I responded. "This happened ten, fifteen minutes ago." I started at the beginning, with dinner for Milo and his talk at the library.

"Alfred Cobb!" Vida exclaimed when I got to the part about the accident. "The old fool! He should have had his license revoked years ago! He must be ninety if he's a day!"

"He has an outstanding guardian angel," I remarked.

"Worn to a frazzle, I should think." But Vida still had objections about my sighting. "I can't imagine Old Nick—or any other of those hermits—staying so long in town, especially in the summer. They come for a day or two, get what they need, and go back to their lairs. It's utterly uncharacteristic for one of them to linger."

Vida had a point, but I wondered if she wasn't dubious because it would mean her search—*Roger's* search—was in vain. "All the same, I'm going to tell Milo," I said.

"Oh, Milo, my foot! He couldn't find Old Nick under his desk!"

"Well," I said, piqued by Vida's disbelief, "Roger and his buddies didn't find Old Nick in my backyard."

"What do you mean?"

"That's where I found them when I came home from work a half hour early."

"You did?" Vida paused. "They were resting, of course."

It was useless to reveal the truth to Vida. She'd accuse me of lying, of causing trouble, of being blind as a bat. Worse yet, she'd be on the peck—as she'd put it—for the rest of the week.

"Ask Roger," I said, and let it go at that.

There was another pause at the other end of the line. "They'd probably been to the cul-de-sac, looking for clues. Or at the abandoned house."

"You haven't talked to him this evening?"

"No," Vida admitted. "I only got home about ten minutes ago. I had dinner with the Thorvaldsons in Sultan. They're distant cousins, you know."

If I'd ever known, I'd forgotten. It was impossible to keep up with all of Vida's relatives.

"I tried to drop off those geranium cuttings for Mandy Gustavson on my way to Sultan. Unfortunately, she wasn't home," Vida continued. "I'll try again tomorrow, or perhaps Saturday. She may be working evenings at the Venison Inn. I certainly don't want to meet her in the bar."

I assumed she shuddered at the mere thought. "Bars are good places for gossip," I pointed out.

"Anywhere is a good place for gossip," Vida retorted.

"I'll call Roger right now. Don't you dare phone Milo until I call you back."

I agreed. For all I knew, Milo had gone off to Mugs Ahoy with Coach Ridley and Cal Vickers. The sheriff was, after all, off duty.

It was going on ten o'clock. I hadn't checked my e-mail since I got home from work. Sure enough, there was a message from Adam.

"Mom," he wrote. "If Toni was seeing Tim Rafferty, that'd explain the e-mail I got from her today. I'm forwarding it on to you. Make of it what you will. Love and prayers, Adam the Popsicle."

Lucky Adam. Apparently, he wasn't suffering from ninety-degree heat.

Quickly, I read through Toni's message.

"Hi, Adam—I'm not at work today because I don't feel good. Is it true that men outnumber women in Alaska? I'm thinking of moving there. Where's a good place? I don't think I can live in Alpine anymore. I trust you. Please help me. Your friend, Toni."

The message sounded like Toni: immature, naïve—and trusting. If she'd trusted Tim Rafferty, she'd made a big mistake. But at least she'd had the good sense—or dumb luck—to confide in Adam. I suspected that Toni always trusted the men she dated. My son was probably one of the few that she could still locate, let alone trust.

I thought about the matter for several minutes before finally replying to Adam. Maybe he was still online. His message had been sent only a half hour ago, our time.

"Dear Adam—Upon sober reflection (no, your mother hasn't been drinking, not for the past four hours anyway), I've decided that this is a perfect opening for me to talk to Toni. But first, you should e-mail and tell her what she needs to know about jobs and locations and such. Then I can take it from there. Are you really cold? I envy you. Love, Mom."

I waited, hoping that Adam would respond. The phone rang a minute or two later.

It was Vida. "I spoke to Roger," she said in a brusque voice. "I was quite right. He and the other searchers were merely taking a break on their way back to Old Mill Park. They'd decided to do a thorough search of the abandoned house and the murder site."

"And?"

"They were impeded by smoldering rubble at the house," Vida replied in a hostile tone. "There's still a danger of flare-up there, though I can't think why. Doe Jameson was patrolling the site and shooed them away. Honestly, you'd think that with all the water and chemicals they use on fires now, there wouldn't be a problem. It's been four days."

"Only three, really," I pointed out. "The fire was late Monday night. This is only Thursday."

"Well," Vida huffed, "it seems like much longer. In any event, Roger and the other brave souls went through the vacant property, though why Milo put up crime-scene tape around the house, I'll never know."

"To keep out trespassers?" I suggested.

Vida took umbrage. "Roger and his chums certainly aren't trespassers, they're on a mission. The sheriff should thank them. But they did get in and had a very good look around before Doe showed up a second time and made them leave."

Doe had had a busy day. Maybe I could learn to like her.

"What did they find?" I inquired as a new message from Adam showed up in my in-box.

"All sorts of things," Vida said cryptically. "Of course, Milo had taken away items that might have fingerprints or be traceable. But there was still a great deal to sort through."

I was torn between reading my son's e-mail and listening to Vida puff up her grandson's importance. "Such as?"

"What you might expect from hippies and squatters," Vida said in a self-righteous tone. "Wine bottles, candles, drug paraphernalia, music tapes, artsy-craftsy things, even some kind of kiln. Or that's how Roger described it, though he thought it was an oven. Which, of course, it really is."

"Yes." I was distracted. "Good for him," I said, trying to sound enthusiastic. "I'm still going to call Milo."

"If you must."

I would—but as soon as I hung up, I read my son's latest missive.

"Mom—Will do, along with a warning for Toni to ignore ads that promise big bucks and may sound like they're some kind of official Alaskan site but are a scam. I'll do it now while I have time and CC the message to you. I'm not cold now, but I will be in about two weeks. Envy is a sin. You'd better stick to drinking."

I smiled, as if I could see Adam's face on the laptop's screen. I tapped out a brief reply. Then I called Milo on his cell. He picked up, sounding irritated.

"Why didn't you call me at home?" he demanded. "I thought this was another damned emergency."

"I didn't know you were home," I said innocently. "I thought you might be out drinking with the boys."

"What boys?" Milo grumbled. "Cal Vickers isn't far from sixty, and Coach has got to be over fifty. Hell, they're as old as I am. As for Myron Cobb, he's close to seventy. Myron rode a bicycle to the library, for God's sake."

"You can't blame him for not wanting to ride with his father," I pointed out. "Guess who I *think* I saw coming home?"

"Roger?"

"No. Old Nick."

"The hell you did."

"This guy fit the description," I insisted before describing the encounter.

"That's weird," Milo said when I'd finished. He knew that I wasn't given to flights of fancy, so his tone was thoughtful. "Maybe he got wind of those goofy kids and their search party. Maybe he decided the best place to hide was in town."

"Did any of them find a shack or any kind of place where a hermit might hole up in the woods?"

"Oh, a couple of old lean-tos we already knew about," Milo replied. "They've been there forever, but nobody lives in them. There's an abandoned cabin up on Martin Creek—some others around the county, too. From time to time, they've been occupied, but not lately. Summer people, homesteaders, whoever built those places a million years ago just left them standing vacant. They should be torn down, but that's not my worry. Most of them are on what's now state or federal forest service land."

I already knew that story. Over the years, we'd run articles on the subject, hoping that rightful owners or their heirs might step forward. The only responses we'd gotten were bogus. As for the hermits, they wouldn't set up housekeeping on property that the authorities had on record.

"One thing bothers me," I said. "If this was Old Nick, he's in terrific shape. He ran like a racehorse. How old is he supposed to be?"

"How should I know?" Milo retorted. "He's always been described as having a long gray—sometimes even white—beard. That goes back twenty, thirty years. If I had to guess—which I hate to do—I'd say in his seventies."

"He ran like he was eighteen," I said. "Or closer to that than to eighty."

"That's possible," Milo said after a pause. "Those hermits have to keep fit just to survive. They have to haul their supplies, often uphill. You've heard about the Iron Man of the Hoh?"

"Of course," I replied, "but he wasn't a hermit. He had a ranch on the Hoh River over on the Olympic Peninsula." The old guy had been so strong that he'd allegedly carried a cast-iron stove for miles and miles over rough country trails and streams. When encountering a neighbor who asked if the stove was a heavy burden, the Iron Man responded that it wasn't too bad—but the hundred-pound sack of flour inside the stove kind of slowed him down.

Milo's point was well taken, however. Forest-dwelling recluses didn't need to work out in a gym to keep in good physical condition.

After assuring the sheriff that he'd made a very effective presentation at the library, I rang off. My work was done. But I had a busy Friday ahead of me.

Vida goes to all the funerals. She always has a wonderful time, despite the tragic circumstances or her criticism of the deceased. I go only when it's someone I've known well. It's not that funerals disturb me so much, but that I can't endure the Wailers, a trio of black-clad women who attend every service for the dead whether they know the person or not, and who constantly moan, shriek—and wail. I've tried to ignore them—as Vida manages to do—but they drive me nuts.

I'd heard back from Adam shortly before going to bed Thursday night. The message he'd sent Toni was informative and relatively concise, directing her to the state of Alaska's web page. He also wanted to make sure that she understood the size of Alaska, not to mention the harsh weather conditions. He'd suggested that she might consider seasonal work, particularly in the seafood industry, rather than making a permanent move.

I don't know why, but I always find it surprising when my son exhibits a mature and compassionate nature. Priest or no priest, I still think of him as seventeen and utterly irresponsible. I suppose it's one of the occupational hazards of being a mother.

Adam had also told Toni that I'd be checking in with her, as I was familiar with the situation in Alaska. That wasn't exactly true, but what he really meant was that at least I knew where to find it on a map.

Thus, the first thing I did after securing coffee and a glazed doughnut was to call the sheriff's office and find out if Toni was at work. She wasn't, Doe Jameson informed me rather testily. Toni was still ailing. It was possible, Doe added, that Toni might come in later in the day.

I tried Toni at her home. She didn't pick up. All I got was a prerecorded message informing me that the party I was trying to reach wasn't available. And all I could do was wait.

"You really must come," Vida declared, standing in the doorway to my office. "The funeral could be very revealing."

"How so?"

Vida began ticking off reasons on her fingers. "Tiffany's reaction. The attitude of her parents. Beth's manner. Dot and Durwood, not to mention anyone else who shows up and makes us wonder why."

"You're referring to suspects we haven't suspected?"

Vida shrugged. "Something like that. Still," she added quickly, "I think finding Old Nick is important. If not the killer, then he may be a valuable witness."

I considered Vida's proposal. "It's a memorial service, right? It won't go on forever, right?"

"Well . . . it *is* at the Lutheran church. Some of them tend to be quite long-winded, though Pastor Nielsen isn't too loquacious. He's Danish, I believe. It's the German Lutherans you have to worry about. Of course, the problem with you Catholics is that your clergymen give rather short sermons. You get very restless if anyone speaks for over ten minutes."

I couldn't argue the point. My brother, Ben, had counseled Adam about long homilies. Ben recalled that when he was in the seminary a priest had insisted that each of his students deliver a sermon while holding a twenty-pound squirming pig. This, the veteran priest asserted, was the equivalent of a parishioner trying to control a baby while attending Mass. It was a lesson my brother never forgot, and one that, I gathered, Adam had taken to heart.

"I can't promise," I told Vida, "but maybe I'll look in. Okay?"

Vida seemed satisfied. I spent the next hour working on my Wild Sky Wilderness editorial, urging the state's congressional delegation to unite across party lines and get the bill passed. The issue had been pending for some time. The vast area, with some of the oldest forests in the state, was north of Highway 2, and included Mount Baldy and the north fork of the Skykomish River.

I got so caught up in seeking the right verbiage to move lawmakers that I lost track of time. It was five after ten when I glanced at my watch. Vida had already left around nine-thirty, presumably to make sure she got an excellent vantage point in the church.

She needn't have worried. The church seats approximately four hundred people, but no more than fifty were scattered among the comfortably padded pews. Vida was in the third row on the aisle. Her broad-brimmed black hat with the white daisies was easy to find.

Not wanting to be noticed as a latecomer, I kept to the

rear. The Wailers sat a few rows in front of me, like a trio of vultures. At the moment they were mercifully silent, perhaps in deference to Beth Rafferty, who was on the altar, speaking of her brother.

"Tim heard many people's troubles over the years," Beth was saying. "That's part of the job when you work in a restaurant."

I noticed she didn't say "bar." Maybe that was because some of the mourners were anti-alcohol. At least a dozen of those present weren't known to me, even by sight. I assumed they were relatives or friends who lived out of town. But I knew many quite well. Dot and Durwood Parker seemed to have shrunk since I'd last seen them. They sat very close to each other in the second pew, right in front of Vida. Tiffany was with her parents. I couldn't see anything but the back of their heads. Poor old Mrs. Rafferty was sitting next to Al Driggers. I hoped she didn't know what was going on. I also spotted Dwight Gould in attendance, wearing his civvies. He was probably doing double duty. Not only had he known the Parkers quite well, but Milo always attends a funeral involving a homicide or else sends one of his deputies to observe.

Beth was still talking. ". . . the radio where Tim made many new friends . . ."

Sure enough, Spencer Fleetwood was sitting off to one side. He was wearing an earpiece. I noticed that Beth wore a microphone. Damn all, Spence was broadcasting the service live over KSKY.

Well, I thought, Tim had been Spence's employee. Why not? I scrunched farther down in the pew as Beth continued: ". . . his love of baseball and his memorabilia collection. Tim hated to part with any of it, but he wanted to share with other fans so he . . ."

Tiffany was shifting around in her seat. Her back probably bothered her. It was a good thing she didn't

attend St. Mildred's, where the old fir pews are as un-
yielding as steel and no pastor has ever suggested replacement or padding.

Beth had finished. The organ was playing "Just a
Closer Walk with Thee." Pastor Nielsen returned to the
middle of the altar. The Wailers were wailing. I tried to
shut them out, but it was impossible. They covered the
scale from deep, dark moans to high-pitched, shattering
shrieks.

I tried to focus on my immediate surroundings and ignore the Wailers. It was impossible, of course, but move-
ment out of the corner of my eye caught my attention. I
saw a side door open ever so slightly. Through a pane of
frosted glass, I could make out a curly dark head I
thought I recognized. I scooted out of the pew and went
over to the side aisle. The door closed quickly. I kept
moving, if only to escape the Wailers.

I wasn't really surprised to see Toni Andreas going
toward the main entrance.

"Toni!" I called to her. "I've been trying to reach
you."

Toni blinked several times. "You have? Why?"

"Did you get Adam's e-mail about moving to Alaska?"
I didn't wait for an answer. "He asked me to talk to you
about it."

"I—" She stopped, lowering her gaze. "I have to go
outside. I can't breathe in here."

The foyer hadn't yet grown stuffy from the morning
heat, but I pretended to agree with her. "I don't blame
you. I can't stand listening to those Wailers."

I helped Toni push the heavy door open. She seemed
not only agitated, but weak. Maybe she really was sick.

"It was nice of you to come to Tim's service even
though you've been ill," I remarked as we stepped outside. "I didn't realize you were close to the family."

Toni stared across the parking lot to the nursing home

where Mrs. Rafferty now resided. Her long curly black hair made her look even more waiflike. "I knew Tim," she said softly.

"Oh?"

"I used to talk to him at the Venison Inn." Toni continued to stare.

"He must have been a good listener," I remarked.

"Yes."

"How are you feeling?"

"Okay." She finally turned slightly but didn't look at me. "Better."

"Flu? Or just this awful heat? It can make people sick, you know."

"Yes. It must be the heat."

"Why don't we go over to that bench? We can sit under the shade of the horse chestnut tree."

Toni didn't move. "I really should go."

"Why? You just got here, didn't you?"

"Well . . ." Toni looked in every direction, her movements jerky. "I really don't like funerals."

"Nobody does," I said, "except people like the Wailers." And Vida, who considered such occasions as sources of unfettered gossip. People, she once said, let their defenses down when they were mourning.

"I should go," Toni muttered, glancing anxiously at the front entrance. "The service must be almost over."

"They'll be going to the reception in the church hall," I said.

Toni shifted from one foot to the other. "Not everybody will stay."

The sun was getting in my eyes. "Is there someone you don't want to see?"

"I'm going now." Toni turned her back on me and started walking toward the street. I followed.

Toni crossed Cedar, moving toward John Engstrom Park. I saw an older dark blue Nissan parked in the middle of the block. I'd seen it often outside of the sheriff's headquarters, and figured it was her car. Sure enough, she jaywalked to the driver's side. I did the same, reaching her just as she slid behind the wheel.

The window was halfway down. I leaned against the door. "Come on, Toni. Don't act like a goose. Adam asked me to help you with your move to Alaska. What's wrong with you?"

Maybe it was the hint of maternal concern in my voice—something that I thought might be missing from Toni's life in recent years. God knows it's hard to keep a long-distance relationship going, even when you try. I wasn't sure how hard the ex–Mrs. Andreas was trying. Second marriages can create problems with children of all ages.

"Why do we have to talk now?" Toni asked in a petulant voice.

I noticed that her eyes were bright with unshed tears. "Because you're not working at the moment and I'm taking a break. Let's go get a cup of coffee somewhere."

"No." She shook her head defiantly.

"Then," I said, "let's sit in the park. It's cool with all those trees."

Toni stared straight ahead through the windshield. A minute passed. I heard voices in the distance. Glancing over my shoulder, I saw a half-dozen people coming out of the Lutheran church. Apparently, Toni had spotted them in the rearview mirror. She looked in the direction of the park with its statue of John Engstrom, one of the Alpine Timber Company's early and much loved superintendents.

"Okay." She seemed defeated, as if her will had been sliced in two by a buzz saw.

She got out of the car on the passenger side, scurrying into the park like a hunted animal. I followed at a more leisurely pace. The mourners who were leaving had gone straight to the parking lot. As far as I could tell, they weren't paying any attention to us.

Two curving benches flanked the life-size statue. We sat under a big maple tree. Its leaves didn't stir in the still, warm air. Only the sound of water rippling over rocks into a small pond offered any sense of coolness. But the grass was green and lush, watered regularly by Fuzzy Baugh's command.

"Let's talk about Alaska," I said. "It's huge, you know, and very different from Alpine."

"We have snow," Toni replied. "We have rain. I don't mind bad weather."

"Do you want to live in a city?"

"I think so. Fairbanks, maybe. Or Anchorage."

"Anchorage has about a quarter of a million people," I said. "Do you want to live in a city that large? Fairbanks is much smaller, maybe twice the size of Monroe." I was guessing about the comparison, but figured I was close enough to show Toni the difference.

She surprised me. "I looked up Anchorage on the Internet. They have over three thousand more men than women."

That, I gathered, was Toni's main interest. "You're assuming that all three thousand of them aren't losers?"

"There's bound to be some good ones," Toni replied. "They can't all be like the men around here."

"How's that?"

For the first time, she looked me right in the eye. There was no sign of tears now. "You've never gotten married. How come?"

"I was engaged. You know what happened." I couldn't keep the bitter note out of my voice.

"But the guy was married," Toni said. "I mean, he was married for a long time. Adam's dad, right?"

"Yes. Tom couldn't leave his wife. She wasn't well."

"I'll bet he told you he'd leave her."

I sighed. "Sometimes he did. But I knew he never would. He felt a great responsibility toward . . . his wife." I still found it hard to say Sandra's name out loud.

"They're all like that, I guess." Toni shifted around on the bench, gazing at a bed of petunias, pansies, and lobelias. "Maybe they're different in Alaska. It's a different kind of place."

"It is at that," I agreed, angry at her, angry at myself for letting the conversation turn to Tom. "You sound as if you've been burned."

It was an unfortunate choice of words. Toni's body convulsed, as if I'd hit her in the stomach. "How can you say that?" she cried, covering her eyes with her hands. "Oh, my God!"

I was tired of playing games with Toni. "It's Tim, right? You were in love with him."

She was sobbing, shoulders shaking, hands curled into fists against her eyes.

"Toni," I said, more softly, "I understand. You just said so yourself. I lost my lover to an early death. Please, talk to me."

She kept crying. I was afraid she was about to have hysterics. Firmly, I grabbed her by the shoulders. "You're making yourself sick. I understand. Truly. I had to be hospitalized after Tom was killed. I felt like I'd died, too. I wished I had. Come on, Toni. Be brave. Show some courage."

It seemed to take forever, but finally Toni began to compose herself. I'd used up almost an entire packet of Kleenex on her tears, sniffles, and coughs. Depleted, she leaned against the back of the wooden bench and closed her eyes.

"I really loved him," she whispered.

"I'm sure you did." A pair of boys went by the park on skateboards. I waited until they were out of hearing range. "Did Tim tell you he wanted to leave Tiffany?"

Toni sniffed several times. "He never wanted to marry her in the first place. But she got pregnant. I mean, she told Tim she was pregnant. She must have lost the first baby. Or she lied. They would have been married a year by the time this one comes."

"Were you seeing Tim before he got married?"

She shook her head. "Only to talk to, at the Venison Inn. He was always so nice. Tim was the most sympathetic person I ever met."

That might be true as far as Toni was concerned. Apparently, he was a good listener in his bartending guise. My own perception of him was that he was shallow and self-absorbed. Maybe he came off differently to someone like Toni, a member of his peer group, holding similar values, and speaking the same glib, cliché-ridden language.

"I take it Tim wasn't happily married."

"He was miserable." Toni shook her head sadly. "All Tiff could do was think about the baby. It was as if Tim didn't exist. He was just a paycheck to pay for baby things. Poor Tim felt like he was worthless. It seemed to him that all Tiff had ever wanted was to have a baby. She used him for that. He had no self-esteem. It was really tragic. He said he might have killed himself if I hadn't been there for him."

"He told you that?" I tried not to sound incredulous.

Toni nodded solemnly. "Often. I was like his . . . his safe harbor, he called it."

"Did Tiffany know about the two of you?"

Toni shrugged. "I'm not sure. If she did, she didn't care. All she could think of was the baby, the baby, the baby. Unless," she added with sudden bite in her voice, "Tiffany did care."

My patience was wearing thin. "Well? Do you think she did?"

"If she did," Toni said, looking me right in the eyes, "then she killed him."

Chapter Twelve

MY FIRST REACTION was that Toni wasn't serious. Surely she didn't believe that Tiffany had killed Tim and then set their house on fire. But Toni wasn't a kidder. Indeed, she had virtually no sense of humor, which was another reason Adam had stopped dating her.

Yet Toni's opinion was just that. She saw Tiffany as the enemy. Toni had ranged all over the map in responding to my questions. Most people, including me, considered her simpleminded. But that didn't mean that Toni couldn't also be single-minded. She seemed to have finally come to the conclusion that Tiffany was to blame for whatever reason Tim hadn't been free—or alive.

The church bells chimed eleven. Coincidentally, the sprinkler system turned on in the park. The lazy spray from the nozzle nearest to us was coming in our direction.

"We'd better go," I said to Toni as I stood up. "I don't know why they don't water in the middle of the night. The rest of us are told we can't water at all until it rains."

"Oh?" Toni looked disinterested, but she rose, too. "What about Alaska?"

Toni's allegation about Tiffany had driven the entire state out of my mind. "I have resources and contacts through the newspaper office that you might not be able to find," I said, keeping one step ahead of the sprinkler.

"Do your own Internet research as Adam suggested, and we'll take it from there. I think the crab season may be coming up. You might want to try something temporary to see how you like it up there."

We had almost reached her car. "Do you think I'm stupid?" she asked suddenly.

More people were coming out of the church. I'd been caught off guard by Toni's earnest question. "Why do you ask me that?"

"Because you're not taking me seriously. I mean it about Tiffany. Who else would want to kill Tim?"

She had a point. Old Nick was the best suspect anyone had come up with so far, and I wasn't buying it. "I think you're naïve," I said in what I hoped was a kindly voice. "But Tiffany was at work that night."

"Not the whole time," Toni replied. "She had a dinner break. I know that, because Tim always had to leave my place in case Tiff went home to eat. She didn't eat, actually, at least not when she first got pregnant. She couldn't. She'd throw up. So she'd just lie down for a while."

I didn't know if Milo had checked Tiffany's alibi. For a moment, I just stood there on the sidewalk, staring at Toni. She looked belligerent. During our fifteen-minute conversation, she'd run a gamut of emotions. Had she only convinced herself in the last quarter of an hour that Tiffany had murdered Tim? I wasn't sure how to deal with her. It was like trying to catch a butterfly without a net.

"You and Tim planned to go to Hawaii together, didn't you?"

Toni's eyes narrowed. "How did you know that? Never mind." She whirled away from me and stepped out into the street. "That blabbermouth Janet Driggers! I've never liked her! She has a nasty mind!"

Before I could stop her, Toni got into the Nissan and slammed the door.

I walked back to my car, which was parked down the street about a block away. Dwight Gould was going into the parking lot. I hailed him before he got to his car.

"I want to check on something," I said, jaywalking across Cascade Street and hoping the curmudgeonly Dwight wouldn't arrest me.

"Is this business?" he inquired, looking wary.

"Yes," I said, making sure no one was around to hear us. "Has Milo verified Tiffany's whereabouts the night of the murder?"

"Christ." Dwight looked even more cantankerous than he usually does. "Ask him. And this is a hell of a time to ask me anyway."

"I'm sorry," I apologized without much conviction. "I know you're an old friend of Dot and Durwood's. I didn't realize you were close to Tim and Tiffany."

"I wasn't. I hardly knew her." Dwight started to move away. "I came today for the Parkers and for Beth."

"How are they?"

"How do you think?" Dwight opened the door to his pickup. "Beth should take some time off, if you ask me, but nobody ever does. I could tell 'em a thing or two." He climbed into the cab and shut the door.

I had asked Dwight. But he hadn't told me anything.

I was mortified. The week seemed to have flown by. I'd completely forgotten to call Rolf back. I couldn't believe it.

"It's this murder story," I explained in my most abject voice when he called me just before noon. "I've been so focused on it that my mind has fallen apart."

"No kidding."

I couldn't tell if Rolf was being humorous—or acting like Dwight Gould.

"I can leave here before five," I said.

"Don't."

"What?"

"I gave the tickets away. I figured you didn't give a damn."

This was our first quarrel. I braced myself. It had been a long time since I'd been involved in a romantic squabble.

"It isn't as if I haven't been thinking about you," I said in a pleading voice. "I have." That much was true. During brief respites from focusing on murder, I'd envisioned Rolf in an abstract sort of way. Not, unfortunately, as the man I was supposed to be meeting in a few hours for a lovers' tryst.

Apparently, the story didn't always come first for Rolf. "You should never date a journalist," I said flatly.

"I *am* a journalist," Rolf replied in the same tone. "Maybe I should have stuck to dating myself. I'm always there for me."

"How mad are you?"

"Mad? I'm not sure that's the right word. Disappointed, hurt, pissed off. That covers it, I think. I could throw in *disillusioned,* but that's probably too strong. Besides, I've never been one for illusions in the first place. I got the impression that you were real."

"You're not bad at this guilt thing," I said, my temper flaring up. "I had enough of Irish Catholic guilt with Tom Cavanaugh. Do I have to put up with Jewish guilt, too?"

"It would appear not," Rolf said coolly. "Who's feeling guilty? Not me."

"Okay," I said, "concert or no concert, I'm coming down to see you."

"I won't be here," Rolf replied. "I'm flying to Spokane this afternoon to cover a story."

"Oh. So you were going to cancel on me, is that it?"

"No. I volunteered this morning to fill in for a sick colleague. You know I usually work the desk, not the field."

That was the difference between us: Unlike me, Rolf didn't have to chase the news on a regular basis. It came to him. We seemed to have reached an impasse. "I don't know what to say. I feel miserable."

"Good. I have to go now. The airport shuttle is picking me up in ten minutes. Goodbye, Emma."

Rolf hung up before I could say another word.

"Well?" Vida demanded, standing on the threshold of my cubbyhole. "You look like the pigs ate your little brother. Or, in your case, your big brother. What's wrong?"

I told her. "I can't believe I forgot," I finally said. "Am I so caught up in my work that I don't have time for a real life?"

Vida shrugged. "He's a man, and you've hurt his vanity. He'll get over it." She sat down in one of my visitor's chairs. "I noticed that you dropped in for the funeral, but you didn't stay. What happened?"

I'm convinced that Vida has eyes in the back of her head—or her hat. She takes in every detail, no matter how trivial. Maybe she absorbs it, like osmosis. "Can we wait to talk about it?" I asked. "I don't feel very clearheaded right now."

"Oh, for heaven's sake!" Vida looked up at the ceiling in exasperation. "You're acting like a teenager! It's a good thing I don't go mooning around whenever Buck and I have a disagreement."

Given that Buck was a retired air force colonel and almost as strong-minded as Vida, I imagined that their "disagreements" were frequent. Yet they had been companions for years.

She was right about my adolescent reaction. "Okay," I said, and revealed what Toni had told me.

"Well now." Vida pursed her lips. "Toni isn't reliable, and a very poor judge of human nature. I wouldn't put much stock in what she said about Tiffany killing Tim. Still . . . the spouse is always the prime suspect."

"Surely Milo's checked her alibi."

"One assumes so." Vida reflected for a moment. "There were serious marital problems. Dot and Durwood hinted as much to me at the reception this morning."

I nodded. "Tiffany and Tim could live together, but a legal union spoiled the fun?"

"So it seems. Not to mention the responsibility involved. Of course," Vida continued, removing the black hat and fluffing up her gray curls, "the Parkers aren't the kind to talk about family matters." She frowned, apparently at the virtue of discretion. "But I could tell they weren't happy about their granddaughter's marriage. I got the impression—well, I've had it all along—that Tim was a very controlling sort of person. So protective, you know, which can indicate a much darker side, such as cutting Tiffany off from her friends and even family."

"It sounds to me as if Tiffany should've considered having a baby on her own," I remarked. "Speaking from experience, I don't encourage it, but if she was that desperate, it might have been better."

"Oh," Vida said, waving a hand, "she's the sort who'd have to have a man in her life somewhere. Very dependent, very needy. Unless . . ." She frowned. "Unless she felt that the baby was all she needed to be complete."

"That happens," I said.

"It's Beth that worries me," Vida said. "She's not herself. Billy mentioned that the other day. Oh, she's keeping up a valiant front, but she's very troubled. I could scarcely get her to make eye contact while we were chatting over some lovely pilchard sandwiches."

"How was her mother?"

Vida shook her head. "Mrs. Rafferty just sat there in her wheelchair. She had no idea what was going on."

"She's confined to a wheelchair in addition to having Alzheimer's?"

"Not completely," Vida replied. "She can walk a bit. Though that's part of the problem. She wanders off. So many Alzheimer's patients do, you know."

"Yes." At least twice a year we ran a story about some poor soul who had left a nursing home or even a private residence and disappeared, only to be found later, dead from hypothermia. A small town on the edge of the forest was a dangerous place. "She wasn't aware of what was going on, I take it?"

"Not as far as I could tell," Vida answered sadly. "I greeted her when we got to the church hall, but she didn't seem to recognize me. All she said was, 'That hat. It's big. Like you.' "

Frankly, that sounded fairly cogent to me. But it didn't mean that Mrs. Rafferty could identify the large person wearing the large hat.

I suggested that Vida use her clout with Bill Blatt to find out if Tiffany did indeed have an alibi. She agreed. "Perhaps I could treat him to lunch if he can get away," Vida said. "Though I'm rather full. The pickled herring at the reception was delicious."

Vida could take on Tiffany. I decided to burden myself with Beth. I liked her, and always felt we could be friends—if I made the effort. I'd try to call her later, after she'd had time to recover from the funeral. Since that was homicide-related, I thought grimly, I might actually remember to make the call.

Milo wandered in shortly after one o'clock. "Back from lunch, I see," he remarked, easing into a visitor's chair.

"I never went," I said. "I wasn't hungry."

"That doesn't sound like you." He removed his Smokey Bear hat and set it on one knee. "How come?"

I didn't feel like telling Milo about Rolf. "I just wasn't. What's new?"

"We've been checking deeper into Tim's money-making schemes," Milo replied. "Nothing new, really. No trace of the baseball stuff. He must have kept it at the house. We did find out that he'd put some of it on eBay and sold a few items over the past few years. Nothing big. An Alex Rodriguez rookie card got the top price—forty-five bucks, unsigned."

"And the online trading?"

Milo shrugged. "Nickel and dime. Tim didn't invest other people's money, as far as we can tell. He made some, he lost some. He liked to brag about the good ones, though. Oren Rhodes told me that every time Tim made money, he'd try to get him—Oren—to follow his lead. But Oren wouldn't bite. Oren said his wife, Sunny, provides the extras with her Avon lady job."

"Oren probably does okay with tips at the Venison Inn," I remarked. "That's your news?"

"Hey," Milo said, scowling, "what did you expect? We got no evidence, we got no witnesses, we got no motive. And nobody's seen Old Nick since you thought you did."

I felt defensive. "I'm ninety-five percent certain it was him. Who else would run off like that?"

"Whoever it was didn't come out of Mugs Ahoy," Milo replied. "We checked."

The sun, which was now directly overhead, felt as if it were beating down on the newspaper's tin roof like a blowtorch. "Is Beth coming to work this afternoon?" I inquired.

"Yep. She's a trooper. I wanted her to take it easy, wait until Monday, but she told Dwight Gould she'd work a short one-to-six shift. She should be on duty now. Beth had to haul her mother back to the nursing home, but that wouldn't take long since it's right across from the Lutheran church."

After Milo loped away, I called Beth on her nonemergency number and asked if she'd like to have dinner with me.

"That's really nice of you," she replied, sounding a bit cautious. "But I'm doing okay. And frankly, I don't have much appetite."

"Neither do I," I confessed, "but I felt bad because I was only able to stay for part of Tim's service. I didn't get to talk to you afterwards. Why don't we meet at the ski lodge? It's air-conditioned."

"That part sounds good," Beth declared. "All I have is a fan." She paused. "Six-fifteen?"

"Perfect." I decided I could kill an hour by keeping the promise I'd made to Donna Wickstrom to visit her art gallery.

For the rest of the afternoon, I felt restless, hot, and upset. Angry, too. I shouldn't have been, but I'm not always rational. The fault was mine. I didn't take much comfort in the fact that if it was ninety on this side of the mountains, it would probably be over a hundred in Spokane. Maybe Rolf would melt, though the most I could really wish for was a thaw in our suddenly chilly relationship.

At exactly five o'clock, I left my stuffy cubbyhole and walked out into the bright sunshine. The Alpine Building is directly across Front Street, but I was sweating when I arrived at the gallery. Donna had just put up the OPEN sign and unlocked the door for me.

"You came," she said, apparently surprised.

"I wanted to." It wasn't exactly a lie, but of course I should have been on my way to Seattle to meet Rolf. "Everything looks very elegant." That much was true. Donna had an artistic eye. The space was small, no bigger than my living room, but she had managed to make the most of it without a sense of clutter. There were the expected mountain and forest paintings, some abstract works, a couple of gorgeous vases, sculptures done in various media, and jewelry. What caught my eye was a river scene, with dark green water tumbling over boulders gilded by the sun.

"That's very nice," I said, pointing to the painting.

"It's called *Sky Autumn*," Donna said. "It's my favorite, too."

I read the label attached to a corner of the painting. The artist's name was Craig Laurentis and the price was five hundred dollars. "Is he local?" I asked.

Donna shook her head. "Not really. That is, he doesn't live in Alpine. I have two more of his paintings in storage and one that's already been sold. The couple who bought it are from Monroe. They'll pick it up tomorrow."

I'm a sucker for rivers. Others may prefer seascapes, or just watching the surf at the ocean. But for me, the tide goes in—and the tide goes out. It just keeps doing that, and I get bored. Rivers are unpredictable, from sudden surging floods to lazy ripples over rocky beds. Rivers turn color, from brown to blue to gray to black to green. They change course; they cut new channels; they go wherever they will. Maybe it's that sense of reckless freedom that appeals to my inherently cautious nature.

"This Laurentis has really captured the feeling of a river," I said. "It looks like you could touch the water and get wet."

"Do you want to see the two I have in storage?" Donna asked.

"Rivers?"

"One river, one waterfall," she replied. "Craig paints only scenes from this side of the Cascades. I'll be right back."

While she was gone, I studied some of the other works. Two or three were done by locals, including Nina Mullins, Deputy Jack's wife. I had no idea Nina painted, but she didn't do it very well. It was no wonder that the asking price was only fifty dollars. Her rendition of a red barn in a snow-covered field was amateurish, even to my untrained eye.

The two vases, however, were a different matter. Both were tall and graceful, with cherry blossoms around the rim. One was pink, the other white. The price made me reel: Each one cost nine hundred dollars. I didn't know the artist, whose name was Anton Kublik.

"Who's this?" I asked when Donna reappeared.

"A Colorado glassmaker," Donna replied. "He's a Nordic skier, and stopped by last winter on his way to Stevens Pass. He showed me some pictures of his work and asked if he could send a couple of items. I was thrilled. I've already sold one to a couple from Everett. It's surprising how many western artists want to exhibit their wares in small-town galleries. At least, the ones that get some tourist trade."

Carefully, Donna removed the protective packaging from the Laurentis paintings. The waterfall was a spring freshet that could have tumbled down the slopes of Highway 2. The earth was a rich, damp brown, after a heavy rain.

"Lovely," I said.

The second picture was even more vigorous. A river poured white water through a narrow canyon, sweeping an uprooted cedar on its crest. It was Nature on the rampage, an unstoppable force that the artist had captured so realistically that I could almost feel the spray as river struck rock.

"I'd wear hip boots if I owned that one," I said. "But it's quite stunning."

"These just came in this week," Donna explained.

"I'll leave them out now and set them up. Craig wasn't sure he wanted me to have them, but I talked him into it. All of the works I have are of the Sky—or along it, in the case of the waterfall. I'll say this for him—he's loyal."

"But not from here?"

"No. In fact, I've never met him. We handle everything by e-mail. I think he lives in Monroe or around there someplace. The paintings are always sent from there."

"Interesting. So you don't have him hovering over you telling you how to display his works?"

Donna shrugged. "Half of the works I show are by out-of-towners. The other half are locals, or at least summer people. Frankly, we don't have many truly good artists in Alpine, although there are a couple of promising students at the college."

My gaze returned to *Sky Autumn*. "I really like that. I've had Monet's water lilies in my living room forever. I like it, but this is so evocative of the area." I grimaced. "Can I think about it?"

Donna laughed. "Most people do. I never encourage people to buy art on impulse. My husband's always loved paintings, but he's bought at least three over the years that are now in the garage. It was love at first sight, and complete loathing after he hung them up at home. That's how I got interested in opening the gallery. I didn't want him making any more mistakes."

"Five hundred dollars," I murmured. "That's a serious investment for a poor newspaper person."

"I know." Donna looked sympathetic. "Steve's high school math teacher's salary doesn't go very far, either. That's why I still run the day care. As for the gallery, I figure if I can pay the rent, I'm doing okay."

I nodded. "I'd better be going. By the way, you haven't had any more thoughts about Tim and Tiffany, have you?"

She shook her head. "Frankly, I try not to think about them."

"I don't blame you."

"Tiffany's lucky she didn't lose the baby," Donna said. "That happened to me when Art was killed. Of course, I was only six weeks along, but his death triggered the miscarriage. Or so I've always felt."

I hadn't known that. "I'm sorry," I said, realizing that Donna and Tiffany had more in common than I realized. Both had been widowed young, and their husbands had died violently. "Tiffany seems to be holding up pretty well, all things considered."

"Maybe she's tougher than she looks." Donna's expression was enigmatic. "Let me know if you want the painting. The best time to call me at home is early afternoon. Most of my charges take naps then."

I thanked her and said we'd be in touch.

But I could hardly take my eyes off of *Sky Autumn*. In my mind, it followed me out of the Alpine Building. It seemed to speak to me.

It would take me some time to find out what the painting was trying to say.

Chapter Thirteen

I JUST HAD time to go home and change into something that didn't reek of perspiration. By the time I got to the ski lodge it was ten after six. Beth Rafferty hadn't arrived yet, but the hostess who had replaced Heather Bardeen Bavich showed me to a corner table.

The Norse gods and goddesses who stood guard over the dining room looked blessedly cool. As I waited, I kept thinking about *Sky Autumn*. I could hardly do much else, given that the ski lodge's décor is forest and streams and waterfalls. Maybe the painting was meant for me. Or, possibly having lost a lover, I wanted to replace him with a live-in extravagance that didn't require care and coddling. It would be better, I supposed, than changing my hair color as many women seem to do when they break up with the man in their lives.

Beth appeared, looking tired and hot. Her blond hair clung damply to her fair skin.

"I should've changed," she said, allowing the hostess to seat her. "But then I'd have been late. It was awfully nice of you to invite me."

I shrugged. "I felt remiss about not talking to you this morning."

Beth smiled grimly. "Better to talk where liquor's available. Unlike you Catholics, the Lutherans don't allow alcohol on church premises."

"I've never understood that," I admitted. "Jesus's first

miracle was changing water into wine at his mother's urging. I assume Mary wanted to see the good times roll. It was a wedding, probably family, and she didn't want the host to look cheap. It was a small town; think how people would carp and criticize." A small town like Alpine—where even now Beth and I were attracting covert glances. *Sister of murder victim dining with newspaper editor. What can it mean?*

Beth looked pensive. "Goodness, I never thought about the Bible story that way. In fact, I guess I've never thought about it much at all."

I smiled. "Father Kelly is very bright, but that's part of the problem. His sermons tend to be intellectual exercises. If I didn't know better, I'd think he was a Jesuit. In any event, sometimes I drift during his homilies. That's when I mull over the readings."

"Our parents never took us to church," Beth said. "At least, not very often. Christmas and Easter, sometimes. We'd go to whichever church had the best choir."

"That probably wasn't St. Mildred's," I replied dryly. "We've never attracted very good singers, and only recently have we had an organist who can play well."

Our waitress, Becky Erdahl, came to take our orders. Beth requested a gin and tonic; I asked for a margarita. Scandinavian restaurant or not, it was summer, and a margarita sounded cool.

"I'm so sorry about your brother," Becky said in a low voice. "He was here for dinner just last week."

Beth looked surprised. "He was? I didn't think Tim and Tiff ate out that often."

Becky is the daughter of Ione Erdahl, who owns the local children's store and had been the unfortunate victim of Alfred Cobb's crash landing in her lap at the library. "Tiff wasn't with Tim," Becky said. "He came with his father-in-law."

Beth looked puzzled. "With Wayne Eriks?"

"Yes, Tiff's dad." Becky suddenly seemed uncomfortable. "I'd better get your drink orders in. The bar is beginning to get busy." She hurried away.

I waited for Beth to say something, but she was studying the specials on the menu. "Were Tim and Wayne close?" I finally asked in what I hoped was a casual voice.

Beth put the menu aside. "No," she said frankly. "They never bonded, not even after all the years that Tim and Tiff were together. I suppose it was because Wayne was old-fashioned and didn't believe in couples living together without a marriage license." She laughed scornfully. "I couldn't wait to get married—and after six months, I wished I had. I was too young, so was my ex. We'd have been better off living together to find out we couldn't really stand each other."

"So you find it odd that Tim and Wayne had dinner together?"

"Oh . . ." Beth's gaze roamed around the dining room's beamed ceiling. "I guess not. Maybe Wayne decided it was time to give Tim some fatherly advice about raising kids."

Her face seemed to shut down. I decided to change the subject. "How is your mother?" I inquired.

"Pitiful," Beth answered. "She used to be so spunky. She's tiny, you know, but she had to be tough to stand up to Dad. He could give her a bad time when he'd had a few too many." She shook her head. "That's the flip side of putting pottery bowls on your head, I guess."

"That's true," I agreed. "Drinking isn't funny when people overdo it."

"The Irish, you know," she said with an ironic expression.

"It's a cliché, of course." Tom Cavanaugh hadn't been a big drinker. "Tim wasn't a big boozer, was he?"

Beth frowned. By coincidence, our own cocktails arrived. Beth waited to answer until Becky was out of earshot. "He drank more than he should have. Being in the bartending business causes that, I think." She tapped her glass. "I keep to one drink, just enough to take off the edge."

I raised my glass. "To Tim."

"Tim," Beth echoed, a hint of tears in the single syllable. We tapped glasses. "He wasn't an alcoholic. Don't get me wrong. Maybe I overreact because our dad went on the occasional bender."

"Sometimes alcoholism is hereditary," I remarked. "That is," I added hastily, "I'm not saying your father was . . ."

Beth waved a hand. "I know what you mean. But Dad only drank on paydays. Unfortunately."

"How's Tiffany? She seemed to be making it through the funeral."

"Oh, yes." Beth sighed. "Maybe it hasn't hit her yet. That's just as well."

"She's very wrapped up in the baby," I noted.

Beth sipped her drink. "Isn't she, though? I've never had children, so I don't know how you're supposed to act."

"Everyone is different." I'd not only been sick as a dog, but frantic. If Ben hadn't insisted I join him down on the Mississippi Delta, I don't know what I would have done. Except, of course, that I'd have done whatever it took. I supposed that Tiffany would do the same. "I hope she hadn't bought a lot of expensive baby things."

"A few," Beth said. "She was waiting for the showers. I think she'd gotten a crib and a stroller and some newborn clothes. Luckily she stored them at her parents' house."

"That *was* lucky," I agreed. "How come?"

Beth shrugged. "I guess she didn't have room until she

put the nursery together. Tiff's not terribly organized. Of course, she has plenty of time."

"Yes." I didn't say anything for a few moments. Beth again studied the menu. Something was wrong about her, but I couldn't put my finger on it. Finally, the word came to mind: dispassionate. I was sure that she was mourning for Tim. Yet when I thought about how I'd feel if something had happened to Ben, I'd be a wreck. I certainly wouldn't be going out to dinner with a mere acquaintance the evening after his funeral. I probably wouldn't even go out with a close friend.

It occurred to me that maybe Beth didn't have friends. So many people don't. I could count but three—Vida, Milo, and my old buddy from the *Oregonian,* Mavis, who still lived in Portland. Perhaps Beth was looking for a friend. Perhaps that's why she was here, sitting across the table from me, scanning the menu, but—I decided— not actually reading it. Most would-be diners made comments: "Oh, good, fresh halibut" or "What's with this *white* salmon?" Beth said nothing.

"The sheriff's office has been undergoing some changes lately," I remarked. "That must be kind of hard."

Beth eyed me curiously. "You mean the addition of Doe Jameson?"

"Well—yes. Sometimes men—especially macho types like the deputies—aren't keen on working with a woman."

Beth gave a little shake of her head. "Dwight complains about everybody and everything. But even he hasn't criticized Doe much since she started working. I think she's fitting in quite well. She's a real no-nonsense type. If I wanted someone covering my back, I wouldn't hesitate having her do it."

"That's good to know," I said, traveling a circuitous route to my destination. "I guess it was Toni who was having some problems."

Beth smiled wryly. "Toni's used to being the office princess. The approval of men is very important to her. She doesn't like the competition. Not that Toni and Doe are at all alike. To be honest, I don't get mixed up in office politics. I stay in my little dungeon and keep away from all that. I have to keep focused."

I didn't respond. Having had to supervise interns occasionally on the *Oregonian,* I'd been forced to attend a workshop on managerial skills. One of the few I remembered regarded listening responses. Saying nothing at all was supposed to coerce the speaker into revealing more than he or she had intended.

It didn't seem to work. Beth announced she wasn't very hungry. That was hardly the revelation I'd hoped for. "I'll have the crab cakes on the starter menu and a small salad."

"I'll bet you haven't eaten much all day," I said. Indeed, neither had I, but my appetite seemed to have returned. "You need to keep up your strength."

"I munched a bit at the reception," Beth said.

"You also worked this afternoon," I pointed out. "You've had a long, exhausting day."

"I'll be fine." Beth looked up as Becky approached again.

"Another round? Or would you like to order?" she asked. A pert blonde a few pounds overweight, Becky was typical of Alpine's younger waitresses, who all seemed to be fair-haired and of Scandinavian descent. I'd often wondered if those qualities were a job requirement at the local eateries.

"We can order," I said. "I'll have the smoked salmon platter and a Caesar salad on the side."

Beth made her request. Becky nodded, but instead of walking away, she leaned closer to Beth. "I meant to tell you, my mother feels bad about that call she made to you a week or so ago."

Beth looked puzzled. "What call?"

Becky blushed. "Maybe she didn't give her name. Maybe I shouldn't have mentioned it. Never mind." Uttering an embarrassed giggle, she hurried off.

"Ione Erdahl called 911?" I said.

Beth looked stony-faced. "I don't remember."

Ione lived on Fifth Street, between Fir and Spruce, just around the corner from Edna Mae Dalrymple. And a stone's throw from the Rafferty property in the cul-de-sac. I was convinced that Beth definitely remembered the call.

"I thought you had a memory like Vida's," I said lightly. "Milo told me once that you had just about everybody's address in Alpine memorized."

Beth didn't look at me. She removed the napkin from her lap and put it on the table. "I'm not feeling well. I'm sorry, Emma. I've got to go." She fumbled for her purse and began pushing back her chair.

"Beth!" I spoke sharply, but softly, aware that we were being watched by several of the other customers. "Let me help you."

Beth shook her head. "No. No, I don't need help." She scrambled to her feet and all but ran from the restaurant.

I swore under my breath. I could chase her, but that would cause a scene. Becky was at a nearby table, waiting on two of Vida's sisters-in-law, Mary Lou Blatt and Nell Blatt. Both women had married Vida's brothers and had been on poor terms with her for years. I didn't want to draw any further attention and create a gossip fest that inevitably would involve Vida. I waited until Becky had left their table.

Luckily, Becky saw me wave. "I'm afraid Beth suddenly became ill," I explained. "The strain, you know. Can you cancel her order and make mine to go?" Having been dumped by Rolf and now by Beth, I didn't feel like eating alone at a table for two.

Becky clenched her fists. "I knew it! I shouldn't have said anything about Mom calling 911! But I feel so bad about Tim, and Mom has been having a fit ever since he died!"

"Why is that?" I asked, keeping my voice low.

Becky struggled for composure. The couple at the next table—thankfully unknown to me—were discreetly gazing at us. "I can't say. Honest." Her plump features contorted with distress. "Ask Mom. God, she's going to be so mad at me!" She smoothed the skirt of her apron with its blue and white Norwegian snowflake pattern. "In fact, please don't say anything to her. It'll only make it worse."

"Wait, Becky," I said. "I don't understand."

But she shook her head. "It doesn't matter. Honest. Let me cancel Beth's order and get yours to go. Excuse me." She moved away almost as quickly as Beth had done.

Annoyed, I finished my drink and waited. Not patiently. Mary Lou and Nell had noticed me and were staring. I waved. They waved back. They must have noticed Beth's departure. Neither of them was as curious as Vida, but they were equally opinionated and strong-minded, which was why my House & Home editor had never gotten along with her sisters-in-law.

They had turned back to each other. I knew they were talking about me—and Beth. Not to mention Tim and Tiffany and her parents and the Parkers and whoever else was connected to the tragedy. No doubt everybody in the restaurant—except the out-of-towners—were also chattering about the homicide. I could sense the speculation clinging to the air, along with the Edvard Grieg sonata for cello and piano that played in the background.

I decided not to wait for Becky to deliver my meal and the bill. Beth's bill, too, I realized, though I'd only have to pay for her cocktail. As soon as I reached the desk, Becky appeared, carrying a takeout box featuring a Viking ship motif.

"I can't tell you how bad I feel about upsetting Beth," Becky said in a low voice. "I ruined dinner for both of you. Never mind the bill. It's on the house."

"Nonsense," I declared, opening my handbag and taking out two twenty-dollar bills. "I insist," I said, pressing them into Becky's hand. "You can't blame yourself for Beth's behavior."

Reluctantly, she took the money. "Gee, Emma, that's really nice of you. That's more than enough. Don't you want change?"

I shook my head. The only change I wanted was to see some progress in finding out who killed Tim Rafferty. Still, I'd seen a big change come over Beth, and I wondered how it might help find a solution to her brother's murder.

Even though Becky had asked me not to talk to her mother, I hadn't promised any such thing. Journalists can't make promises when they're on the trail of a hot story. I ventured out of the house at five to ten Saturday morning, heading for kIds cOrNEr. Its quirky lettering, etched on oversize children's blocks, highlighted the owner's first name, Ione.

I parked in front of Francine's Fine Apparel, next door to kIds cOrNEr. Luckily, Ione had just opened the store and had no other customers. I wasn't going to bother with subterfuge.

"I'm out of line," I declared. "But I have to ask you a question."

Ione, who is as dark as her daughter is fair, frowned at me. "What kind of question?"

"You called 911 last week. Why?"

Ione seemed prepared. I guessed that Becky had confessed her indiscreet remark to Beth Rafferty. "I could say it's none of your business, Emma."

"Yes, you could," I replied. "You're not a fanciful person, Ione. If you called 911, it should be a matter of public record. Your call was never logged. Scott Chamoud checks the police log every workday. There was nothing listed for your neighborhood. I want to know why not."

Ione's sharp features didn't soften one jot. "I've never been a troublemaker. I'm not going to start now."

"Would you rather get Beth into trouble because she didn't make an official entry in the log and didn't respond in any way?"

Ione uttered a four-letter word she wouldn't have dreamed of using in front of her clientele. "You're blackmailing me," she accused.

"No," I asserted. "I'm doing investigative reporting. Oh, I know that some people call 911 for really stupid reasons or because they imagine something. But that's not your style. I'm guessing your call was about Tim and Tiffany. That's why Beth didn't log it. Milo thought she'd simply forgotten."

Ione's eyes widened. "Dodge knows?"

"He knows she skipped a beat," I said. I'd let Ione figure out what else he knew—or in this case, didn't know.

"Okay, okay," Ione barked. "So I overreacted." She paused, the faint lines in her high forehead deepening. "You never knew my husband," she said in a more matter-of-fact tone. "Kris was a logger who lost a leg in the woods. He blamed me. Can you beat that?" She made a disparaging gesture with her hand. "He was verbally abusive, day in, day out. Finally, he blew his brains out with a twenty-gauge shotgun. The girls weren't home, thank God. They were staying at their grandmother's. I was the one who found him. I threw up, but I never shed a tear. Becky and Dani and I were better off without the bastard."

"That's horrible," I remarked, wondering why Ione was telling me this sad story.

"While I was married to Kris, nobody talked about verbal abuse," she continued. "I guess back then it was called constructive criticism." Ione made a face. "Or if a woman did it, she was just a nag. But it gets to you. It erodes your self-confidence. You get so damned unsure of yourself that you start making mistakes, dropping things, stumbling over your own feet. For six years, I was a nervous wreck. So were our daughters, though Kris wasn't as hard on Dani and Becky as he was on me. In fact, he ignored them most of the time, probably because they were girls. They were two and four when Kris killed himself, and hardly remember him, which is just as well. I'd like to forget him, too."

I was wondering—not too patiently—where all this Erdahl family history was going. Before I could say anything, Ginny Erlandson entered the shop with her two boys in tow. She greeted me with a surprised expression. "Don't tell me you're buying toys," she said with a smile. "Or clothes?"

I hesitated for only a moment. "As a matter of fact, I am. I'm going to send some things to Adam for the young members of his flock in Alaska."

"That's really nice of you," Ginny said, keeping one eye on her sons, who were pawing the merchandise. "Our plastic pool sprung a leak." She looked at Ione. "Do you have any left?"

"Two," Ione replied, her sales smile in place. "Neither is the same as the one you bought, but I've marked these down since summer—hopefully—is coming to an end. They're at the back of the store. The turtle is the best deal, although you'll have to put it on top of your car to take it home. It's fairly big."

Ginny gathered up her children and headed down the main aisle. Ione was still wearing her customer-friendly expression. "What are you interested in, Emma? I don't have much for cold weather right now."

I had to think. Like most men, my son was vague when it came to ages—let alone sizes—of children. "Pants," I said. "Two in each size for boys and girls. And tops—same thing, as long as they aren't sleeveless."

"They're all on sale, too," Ione said, leading me to the round racks that held the appropriate items. "Or don't you read our ad in the *Advocate*?"

"That's Leo's job," I replied. "You know I'm not used to shopping for kids."

We were out of earshot from Ginny and her boys, though they were both making enough noise to drown out a symphony orchestra.

"Are you going to tell me why you called 911," I said in a low voice, "or do I have to give you a rubber check?"

Ione turned grim. "Are you buying toys, too?"

"Yes." What did I know about toys? How was I going to pay for all this? First, she accuses me of blackmail; now she wants a bribe. "Of course I want toys."

Ione nodded once. "I walk our dog, Charley, every night." She was speaking quietly, glancing over her shoulder to make sure that Ginny wasn't coming closer. "Over the years, he got in the habit of doing his business in the cul-de-sac. He won't go anywhere else, even after the Raffertys built their house. I take a baggie, of course. The last couple of months, I could hear Tim and Tiffany fighting, yelling, screaming. It reminded me of my own marriage. That can escalate, you know. Last week, it was really bad. I stayed awake all night fussing about it, so the next day I called 911 before the situation got out of hand.

Beth answered. I told her what was going on. She was really upset, but I don't think she did anything official about it. Now that Tim's dead, I don't know if I did the right thing. Maybe I made the situation worse somehow. If Beth confronted Tim and Tiffany—"

Ione shut up. Ginny and the boys were hauling a large pool shaped like a turtle down the aisle. "We'll take it," she said. "I've got some rope in the car. If you help me, I'll tie it on top."

"I'll help," I volunteered.

Ginny gave me a grateful look. "Thanks, Emma. You're a good boss."

She paid for her purchase and ordered the boys to get out of a fire engine made for two. Ione held the door open for us. Lugging the pool down Front Street, we turned the corner. Ginny had parked halfway up the hill. I was out of breath by the time we got to the car. The boys were whooping and hollering, triumphant over their new acquisition.

It was a struggle, but we managed to get the blasted thing secured. In truth, it wasn't heavy—just very awkward. Ginny thanked me again before settling the boys into the car and driving away. Slowly.

I went back to kIds cOrNEr. "Well?" Ione said, arms folded across her chest. "I picked out the clothes for you. What about the toys?"

"You choose," I said, already perspiring in the morning heat. "Try to keep it under a hundred, okay?" I gave her my credit card number and Adam's address.

"I'll select items for all ages," Ione said, running my card through her machine. "I'll call you later with the total."

"Fine. Thanks." I sounded beat.

"The winter clothes should start coming in by the end of the month," she said, returning my card. "You aren't going to put anything in the paper about what I said, are you?"

"I doubt it," I said. I'd make no promises to her, either. Like mother, like daughter.

"I hope not. I feel like a meddler. But," she added, "I think it's terrible the way Tiffany treated Tim."

I did a double take. "You mean . . . ?"

Ione nodded. "It was Tiffany who was doing most of the yelling. I'd say that woman is a first-class abuser."

Chapter Fourteen

I DIDN'T KNOW what to do or what to think about Ione's account of the Rafferty relationship. I wanted to talk to Beth, but I'd already flunked that course. I hadn't done much better with Tiffany. Cookie Eriks would never admit that her daughter had a problem. If anything, Cookie seemed intimidated by Tiffany. I'd taken the older woman's coddling as concern for her pregnant offspring. But maybe there was another reason for Cookie's humble servitude.

Wayne Eriks might be more forthcoming. He'd had dinner with Tim just a few days before the tragedy. I wanted to know why. It was Saturday, however. Wayne probably would be home with Cookie and Tiffany.

I'd been cruising Front Street, trying to think. KSKY played on the car radio, C&W classics, which was Spencer Fleetwood's standard Saturday-morning fare. As Willie Nelson's "Always on My Mind" ended, Rey Fernandez began the eleven o'clock news. I wondered if I was on Rolf's mind over in Spokane. He'd been on mine—at least, at the back of it. I still couldn't believe I'd forgotten to call him.

Nothing of interest caught my attention in Rey's newscast. At least we hadn't been scooped on a breaking story. I was about to turn onto Alpine Way and head home when Rey delivered the weather forecast: a high of eighty-nine, a low of sixty-four, with gathering clouds and the possibility of thunder and lightning in the Cascades. No rain, though. That wasn't good news.

But the forecast gave me an idea. I turned right instead of left on Alpine Way and headed for the newspaper office via Railroad Avenue. Parking behind the building, I went in through the quiet back shop to reach my cubbyhole.

Unlike Vida, I don't have most Alpiners' phone numbers filed in my head. The phone book had only two listings for the last name of Eriks—Wayne and his cousin, Mel, who worked for Blue Sky Dairy. Cookie answered. I inquired about how the family was doing, especially Tiffany.

"She's resting," Cookie replied. "Jake and Betsy have given her a few days off to recover. With pay. Isn't that nice?"

"Very," I said, though knowing Betsy, she had to grit her teeth to do it. Betsy runs a tight financial ship for her husband's grocery store. "Is Wayne there? I've got an electrical problem at the office."

Wordlessly, Cookie turned the phone over to her husband. "Yeah?" he said by way of greeting.

Since Cookie hadn't bothered to identify Wayne's caller, I told him who I was and asked if he ever moonlighted.

"Sometimes," he said.

"If I call an electrician on a Saturday, I'll have to pay double or triple time," I explained. "I'll make it worth your while, of course."

"What's the problem?"

That was the tricky part. "We've got a satellite dish on the tin roof at the *Advocate*. We're supposed to get thunder and lightning tonight, and I'm afraid something might happen." I didn't want to mention that lightning might cause a fire and burn the place down. Under the circumstances, that seemed tactless. Besides, I had no idea what I was talking about. "Could you check it out and make sure everything is grounded?" Whatever that meant.

"Call the cable guy," Wayne said. "That's his job."

"You know he won't come until Monday or Tuesday," I said, sounding dismal.

"What about Kip MacDuff? Isn't he your jack-of-all-trades?"

"I can't reach him," I lied.

"Do you know how hot it's going to be on that damned roof under the noonday sun?"

"Well . . . yes. I could go up with you and hold a parasol over your head."

To my surprise, Wayne chuckled. "I'd like to see that. Okay, I'll come by and take a look. See you in a few."

My thank-yous were effusive. As soon as I hung up, I rushed outside, got in the car, and drove six blocks down Front Street to the 7-Eleven. Eight minutes later I was back in the office with a six-pack of Henry Weinhard's Private Reserve. Maybe a couple of beers would loosen Wayne's tongue.

Wayne arrived ten minutes later. "I got a ladder on the truck," he said. "This part of the building's so low I could practically jump it."

"It was an add-on," I replied. "Marius Vandeventer had it built thirty years ago."

"Old Marius." Wayne grinned. "Is he still kicking?"

"Yes," I said. "He's alive and well in Arizona. Vida hears from him every now and then. I get a Christmas card. But he was a real help when I bought the paper from him."

Wayne went outside. I followed him. He was right about the overhead sun. It was hot, too damned hot for Alpine or any other place north of the equator, as far as I was concerned.

"Looks fine to me," Wayne called. "Why don't you

put a different roof on this thing? Nobody uses tin anymore."

"They use aluminum or some kind of metal on some of the new buildings in Seattle," I quibbled. "Although I think most of them are ugly."

He descended the ladder, folded it up, and started for his truck, which he'd parked by my Honda. "I can't charge you for a look-see." With ease, he put the ladder in the back of the vehicle, where other tools of his trade were stored.

"At least you can have a beer," I said. "I've got some Henry's, cold."

"That sounds good to me," Wayne said with his gap-toothed smile.

We went back to the newsroom. I'd stashed the beer in the small fridge next to the coffeemaker. "Paper cup or the bottle?" I asked, taking out two beers. Ordinarily, I don't drink beer, although I make an exception during hot weather.

"Bottle's fine," Wayne said, giving me a quizzical look. "How come you got so worried about that satellite dish? Hasn't it been up there for years? We get thunder and lightning all the time."

"But not this much prolonged hot, dry weather," I replied. "And," I went on, tactless or not, "I'm terrified of fires."

Wayne shuddered. "Who isn't?"

Having broached the subject, I plunged ahead. "It was probably what happened to Tim and the house that got me so upset. Of course, I know that fire wasn't started because of the weather. I just wish Milo would find out who did it."

"Don't we all," Wayne murmured.

"This should have been the happiest time of Tim and Tiffany's lives," I remarked, leaning against a file cabinet. "For everyone in the family. I imagine the baby brought you all closer."

After taking a big drink of beer, Wayne shrugged. "That's down the line. When the kid gets here, I mean."

"True," I admitted, "but you and your son-in-law must have been forging a special bond. Fatherhood. It's such a responsibility."

"Sure is." Wayne gulped more beer. "It's got its ups and downs."

I supposed Wayne was thinking of the son he and Cookie had lost in the rafting accident. Ringo. The family had had more than its share of tragedy. I said as much. "You must be very strong. I'm sure Tim could have benefited from your advice."

"I *am* strong," Wayne declared after swallowing more beer. "In lots of ways." He moved a couple of steps closer. "Want to feel my abs?"

"No." I made an effort to smile. "I believe you. How's Cookie?"

If I thought mentioning his wife would deter Wayne, I was wrong. He set the beer bottle down on the coffeemaker table and put both hands on my shoulders. His paunch was almost touching me; I could smell sweat—and beer.

"I could use more of a payoff than a couple of brewskis. How about it, Emma? You didn't ask me here to check your stupid dish. You're the only dish I'm interested in."

He'd certainly caught me off guard. Maybe I'd gotten used to being some sort of authority figure in Alpine. Or maybe it was that in middle age, I'd grown unaccustomed to a man coming on so strong so soon. "Hey!" I barked, yanking at the long sleeves of his shirt. "Knock it off!"

Wayne pulled me closer. His face was hovering over mine. "Come on, sweetie. You're damned cute. You got a good body, too." He began running his hands up and down my sides.

I turned away, burying my face against my shoulder. "Stop. I mean it." My voice was steadier than I'd expected. "Do you want Dodge arresting you for attempted rape?"

His hands froze on my hips. Apparently he'd forgotten my intimate connection with the sheriff.

"Shit." Wayne removed his hands and backed off. "You're a prick-tease, Emma Lord. Go to hell."

He grabbed his beer and stalked out of the newsroom.

I gasped for breath. My investigative skills were not only failing, but they were buying trouble. Going into the back shop, I looked through the peephole to see if Wayne was gone. I couldn't see his pickup from that angle, but a moment later, I heard the engine rev and the sound of the truck pulling away. The vehicle sounded as angry as its owner.

Maybe I should call the sheriff, although it wasn't because of what Wayne had done. It was what he hadn't said that bothered me most.

Milo was home, going through his tackle box. "I can't fish in this weather," he grumbled. "It's too damned hot. Even the trout won't come out of the water when the sun's beating down on the lakes and the streams."

I managed—just barely—not to mention Wayne Eriks's unwelcome attentions. But I did suggest that he talk to Wayne about his relationship with Tim. As I spoke, I realized that my voice was strained. I was more shaken by Wayne's move on me than I realized.

"Just because they ate dinner together?" Milo responded, apparently not noticing that I wasn't quite myself.

"Think about it," I urged. "They weren't close. So why would they go off to dinner together at the ski lodge unless there was an important reason? Why didn't

Tim and Wayne talk at the Venison Inn or have a few beers at Mugs Ahoy? Instead, they chose a place where there was both privacy and no interfering hassles."

"How the hell do I know?" Milo retorted. "You're doing that speculating thing again. That doesn't work in law enforcement."

If I wasn't going to rat out Wayne Eriks, I certainly wouldn't betray Beth Rafferty. "Trust me," I said in my most earnest voice. "Something strange was going on between Tim and Tiffany. How does her alibi hold up for the time of Tim's death?"

"Christ." The sheriff sounded as if he'd like to take a twenty-pound test line and strangle me with it. "She says she went to the employee break room about that time and ate her dinner."

"Witnesses?"

"Buzzy O'Toole saw her leave the check stand and come back an hour later," Milo said in a beleaguered tone. "He was filling in as the night manager."

Jake's brother wasn't the most reliable man in town. His own business ventures had failed. Buzzy was able to cope as the Grocery Basket's produce manager only because Jake and Betsy watched him like a pair of hawks. "Tiffany ate alone?"

"Yeah. They only have three checkers at night and one of them spends most of the time restocking or facing out the shelves or whatever they call it. They close at one in the morning and reopen at six. Don't you read your own ads?"

If one more idiot asked me that question, I was going to explode. "I know their hours," I snapped. "They wouldn't stay open that long if Safeway hadn't forced them into it. Stick to the issue at hand. I'm serious."

"What you're telling me," Milo said in a condescending tone, "is that you think Tiffany killed Tim and set their house on fire, right?"

The sheriff had backed me into a corner. That brought out the contrariness in my nature. "Yes, I'm saying that's possible."

"You don't really believe that."

"I believe stranger things have happened," I declared, growing more contrary by the moment. "Tiffany doesn't act like a bereaved widow. She's still going to have a baby, she gets the insurance money for the house, she's being spoiled to pieces by her mother, and all of the nursery items she's bought were kept at the Erikses' house. Maybe Tim was just a sperm donor, and after that, he'd outlived his usefulness."

"Whoa." Milo sounded taken aback. "What'd Tiffany ever do to you? You really have it in for her."

"No, I don't," I asserted. "I'm hearing things—in confidence. Good journalists never betray their sources. Won't you take my word for it?"

"You've got some bug up your ass," Milo said, but his tone was thoughtful. "Are you okay? You sound like you're sick."

"It's the heat," I said, which was partly true. "I get depressed when we don't get rain."

"Who doesn't?" Milo responded. "I mean, if you're a real native."

"Our roots need watering, just like the trees. Will you really talk to Wayne?"

"Oh—sure, why not? He lives just down the street. I'll drop by this afternoon."

"Good." I smiled in an evil manner, wishing I could see Wayne's face when the sheriff dropped by. A little intimidation—real or imaginary—might make the creep talk.

I was driving the car around from the back of the newspaper office when I spotted Vida coming out of the hobby shop across Fourth. She was carrying a huge box.

"Vida!" I called. "What's that?"

She could barely see over the box. "Meet me at home. I'm parked right there." She nodded at her Buick Regal, which was pulled in at the curb a few yards away on Front Street.

Why not? I drove straight to her house. Vida arrived a couple of minutes later, empty-handed.

"I left the Destroyer in the car," she explained. "It's an incentive present for Roger."

"What kind of incentive?" I asked as we headed for her front door.

"To study hard fall quarter," she replied. "And to reward him, too, for his efforts in trying to find Old Nick. My, but it's warm." She brushed at the damp gray curls under her green straw hat's brim.

"Dare I ask what kind of Destroyer you bought him?"

Vida opened the front door. "It's put out by Lego— over three thousand pieces. Rather pricey. It has something to do with *Star Wars*. He's very fond of the films."

She left the front door open. The house felt stuffy despite the big fan that she'd left turned on in the living room. "I didn't know Roger liked *Star Wars*," I remarked.

"Oh, very much," Vida replied, removing the sun hat. "I believe that's how he first got interested in becoming an actor. Not that I've seen the movies, but I understand they've been very popular. Let's sit for a minute before we go."

"Go? Where are we going?"

"To visit Delia Rafferty," Vida said, collapsing into an easy chair. "Actually, you don't have to go if you don't want to. I wouldn't blame you. It's rather depressing at the nursing home. So many addled old people. Of course, most of them were addled long before they went into the home, but it still makes conversation very difficult."

Coming from Vida, that translated as not being able

to get satisfactory gossip. "Why are you going to see her? Didn't you speak to her at the funeral reception?"

"Yes, but I came away perturbed," Vida said. "I felt there was something odd about Delia. I can't explain it, but as if she wanted to talk to me."

"She mentioned your hat," I noted, omitting the part about Delia also referring to Vida's size.

"Yes, yes," Vida said impatiently. "It was how she looked at me. Searching, perhaps. Or beseeching—that's a better word. It's bothered me ever since. By the way," she continued with an inquisitive stare, "did you ever hear back from Rolf?"

"No," I said. "I told you he had to go to Spokane." I hadn't yet sat down, and now I felt as if I should keep on my feet, perhaps to elude Vida's perceptive eyes.

Vida sighed. "I'm still not sure about him."

"You hardly know Rolf," I challenged.

"I know enough to know I'm not sure." She shrugged. "You never mentioned your weekend once after he made the original call. I think you forgot. Perhaps on purpose. You don't want to get in too deep. That's wise, of course."

I should have known Vida would see through me. "It's not quite like that," I argued. "I got so caught up in the Rafferty case that everything went out of my head."

"Then Rolf wasn't lodged there very solidly in the first place. I'm the last person to give such advice, I suppose, but I do think you should occasionally consider how closely wedded you are to your career. I've been fortunate in that Buck has his own interests and keeps busy when I'm not available. But at our age, that's different. I'm not urging you to become besotted. On the other hand, you need some time for yourself as a woman. You have no family close by. You have very few friends. I think you're lonely, Emma. You don't think about it because you make sure your brain is otherwise occupied. That's too bad." Vida stood up. "Come, we must go."

I had been standing a few feet away from her, ostensibly to take in the benefit of the fan's cooling breeze. But her presence in the easy chair had reminded me of a teacher lecturing a dull-witted student. Maybe that's what I was.

"You're my friend," I asserted. I couldn't think of anything else to say. I was quite dumbfounded.

"Of course." She put the straw hat back on her head. "I wouldn't speak so frankly if I weren't."

I lingered in the living room as Vida collected her purse and got out her car keys. "I'm not sure I want to go with you," I said. "Nursing homes are so bleak."

Vida peered at me through her big glasses. "They're also air-conditioned."

"Oh." I decided to join her.

The Lutherans had done their best to make the facility homelike. Three years ago, they had bought the small block across Seventh to build a nursing and hospice addition. The fact that the other side of the block was on the service road in back of the cemetery had struck some people as morbid and others as practical.

Delia Rafferty lived on the first floor, officially called the assisted-living residence. The top three stories were individual apartments, added over the years as the retirement population grew. According to Vida, they were very nice units, complete with kitchenettes. She had said at one point that she might consider moving there someday—if the facility were run by Presbyterians.

The lobby resembled a pleasant boutique hotel, with fresh flowers on the main desk. Vida approached a fair-haired middle-aged woman and asked to see Delia.

"You're a Peterson," Vida said. "Which one?"

"Margaret," the woman replied with a stiff smile. "My sister-in-law, Constance, is a nurse at the hospital."

"Of course." Vida nodded sagely. "How is Delia today?"

Margaret tipped her head to one side. "Well . . . you know how it is. She's in her room, watching TV. She's not one to mix with the other guests."

"She was never particularly social," Vida noted. "Which room?"

"One-thirty-four," Margaret replied.

Vida nodded. I trotted along, feeling, as I often did, that I was her stooge. Margaret had scarcely looked at me. I could have been a terrorist with a suicide bomb attached to my head.

The hotel atmosphere was quickly dispelled as we walked down the corridor. Instead of stargazer lilies, the air smelled of disinfectant. Several old people sat in wheelchairs, some of them asleep, a few moaning pitifully, and a couple of the others eyed us as if we'd come to rob the place.

Delia Rafferty's room was small and crowded. Apparently Beth—and possibly Tim—had wanted their mother to keep many of her own possessions and trinkets. The TV was turned on to a cable news program, but there was no sound. Delia stared at the screen as if hypnotized.

Vida was undaunted. She tromped over to the wheelchair where Delia was sitting and put a firm hand on her shoulder. "Delia," she said, "it's Vida. See my hat?"

Delia's gaze slowly moved from the TV screen to Vida's looming presence, and she spoke quite firmly. "Vida. Big woman. Big hat."

"That's right," Vida replied. "Emma is here, too." She motioned for me to come forward. "Emma is a friend of Beth's."

Neither my name nor Beth's seemed to register. But Delia did stare at me curiously. I hadn't seen the woman up close in years. She was much younger than I'd realized—perhaps no older than Vida. Delia's skin was virtually unlined, though her short-cropped hair was almost white. She had big blue eyes and probably had been a pretty young woman. The bone structure was good—though her body was petite. I couldn't guess accurately because she was seated and slightly hunch-backed. I figured she probably wasn't much over five feet tall. Her late husband, Liam, had been a six-footer with red hair going gray.

"Eggs," Delia said.

"Eggs?" Vida was wearing her Cheshire cat smile. "What eggs, Delia?"

"Brown eggs. For omelets." Delia was looking down at the afghan that covered her lap. Apparently, her circulation was poor. Even with the air-conditioning, the room's temperature felt like eighty degrees.

"You raised chickens during the war, didn't you?" Vida inquired, sitting down on a straight-back chair while I remained standing by a curio cabinet filled with ceramic figures.

"My parents did," Delia responded. "We had a victory garden."

"So did we," Vida replied. "Many people did, even in the city."

"Tim died in the war," Delia said.

"Did he now?"

Delia nodded. "In Italy. Or was it Idaho?"

"I don't know," Vida said. "What happened?"

Delia's lips trembled. "He was burned up."

"Gruesome," Vida remarked with a sharp glance at me. "So sad."

Delia didn't respond.

"Would you like to talk about Tim?" Vida coaxed.

Delia shook her head.

"What about Tiffany?" I asked, venturing to include myself.

Delia shook her head again.

Vida wasn't giving up. "How is Beth?"

Delia was still staring down at the afghan. "Beth didn't break the eggs."

"That's good to know," Vida said. "Beth's a nice girl. Who did break them?"

Delia's blue eyes gazed around the room. There were several photographs, showing Tim and Tiffany's wedding, Beth and Tim's high school graduations, Delia and Liam in middle age, and various babies.

"It's cold in here," Delia finally said. "Tell the boy to turn up the heat."

Vida moved about in the chair, obviously pondering her next move. "You're going to be a grandmother," she said at last. "I've had grandchildren for years. They're such a joy. Are you excited about your grandbaby?"

Delia's gaze shifted to the baby pictures. "That's my baby. That other one, too."

"Yes," Vida agreed, though her patience was becoming strained. "I mean the baby that's on the way."

Delia didn't respond.

Vida sighed and stood up. "We must go now, Delia. Thank you for having us."

To my amazement, Delia struggled to her feet and put out the hand that wasn't clinging to the afghan. She shook Vida's hand, then reached for mine. "Thank you both." Her grip was surprisingly strong. She looked back at Vida. "I want your hat. I can put eggs in a hat."

Vida seemed uncharacteristically flummoxed. "Oooh . . . here." She removed the hat and carefully set it on Delia's white hair. "There. It looks very nice."

"Thank you. Goodbye." Awkwardly, Delia sat back down in the wheelchair.

We left, Vida shaking her head all the way down the hall. "Hopeless," she declared as we reached the lobby. "Is it Alzheimer's or dementia? Goodness, the woman's not as old as I am!"

"That surprised me," I admitted as Vida waved farewell to Margaret Peterson, who was talking on the phone at the main desk. "I remember her as always being elderly."

"She's two years younger than I am," Vida said as we stepped out into the midday sun. "She has osteoporosis and her hair started turning gray when she was in her early thirties. Living with Liam did that, no doubt. He was poor husband material. Oh, good grief! My head feels like it's on fire without my hat!"

"That was very generous," I declared. "I've never seen you part with a hat before."

"I almost never have," Vida replied as we got into her Buick. The Lutheran home was only a block and a half from her house, but we didn't want to walk in the heat. "That straw hat was very cheap. I have four others just like it, three dollars apiece at a street fair I attended in Bellingham with my daughter Meg."

"What's with the eggs?" I inquired while Vida turned the car's air-conditioning on full blast.

"Delia's family did have chickens during World War Two," Vida explained. "That part made sense. For all I know, there was some relative named Tim who was killed in combat. Or in Idaho. Perhaps Delia named her son for him. Whatever I thought she wanted to tell me apparently was a figment of my imagination. We wasted our time, and I lost my hat. Oh, well."

"Maybe Delia liked having company," I said.

"I doubt that she remembers we were even there," Vida retorted.

"But she'll remember your hat."

Vida sniffed. "Indeed. A pity there's no longer a brain operating under it."

I didn't know why, but I wondered if—for once—Vida could be wrong.

Chapter Fifteen

I KNEW VIDA'S criticism of Delia Rafferty was born of frustration, not a lack of kindness. Knowing how keenly she felt about unraveling the mystery that was Tim and Tiffany, I couldn't blame her. After I left Vida's house, I drove to Icicle Creek. I wanted to find out if Milo had spoken with Wayne Eriks.

The Grand Cherokee was in the driveway, but the house was closed up. Maybe Milo was at the Erikses' home, grilling the man I'd suddenly decided was my favorite suspect. I went to the door and rang the bell anyway. I'd rung it a second time when Milo appeared.

"I was in the basement," he said. "What's up?"

I asked if he'd seen Wayne.

"He wasn't home," Milo replied as I stepped inside. "At least, that's what Cookie told me, although his truck was parked outside. Come on downstairs. It's cooler there."

The basement was also tidier than the living room. Upstairs, empty pizza and TV dinner boxes usually littered the sofa, chairs, and carpet. I hadn't seen the surface of the dining room table in years, and I avoided the kitchen at all costs. It was as if once his ex-wife had walked out, he'd never bothered to keep house. Yet in the basement, he kept his fishing and hunting gear in perfect order. Even his tool area was organized, includ-

ing a large plastic file container that held back issues of
his favorite outdoor articles.

"Do you think Cookie was lying?" I asked as Milo
rolled an office chair in my direction.

"Probably." The sheriff leaned against his worktable.
"So maybe you're right. Something's going on with
Wayne." His hazel eyes narrowed. "I wish I knew what
the hell was going on in your head about this Eriks and
Rafferty bunch. You don't know them that well. What's
the deal?"

I wanted to level with Milo. But I couldn't. At least,
not about Beth. She could lose her job for not logging a
911 call. I decided, however, to tell him about Wayne.

Milo laughed. "The SOB made a pass at you? Jeez,
Emma, weren't you kind of flattered?"

"Are you out of your mind?" I all but shouted. "He's
married, he's just lost his son-in-law, he's *gross*!"

Milo was still laughing, though he apologized. "Sorry.
But haven't I told you it's risky to go around sleuthing
on your own? Hell," he continued, growing serious,
"you've almost gotten yourself killed a couple of times.
Maybe you should keep your investigating to the telephone."

"I usually do just fine," I declared, shooting Milo a
few daggers from narrowed eyes.

He shrugged. "You're okay for an amateur. Want a
beer? Or did you get your fill with Wayne?"

His words provoked a small smile. "I guess it *is* kind
of funny," I said. "Wayne, I mean. A little groping might
be considered an improvement over the phone calls and
letters I get calling me everything from a moron to a
whore."

"At least the jerk knew when to stop," Milo remarked. "We get some of them who don't. The word *no*
isn't in their dictionary."

"But you will talk to him again?"

The sheriff nodded. "Especially if he's avoiding me. Maybe he thought you'd carried out your threat to rat on him. Who knows? I can always start by asking him a few more questions about his sighting of Old Nick. Did his description mesh with yours?"

"Yes—but it was getting dark when I saw Old Nick. Neither Wayne nor I could describe features or details. 'Ragged old guy with a beard' is vague. Do you think he's still around town?"

Milo considered the question in his usual deliberate manner. "Hard to say. It's not typical. They come to get what they need, they take off. They don't like civilization. They don't like people. And in this hot weather, they're bound to be cooler in the forest."

"Good point," I said. "So why is Old Nick wearing a bunch of ragged clothes in ninety-degree heat?"

"Who knows? He's like the Arabs, thinking that clothes keep out the heat." Milo turned to the near wall where his fishing poles were lined up on racks. He took one down and fondled it like a baby. "See this? I treated myself. Top of the line, for salmon and steelhead. I got it through a catalog from the NRA. Graphite, cork handle, terrific action in this spinning rod."

"Nice. Now if you could only catch some fish . . ."

Or a killer.

The day was slipping out of my hands. Everywhere I turned, everybody I spoke with, every lead I tried to follow eluded me as craftily as a ten-pound steelhead would defy Milo's expertise—and expensive new fishing rod.

I felt glum. My weekend was ruined, my investigative reporting skills were a shambles, and I'd probably wrecked the best chance for romance that I'd had in years. How could I make it up to Rolf? Did he want me to try? Did he really care? I felt like writing myself a "Dear Moron" letter.

If Milo could treat himself, so could I. Although I'd started to head for home from his house, I took a detour off the Icicle Creek Road and went back to Front Street. Parking was no problem. It was too hot to shop, except at the air-conditioned Alpine Mall. I had no problem finding a space right in front of Donna Wickstrom's art gallery.

Donna was talking to a young couple I didn't recognize. They were admiring one of the spectacular vases by the glassmaker from Colorado.

"If she has to have it," the young man said to Donna, "then let's do it. Her birthday's next Thursday."

The young woman leaned over and kissed the young man. "I love you, Derek."

"You'd better," he said with a smile. "Are you sure which one you want?"

She grimaced. "That's the problem. I can't make up my mind between the two of them. One is perfect for the entry hall; the other would look wonderful in the guest bathroom." She paused. "We do have a wedding anniversary coming up in September."

"Oh, why not?" The husband hugged the wife, but spoke over her shoulder to Donna. "Can you ship it? We're off to British Columbia for a few days to visit friends in Osoyoos."

I had drifted over to *Sky Autumn*. The painting was every bit as glorious as I'd remembered. I stared at it the entire time that it took for the young couple to give Donna their billing and shipping information. Five minutes later, they walked out of the store, arm in arm.

"Mercer Island people," Donna noted, referring to the Seattle suburb in the middle of Lake Washington. "Aren't they all rich?"

"Not all," I replied. "But quite a few of them are. It's

prime property, if you don't mind having to take the floating bridge to get there."

"Anton will be really pleased," Donna said. "I know he'll send me a couple of other pieces. Vases, I hope, though he does some beautiful bowls and pitchers."

"Thank God for tourists," I murmured. "It's too bad we don't have more rich people in Alpine. Tell me, has Ed Bronsky—or Shirley—ever bought art from you?"

Donna held her head. "Shirley's been in several times, but she's never bought anything. She looks and looks, but always says she can't make up her mind. She wants cherubs—and I haven't got any unless I order prints from a catalog. Ed told her they'd go with the Italian décor of their so-called villa. In fact, Shirley was in last week. She says Ed is thinking of having his portrait painted. She wanted me to recommend an artist. I stalled her. I can't think of anyone who would want Ed sitting for them."

"Sitting or squatting?"

Donna laughed. "You choose." Suddenly, she shifted into her gallery-owner mode. "Are you still tempted by the Laurentis?"

"I'm hooked," I admitted. "I want it. Can I pay for it on the installment plan? Five hundred dollars is a bit of a stretch for my overextended credit cards."

"Well . . ." Donna looked pained. "Craig doesn't like credit sales of any kind. He wants cash—certified checks, I should say."

I frowned. "I understand about creative types," I said. "Unless they have a day job, they get paid very irregularly. Not to mention the matter of taxes. I assume some artists don't declare sales on their IRS returns."

"I wouldn't know," Donna said, looking innocent. "Craig Laurentis is the only artist I've dealt with who insists on cash. I mail it to a PO box in Monroe."

"How about this?" I ventured. "I write you a check

for two-fifty now and the rest next month? Would you be willing to hold the painting for me until then?"

Donna nodded slowly. "Yes, I could do that. I'll wrap it and put it in the back. I should point out that in my opinion—and I'm really not an expert—Craig's works are undervalued. I've tried to get him to raise his prices, but he refuses. He thinks art belongs to the world."

"That's very idealistic," I said. "Does he have another job?"

"No." Donna shrugged. "He doesn't seem interested in money or material things. I don't believe he's ever married."

"He sounds like someone with a busted vocation," I remarked. "Maybe he should have gone into the clergy. Is he Catholic?"

"I've no idea," Donna replied. "What do you mean?"

"My brother, Ben, has a theory that many Catholics in today's secular world ignore their religious calling," I explained. "They often end up making bad marriages or not marrying at all. Sometimes they live a very ascetic life, even if they don't always attend church. He also thinks that happens with Protestants. That is, some of them may become ministers and marry and have families, but others ignore the call. Am I making sense?"

"I guess," Donna replied, though she looked puzzled. "Really, I wouldn't know about Craig's beliefs. He never talks about anything but art, and none of it has a religious theme."

"That depends on how you define *religious*," I said. "I think *Sky Autumn* is quite spiritual."

Donna looked at the painting. "Well . . . yes. The forces of nature, water and earth. Very . . . visceral. I can see that." Suddenly, she looked distressed. "I guess I have a love-hate relationship with Craig's art. At least with the river scenes." She stopped and turned to me. "You understand."

It took me a few seconds to realize what she meant. The murdered body of her first husband, Art Fremstad, had been found by a river. Ironically, his killer eventually had been murdered, too. "Yes, of course."

Donna looked away. "It's been thirteen years. I was lucky to find Steve. I hope Tiffany gets lucky, too."

"Yes," I said again. But I also hoped Tiffany was as blameless as Donna.

At home, an e-mail from Adam awaited me.

"I heard from Toni again," he wrote. "She said she talked to you about Alaska. She thought it all sounded too complicated. Cannery work doesn't appeal to her. She thinks it must smell bad. She'd like to do what she's doing now—some kind of office work, but not in law enforcement. She looked up the state's 2000 census and learned that the male-female split is fifty-two to forty-eight percent, but she can't figure out how many of the men are eligible. All I can say is thank God I'm not one of them. Toni's driving me nuts. Patience and compassion are great virtues, but I've got people up here with REAL problems, like survival. About now, I'm one of them . . . Love and prayers, Adam the Nonmatchmaker."

I smiled at the laptop's screen. Religious vows or not, Adam was still Adam. Like his mother, he had little patience with people who couldn't get a grip on real life. I replied to him, saying that Toni's quest was for a husband. Her vision was no wider than that, and it probably wasn't the worst goal she could have, but it was the only one that seemed to matter. Meanwhile, I added, his dim-witted mother had managed to blight her own romantic prospects with Mr. Fisher. When it comes to romance, even bright people behave stupidly. I ought to know; I'd just done it.

I tried to put personal and professional problems

aside for a few moments. Instead, I gazed at Monet's water lilies and decided that I still liked it. It would look nice in my bedroom. I tried to visualize *Sky Autumn* in its place above the sofa. Artistically, Laurentis was no Monet. Yet he had captured the river scene so vividly that my heart and soul overruled my taste and intellect. I grew curious about the artist. He must be a native. His affinity for the area's elements seemed inherent, rather than acquired.

What the hell was I talking about?

My mind had gone off on a tangent. In fact, my brain seemed scattered, rambling, disconnected. It was the weather. Unrelenting sunshine has that effect on natives from the Cascades' western slopes. The rivers dwindle, the lakes shrink, the waterfalls dry up. So do our brains. Maybe that was another reason that *Sky Autumn* beckoned me. Its churning waters ran deep and plentiful. It reminded me of what I was missing during this hot, sometimes humid summer.

That was when I realized I had to learn more about Craig Laurentis. A strange suspicion was growing in my mind.

I checked the Internet. His name came up, but the only information was about his paintings that were for sale in galleries around the Puget Sound basin: Seattle, Tacoma, Bellevue, Everett, Bellingham, and Olympia. I saw several reproductions, all of rugged mountain, lake, and forest scenes. No people, no animals, not even a seascape. He concentrated on the Cascades and the range's surroundings. The prices were from four hundred to nine hundred dollars. I found no biographical information except that Laurentis was an artist who lived in the Puget Sound area and had been painting for almost thirty years.

Donna Wickstrom didn't have a website. I guessed there were other small galleries that didn't either, but might also feature Laurentis's work. Apparently, he was fairly prolific.

I couldn't locate him anywhere else on the Internet, and a call to directory assistance proved fruitless. After an hour, I had become obsessed. I felt a pressing need to find out about Craig Laurentis. I telephoned Donna.

"I have a strange question for you," I said. "Remember, I'm a journalist, and therefore a professional snoop. What bank do you send Craig's money to?"

Donna sounded surprised. "Does it matter?"

"It matters to me for some reason I can't explain," I admitted.

"Let me double-check." She went off the line for a few moments. "It's Washington Mutual in Monroe, right on Highway 2. Do you have a line of credit there or something?"

Apparently, Donna thought I was trying to figure out a way to pay for the painting all at once.

"No," I replied. "I'm just a snoop. Thanks."

"Of course." Donna still sounded curious.

My next call was to Rick Erlandson, Donna's brother and Ginny's husband—as well as the assistant manager at the Bank of Alpine. Ginny answered on the fourth ring. She sounded out of breath.

"Are you okay?" I asked.

"Yes, I'm fine. We're out in the turtle pool. Rick finally got it put together and filled. The boys love it."

"Can Rick come to the phone?" I asked.

It was Ginny's turn to sound surprised. Naturally, she assumed I must be calling about an *Advocate*-related matter. "Well . . . yes. I'll take the phone out to him. We won't leave the boys alone in the pool even if it isn't very deep. You never know what might happen."

I could hear the raucous sound of children grow closer as Ginny moved outdoors. She called to her husband, explaining that I wanted to talk to him.

"He'll be right there," Ginny said. "He's all wet."

If Ginny had possessed a sense of humor, I would've made a lame joke. Since she didn't, I merely said that was okay and that I was sorry to interrupt their family fun.

"It's all right," she assured me. "I was coming inside soon to make lemonade."

Rick finally responded. "This pool's a godsend," he declared. "I don't know who likes it better—the boys or Ginny and me. The only problem is we all can't get in it at once."

Rick has a sense of humor—though not greatly developed. I chuckled obligingly at his comment. "I won't keep you. Do you know anyone who works at Washington Mutual's Monroe branch?"

"Gee . . . not really. I used to. The manager there was Felicia Royce until she quit to have a baby about a year ago. I don't know her replacement very well," he said, sounding apologetic. "But Felicia married one of my college roommates, Jeff Royce. He works at Bank of America. Does that help?"

I told Rick it'd help if he could give me Felicia's phone number. "I'm doing some research," I said. "It's a long story, and I'll explain it to Ginny on Monday."

"Hang on."

Rick must have set the phone down outside. I could still hear the Erlandson boys yelling and yipping, along with an occasional word of caution from their mother. At last, Rick returned and gave me the Royces' number in Monroe.

I got their answering machine, which informed me that they were unable to take the call, but would get back to me—or whoever was calling—as soon as possible. Temporarily stymied, I wondered what I could do next to occupy myself. Nothing strenuous—it was too hot for real work. Maybe I'd write an e-mail to Ben in

Milwaukee. I hadn't been in touch with my brother for over a week.

I'd just gone online when there was a knock at my open front door. I looked up from the sofa and saw Cookie Eriks, looking agitated.

"Come in," I said, setting the laptop aside and getting up. "Is something wrong?"

"No." Cookie shook her head in a frantic manner. "Not really. Could I get a glass of water?"

"Sure," I replied, starting into the kitchen. "This way. Don't tell me you're out walking in this heat."

Cookie shook her head. "My car broke down."

I filled a glass with ice. "Right here?"

She shook her head again. "About a block away, at Third on Fir. I was going to the mall."

Cookie had gone out of her way to reach the mall from her home in Icicle Creek. After filling the glass with water from the tap, I handed it to her. "I don't get it," I said frankly. "Let's go back in the living room. It's cooler there, with the fan."

Cookie flopped down into one of my easy chairs. "I couldn't help myself. I had to drive by the house. I mean, what's left of it."

"Oh." That made sense, at least in terms of Cookie's route. "Unfortunately, it's just rubble."

"Yes." Cookie's expression was dismal. "It's not smoking or anything now. It's just . . . nothing."

"Everyone feels terrible about it," I said. "How are you coping?"

"Not well." Cookie regarded me as if the question was futile. It was, of course. "Anyway, I got as far as Third and that was when the car broke down. I think the radiator overheated. May I use your phone to call Cal Vickers?"

"Sure." I picked the receiver up from the end table and gave it to Cookie. "Do you know his number?"

"Yes. It's an easy one to remember."

I went in the kitchen to get a cold Pepsi while Cookie made the call. She was disconnecting when I returned.

"They're coming with the tow truck in half an hour," she said. "I don't need to be there. I'm glad. There's no shade where I left the car."

"How's Tiffany?" I inquired.

"She's feeling better, I think." Cookie sipped her water. "She's exhausted, of course. I don't know when she'll be able to go back to work. Maybe she shouldn't."

"Dr. Sung can advise her about that," I said. "It's a fairly long time until the baby arrives."

"Well . . . yes, but . . ." Cookie's voice trailed off. "You know Sheriff Dodge quite well, don't you?"

The question seemed guileless. "Of course. We're friends as well as working colleagues."

"Does he know what he's doing?"

"You mean with the homicide investigation?"

"Yes." Cookie shifted uneasily in the chair. "He came to our house twice this afternoon, asking for Wayne. The sheriff was wearing regular clothes, but he acted as if he'd come on business. I know he lives just a few doors down from us, but it seemed . . . odd. In fact, it upset me."

"Did Milo talk to Wayne?"

"No." Cookie lowered her eyes. "Wayne wasn't there."

"Then why would you be upset?"

Cookie started to take a sip of water, but the glass slipped out of her hand. It bounced on the carpet, spilling the contents all over her sandal-clad feet. "Oh! I'm sorry! I'm so clumsy!" She bent down to retrieve the glass.

I was on my feet. "I'll get a towel," I said. "Don't worry about it. In this weather, ice water probably feels good."

"What?" Cookie picked up the glass—and dropped it again. "Oh, no! What's wrong with me?" she wailed.

I stopped halfway to the kitchen and turned back to her. "Hey—you've been through a terrible time. You're probably ready to collapse. Sit, take a deep breath. I'll take care of the water. The glass isn't broken." I gave her a gentle shove into the chair. "I'll be right back."

I collected the glass, went to the kitchen, got out a clean glass, filled it with more ice and water, and grabbed a towel off the rack by the sink. When I returned, Cookie was crying softly.

"Go ahead," I said, setting the glass down on the side table and putting a hand on her shoulder. "You're entitled."

Cookie dried her eyes with her fists and shook her head. "I'm . . . trying to be . . . brave . . . for Tiff. She . . . needs . . . me."

"Of course she does," I soothed. "But she seems to be holding up rather well."

"She's strong," Cookie replied, the tears staunched. "She's tougher than she looks."

Was there irony in Cookie's voice? Probably not, though I felt there should have been. Maybe *tough* wasn't the right word. *Selfish* could be more apt.

Cookie made no attempt to reclaim the water glass. Maybe she was afraid she'd drop it again. Instead, as I sat back down on the sofa, she leaned forward and stared at me with searching eyes. "Why do you think the sheriff wants to talk to Wayne? What could he possibly know?"

I shrugged. "Maybe Milo wanted to hear more about Old Nick. Maybe he's trying to figure out if Tim had any expensive sports memorabilia stored somewhere other than in the house. Maybe he's just double-checking alibis."

"Alibis?" Cookie's body jerked into a rigid position. "That sounds awful! As if Wayne was a suspect!"

"A poor choice of words on my part," I said in apology. "It's routine. I'm sure he's asked everyone connected to the family about where they were that night. Hasn't he asked you already?"

Cookie scarcely moved a muscle. "We were home. We watched TV until we went to bed around eleven. The phone woke us up a little after midnight with the terrible news."

She'd rehearsed that story. Maybe it was true. "That's what you told the sheriff?"

"Yes." She still didn't move, except for her thin lips. Suddenly, jerkily, she got to her feet. "I must go. Cal should be coming. I'd better ride with him to the service station."

I followed her to the front porch. Cookie didn't turn around. She kept walking at a brisk pace, turning left at the street's edge until she was out of sight.

But not out of mind. Cookie Eriks hadn't come to my log house by chance. She'd never visited me before. Obviously, she was desperate to pick my brain about the official investigation. I sensed that Cookie was scared. She had at least two reasons—Wayne and Tiffany.

Or maybe there was a third. Cookie might be scared for herself.

Chapter Sixteen

I FELL ASLEEP on the sofa a few minutes after Cookie left. To my dismay, I didn't wake up until after five o'clock. The heat had gotten to me. Ninety-degree temperatures not only rob me of my appetite, they steal my energy. I woke up cursing myself for wasting the rest of the afternoon.

Groggily, I went into the kitchen to get something to eat. Nothing appealed to me. Cooking—even heating a bowl of soup in the microwave oven—made me cringe.

The phone rang while I was staring at the refrigerator. A pert voice at the other end announced herself as Felicia Royce. "You called earlier," she said. "So did Rick Erlandson, who told me you were trying to get in touch. His sister, Donna, asked him to give me a ring. I know your name from the Alpine paper, Ms. Lord. I see it sometimes. My grandmother lived there years ago."

I apologized for bothering her and told her about the Craig Laurentis painting I'd put on hold. "I'm very interested in the artist," I continued, "but I can't find any information about him. He could be a wonderful subject for an article in the paper. It turns out that Donna Wickstrom has never met Laurentis. She sends his money to your bank. That is, the branch where you used to work. I wondered if you knew more about his background."

Felicia laughed, a cheerful trill. "Even though I don't work at the bank anymore, someday I may have to if we can't get along on one income. You know I can't reveal customer information." The mirth evaporated from her voice. "I'm really sorry."

"I understand." I paused. This was hardly the first time I'd encountered client confidentiality or a variation thereof. "How about this? Let me make some suggestions. You can say yes or no—or whatever wouldn't breach banking ethics. Okay?"

"Well . . . Go ahead, try it. I can't promise anything."

"Let's play true or false," I said. "You've never met Craig Laurentis."

The concept apparently amused Felicia. She uttered that trilling laugh again before answering. "True."

"He does all his banking online."

"True. This is sort of fun."

"Good. Let's try this one. You've never spoken to him on the phone."

She hesitated. "False."

I was surprised. "You often talked to him on the phone."

"False. Do I get a prize?"

"A free subscription to the *Advocate* for your grandmother," I replied. "But we're not finished."

"Oh." Felicia didn't sound overly disappointed. "Okay."

"You only spoke to Craig Laurentis once or twice."

"True."

"He was . . . terse."

Felicia didn't respond immediately. "I don't know how to answer that."

"He was abrupt."

"False."

I considered other options, assuming my crazy premise was correct. "He wasn't very articulate. He sounded as if he wasn't used to dealing with people, over the phone or otherwise."

"True. Yes, that's true."

"That makes sense," I responded, wincing as I noticed that the thermometer outside my kitchen door had edged over ninety-one. "Let's try one last question. His voice wasn't that of an old man, but somewhere between forty and sixty."

"Huh." Felicia was silent for a moment. "That's tricky, over the phone. But basically, I'll say true."

"Good. Your grandmother just won two free years' subscription to the *Advocate*."

"Wow! She'll love that!" Felicia sounded as excited as if I'd given away a sports car. "Let me give you her name and address. She's a Larson, spelled with an *O*."

I wrote down the information. "I really appreciate your help," I said. "I suspect that Craig Laurentis is a dedicated artist who doesn't have much of a social life. I also assume the bank has no address for him."

"True. Do I get a bonus?"

"Sorry. I already knew that. Donna told me he has a PO box in Monroe. If there's a phone number, the bank probably has it, and I'll bet it's a cell."

"They won't give it to you, I'm afraid," Felicia said. "Are you really going to write an article about Craig?"

"I hope so," I said.

I could hear a baby crying in the background. Yelling, actually. "Excuse me," Felicia said. She must have turned away from the receiver. I could barely hear her asking Jeff to get Parker out of the cupboard. Or maybe it was Barker. Parents pick some odd names for their offspring these days. "I'd love to read it," Felicia said, again speaking into the phone. "I'm sorry I made this so tricky for you."

"I respect confidentiality," I replied. "I have to regard that in my business, too. You've been a big help." The baby had stopped squalling. I took a chance. "Is Barker okay?"

"Barker? Oh!" She laughed once more. "Her name is Marker. My grandmother—the one who lived in Alpine—was a huge Shirley Temple fan. She came up with the idea from one of Shirley's movies, *Little Miss Marker.* Jeff and I loved it."

"Cute," I said, not adding that the younger generation wasn't the only peer group who came up with weird names. I thought it was too bad that Grandma hadn't liked Shirley's version of *Heidi* better.

The bank in Monroe might not give me Craig's phone number, but they'd give it to the sheriff. If I could get Milo to ask.

"You've got more weird ideas lately than any of the psychos we pick up," the sheriff declared when I called him a few minutes later. "Why the hell do you think this artist guy is Old Nick?"

It had taken me a while to give voice to my suspicions. "Because it fits. I saw him near the art gallery in the Alpine Building. Maybe he comes into town to take a peek through the windows or to be near his paintings. The kids who went looking for him found some art supplies—paints or brushes or something. He has no known address, deals only through the Internet, and apparently isn't accustomed to social situations. I figure he's some creative type who can't deal with people, only with nature. Maybe he was a hippie. I'll bet he's not more than fifty or so and went gray prematurely. He certainly ran like a reasonably young man."

"So he's this crazy artist who goes off his nut and kills Tim Rafferty because . . ." Milo was definitely irked. "Hell, because why?"

"I never said he killed Tim," I replied, trying to stay calm. Maybe I could keep composed if I stuck my head in the fridge's freezer unit. The thermometer read ninety-two. "But if he was hanging out at that vacant house, he might have seen or heard something that'd help find the killer. You should try to question him. Wasn't that your whole point all along?"

Milo hesitated. "Well . . . he could have been a witness."

"Right."

"A hermit with a cell phone?"

"Why not? He's also a businessman."

"Jesus."

"He's trying to earn a living," I contended. "Not that he's in it for the money. Donna says his prices are far under market value, considering his talent."

"Good for him." There was, however, a note of resignation in Milo's voice. "We've been looking for him, goddamn it. The guy's elusive as hell, like all those other hermits. He doesn't want to be found."

"But you could get his cell number."

"And then what? Call and say, 'Hi, Nature Boy Artist, this is the sheriff. How about a sit-down at my office?' Gimme a break."

"You're smarter than that," I said.

"He won't come," Milo replied doggedly, "and we won't be able to find him. Even," he added grudgingly, "if you're right."

"Then you'll have to set a trap," I said.

"Oh, there's a good idea," the sheriff said sarcastically. "Ever hear of entrapment?"

"Not like that," I argued. "Something to do with his art. Maybe we can talk Donna into doing it once you have his cell number. He's underpricing his work. She could play on his vanity, tell him that he has to come in to discuss prices with her, because money talks. She could say how he'll never be recognized as a serious or important artist unless he triples his market value."

"Think Donna could handle that?" Milo sounded skeptical.

"She's a surprisingly astute businesswoman," I replied.

"It sounds more like a job for you."

"Well—I'd do it if I had to," I allowed. "But he knows Donna—in an Internet kind of way. He must trust her."

"That'd break the trust," Milo pointed out.

"Maybe not. It would depend on how it was handled."

Milo still didn't sound convinced. "Why couldn't they discuss that stuff on the phone or the Internet, like they always do?"

"Because she'd want to show him things," I said a bit vaguely. "Catalogs from other artists. Comparative prices. Comments from art buyers. Whatever. It has to be visual. Donna could do this. She knows how to handle patrons. I can vouch for that. And she certainly has a knack for dealing with other artists and craftsmen. Besides, it's in her interest. She gets a hefty commission. I'm guessing, but I think I've heard that gallery owners receive anywhere from thirty to fifty percent of the sales."

"This all sounds pretty wacky to me," Milo said glumly. "I'll bet you fifty bucks that even if you can pull this off, it won't help solve the homicide."

"You're on," I said, although I didn't blame the sheriff for being dubious. "You make the call to the bank. I'll take care of Donna."

"I still think it's dumb."

I didn't argue. But as I hung up the phone, I smiled.

Donna was about to close up shop when I arrived at exactly six o'clock.

"You decided you had to have the Laurentis now?" she asked with a smile of surprise.

I offered her a regretful expression. "I'm sorry to keep disappointing you, but unless I win the lottery, it'll have to wait until next month. Actually, I'm doing some weekend work. I want to write an article about Craig Laurentis. I checked him out on the Internet, and it's obvious that many of his paintings have been done in Skykomish County."

"I believe that's true," Donna said, though her smile had been replaced by a slight frown. "I have to say that I doubt he'd be open to publicity. He's an intensely private person."

"I realize that," I said. "I understand creative types. Many reveal themselves only in their art or writing or whatever it is that they create. But from what I can tell— and from what you told me—Craig is undervaluing his work to the point that he's practically giving it away. That discredits his talent. It almost equates him with people who sell their paintings at shopping malls."

"Please! You're talking about one step beyond paint-by-numbers," Donna declared fervently. "Craig's very close to being a genius when it comes to his genre."

"I know," I agreed. "That's why it's so unfair to him. Not to mention," I added, "that it also cheats gallery owners."

A spark glittered in Donna's eyes. I had the feeling she'd give up her day care business in a wink if she could improve art sales profits. For all I knew, some of her other artists were also lowballing their work.

"It's true," she admitted. "I could sell a Laurentis like *Sky Autumn* for two thousand dollars. Still, I doubt that he'd talk to you."

"But he'd probably agree to meet with you," I pointed out.

Donna remained doubtful. "I think he'd insist on using the Internet. Besides, I don't have a phone number for him."

"That can be arranged," I said cryptically. "Anyway, I wouldn't have to conduct a face-to-face interview." Like hell, I wouldn't. But Donna didn't need to know that yet. "I could give you some questions, and you could describe him as a person. The story has to have some personal touches."

"Well . . . I can see that." Donna's eyes roamed around the gallery. Maybe she was trying to calculate how much she could bump up the prices on her other artwork. "When should I call Craig?"

"I'll have the number Monday," I replied. Milo might need reminding. In any event, he wouldn't try to get hold of the bank manager in Monroe until after the weekend. "Thanks, Donna. I really appreciate your help. And I hope it benefits you, too."

Donna, however, still looked uncertain.

The old song claims that Saturday night is the loneliest night of the week. Certainly this Saturday in August was just that for me. I spent the evening watching the Mariners, and even though they won, my spirits didn't lift much. Maybe I should have asked Milo to join me. But the truth was that I was afraid I might seek consolation in his arms, which wouldn't have been fair to either of us—or to Rolf.

At least Father Kelly showed Christian mercy by keeping his homily short Sunday morning. St. Mildred's is a small wooden church with poor ventilation. Indeed, it had been built when winters were colder and longer. The architectural premise—I assumed there had been one—was to keep the heat inside the church and the fresh air out where it belonged. I suspected everyone was perspiring. Certainly Ed Bronsky looked like a greased pig. I felt like one.

But there was no escaping Ed and Shirley and their brood after Mass. The entire clan confronted me at the bottom of the church steps.

"I need help," Ed declared, wiping his brow with a soiled napkin from McDonald's. "This bond issue deal for the Mr. Pig theme park is darned complicated. Can you write some kind of think piece on the editorial page about it?"

That meant the thinking would all have to be done by me. "Ed," I replied, trying to remain calm if not cool, "that's not something I know much about, either. You need to talk to a lawyer." I pointed toward Marisa Foxx, who was heading toward her dark green Saab in the parking lot. "Marisa can steer you in the right direction. She's the parish attorney, after all."

Ed shuddered. "You know what attorneys charge. Hundreds of dollars an hour just to sit and think about stuff. Gosh, Emma, you've had to research bond issues and referendums and all that legal gibberish for your election editorials. You must know quite a bit."

Flattery—if that's what it was—would get Ed nowhere, especially on an overly warm August morning. I shook my head. *Can't. Won't. Would prefer going to guillotine than help Ed with his stupid bond issue.*

"This is something so special for the two of you," I said, glancing at Shirley. "For the whole family, in fact. Now that your kids are older, they should join in with the project. After all, some day the Mr. Pig theme park will be part of their heritage."

Shirley nudged Ed. "Emma's right, honey. You're building something for the ages."

Ed scratched a mosquito bite on his bald spot. "When you put it like that . . ." He turned to his children, who were looking as if they wanted to be someplace else. "Joey," he said to his teenage son, "you're a computer whiz. See what you can find out on the Internet." His gaze shifted to Molly, who was attending Skykomish Community College. "Aren't you signed up for political science this fall?"

"Economics, Dad," Molly replied.

Ed shrugged. "Same thing. Sort of. Anyway, somebody at the college must teach political science. Talk to whoever it is."

Even Ed could sense the lack of enthusiasm on all five of his children's plump faces. "Hey, hey, you guys— don't worry. I'll do my share. I'll take a meeting with the mayor. Fuzzy must know how to work this."

"Don't forget the county commissioners," Shirley put in.

Ed looked as if he'd like to, but nodded. "I already talked to them. You know what happened at the last meeting. They don't get it. Progress stopped for them around 1975."

Ed had a point there. "Once you put everything to- gether for them," I said, edging away from the group, "the county commissioners will probably approve the idea. Besides, you have such a gift for selling things." How could I lie so blatantly after I'd just been to church? Ed had been a terrible salesman, frequently con- vincing merchants that nobody read newspaper ads, ex- cept maybe for the grocery specials.

"You're darned tootin'," Ed responded, moving his fists as if he were in a sparring match. "I can do that."

"Great," I said with what I hoped passed for a genu- ine smile. "I'd better get out of this sun. It's making me cross-eyed."

I headed not for home, but to the Bourgettes' diner. I'd slept just late enough that I'd had no time to make breakfast, and the idea of turning on the stove—or even the toaster—hadn't appealed to me in my muggy kitchen.

The diner wasn't air-conditioned, but ceiling fans that actually worked were part of its 1950s décor. The restau- rant was reasonably cool. But it was also crowded, ap- parently with the rest of the churchgoing residents. I could tell that they were mostly Protestants because they were wearing their Sunday best, unlike Catholics, who seem to dress as if Saint Vincent de Paul himself had handed out their wardrobes.

Terri Bourgette, who served as hostess for her brothers' enterprise, greeted me with a frazzled smile. "I'm sorry, Emma," she said, "but there's a twenty-five-minute wait, even for the counter. Everybody seems to want to eat breakfast out this Sunday."

"That's okay," I said. "I'll wait. It's cool in here."

I joined the dozen or more patrons who were crammed into the area by the door. The oldsters had managed to find seats on a couple of red vinyl couches. I nodded at some Gustavsons; said hello to my dentist, Dr. Starr, who was with his wife, Carrie; and smiled at a couple of faculty members I recognized from the college. I was trying to find a spare bit of wall so that I could lean when I spotted Beth Rafferty standing at Terri's podium. Beth and Terri were speaking in a serious manner. I couldn't help but watch them. And then I stared. Beth and Terri were both looking at me.

Terri came from around the podium. "Emma?" she called, beckoning with a finger.

I advanced toward Terri, smiling at Beth en route. "What is it?"

Terri lowered her voice. "Beth invited Tiffany to breakfast but she hasn't shown up. Beth's been waiting for half an hour. I couldn't seat her until Tiffany got here. There's a booth for two free now. Would you like to join Beth? She says it'd be okay with her."

"I'd love to," I said, giving Terri and Beth big smiles.

They both thanked me. Terri led us to the section that was decorated with photos of Dean Martin and Jerry Lewis in their comic duo heyday. I was suddenly so hungry that I wouldn't have cared if there'd been pictures of Ivan the Terrible and Attila the Hun.

"I appreciate this," I said after Beth and I were seated.

"I have no appetite unless the temperature is under seventy-five degrees. Those big fans really help."

Beth glanced up at the ceiling. "Yes," she said in a vague voice. "They move the air around."

An awkward pause ensued. Beth seemed as ill at ease at breakfast in the diner as she'd been at dinner in the ski lodge. Once again, she appeared to be studying the menu, but didn't really appear to focus.

"Is Tiffany feeling ill?" I finally asked.

"I've no idea," Beth replied, putting the menu back behind the chrome napkin holder. "I tried to call her at the Erikses' house, but nobody answered. We made the date for ten-thirty. It's twenty after eleven now. I thought about driving over to her parents' house, but I was afraid we'd cross paths and lose our place in line for a table." Beth made a face. "That's typical. Tiff really isn't reliable."

"Or considerate," I noted, and promptly apologized. "Sorry. I realize she's going through a horrible time."

Beth's expression was skeptical. "Is she? Tiff never has been somebody who thinks much about other people. I've been pretty inconsiderate myself, walking out on you at dinner the other night. The least I can do is treat you to breakfast."

"No need," I asserted.

Our waitress was not one of the typical blondes who worked as servers in the Alpine restaurant business, but a rail-thin brunette, possibly another Bourgette. I ordered pancakes, ham, and eggs, my standard fare when I ate breakfast out. Beth took some time to think over her decision, but didn't refer back to the menu.

"I'll have the mushroom omelet," she finally said. "No hash browns, white toast, and just two eggs, please. There's no point in breaking more than you have to. I couldn't eat it all."

The waitress, who had identified herself as Clare, assured Beth that would be no trouble and that she wouldn't charge her for the three-egg omelet on the menu. After filling our heavy white mugs with coffee, Clare hurried away.

"My plan," Beth said, "was to go from here with Tiff to visit my mother. I suppose it's silly, but I thought if Mom saw Tiff pregnant, she might understand that there's a baby on the way. I don't think Mom realizes that, especially since Tiff's only beginning to show now."

"It can't hurt," I allowed.

Another uncomfortable silence arose. "Beth," I said, leaning forward, "how well did Tim and Tiffany really get along? I have to be frank; I've heard some rumors."

Poor Beth, I thought. She looked so tired. Her usually flawless skin was reddened from the sun, and the dark circles under her eyes made a stark contrast. She seemed to have aged overnight.

"I think," she said slowly, "that Tiff was hard to get along with after she got pregnant. She should've been happy, but I guess all those hormonal changes can alter a woman's personality. These last few months were hard on Tim." Beth turned away, staring at one of the Martin and Lewis photos. Judging from her miserable expression, she found nothing funny in their staged antics.

"Tim always seemed to be the one in charge," I remarked.

"Yes." Beth turned back to me. "He was very protective. My brother was basically a good guy. He had his faults, but there was never a mean streak in him. That was lucky, in a way. I mean . . ." She made an unhappy face. "Our dad drank. I think I told you that. It wasn't all the time, usually paydays, but when he'd come home, he'd be ornery. More than ornery. He—"

Beth stopped as Clare delivered our orders. "Violent?" I said after Clare had left us.

"Yes." Beth sighed heavily. "He'd beat Mom, and

sometimes go after Tim and me. That's when Mom would step in. She's tougher than you might think. Or at least she was back then. The next day Dad would be full of remorse, swearing he'd never do it again. He'd even cry. But it was a cycle he couldn't seem to break. The worst of it was, neither Mom or Dad would consider counseling. They were too embarrassed." Beth hadn't even looked at her food and seemed on the verge of tears. "Oh, Emma, why am I telling you all this?"

"Because you've probably kept it all bottled up inside, simmering until you must be ready to boil over," I said, looking sympathetic despite slathering butter on my pancakes and putting salt and pepper on my egg. "Besides, you know I can keep a confidence. It's part of my job."

She sighed again, but this time the sound was more like relief. "Yes. That's true. Anyway, Tim wasn't like some children who grow up with an abusive parent and believe that's how a relationship should be. Or whatever they think. And of course I never let my own anger get out of control, even when I was married and things fell apart."

"You learned that violence doesn't solve problems," I said. "It only creates more. Unfortunately, some victims don't understand that. They think it's acceptable behavior because that's the way they were brought up."

"I know," Beth replied. "How many 911 calls do I get in a week involving domestic violence? Maybe a half-dozen, even in a town like Alpine." She grimaced and shook her head.

Even as I stuffed my face with ham and pancakes I wondered if Beth was thinking about the call from Ione Erdahl that had never been logged. I was trying to figure out how to tactfully approach the subject when my cell phone rang.

"Damn," I said softly. "I hate it when people answer phones in restaurants. I think I'll let it ring."

But I couldn't. It might be Adam, wrestling with a bear. Or Ben, in a car accident in Milwaukee.

It was the sheriff. "Emma?" he all but shouted, since the reception inside the diner was poor. "That you?"

"Yes." I tried to keep my voice down. "What is it?"

"I'm giving you a heads-up," he said over the buzz and hum of the phone. "We just arrested Wayne Eriks for Tim's homicide."

Chapter Seventeen

BETH, WHO WAS nibbling on a piece of toast, stared at me. I must have looked shocked. I certainly felt that way. For her benefit—and to make sure I'd heard Milo correctly—I repeated what he'd told me.

"You arrested Wayne for killing Tim?"

Beth dropped the toast and collapsed.

"Gotta go," Milo shouted.

"Wait! Send an ambulance to the diner!"

"What?"

"Beth just passed out."

"You need—" The connection was lost.

The Starrs, who had just been seated in the *I Love Lucy* booth across the aisle, were already at Beth's side. Clare came up behind them, followed by Terri Bourgette. Beth was lying at an awkward angle, half on the vinyl seat, half under the table.

"What happened?" Terri demanded, looking apprehensive.

"I think she fainted," I said.

Dr. Starr was bending over Beth, trying to see if she was conscious.

"Pour water on her," Carrie Starr said.

"No!" cried Deputy Mayor Richie Magruder, who had suddenly appeared in the aisle. "Pinch her!"

"You're crazy, Richie," said his wife, Stella. "Put her head between her knees."

"I think she's coming around," Dr. Starr murmured.

"Should I call 911?" Terri asked, her hands trembling.

"I think I already did," I said, sounding stupid. "I mean . . ."

Terri, however, was now engaged in trying to keep some of the other customers away from the area. "It's fine, it's nothing serious. Please, go back to your places. Everything's under control."

Dr. Starr had Beth sitting up. Her eyelids were fluttering and her lips were moving, although she made no sound. Clare offered a glass of water, but Beth shook her head.

"I'm . . . okay," she murmured. "I don't think I even blacked out."

The gawkers were reluctantly returning to their seats. Terri stood guard in the middle of the aisle. She had stopped shaking and seemed in control of herself as well as the situation. I still felt stunned, but pulled myself together. My appetite had fled, however. I glanced at my half-eaten breakfast with a tinge of regret. Beth hadn't eaten anything except a bite or two of toast. The two eggs had been broken in a lost cause. Poor Beth didn't seem able to share a meal with me.

The ambulance siren announced its approach. Beth heard it and went rigid. "Is that for me?" she asked with a stricken expression.

I nodded. "Let the medics tend to you. Frankly, you're a nervous wreck. You may be suffering from exhaustion— not to mention this damned heat."

Beth looked as if she wanted to argue, but maybe she lacked the strength. She merely pressed her lips together and hung her head.

"I'll get out of the way," I said, scooting across the seat. "I'll check in with you later, okay?"

Beth nodded once. The familiar medics were already

headed toward our booth. I turned tail and took the longer route out of the dining area. Terri met me at the front.

"What made Beth collapse?" she asked. "It couldn't have been anything she ate."

"No. It's nerves," I said. "Here." I handed her my overworked Visa card. "Run it through, I'll sign it, and you can figure out the total later. Add a tip for Clare. She looked sort of pale, too."

"Forget the bill," Terri said. "Besides, I have to go back to the kitchen and bring my brothers up to speed. They can't leave the food cooking. The poor guys must wonder what's going on."

I didn't argue. I was in too much of a hurry to get to the sheriff's office. Before I started the car, I called Vida to tell her what had happened. But Vida wasn't home. Maybe she'd stayed for the fellowship hour at the Presbyterian church. It was a good place to pick up gossip.

I spotted Milo's Grand Cherokee in front of the sheriff's office, but saw no sign of Spencer Fleetwood's BMW. Maybe my archrival hadn't been contacted. Not that it mattered—Spence would still beat me with the story. Whoever was manning the radio station would pick up the arrest on the police scanner.

The only person in the reception area was Dustin Fong. Whoever else had been called for extra Sunday duty must be in the back, either in the interrogation room or the waiting area for friends and relatives of suspects and witnesses.

"Sheriff Dodge said he called you," Dustin said, polite and calm as ever. "He thought you'd want to know."

"Of course." I smiled, always amazed that even after several years as a deputy, Dustin never seemed to grow callous or indifferent. "What happened?"

He also remained discreet. "I'd better let Dodge tell

you," he said. "He and Bill Blatt made the actual arrest about an hour ago."

"Is Cookie with Wayne? What about Tiffany?"

"Cookie's here," Dustin replied, looking troubled. "She's pretty distraught. Tiffany's still at the Erikses' house."

"That's just as well." But I didn't like the idea of her being alone. "Do you know if she's okay?"

Dustin's expression changed only slightly. "I believe Mrs. Runkel is with her."

"Vida?" I cried. Before Dustin could respond, I waved a hand. "Of course. Bill, her nephew, was one of the arresting officers." I had no idea how Vida had found that out, but didn't doubt for a moment that she'd gotten the news before I did.

I leaned on the mahogany counter. "How soon before I can talk to Milo?"

Dustin shook his head. "I've no idea. Eriks claims he's innocent."

"I suppose he would," I said thoughtfully. "I'm trying to figure out the motive."

"Who knows?" Dustin looked as skeptical as I'd ever seen him. "One thing I've learned in law enforcement is that people can be unpredictable. Sometimes they just go off their heads for no reason, especially when drugs or alcohol are involved."

"Yes." I, too, had encountered murderers who didn't fit the popular profile of jealous lovers, blackmail victims, or just plain crooks. Some were people I'd known for years, with reputations above reproach. But they'd snapped. And neither substance abuse nor addictions had influenced their homicidal actions.

"Does Toni Andreas know?" I asked.

Dustin looked surprised. "No. I mean, I doubt it. There was no reason to call her in on a Sunday. Besides, she hasn't been feeling very good lately." He frowned slightly. "Why do you ask?"

I hedged. "She seemed very upset about Tim's death. I thought she might want to know that an arrest had been made."

Dustin looked beyond me to the entrance. "She'll know soon enough," he murmured. "Hello, Mr. Fleetwood."

Spencer Fleetwood had brought along some of his remote equipment. He flashed me a big smile—of triumph, I assumed—and nodded at Dustin. "Rey Fernandez just heard the news on the police scanner. It only seems fitting that we should break the story, since Tim worked for KSKY."

That was true enough. "Didn't you threaten to fire him at one point?" I said in a sarcastic tone.

Spence chuckled. "Station owners always threaten to fire their people. Sometimes they actually do it. But even if Tim did screw up a while back, he made the mistake newsworthy. We got more listener response to his apology than to any other program—except for Vida's, of course."

I recalled the incident only too well. Tim had gotten himself involved in a murder investigation and although he was innocent, he'd managed to tamper with evidence—and lie about it. It had been cowardly, but he'd never been charged with a crime. He'd been scared, and insisted he was protecting Tiffany's sensibilities.

"You're right," I said softly. "Tim was never what you'd call heroic."

Spence shot me a quizzical look, but said nothing. He started to set up his equipment, a process Dustin seemed to find fascinating. I remained leaning against the counter, my stomach growling again, and wishing I'd brought the rest of my breakfast with me.

"You don't seem to need much except a microphone and headphones," Dustin remarked to Spence.

"Technology," Spence replied. "This is radio, not TV. Rey's at the other end in the studio." He pinned the tiny mike to his safari shirt. "Rey? I'm all set. Five, four, three . . ."

Dustin and I looked at each other.

"This is Spencer Fleetwood, broadcasting live with breaking news over KSKY-AM, the voice of Skykomish County," Spence began, his usually mellow voice charged with just the right amount of urgency. "We're here at the sheriff's headquarters in Alpine, where a suspect has been arrested in the homicide death of Tim Rafferty. Wayne Eriks of Alpine was taken into custody this morning by Sheriff Milo Dodge and Deputy Bill Blatt. Eriks, fifty-four, and a longtime employee of SkyCo PUD, is the victim's father-in-law."

Spence always sounded so damned professional. He could have worked for any number of major-market radio stations, even television, since he was also good-looking in a somewhat hawklike manner. But for reasons of his own, he preferred Alpine. He also liked being his own boss. I understood that part very well.

Spence was motioning to Dustin. "We're here live and direct with Deputy Dustin Fong. What can you tell us about this startling development in the Rafferty case, Deputy Fong?"

Although he had leaned across the counter to face Spence, Dustin looked startled. "I'm afraid," he said carefully, "that I can't say much at this point. Sheriff Dodge is interrogating the suspect right now."

"Has Eriks made a statement?" Spence inquired.

"Not a formal statement, no, sir."

"In other words," Spence went on, "Eriks hasn't confessed to the crime?"

"No, sir. He insists he's innocent."

"Has he contacted an attorney or asked for legal counsel?"

"I don't know."

Spence knew the drill as well as I did, but that didn't stop him from asking questions. "Can you tell us where Eriks was arrested this morning?"

"I believe Mr. Eriks was at home."

"When will the sheriff release any information about the evidence that led to the arrest?"

"I don't know." Dustin was looking very serious, as if he could imagine SkyCo residents leaning into their radios to catch every word, every nuance. "Usually, evidence isn't revealed until the trial or at least a formal hearing."

"Thank you, Deputy." Spence flashed Dustin a big smile. "We're staying right here at the sheriff's office, awaiting further developments. Stay tuned for our next update. Meanwhile, here's a word from one of our friendly Alpine merchants, Barton's Bootery."

Spence clicked off the mike. "Thanks again," he said to Dustin. "I understand the constraints of your job. Of course, I have to do mine, too."

"I know." Dustin looked relieved.

Spence turned to me. "I see you got here first."

The implication was obvious. I didn't say a word.

"Vida?" he asked.

I just stood there, looking innocent.

At that moment, Milo loped into the outer office. He was wearing his civilian clothes—tan pants and a blue summer shirt. "The media," he muttered. "Both of it." He shot a dark look at Spence. "Don't even think about turning on that mike. It's not already on, is it?"

Spence held up his hands in a guiltless gesture. "I've already finished my preliminary broadcast, Sheriff. I was waiting for you."

"Hunh." Milo glanced at Dustin.

"I couldn't tell Mr. Fleetwood anything but what we already announced over the scanner," Dustin said.

"Good." Milo went over to the coffeemaker next to the door of his private office. "Shit, didn't anybody make coffee?"

"Sorry," Dustin apologized. "I didn't think of it."

I couldn't resist. The sheriff's coffee was too vile for me to keep my mouth shut. "Just pump out some sewer bilge and throw in a little dirt. You won't know the difference."

Milo scowled at me before turning back to Dustin. "Go over to the Burger Barn and get us some coffee, okay?"

Dustin moved quickly. Maybe he was glad to get out of the line of fire.

"Well?" I said after the deputy was gone. "Can you tell us anything?"

"Hell, no." Milo pulled out a pack of cigarettes, his usual Marlboro Lights. Spence followed suit, with his exotic gold-filtered black brand. "We won't be able to say anything until the arraignment tomorrow," the sheriff said after his first puff.

"Is Eriks still protesting his innocence?" Spence asked.

"Right." Milo looked cynical. "They often do, you know. Sometimes the bastards even believe it."

"But you don't?" Spence persisted.

"No comment."

The main door opened. I expected to see Dustin returning with coffee, but it was Doc Dewey instead. He greeted Spence and me before speaking to Milo. "Sorry, Sheriff," Doc apologized, beads of sweat dampening his balding head. "Babies don't wait, and Dr. Sung had an emergency surgery this morning."

"It's not an emergency," Milo said, "but the county

doesn't want to be liable. Come on, let's go back so you can tend to the patient."

Without so much as a backward glance for Spence and me, Milo led the way out of the reception area.

Spence looked as puzzled as I felt. "What did they do, beat up on Eriks?" he asked.

"Not likely," I said. "You know Milo and his merry men well enough to realize they don't strong-arm anybody. Maybe it's not Wayne. Cookie might have collapsed."

"Cookie?" Spence frowned. "Eriks's wife is here?"

I nodded. "She came with him. Maybe Wayne put up a fuss. Maybe he had some kind of accident." I gazed at the empty corridor that led to the interrogation and holding areas as well as the jail cells. "Damn. This is more frustrating than I expected. Stalling, yes. Doc Dewey showing up, no. It'd make more sense if Tiffany was here, but she's at home."

Briefly, Spence looked blank. "Oh." He fingered his beaklike nose. "That's right, she's pregnant." He was quiet for a moment. "Car chase? Wayne, eluding arrest and hitting one of his own PUD poles?"

"That would have been on the scanner."

"True." Spence studied the area around the reception desk. "Let's check the log. It's public property."

The log showed only three items for Sunday so far. The first had occurred at 2:17 A.M.; the second at 3:40 A.M. Both were traffic violations—one for speeding, the other for running an arterial stop sign on Alpine Way. The third and last entry, written in Dustin's perfect penmanship, was the arrest of Wayne Eriks on suspicion of homicide and arson.

"I wondered if they'd charged him with the fire," Spence said. "I can mention that in my next bulletin."

"But nothing logged about resisting arrest," I noted.

Dustin returned with a half-dozen cups of coffee in a cardboard container. "Anybody?" he inquired.

Spence declined, but I accepted, adding a packet of raw sugar to my cup. The deputy headed toward the interrogation room.

Spence watched Dustin disappear down the corridor. "How can we lure Mrs. Eriks out here?"

"Yell 'fire'?" I said facetiously.

Spence's expression was ironic. "You newspaper types really are callous."

Neither of us spoke for a minute or two. I stirred my coffee and sipped slowly. When Dustin returned, Spence leaned on the counter. "Is there any way we could talk to Cookie Eriks?" he asked the deputy.

Dustin considered the request. "I don't think that's appropriate, sir."

Dustin was probably right. But that didn't mean it was impossible to see Cookie. "Is Doe here?" I asked.

Dustin shook his head. "She had the night shift. Sheriff Dodge didn't think it'd be right to ask her to pull extra weekend duty."

"You mean," I said, looking as severe as I could manage, given my liking for Dustin, "that poor Cookie is all alone while her husband's being interrogated? Or is there another deputy with her?"

"Emma . . ." Spence began in a warning voice.

But I kept talking. "Cookie's not charged with anything. She's got a pregnant daughter at home, she already lost a son years ago, her husband's been accused of killing her son-in-law. If nobody else is available, I'm going to sit with her. We'll go into the women's restroom where it's private."

I heard Spence swear under his breath. I'd trumped him. Dustin uttered only the most feeble of protests as I circumvented him and headed down the corridor.

I found Cookie Eriks sitting in the small room reserved for inmates' visitors. She had her head down and appeared to be asleep, but jumped when I came through the door.

"Oh! Emma! What's happening?"

"I don't know as much as you do," I said, sitting down on the hard wooden chair next to her. "Can I get you something?"

Cookie shook her head. "Dustin Fong brought some coffee a few minutes ago, but I didn't want it."

I gazed around the stark room. Prisoners were seldom kept very long in the local jail. There were only a half-dozen cells, and the usual occupants were drunks or drug addicts who needed time to sober up. More serious criminals were shipped off to Everett or the correctional facility in Monroe. Thus, the visiting room was rarely used. Under close surveillance, visitors were allowed to talk face-to-face with the inmates. The room contained six chairs, a table, a magazine rack attached to the wall, and—just to make sure everybody knew where they were—a map of Skykomish County covered in heavy plastic wrap. There were no windows, only one-way glass on the outer corridor. The room smelled stale and felt oppressively stuffy. The women's room had to be an improvement.

I made the suggestion to go there, but Cookie rejected the idea. "I'm not budging until I find out what's going on with Wayne."

"I understand," I said, searching for tactful words. "So why do you think Dodge arrested him?"

Cookie twisted her fingers together. The plain gold wedding band looked dull under the fluorescent ceiling lights. "I'm not sure. Dodge showed up this morning. He'd been at the house yesterday, but . . . Wayne wasn't home." She paused, not looking me in the eye. "I tried to tell him—the sheriff—that Wayne was in the shower and that Tiffany was still asleep. Dodge insisted on coming in. Well, he *is* a neighbor, and I didn't know what to do. Anyway, before I could let Wayne know the sheriff was in the house, he—Wayne—oh, dear, I'm so rattled!" She stopped and shoved a lank strand of hair off her forehead. "Wayne came upstairs from the bathroom in his underwear. That's when Dodge saw the burns on his—Wayne's—arms."

"Burns?" I suddenly recalled that every time I'd seen Wayne in the past week he'd been wearing a long-sleeved shirt despite the hot weather. "How did he get burned?"

"On the job." Cookie's jaw jutted, though she still avoided my gaze. "Live wires. It happens sometimes."

My brain did some mental gymnastics. Cookie could be telling the truth—or merely relaying the version Wayne had given her. But if her husband had gotten those burns when he started the fire to cover the murder, he might not have wanted to seek medical help. Perhaps the blisters had festered. That would explain Doc Dewey's presence at the sheriff's office. Milo was duty-bound to make sure that any suspect requiring medical treatment got it at county expense.

"I assume," I said casually, "that Wayne had reported his on-the-job accident to the PUD."

Cookie sighed. "He gets banged up every now and then. His work's dangerous. He started out as a logger, you know. I thought he'd be much safer when he started with the PUD. But things happen. And Wayne is too macho to tell the bosses about every little scrape or bruise. He doesn't want anybody to think he's a whiner."

"Well," I said, not entirely convinced, "I certainly can't imagine why Wayne would want to harm Tim. I understand they had dinner together about a week ago."

"They did." Cookie darted a glance at me, but didn't elaborate.

"So they must have gotten along," I remarked. "There doesn't seem to be any motive. It doesn't make sense."

As I'd hoped, the provocative comment evoked a reaction. "What evidence? Dodge didn't search our house. He just called Bill Blatt and told him to come on over. The next thing I knew, Wayne was being hauled off to jail. I followed them in my car." She began to twist her fingers again. "I don't know what to do. Thank goodness Mrs. Runkel happened to come by. I hated leaving Tiffany alone." Finally, she met my gaze head-on. "Should I call a lawyer?"

"I honestly don't know, Cookie," I admitted. "Sometimes that isn't a good idea. I mean, if Wayne can get this cleared up with the sheriff, he may not need one. Milo's fair."

"He's wrong," Cookie declared. "Why are men so aggravating?"

The rhetorical question didn't quite seem to jibe. "You mean the sheriff or men in general?"

"I don't know what I mean." Cookie's jaw jutted again. "I just want to get Wayne out of here and go home."

The door opened and Bill Blatt appeared. For the first time, I noticed that his boyish face had begun to age. Or maybe the strain of the weeklong investigation had gotten to him.

He nodded at me before speaking to Cookie. "I'm afraid we're going to have to hold your husband overnight. We can't formally charge him on a Sunday because the courthouse is closed. I'm sorry. Can I do anything for you?"

"Can I see Wayne?"

Bill nodded. "Of course." He gave me an apologetic look. "You'll have to wait out front, Ms. Lord."

"Sure." I attempted to give Cookie a reassuring smile, but she'd already turned away from me.

Spence was still at the reception desk, chatting with Dustin. Mr. Radio interrupted himself when he saw me.

"That was a dirty trick," he asserted, though he didn't really seem angry.

"Girl talk," I replied. "I assume you and Dustin here have been doing the male bonding thing."

Dustin looked embarrassed, but Spence shrugged. "Deputy Fong doesn't exactly run off at the mouth." He winked at the younger man. "We were discussing international politics."

That may have been true. "Have you done another bulletin?"

"Not yet." Spence stood up and stretched. He was definitely a cool customer in more ways than one. There were no sweat stains on his shirt, despite the fact that it felt very warm in the sheriff's front office. "I thought I'd interview you, now that you've spent time with the suspect's wife."

"Don't you dare," I snapped.

"Chicken." Spence made a clucking sound.

"Okay. Why not?"

He flashed me his big smile. "You're a good sport." Spence turned on the mike while I moved closer. "Rey? What's airing?" He waited a moment. "Okay, as soon as the Pentecostal reverend winds down, break in. I'll stay on until you give me a countdown."

Spence's dark eyes danced as he waited. "You can pour it on, Emma," he said in a low voice. "Real sob-sister stuff. This is your chance to shine."

I smiled.

Spence cupped his ear. "Got it," he said to Rey, and gave me a thumbs-up sign. "This is Spencer Fleetwood," he began after a few beats. Briefly, he continued with his standard self-aggrandizing introduction. "I'm here live and direct with Emma Lord, editor and publisher of *The Alpine Advocate*. Emma has just had a heart-to-heart talk with Cookie Eriks, wife of Wayne Eriks, who, as we announced earlier, has been arrested in the homicide and arson case involving the death of Tim Rafferty. Emma," he continued, making sure I was close to the mike, "what was Cookie's reaction to this latest turn of tragic events?"

"Thank you, Spence," I said. "Unfortunately, I'm not at liberty to disclose what Cookie Eriks told me in our remarkable conversation. You can read all the details in the next edition of the *Advocate*. We'll have the entire story, along with comments from Sheriff Milo Dodge and other revealing aspects of this unfortunate crime."

I smiled even more broadly at Spence and backed away from the mike.

That was one of the rare instances when I'd seen Spence look flabbergasted. There was dead air for at least four seconds before he spoke to his audience again. "I appreciate your discretion, Emma. I understand that you—as is true with all of us in the media—must protect our sources. Stay tuned for more breaking news on KSKY—the only place you can get on-the-spot coverage in Skykomish County." Angrily, he switched off the microphone. "That was a really low blow."

I shrugged. "You didn't actually expect me to tell all, did you?"

Before Spence could respond, Evan Singer came out from the hallway on the other side of the reception area. "Is Dwight Gould the only deputy on patrol right now?" he asked Dustin.

Dustin nodded. "Bill's supposed to be out there, but he had to help out Dodge with the arrest. Why?"

"Because," Evan replied, "I just got a call from the nursing home. The old Rafferty lady has wandered off again. It may take more than one deputy to find her."

Chapter Eighteen

MY IMMEDIATE THOUGHTS went to Beth Rafferty. The last thing she needed was to have her mother roaming around Alpine in ninety-degree heat. There should be limits to what one person had to endure in the course of a week.

"What about Roger Hibbert's volunteer searchers?" Spence said to Dustin. "As far as I know, they haven't done much since that first foray."

"You're right," I put in. "Vida has been very quiet about Roger and his band of blunderers."

"I'll check with Dodge," Dustin said. He asked Evan if Jack had been contacted.

"Right away," Evan replied, his lanky frame restless as always. He'd been in Alpine for over ten years, and was not only a serious student of film, but an artist. He was also a bit of an eccentric and rarely showed off his drawings, which were usually rather morbid. Instead, he restricted his commercial efforts to more conventional art for local merchants. The rest of the time he ran the Whistling Marmot Movie Theatre and filled in taking 911 calls. He was a loner whose nervous energy seemed to be expended in various pursuits. It suddenly dawned on me that I should have talked to Evan earlier.

"How long are you on duty today?" I asked him.

"Until six," he replied with a curious expression.

"Can we meet for coffee after you get off?"

He ruffled his unruly reddish hair. "How come?"

"I have some art questions for you."

"Sure. Fine. Starbucks okay?"

I said it was. Evan returned to his inner sanctum.

"I wonder," I said, "if Beth's been told about her mother."

"The nursing home would've called her," Dustin said. "They always notify family when one of the residents disappears. That is, if they have family or anyone who cares." There was a sad note in his voice.

I was torn. I wanted to wait for Milo, but I felt I should try to get in touch with Beth. If not yet friends, we'd formed a bond in the past week. I realized, however, that even after the sheriff had put Wayne Eriks in a cell, there'd be no further news. Spence could fill up the airways with words such as *alleged, possible, awaiting developments,* and promises of bulletins to come, but he'd have nothing hard-core—and neither would I. As for Cookie, she'd go home—where Vida waited like a duck hunter in a blind. That situation was covered.

I made my brief farewells and went out to the Honda, where I immediately called Beth on my cell.

She didn't answer. Maybe she was still at the hospital. I called the emergency room, but was informed that she'd been released. Perhaps she'd been summoned to the nursing home. I decided it was worth a try, and pulled out onto Front Street.

Margaret Peterson was behind the front desk. She recognized me at once and frowned. "Are you looking for Beth?" she asked.

"Is she here?"

Margaret nodded. "She's talking to some of the other residents, trying to figure out where Mrs. Rafferty may have gone. This isn't the first time, you know."

"Delia seems so feeble," I remarked. "How could she get far?"

"Where there's a will, there's a way." Margaret sighed. "You'd be amazed at how some of our residents find the strength to do what's impossible. Two weeks ago Dorothy Phipps moved a bookcase from one side of the room to the other. She's been in a wheelchair for five years, but she suddenly got the notion that the bookcase shouldn't be by the TV. It must have weighed fifty pounds, but she did it—and then she couldn't get out of the wheelchair to use the toilet."

"Malingering?"

"No." Margaret gave me a doleful look. "Oh, for some, maybe. But so many people who end up in the nursing facility—not the retirement residence," she added hastily as two well-dressed couples in their seventies came through the lobby and headed for the elevator. I guessed that they'd been to church and out for brunch. Margaret greeted them before she spoke to me again. "People like that. They keep active, they're in fairly good health, they have outside interests, but they don't want to be bothered keeping up a house. It's the other type that simply give up. Their families have given up on them, too. I've seen some sad cases of neglect and indifference."

"But not with Delia Rafferty," I said. "She has Alzheimer's. She can't live alone."

Margaret nodded. "True. The situation became impossible for Beth. Her job is very stressful, and she'd gotten to the point where she couldn't focus on it as she should because she was always fretting about her mother being alone and doing heaven-knows-what. Beth tried to get help during the day, but that's so difficult in a small town like Alpine. Caretakers are hard to find, and frankly, there's always the danger of elderly abuse. Alzheimer victims are particularly hard to deal with."

"Where did Delia go the last time she wandered off?" I asked.

"Downtown," Margaret replied. "Ione Erdahl found her at the children's store. They often go somewhere that's familiar, usually from the distant past. Delia wanted to buy something for Tim—in a toddler two size."

"I've heard that's typical," I said as Beth came into the lobby.

"Emma!" she said in surprise. "What are you doing here? Have you news?"

"I'm afraid not," I said in apology. "I thought I'd see if I could help you in any way. How are you feeling?"

"Fine," she replied, despite the fact that she looked even worse than when I'd last seen her slumped in the diner booth. "I mean, I just sort of caved in at breakfast when I heard about Wayne's arrest. It was such a shock. One of the nurses checked me out and agreed that I was overwrought, so I went home. I hadn't been in the house five minutes when Margaret called about my mother. Is there no end to this?"

I went to her and put a hand on her shoulder. Beth had never been fat, but she'd always seemed substantial. Now I could feel bone instead of only flesh. I realized she'd probably lost at least ten pounds since I'd last noticed.

"It's a nightmare," I agreed, "but you'll manage. You're strong. Did you find out anything from the other patients?"

"No." Beth lowered her voice, apparently to prevent Margaret from overhearing. "They're mostly gaga in that wing. Half of them don't even know who my mother is."

I nudged Beth over to a Victorian love seat away from the front desk. "Tell me what happened. When did they realize your mother was gone?"

Beth gazed up at a grandfather clock, which stood in the corner. Its elegant hands indicated that it was ten minutes after one. "Her lunch was brought to her room at a quarter to twelve," Beth said, trying to keep her voice calm. "Mom rarely eats in the dining room. The first week she was here, she got into the kitchen and turned the stove on high under a kettle of water. It boiled over, and I guess one of the orderlies chewed her out about it. Those people ought to know better. But she wouldn't go back into the dining room unless I was visiting and insisted. Anyway, whoever brought her meal—her name's Cristina—said Mom wasn't in her room. Nobody could remember when they'd seen her last except after breakfast when they cleared away her tray. That would've been around nine, nine-thirty."

"Did she take her wheelchair?"

"No." Beth grimaced. "She took her walker, though. At least, I think so. Sometimes the patients steal each other's walkers, even their dentures." Putting her head in her hands, she shuddered violently. "If only I could have kept her at home! This is such an awful place!"

Margaret's head jerked up. She stared at us, looking annoyed. I didn't really blame her. Hopefully, Margaret and the rest of the staff were doing the best they could—given the pathetic circumstances.

"Milo may ask those students to help look for your mother," I said. "She can't have gone far in this weather."

Beth shook her head. "Heat doesn't affect her the way it does the rest of us. Her circulation is so poor. She's always cold."

"Still . . ." I began, and stopped. "Shall we go together and look around Front Street? Not that many stores are open on Sunday."

"She'd have been seen by now if she'd gone there," Beth said.

That was probably true. The eating places on Front

Street were doing business, as were assorted other establishments, including Donna's art gallery, the movie theater, and Videos-to-Go. But most Alpine merchants firmly believed that "if you can't make it in six days, you won't make it in seven."

"Would she go to the mall?" I asked.

"Mom hated the mall," Beth replied. "She was old-fashioned. She liked the stores on Front Street, even during those years when many of them closed or moved because of the downturn in the timber industry." Beth paused, obviously considering the possibilities. "She might have gone anywhere, even back to the house. I asked the neighbors to watch for her."

"What about Tim's? I understand Alzheimer victims often go to familiar places. Could she make it uphill?"

Beth calculated. "It's only two blocks up, and then two more on the level when you reach Fir. She might, if she has her walker." A flash of fear crossed Beth's face. "But if she did, she could have gone off into the woods. The cul-de-sac is surrounded by trees. That's another thing," Beth added fretfully, "the patients often wander off into the wilds, especially around this part of the world."

Nobody knew that better than I did. "Let's go that way," I urged. "If she's around town, someone will find her. We can take my car."

"No. I'll follow you," Beth insisted.

"Fine."

As soon as I got into the Honda, I called Milo's headquarters. Dustin answered. He told me that Bill Blatt had been trying to contact his nephew or cousin or whatever relation Roger was to the deputy, but that Amy Hibbert said her son wasn't home. He'd taken an inner tube with him and presumably was going to float His Royal Chubbiness in the Skykomish River.

Despairing briefly because the river was so low that

Roger couldn't possibly drown, I realized that neither could Delia Rafferty, should she also head in that direction.

I could see Beth in the rearview mirror, keeping just a few yards between our cars. It took less than five minutes to reach what was left of the Rafferty home. The crime-scene tape remained, sagging under the bright sun.

I knew how hard this was for Beth. She didn't get out at first, but sat behind the wheel, staring through the windshield. I waited between our two cars, already feeling enervated by the heat.

"This is hopeless," she declared, finally joining me. "Everything is such a mess. How could we tell if Mom had been here?"

"Somebody has," I said, pointing to a strip of crime-scene tape that had been pulled off from one of the temporary supports.

"You think so? Maybe it was those kids, when they were searching for the hermit."

"Maybe." I walked over to where the tape had been removed. Judging from what I knew of the original house layout, the section could have been a bedroom. There had been two, as I recalled—one for Tim and Tiffany, the other for the nursery.

"That's odd," I said.

Beth had stayed put, staring blankly at the pitiful scene. "What?"

"There are footprints in the ash," I said, leaning down to get a better look.

Beth still didn't move. "So? Those kids, probably."

"No. The kids I saw wore sneakers or hiking shoes or sandals," I said, standing up. "Whoever came here was barefoot."

Beth finally walked over to where I was standing. I noticed that she was trembling. I didn't blame her. We were probably very close to the spot where her brother had died.

"Good lord," she whispered. "You're right."

"They had to be recent prints," I said. "No one would have walked barefoot through this . . . debris until it was completely cooled down. That took at least two or three days, as I understand. Whoever was here had fairly big feet and didn't seem to go very far, though it's hard to tell because of the rubble. We'd better notify the sheriff. They can make casts from the footprints."

"Yes," Beth agreed. "I've heard about that, but usually it's from shoes."

"True." I had no idea how footprint casts would help unless the sheriff happened to have access to the feet's owner.

"Shall we start walking through the woods?" Beth asked. "We could go in different directions."

I surveyed our surroundings. Most of the wild berry vines, ferns, and other underbrush had been cleared away when the Rafferty house had been built. The small garden area—like my own—abutted onto the encroaching forest, which marched up the face of Tonga Ridge.

I was wearing sandals—my churchgoing footwear; Beth was more sensibly shod, in Birkenstocks. On the other hand, if Delia Rafferty had tried to climb the hill, she may have been wearing bedroom slippers. Certainly she couldn't get far.

There was a rudimentary trail, perhaps made by the Bourgettes when they built the house or used by Tim and Tiffany to gather kindling or mushrooms or whatever the younger Raffertys may have sought. Beth and I decided to stick together and follow the trail. It seemed like the most likely place that Delia would go.

It was somewhat cooler under the tall trees, and the air smelled of evergreens. The footing, however, was tricky:

dry dirt in places, exposed roots, rocks, fallen branches, and scatterings of brown evergreen needles.

We had meandered along the switchback path for about a hundred yards when I stopped, leaning against a hemlock tree and catching my breath. "I haven't seen a single sign of anybody using this trail recently. I can't imagine your mother managing to get this far, given so many obstacles."

Beth, who was about six feet behind me, shook some fir needles off her Birkenstocks. "Maybe she didn't follow the trail. Should we go back and search closer to the cul-de-sac?"

I was dubious. "I wonder if she came here in the first place."

"Yes. It was just a guess, after all." Beth pondered for a moment. "Okay. We'll head back down. The going seems to get rougher from here anyway."

I agreed. The trail became narrower, the terrain much steeper. Beth turned around and started the descent. As I took a step forward, the sole of my sandal caught on a half-hidden root. I tripped, falling to my knees before I could grab a rotting log to steady myself. The only damage was a few splinters in my fingers. Carefully, I pulled them out before I started to move again, this time keeping my eyes focused on the ground.

I'd gone only a few feet when I heard a noise. At first, I thought it was Beth, out of sight, but somewhere below me on the zigzagging trail. But the sound—a branch, a bird, a deer?—had been either behind or above me. I looked up into the ceiling of fir and hemlock. I saw no chipmunk, no jay, no crow, no wildlife of any kind. I stood very still and listened.

Nothing but the silence of the forest. Any creek that had tumbled nearby had dried up by early August. Even at this level of over three thousand feet, there was no snow. The only living creature I saw was a deerfly. I waved it away, not wanting to become its next meal.

But I definitely felt a presence. I was being watched. I'd lived next to nature for too long not to be able to sense intrusion, if not actual danger. I'd had the same feeling several times over the years when I'd been out in my backyard, and later found fresh deer tracks in the damp ground just beyond the tree line.

But the noise could have been made by a bear, even a cougar. I debated about whether or not I should move. Bears won't bother you if you don't bother them—or so I'd been taught. Cougars were another matter. I decided to start down the trail.

But I was unnerved, and when I slipped again in my frivolous sandals, there was nothing to grasp. I tumbled into a heap at the bend in the trail. And swore.

I'd twisted my right ankle, skinned my knees, and bruised my left arm. For a few seconds after I stopped cursing, I huddled on the ground, wondering if I dared test the ankle to make sure it wasn't broken. Like an idiot, I'd left my purse—and cell phone—in the car.

I didn't hear the sound again. But after I flexed my ankle enough to make sure it was still in one piece and brushed the dirt and gravel off my knees, I finally looked up.

That's when I saw him.

He was a scant four feet away from me, standing on the trail in a ragged tank top and tattered pants, barefoot, and with a long gray beard.

I was so startled that I couldn't speak. I knew he was Old Nick.

But when I finally found my voice, I took a deep breath and a big chance. "Hello, Craig," I said. "How are you?"

Chapter Nineteen

HE DIDN'T RESPOND. The man simply stood there, studying me as if I were part of the landscape.

"Can you help me?" I asked, anxiety overcoming pain.

He still didn't budge.

"I can't get up," I said in a plaintive voice.

At last, he came toward me. I was beginning to tremble. Wordlessly, he bent down to peer at every inch of my battered body. Crazily, I thought of Hansel and Gretel, with the old witch speculating about how much meat they had on their bones before she put them in the oven.

"What hurts?" The words were raspy, as if his voice had rusted from lack of use.

"My ankle, mostly," I said.

His eyes were green, dark green like pine needles. He didn't smell like pine, though. Old Nick—or Craig, or whoever he was—smelled of sweat and poor hygiene.

With astonishingly gentle fingers—long and lean—he felt the ankle. It didn't look as if it had begun to swell, but it still hurt.

"Hold on." He put his hands under my armpits and slowly lifted me to my feet. "Don't walk. Test the weight."

I shifted from one foot to the other. My ankle was painful, but not unbearable. Could I manage a hundred yards on it? The length of a football field, I thought irrelevantly. Or maybe not. The end zone meant safety.

Suddenly it dawned on me. My rescuer didn't appear to have any intention of harming me. All he'd done so far was help. I was still shaking a bit, but my fear began to ebb.

"You are Craig Laurentis, aren't you?" I finally said.

He looked exasperated. "So?"

"Don't you care how I know who you are?"

"I already know."

I stared at him. "You do? How?"

He shrugged. "Does it matter?"

"I'm curious, that's all." I paused, but he said nothing. "How can I thank you?" I asked.

"You already did." He turned around and started walking up the trail.

I opened my mouth to call his name, but realized it wouldn't do any good. I was in no shape to chase after him. I'd be lucky if I could get back down to the cul-de-sac. A moment later, he'd made a sharp turn in the trail and disappeared.

It seemed to take forever to navigate my descent. Every step was painful, and I hung on to whatever branch, root, or rock I could find to keep myself upright. At last I moved out from the trees and into the clearing. The sun blinded me for an instant before I saw Beth, pacing around the area by her car.

"Good Lord!" she cried. "What happened to you? You look like a wreck!"

"I fell," I said, reluctant to give her the details. "I'm okay."

"You don't look it," she said with a frown. "You're limping, and your slacks are torn. Do you need to see a doctor?"

I shook my head. "Any luck?"

"No." She grew despondent. "I searched around here while I was waiting for you, but I couldn't see any sign of Mom. Should we go to the sheriff's headquarters?"

We didn't need to. Bill Blatt was pulling up in his patrol car. He got out and hurried over to us. "Dodge has been trying to get hold of you," he said to me before turning to Beth. "A couple walking their dog found your mother in John Engstrom Park. She's okay."

"Thank God!" Beth cried. "The park's right by the nursing home! Why didn't anybody look there sooner? Why didn't I?"

"She was asleep," Bill said, taking off his regulation hat and mopping his brow with a blue and white handkerchief. "It was the dog who found her, actually. Your mother was under some of those big rhododendron and azalea bushes."

"Where is she now?" Beth asked.

"In the nursing home infirmary. Just to make sure she's okay," Bill explained. "Doc Dewey's checking her out."

Doc was having a busy Sunday. Bill finally took a long look at me. "What happened? You look like you've been in a brawl."

"Just a dumb fall," I said. "Where's Milo?"

"Doing paperwork," Bill replied. "Eriks is locked up, Cookie finally went home, and Fleetwood got tired of waiting for news that wasn't going to break. Oh," he added as an afterthought, "Toni Andreas called to say she's quitting her job. In fact, she's moving to Alaska."

I shook my head. "That's sort of precipitous. But I'm not surprised."

Beth obviously didn't care if Toni moved to Mozambique. "I'm going to the nursing home," she said, getting into her car. "Thanks, Emma. I really appreciate your help." She drove off before I could respond.

"Poor Beth," Bill said. "Well, I'm glad I found you two together. That made things simpler." He nodded in the direction of the rubble. "It looks like we've got this whole thing pretty well wrapped up. Gosh, who would've thought Wayne Eriks would kill his own son-in-law?"

"People are very complex," I said.

But I wasn't convinced that Wayne had done it.

Looking back, I'm not sure why I had doubts about Wayne's guilt. He had been so eager to report that he'd seen Old Nick—or maybe I should start calling him Craig—near the crime scene. But Wayne had gone to the sheriff after the fact, and his story had sounded contrived. Wayne certainly wasn't one of my favorite local citizens since he'd made a pass at me, but that hardly qualified him as a murderer—just a jerk. I couldn't even envision him in a rage, quarreling with Tim and coming to blows that resulted in death.

All these thoughts went through my head as I drove to the sheriff's headquarters. That short trip wasn't easy. It hurt every time I put my right foot on the gas pedal or the brake. By chance, I reached my destination just as Toni Andreas was getting out of her car.

"Toni," I called out, limping toward her. "I heard you quit."

Toni frowned and peered at me over the top of her sunglasses. "How did you learn that so fast?"

"I ran into Bill Blatt," I replied.

"Oh." Toni proceeded to the main entrance. "I've come to collect my personal stuff. I'm leaving for Fairbanks tomorrow."

"That soon?" I was surprised. "Don't you have to give notice?"

"I guess not," she said, going through the door.

Dustin was still behind the counter, talking on the phone. When he saw us enter, he rang off abruptly. "Hi," he said to both of us, but his gaze was fixed on

Toni. "Are you sure about this? Don't you want to talk it over with Dodge?"

Toni shook her head. "I got a last-minute cheap fare. It's almost the end of the month, so I won't lose much on my rent, if I get my damage deposit back. I've made up my mind." She went behind the counter to her desk. "This won't take long."

"Toni," Dustin pleaded, "this is crazy. How do you know you'll like Alaska? Do you have a job up there? Have you any friends?"

Toni gave him a baleful look. "I'm not sure I have any friends here. And I'm sick of this job. I'm sick of Alpine." She began to pull out drawers. "Have you got a carton around here somewhere?"

"Yes." Dustin sighed and headed down the corridor.

I considered arguing with Toni, but knew it was hopeless. Furthermore, the only person she seemed to take advice from was my son. I knew he'd been cautious, but Toni must have taken his lack of negativism for tacit approval. Besides, I had other matters on my mind.

I'd seen Milo's Grand Cherokee parked outside, so I assumed he was still in his office. Toni paid no attention to me as I went through the counter's swinging gate and limped over to Milo's closed door. I knocked twice and announced myself.

I heard him tell me to come in.

"Jeez, Emma, what's with you? Did you get in a fight at Mugs Ahoy?"

I flopped into his visitor's chair. "I fell down. Old Nick helped me get up."

"Right." Milo pushed his chair back a few inches from the desk. "Man, your arm's turning some funny colors. Do you want an ice bag?"

I glanced at the bruise. It wasn't pretty, but it didn't hurt as much as my ankle. Or even my knees. "I'm not kidding," I declared. "Old Nick is definitely Craig Laurentis. I met him in the woods above the cul-de-sac."

Milo turned serious. "No shit. When?"

"About twenty minutes ago. I was with Beth, looking for her mother."

"They found her in the park," Milo said absently. "Did Beth meet this guy, too?"

"No. She'd gone on ahead back down the trail that leads up from the Rafferty property."

He got out his cigarettes and offered me one. I took it, wishing he were the kind of lawman who kept a bottle of booze in the desk drawer. "So what happened?" he inquired.

I explained in careful detail. "Then he just ambled off, up the trail. Maybe he lives around there."

"Hunh." Milo stared off into space. "I thought you were nuts when you told me your theory. It makes sense, though. Reclusive artist, probably a hippie dropout, antisocial, antigovernment, antiestablishment—the whole bit. I wonder if his family knows where he is and what he's doing."

"They probably gave up on him years ago," I said. "Or they think he's dead, probably from an overdose."

"Could be. It wouldn't be the first time." Milo tapped ash into his Marlboro Man ashtray. "He still could be a witness."

"Not a suspect?"

Milo grunted. "We've got our man." He gestured behind him. "Eriks is locked up and feeling very sorry for himself."

"He still claims he's innocent?"

"Oh, yeah. Cookie is his alibi. You know what that means."

I didn't express my doubts. They were too ill-founded. "Motive?"

"I figure Tim wasn't a very good husband," Milo said.

"He may have been physically as well as verbally abusive. I suppose Wayne and Tim got into it, a fight broke out, and Wayne cracked him with a baseball bat. I'll admit, he probably didn't mean to kill him. It may even be self-defense. Once he's got an attorney, that could be the plea. It might even work. Of course, there's still the arson charge. Wayne started the fire to cover the murder. It all fits."

"Evidence?"

"The burns on his arms," Milo said. "The flimsy alibi. We'll find more, like traces of kerosene on his shoes or some other signs of how the fire started. That's up to the crime lab folks."

"What if Wayne destroyed what he was wearing that night?"

Milo shrugged. "Why didn't he have those burns treated if he got them on the job? Why was he coughing a day or so after the murder and fire?"

I remembered how Wayne had coughed and blown his nose when he'd come into the *Advocate* office. I hadn't thought anything of it at the time—a cold, allergies, a chronic condition. People who work outdoors often have allergies year-round, whether from pollen or mold or whatever other natural source agitates their respiratory systems.

"That's true," I murmured. "It could have been from smoke inhalation. Maybe one of the doctors should check his lungs. Could there still be some signs of the smoke?"

Milo gazed at his cigarette. "Wayne's a smoker. I honestly don't know if the docs could tell at this late date. I'll ask."

I put my own cigarette out even though I'd smoked only half of it. What I really needed was some aspirin. "Will you look for Old Nick—I mean Craig—in the area above the cul-de-sac?"

Milo nodded. "We'll give it a go. It gets pretty rugged up there, but at least we won't have to fight the snow this time of year." The sheriff pulled his chair up closer to the desk and peered at me. "You sure you're okay?"

I made a face. "I'm not in pieces. I'm just banged up. By the way, I think Craig's been tromping around in the Rafferty rubble. I saw some footprints there today. Bare feet. I wonder why he did that."

Milo shrugged. "He's not the only one who goes barefoot around here in this weather."

That was true. I frequently shed my shoes when I was home, even when I went outside. "I'd better go," I said, getting up from the chair and discovering that I felt stiff all over. "Let me know what you find out."

"I'll do what I can," Milo replied. "Take care of yourself, Emma."

He sounded as if he meant it.

Dustin was on the phone again as I went through the reception area. He nodded politely. There was no sign of Toni. She must have made short work of her task. Maybe there were few souvenirs she wanted to keep; maybe she had too many bad memories.

My cell phone rang as soon as I got in the Honda. "Goodness," Vida cried in my ear, "I've been trying to reach you for ages! I heard you had a bad fall. You'd better come over here and see Doc Dewey."

"Come over where?" I asked in a puzzled tone.

"To the Erikses', of course. I'm still here." Vida lowered her voice. "I've been trying to call you at home. That's where I thought you'd go after you found out Beth's mother was all right."

I was still confused. "What's that got to do with Doc Dewey? He's supposed to be at the nursing home, looking after Delia Rafferty."

"He is. He was. She's fine. But he's on his way here now to give Cookie a sedative. She's an absolute mess.

No emotional stamina. Good grief, whatever happened to *backbone*?"

"What about Tiffany?" I inquired.

"What about her?" Vida sounded disgusted. "She's fine. Whining about her father being arrested, of course. Whining about her backache. Whining about not having any potato chips in the house. Honestly! I'm sick of listening to her."

"Can't you leave now?" I asked, flexing my ankle before turning on the ignition.

"Not until Doc gets here," Vida replied. "Do come. I need to be restrained, or the next homicide in Alpine will be committed by me on Tiffany."

I couldn't refuse. Doc might have some proper bandages for my knees. They were still bleeding a little through the inadequate Band-Aids I'd used from my emergency kit in the glove compartment.

The Erikses' house in Icicle Creek looked the same as when I last visited. But of course it had changed. Tragedy had buffeted the place, lending it a defeated air. If the exterior's beige paint had been peeling before, I hadn't noticed; if a couple of shingles were missing from the roof, I'd missed seeing the bare spots; if the camellia bush near the front door had already withered, I'd paid no attention. But now I did, and the property almost looked abandoned. In a way it was—abandoned by happiness and hope. Houses were built on sale value. Homes were created by love. If love was here, it seemed to have turned to ash—not unlike what was left of the Raffertys' burned-out bungalow.

Wearily, I trudged to the door. Vida opened it almost immediately. I suspected that she'd been watching for my arrival.

"Doc's not here yet," she announced grimly. "Cookie's drinking tea in the kitchen and crying. Tiffany's on the sofa in the living room, complaining. They should have a sign out front, 'Beware of Family.' "

Tiffany scarcely glanced at me when I came into the living room. "Jake O'Toole just called," she said in a petulant voice. "He wanted to know if I was coming to work tomorrow. What a jerk!"

"It would do you good," Vida declared. "When Doc gets here, you must ask him what's best for you—lying around doing nothing, or getting back to the store to take your mind off yourself."

Tiffany ignored the advice and turned a page in the copy of *Us* magazine that she'd been reading. In the distance, I could hear Cookie sobbing softly.

"She won't stop," Vida lamented just as the doorbell chimed. "Ah. It must be Doc. Thank heavens."

Vida went off to answer the door. I considered talking to Tiffany, decided it was useless, and hobbled out to the kitchen. Cookie was standing by the sink, shoulders hunched, head down, still sobbing.

She didn't turn around, but she must have heard me approach. "I want to kill myself," she moaned.

"How would that help?"

Startled, she looked at me. "Oh! I thought you were Vida."

"Vida's still here," I said. "I think Doc Dewey just arrived, too." I put my hand on one of the kitchen chairs. "Sit down, Cookie. You look like you're about to collapse." The way I felt, maybe I'd beat her to it.

With an air of despondency, Cookie moved to a chair by a mug of tea that looked as if it hadn't been touched. She picked up a crumpled table napkin and wiped her eyes. I could hear Vida and Doc talking to Tiffany in the living room. Hopefully—probably foolishly—I thought they might be able to convince Tiffany that spending almost a week on the sofa wasn't healthy for her or her baby.

The lecture might not last long, which meant my conversation with Cookie would have to be brief. "Look," I said, sitting down, "you can't give in to your emotions. Wayne and Tiffany both need you. If Wayne didn't commit this crime, he won't be convicted. You know the truth, Cookie. You told the sheriff Wayne was with you all of Monday evening. Of course," I continued as she stared into the tea mug, "the two of you will have to account for every moment. Can you remember what happened that night?"

She kept staring. Maybe there were tea leaves in the mug; maybe she was trying to read the future.

If so, it must have looked as bleak as the present. "It was just the usual," she murmured. "We watched TV, we went to bed around eleven. That's our routine."

"Just like you usually do?" I remarked, hearing Vida raise her voice in annoyance.

Cookie nodded. "We don't socialize much, except to visit Tiff and Tim sometimes, or they come over here. But we hadn't left the house at night for several days."

Vida appeared in the doorway, looking disgusted. "Doc wants to see you, Cookie. Shall I bring him in here or would you rather go out into the living room?"

"I don't care," Cookie said listlessly, but she rose from the chair.

Vida remained by the door. "Feckless," she said. "Tiffany is lazy, self-centered, and utterly worthless. Doc can't talk any sense into her. I'm leaving."

"You've done your duty," I said. "Maybe I should leave, too. I've got some things I want to tell you."

"Oh?" Vida looked intrigued. "Let me get my hat. I intend to go see Delia Rafferty. This is Sunday, my day to do good works. Doc says Delia's none the worse for her little adventure, but I still feel obligated to call on her. Do you want to come with me?"

"No, thanks. I need to rest my beat-up body." Another trip to the nursing home was the last thing I wanted to do.

Tiffany was still on the sofa, once again reading her magazine. Cookie was sitting in a side chair, while Doc asked her some questions. He smiled and nodded at me.

"Busy day," I remarked as I passed him.

"Very." Doc stopped smiling.

Vida picked up her hat from a side table. I'd never seen this particular model before, but guessed that it was one she reserved for going to church. It was definitely a spring or summer hat, a net confection with a nest on the crown and a trio of baby birds poking their heads out of small blue eggs. I assumed that Vida had bought it on an Easter whim.

I said goodbye to everybody in general, but Vida wordlessly tromped out of the living room and down the short flight of stairs to the front door.

"Did Cookie even taste that tea I made for her?" she demanded when we got outside. "Don't tell me. Honestly, those Eriks women have no spunk!"

"Tiffany has her own brand of spunk," I noted. "She takes very good care of Tiffany."

"Not so," Vida huffed. "If she did, she wouldn't be lying around like a heroine in some tragic Italian opera. Exercise. Work. Wholesome food. Mental stimulation. That's what she needs, for herself and for the poor baby. Well?"

Vida had stopped by her Buick, which was parked in front of my Honda.

"You want to talk here?" I asked, surprised.

"Of course not. Shall we go to my house? It's only a block from the nursing home. I could use a cup of tea myself."

"Hot tea?"

"Yes." Vida nodded. The baby birds bounced. "Hot

beverages are actually supposed to be good for you in this weather."

We both drove to Vida's, where she made tea and offered soothing noises to her canary, Cupcake. She insisted that even he hated the heat.

For the next twenty minutes, I updated Vida about everything I knew, including the encounter with Craig Laurentis.

"Fascinating," she declared. "That's very clever of you, Emma, to figure out that Old Nick is this painter person. I should have thought of that myself, especially when some of the search party members found brushes and other indications of an artist. Really, I feel quite dense."

"You shouldn't," I said. "It wouldn't have occurred to me if I hadn't seen one of his pictures at Donna's gallery and fallen in love with it."

"Do you think he's crazy?" she asked, putting more sugar into her English bone china teacup.

"I doubt it," I replied. "Eccentric maybe. He was very helpful."

"You should go home and rest." She glanced at her watch. "It's after three. I must head for the nursing home. I'd like to be back here around four. Buck and I are driving down to Sultan for dinner. He likes to eat early, you know."

I was aware that Buck Bardeen preferred to keep to a strict schedule, no doubt a habit from his career in the military. I took a final sip of tea and stood up. I was getting stiffer by the minute.

"You really should have let Doc Dewey take a look at you," Vida said with a frown.

"Doc's busy enough," I replied. "It's all superficial. I can take care of my wounds when I get home. I don't plan on doing anything for the rest of the day except lie on the sofa and read or watch TV."

"Yes." Vida made a face. "But don't stay there forever like Tiffany."

"No. I—" Something popped into my head. "Cookie's lying. Or else Wayne is."

"What?" Vida wore her most owlish expression.

"Cookie told me that Wayne was home all of Monday night," I replied.

"Yes, yes, his alibi," Vida broke in. "Weak, of course. Spouses tend to do that sort of thing for each other."

"But she went on to say that they hadn't been out in the evening for several days," I explained. "Yet Wayne claimed to have gone up to check that power pole or whatever it was Sunday night when he—allegedly— spotted Old Nick by the football field."

"Ah!" Vida looked as if she'd discovered the secret of the universe. "Most intriguing. Cookie may have forgotten he'd gone out Sunday—or else he didn't and she's lying her head off. Surely Milo can get her to break down. Cookie's not a strong person."

"She doesn't seem to be," I said in a thoughtful voice.

Vida cocked her head at me. "Are you suggesting that Cookie may be the one who went to Tim and Tiffany's?"

I sighed. "I'm not sure what I'm saying. Wayne's the one with the burns. Maybe," I said slowly, "we don't know exactly who's strong and who's weak."

"Yes," Vida agreed. "That's a fair question, isn't it?"

The air was very still and very muggy, with gathering clouds over Mount Baldy. We seemed to be in for a thunder-and-lightning storm. That was bad news. While it might signal a break in the weather, lightning could start forest fires anywhere in the Cascades.

I opened both the front and back doors, but latched the screens. The windows were already open. After taking care of my skinned knees and putting on fresh bandages, I changed into an old cotton shift. Propped up on the sofa, I wrote a quick e-mail to Adam, telling him that in case he hadn't already heard, Toni was on her way to Fairbanks Monday. Fortunately for him, the city was a long, long way from St. Mary's Igloo.

As soon as I shut down the laptop, my eyes shut down, too. The events of the past week, as well as the weather, had sapped my energy. I fell asleep, the second time in the last few days that I'd taken a nap. That was a record. I don't think I'd taken two naps in two years until this August. Maybe I was simply getting older.

It was the clap of thunder that woke me up. I was disoriented at first, thinking it must be morning. It was quite dark, which further confused me because my watch said it was five minutes to seven. Dawn or dusk, the sky should be light at that time of day during summer.

Sliding off the sofa, I walked—stiffly—to the open front door. No rain fell, but twin jagged bolts of lightning flashed vertically across the sky. It was still Sunday. The storm had begun.

Despite the muggy atmosphere, I was starving. I went into the kitchen and turned on the light. Occasionally I tease Milo about subsisting on TV dinners, but in fact, I always kept two or three in the freezer. As I put a turkey entrée into the microwave, the phone rang.

It was Vida. "I just got back from Sultan," she announced. "A good thing, too. The storm hit just as we drove past Skykomish. I had to get Cupcake covered early in this dark weather. How are you feeling?"

I told her I'd slept for almost three hours, but I'd survive.

"Of course you will," she asserted. "You're not a nincompoop like some of the women around here. By the way, that pathetic Delia took my hat—again."

"You mean the one with the bird's nest?"

"Of course. It was a great favorite of mine. I bought it years ago on sale in Seattle. I almost didn't give it to her, but she's so pitiful that I felt I had to. Maybe I can get Margaret Peterson or Beth to return it to me. I don't care about the other one, but this was a one-of-a-kind model, sixty percent off."

I didn't doubt that the hat was unique. "Delia must have liked the birds," I said.

"She adored them," Vida replied wryly. "Unfortunately. Next time I visit, perhaps I'll take her a stuffed animal. I certainly won't wear a hat."

"Excuse me, Vida," I said, "but my microwave timer just went off."

"That's fine. I'm going to observe the storm. Summer lightning is very spectacular, if dangerous."

I devoured my prepared dinner in front of the TV, watching Sunday night baseball. The thunder and lightning continued, sometimes sounding very close, occasionally in the distance. The lights and the TV flickered a few times. Periodically, I limped to the front window to watch the show. The storm was all over the sky, probably stretching the length of the central Cascades.

The game ended, but I stayed tuned for ESPN's *Baseball Tonight*. The sportscasters were doing a National League roundup when I heard sirens. I turned the volume down and tried to judge where the sound was coming from. Not in my direction, I decided. Perhaps whichever emergency vehicles were involved had headed for Highway 2.

But the sirens stopped after about three minutes. Whatever was happening had occurred in town. Then I heard more sirens. Again, they quit after a very short time. I considered turning on KSKY, but decided I couldn't stand being scooped twice in one day by Spencer Fleetwood and his breaking news. For all I knew, there might have been a false alarm or a minor medical crisis. I'd had enough drama for what should have been a quiet Sunday.

I turned my attention back to ESPN. They cut to a commercial just as the phone rang again. I hit the mute button and picked up the receiver.

"Emma!" Vida shrieked. "Have you heard? The nursing home's on fire!"

Chapter Twenty

I'LL BE RIGHT there," I said, not waiting for details. "I'll call Scott first."

Scott was at home with Tamara. He, too, had heard the sirens. "I'm on my way," he said. "Two big fires in one week! Man, that's a record."

Certainly it wasn't one anybody would want to break. As I hurried out to the car, I thought about all those crippled and confused residents in the nursing facility. Maybe the retirement section itself would be spared. Maybe, I prayed, the fire hadn't spread far.

I could see smoke but no flames as I drove down Sixth Street. I could also see several emergency vehicles with their flashing lights. As I stopped near the corner of Sixth and Cascade, a jagged bolt of lightning struck so close by that it lit up the scene as if it were midday. Onlookers had gathered, but were being urged to move on by Sam Heppner and Dwight Gould.

As soon as I got out of the Honda, I started to cough. The same smells, the same heat, the same eye-burning sensations assailed me as I'd endured Monday night. I felt as if I must be having a nightmare. Surely lightning couldn't strike twice. Or, I asked myself, reining in my fantasies, was it really lightning that had started this fire? It was possible. The thunder that followed the last bolt had come quickly and loudly, making me grit my teeth.

Putting a tissue over my mouth and nose, I tried to focus on what I was seeing. That wasn't easy. But another flash of lightning allowed me to see what was happening. The church, which stood between the infirmary-hospice and the retirement home, appeared untouched. So did the retirement home itself. The smoke was pouring out of the newer building to the east. That was where the hoses were spraying big plumes of water. It was also where the pitiful cries of the elderly and infirm were coming from. I could see patients being evacuated on gurneys, in wheelchairs, and in rescuers' arms. Another ambulance was coming down Cascade, perhaps from the nearby ranger station at Skykomish. I suspected that more would come from other parts of the county. Alpine's city budget could afford only one.

I couldn't spot my reporter, but if Scott had arrived, he was probably closer to the fire's source. Finally, I caught Sam Heppner's eye.

"Move back, Emma," he ordered. "Everybody's got to keep away. We need space to get these people out of here."

"Sam," I begged, "please tell me what happened. I have to know."

Sam was wielding his baton at a couple of teenagers. They backed off. The deputy scowled at me, but spoke rapidly. "Fire started in a wastebasket. No known fatalities yet, but that could change with these old, sick folks. Some of them'll be taken to Sultan or Monroe. We don't have room for all of them here. Now step back."

I obeyed. And bumped into Vida.

"Too dreadful," she declared, speaking loudly over the sirens and shielding her eyes from the blinking emergency lights. "But so lucky the fire started in the new section. It appears that it's much easier to contain because of the improved construction and safety methods.

The damage is mostly from smoke, but many of the patients have lung problems." Sadly, she shook her head.

"A wastebasket?" I remarked, trying not to cough. "Was someone smoking?"

"I don't know." Vida grimaced. "Really, it's impossible to learn very much. I can't imagine, though, that smoking would be allowed in the infirmary. Several residents are on oxygen."

"Someone on the staff might have sneaked a cigarette," I speculated as the parade of stricken old folks continued. The deputies were growing hostile as relatives and friends of the victims arrived, demanding to know what had happened to their loved ones. People were sobbing; a woman's hysterical shrieks rose above the din; two small children clung to their father, asking "Where's our nana?" over and over.

Milo stood on the edge of the street with a bullhorn. "Don't come any closer," he commanded in a calm but authoritative voice. "You'll only interfere with the situation. Step away. *Now.*"

Most of the crowd obeyed, but several remained, besieging Milo and anybody else they could collar for information.

I wanted to ask him if Vida and I could do anything to help, but he was completely surrounded by concerned friends and relations. Instead, I put the question to Vida.

"I already asked," she said, removing her glasses and rubbing her eyes with less than her usual vigor. "The Lutherans rallied immediately. So many of them live near the church. They seem well organized, and I must admit, they're generally very strong, sturdy people."

Vida's assessment would have amused me if the circumstances weren't so dire. Two ambulances were pulling away; two more were arriving, along with a pair of EMT vehicles. The smoke was beginning to dissipate. Maybe the worst of it was over. I could see Pastor Nielsen conferring with Milo. I also noticed Scott farther down the block, taking photographs.

"I brought a camera," Vida said. "I took a few pictures but stopped when I saw Scott. He's really very good when it comes to photography."

"Yes," I agreed, though Vida could take adequate pictures, which was more than I could manage.

I felt an urgent hand on my arm. "Emma!" Beth Rafferty cried. "Have you seen Mom? Has she been evacuated? Is she okay?"

I turned to look at Beth, whose face was pale and haggard. "I don't think they're moving people out of the older wing," I replied. "She must be fine."

"No!" Beth exclaimed, frantically yanking at her hair as if she wanted to pull it out by the roots. "Mom was in the infirmary!" For the first time, Beth noticed Vida. "Do you know anything?"

Vida looked pained. "I visited her shortly after you left this afternoon. She was still in the infirmary then. I understood she'd be kept there overnight."

I felt stupid. Somehow, I'd assumed that Delia was back in the retirement home's assisted-living wing. My brain seemed to be clouded by sleep and smoke.

"It's impossible to identify the patients who've been removed," I said, feeling completely inadequate. Even as I spoke, I saw that the only people now coming out of the infirmary annex were walking under their own power. Firefighters, staffers, and volunteers, I guessed. The evacuation must be finished.

Vida was tapping her chin, always a sign that she was contemplating action. The anxious relatives and friends were gathered around Elvis Sung, who, along with the beleaguered Doc Dewey, was evaluating the stricken victims who hadn't yet been put into the ambulances or medic vans.

"Dr. Sung seems to be giving out information," Vida

said. "Come, Beth, let's speak with him. I don't believe anyone will try to stop you at this point."

Naturally, I trailed along. Dr. Sung was on the sidewalk where only a thin pall of smoke remained hanging in the air. Behind him, Doc Dewey worked with the medics. Milo and Pastor Nielsen were speaking with two of the firefighters and a couple of people who appeared to be staff members. After thoroughly spraying the church as a precautionary measure, the fire hoses dwindled to a trickle.

Quickly, I counted how many patients—and possibly employees—were still waiting to be treated. Four in wheelchairs, two on gurneys, one on a walker, and three wrapped in blankets. One of the medics was putting an oxygen mask over the face of a gurney patient.

Beth and Vida were edging up to Dr. Sung. I moved closer to the person on the gurney.

"Beth!" I shouted. "Here! It's your mother!"

"Oh!" Beth ran toward me as lightning struck and thunder rolled. "Where?"

I pointed to the gurney. Even in the darkness I was certain that the patient was Delia Rafferty.

She was wearing Vida's bird's nest hat.

Almost an hour passed before I could talk to Milo. We ended up in Vida's living room. Since she lived only a block away, it was the most convenient place to gather. The sheriff, however, rejected Vida's offer of tea, and looked as if he'd prefer a stiff drink.

"The wastebasket was the source," Milo confirmed, stretching out his long legs on an ottoman. He looked tired and disheveled. "The wastebasket was in a linen closet. Nobody was seen going in there, but someone noticed smoke coming out from under the door. When they opened the door, the rush of fresh air really got the blaze going. It had already burned quite a bit of the stuff that was stored there, but the flames and smoke got into the hall where there were some garbage bags ready to go out. Most of the stuff inside was paper and plastic, so it all caught pretty fast. Luckily, they were able to get the extinguishers and help contain the fire even before the emergency guys got there."

"Goodness," Vida said with a shake of her head. "How lucky! It could have been the worst disaster Alpine's ever suffered. Is there any word yet on fatalities?"

Milo grimaced. "All I know is what the doctors and one of the medics told me. At least a couple of them probably won't make it. There were only twenty patients in the infirmary at the time, about the usual number. It's a hospice, too, so half a dozen of them probably don't have much chance of lasting very long anyway." He spoke dispassionately, but his hazel eyes were melancholy.

"Yes," Vida murmured. "I know several of them. I've been preparing obituary backgrounds."

I'd also declined hot tea and was drinking ice water. "Any idea of how the fire started?" I asked.

Milo shook his head. "Not exactly. Somebody going in there for a cigarette or even a joint is the best guess. A couple of employees have been caught—and canned—for doing that. When the weather's bad in the winter and they don't want to smoke outside, they go to some enclosed space so they don't screw up the oxygen tanks. It happened around the time they change shifts, so the medical staff was meeting to exchange information."

"There will have to be another investigation," I said, noticing that Vida had stiffened in the rocking chair where she was sitting. "What?" I said to her.

She blinked several times. "Oh—nothing. It just makes me so upset to think what might have happened. Not that it wasn't bad enough. But still . . ." She made a dismissive gesture.

"Say," I said, turning back to Milo, "where was Fleetwood?"

"On the other side of the infirmary," the sheriff replied. "He did his broadcast from Cedar, not Cascade. Doe Jameson was over there. She refused to be interviewed. Doe told him she was busy and to buzz off."

I laughed. "I still don't know her, but I'm getting to like her better all the time."

Milo pulled himself up out of the chair. "Doe's not going to like working the desk until we get somebody to replace Toni. I hope I can find a new hire fast. Toni should never have left without notice. That pisses me off."

"Now, Milo—" Vida began.

But the sheriff waved aside her disapproval. "You're lucky I didn't say something worse. Like what Toni could do with herself. She may not have been the sharpest knife in the butcher block, but at least she could handle the job once she learned it."

"Perhaps you should insist that she stay on until you do find someone else," Vida said, rising from the rocking chair to accompany Milo to the door.

The sheriff shrugged. "She's already bought her plane ticket."

"So?"

"Look," Milo said to Vida, "it's a hassle, but frankly, Toni's been a pain in the ass the last few weeks anyway. On top of it, Beth's a mess. I need to get somebody in that office who isn't a train wreck."

Vida neither argued nor reprimanded. "I suppose you know what you're doing," she said.

Milo gave her a dirty look. "I already did what I had to this week. I caught Tim's killer. Now I'm going home and work my way through a half rack of Budweiser."

The sheriff left.

"He really isn't going to do that, is he?" Vida said in a horrified voice.

"No," I replied. "But he needs to unwind."

"He needs to eat," Vida declared. "If I were a wagering woman, I'd bet that he's hardly stopped to have a decent meal all day. I should have offered to make him something. Scrambled eggs, perhaps, or an omelet."

I didn't want to contemplate what outrage Vida could commit with eggs. Years ago, she'd prepared breakfast for me when I was laid up with a minor injury. The toast was barely browned, the bacon was burned to a crisp, and the scrambled eggs had somehow managed to come out both watery and lumpy. There had even been bits of shell in them. I'd been unable to finish the meal and had given the excuse of an upset stomach. Which, after a few bites, was true.

"Good grief!" Vida exclaimed.

"What?"

She stared at me, her eyes wide. "Eggs. It's all about eggs. Why didn't I think of that before?"

I didn't know what Vida was talking about. Nor would she tell me.

"I have to think," she insisted. "I may be wrong. Please, Emma, be a dear and don't ask any more questions."

Baffled, I surrendered. I was too tired to argue, and the Excedrin was wearing off. "In that case, I'll go home."

"Yes, you do that. And be careful. You're limping rather badly."

Despite the cautionary words, Vida practically shoved me out the door.

As I was about to turn off Fir into my driveway, a car came from the other direction. I had my blinker on, so I waited for the other vehicle to pass by. But it didn't. The driver—without any right-turn signal—swerved abruptly, narrowly missed my mailbox, and stopped on the verge where the grass met the gravel that led to the street.

Slowly, I made the turn, keeping one eye on the rearview mirror. In the dark, I could just barely recognize Toni Andreas. She had gotten out and was going around to the trunk. I pulled into the carport. Slowly, I opened the door and emerged on tired, aching legs. Toni was coming toward me, carrying a big carton.

"Can I leave this stuff with you?" she called as she walked toward the carport.

"What is it?" I asked wearily. It was almost ten o'clock. I really didn't need any more burdens or impositions on this hot, horrible day.

She joined me at the back door. "Just some things I don't want to take with me to Alaska. I don't have any place to store them. You're a baseball fan, aren't you?"

I nodded. "I didn't know you were, too," I said, opening the door and letting Toni enter ahead of me.

"I'm not." She dumped the carton on the kitchen table. "Ooof! That's heavier than I thought it was."

The unmarked carton was sealed with strapping tape. "What's in it?" I asked, wondering if I should listen to see if the damned thing ticked.

"I'm not sure," Toni said in her vague manner. "Baseball stuff. Tim asked me to keep it for him. I don't care about baseball, but I hate to throw it away. I'd have asked Sheriff Dodge to store it—I know he's a sports fan—but he's mad at me. Then I thought of you."

"I see." But I wasn't quite sure what I meant. "When did Tim give this to you?"

Toni shrugged. "I forget. Last spring? Around Easter, maybe."

Easter. April. The opening of baseball season. "Did Tim say why he wanted you to keep this box?"

"He wanted it to be in a safe place," Toni replied.

"It wasn't safe at his house?"

"I guess not," Toni replied, then looked at me as if I were the one who was short on brain cells. "It wouldn't have been, would it?"

I thought she meant the fire. But I didn't think that was what Tim had been trying to say.

"Maybe," Toni went on, "I'll figure out what to do with it after I get settled in Fairbanks. I'll let you know." She started for the back door, but stopped. "The thing is, Tim said if Tiffany had a boy, he wanted him to have what's in the box."

I gave Toni my best impersonation of an investigative reporter's stare. "Why don't you give it to Tiffany?"

Toni looked faintly exasperated. "Because," she responded in a tone that suggested she really was dealing with a nitwit, "Tiff would have thrown the box away. That's why he gave it to me in the first place, don't you see?"

"Yes," I said. "I do."

That's what I'd been wondering all along.

Toni left. I gazed at the carton for about ten seconds before I got out my kitchen shears and cut the strapping tape. Inside, the items were safely preserved in varieties of plastic: a baseball signed by members of the 1995 Mariners' team that had played for the pennant; scorecards autographed by Alex Rodriguez, Ken Griffey Jr., Edgar Martinez, and Randy Johnson; a full-color poster signed by Chris Bosio commemorating his 1993 no-hitter; two fielders gloves, one bearing Jay Buhner's autograph, another with Ichiro Suzuki's signature in English and in Japanese; an album of baseball cards in mint condition, most signed by all-star players from all over the major leagues—Derek Jeter, Sammy Sosa, Barry Bonds, Curt Schilling, Roger Clemens, Cal Ripken Jr., and many, many more. There were signed photos, autographed game programs, and even a few roster cards with the players' names written in by several famous managers.

I had no idea how much these items were worth on eBay. Maybe none of them individually would bring in more than a few hundred dollars. But taken altogether, the collection was probably worth several thousand. Yet, from what I understood, Tim hadn't tried to sell many of these treasures. Suddenly I could imagine Tiffany, pregnant, standing on her feet for long shifts at the Grocery Basket, berating her husband for not cashing in. And threatening to destroy his beloved souvenirs in retribution.

As a woman, I felt sorry for Tiffany. As a baseball fan, I sided with Tim. I wished he'd collected coins. Then I wouldn't have been torn.

But while my emotions might be in conflict, my brain was not. The collectibles legally belonged to Tiffany. I should turn them over to her as soon as I got the chance. Whether she had a boy or a girl, the child should inherit the father's belongings. Besides, lots of women—like me—loved baseball.

I closed the box and resealed it. If I hadn't been so exhausted, I would've pored over each item. Tomorrow I'd take the collection to the Erikses' house. Maybe.

The storm seemed to have passed. I hadn't heard thunder or seen lightning for the past half hour. So far, there was no sign of rain. I started into the bathroom to get ready for bed when the blasted phone rang. I was tempted to let it trunk over to the answering machine, but shuffled back into the living room and picked up the receiver on the fourth ring.

"Emma?"

I didn't recognize the agonized voice at the other end of the line. "Yes?"

"Can you come over? Please?"

It was Beth Rafferty, speaking almost in a whisper.

"What's wrong?"

"Everything. Please come. I don't know who else to call."

Desperation seeped from every syllable. "I . . ." Taking a deep breath, I resumed speaking. "I'll be right over." I was already getting my car keys out of my purse. "Can you at least tell me what's going on?"

"It's . . . a . . . confession. I must see you before I call the sheriff."

She hung up.

Even as I drove to Beth's house, I wondered if calling the sheriff might not be a bad idea. I didn't know what I was facing. Had Beth finally gone over the edge? Certainly the last few days, even weeks and months, had taken their toll on what had seemed to be a stable personality. I'd known other people who had cracked with less provocation.

But I'd kept her confidence before. I could do it one more time. I hoped. And prayed. Mostly for Beth.

The Rafferty house looked normal. Despite its own tragedies, it didn't exude the aura of misery that I'd sensed when I'd gone to see the Eriks women earlier in the day.

Beth was waiting for me at the door. "Thank God, Emma," she said in that same voice of muted desperation. "I was afraid you might not come."

"I'm here," I said, feeling wobbly. "What's going on?"

Beth led me into the living room, where we sat down on the sofa. The surroundings were more tangibly poignant than the house itself. Several bouquets, probably from Tim's funeral, were wilting. Dust covered all the surfaces, and a stack of unopened mail had toppled over from a side table onto the floor. Beth had closed the door behind us. All of the windows were shut tight and the drapes were drawn. The room smelled stale and un-healthy.

"I brought Mom home," Beth said. She looked defiant. "Physically, she's okay. Doc Dewey advised against it, but I couldn't bear to put her back in the nursing home. Mom should be in her own environment right now."

I was blunt. "Does she know the difference?"

"I think so." Beth nodded. "She's asleep. Doc gave me some pills for her. I'll pick up the rest of her medication tomorrow."

"You're not going to work?"

Beth shook her head. "I can't." She looked away.

I waited. But Beth remained silent, her nervous fingers tracing circles on the sofa's arm.

"You mentioned a confession on the phone," I finally said, trying to keep my voice casual. "Did you refer to removing your mother from the nursing home?"

"No." Beth still didn't look at me. She shuddered, and I thought she was going to cry. But when she finally met my gaze, her eyes were dry. "I killed Tim."

Chapter Twenty-one

I WAS STUNNED. "You killed your own brother?" I gasped. "Beth, I can't believe it!"

"It's true."

The simplicity of her words struck me like a strong wind. Maybe I should have been frightened. But I was too shocked to have room for fear.

"Why would you do such a thing?" I demanded. "You loved your brother. I know you did. What happened?"

"Let me explain." She swallowed hard, but kept her voice down. "I knew that Tim and Tiff weren't getting along, not after she got pregnant. Tiff had always been a whiner and she was spoiled. Her parents—her mother, anyway—doted on her after her brother was killed in that rafting accident. Tiff could do no wrong. And once she found out she was going to have a baby—which she'd wanted for years—her whole personality changed. In fact, it wasn't unlike the way my mother's did with Alzheimer's. It's chemical I gather, or hormonal, in Tiff's case. She began to criticize Tim for everything. She even got physically abusive. When Ione Erdahl called 911 to report a disturbance at their house, I knew what was happening, but I couldn't log it. I didn't need to send a response; Tiff wasn't strong enough to do any serious damage, and I . . . well, I figured Tim could defend himself without hurting her. I believed—I tried to believe—

he could handle the situation, and that after she had the baby, Tiff would change."

I wanted to mention Tim's affair with Toni, but I couldn't risk getting Beth sidetracked. I was still in shock over her admission of guilt. Beth was uncomfortable in more ways than one. She'd paused to shift her position on the sofa, making an effort to fold her hands and hold them steady in her lap.

When she spoke again, it wasn't of Tiffany and Tim. "Visiting with Mom was so hard," Beth lamented. "It was impossible to carry on a real conversation. I ran out of mundane things to say—not that it mattered. Then I started voicing my concerns about Tim and Tiff. It was like therapy, I suppose, just rambling on about how they weren't getting along and the quarrels and the abuse. Mom didn't seem to pay attention. She never made a comment. Her gaze was always far-off, and if she said anything, it was like, 'Look at the bird out in that tree,' or 'I never did like popcorn.' "

Beth's face suddenly crumpled. "How could I know?" she all but shouted.

I jumped. Until that moment, her voice had been so low and controlled, almost as if she was giving advice to a 911 caller. "Know what?" I asked.

"That she did understand . . . enough." Beth had turned away again. "That she recognized a bad marriage and abuse. That a baby was on the way. And that's why I might as well have killed Tim with my own hands."

It took me a few seconds to understand what Beth was saying. "Your mother killed Tim?" It was incredible. I actually recoiled in horror. "Her own son?"

Beth held a hand to her forehead. "She thought it was my dad. She told me she'd finally stopped Liam. He'd never hurt anyone again."

Footsteps nearby startled me out of my shock. Some-one was coming down the hall from the bedroom. Either Beth didn't hear anything or she didn't care. She simply sat on the sofa, holding her head.

I got to my feet, heedless of the pain in my ankle. The only way out of the living room was through the hall. If Delia Rafferty was strong enough to wield a baseball bat, she might do anything. I'd confronted some danger-ous people in my life, but never a crazed old lady who had no compunction about bashing in the head of the son she thought was her husband. What might she do to a virtual stranger?

I started to speak Beth's name, but before I could say anything, Vida walked into the living room.

"There now," she said in her usual brisk manner. "Your mother finally settled down." Vida stared at me. "You really shouldn't be here, Emma. You're worn out. I could have handled this."

My mouth was dry. I could hardly speak. "Beth asked me to come," I finally said.

Warily, Beth looked at Vida. "Emma's been a good friend. You have, too, Vida, but I . . ." She shook her head. "I'm sorry. I should have told you, too."

Vida looked faintly miffed. She wasn't used to being a secondary confidante. "Yes, you should have. After all, I knew what your mother had done."

Beth and I both stared at Vida. "How could you?" Beth asked in a breathless voice.

"It was the eggs." Vida sat down in an armchair. "You know the old adage, 'You can't make an omelet without breaking the eggs.' Your mother rattled on about that, and I wondered why. Then she was obsessed with my hat and the eggs in the bird's nest. It all dawned on me earlier this evening when Emma was at my house after the fire. Eggs are a fertility symbol, a sign of new birth. I called Margaret Peterson and asked if she knew what your mother was doing in the kitchen when she let the water boil over. Margaret thought she was trying to boil eggs. Delia not only wouldn't have her meals in the dining room after that—unless you insisted—but she never ate eggs again."

Beth seemed dazed. "I don't understand."

"I don't understand how her mind works, either," Vida admitted. "But she associated eggs with babies. She knew there was going to be a new baby in the family— but she was confused. Maybe she thought she was having the baby. She didn't want the baby—or the mother—to be abused in any way, not after what she'd gone through with your father in his drunken rages. Yes, she'd heard you talk about Tim and Tiffany and mention the word *abuse*. It all came back to her."

Beth waved a hand at Vida. "I never told anyone but Emma about my father's—"

"Beth!" Vida interrupted. "Do you think that people in this town didn't know? Your neighbors heard quarrels. Your mother often had bruises. And sometimes your father did, too. We—well, at least *I* always wondered if she didn't wait until he was asleep or passed out, and give him a few whacks in retribution. She was small, but strong. I suppose Tim left the door unlocked, or even open because of the hot weather and the fact that Tiffany would be home later that night. Your mother probably walked in, found Tim asleep, and thought he was Liam. There was a resemblance, of course. She picked up a baseball bat and—" Vida stopped and shrugged. "But my point is, your parents' marital situation was no secret."

There never were any secrets from Vida. Still, Beth looked puzzled. "I didn't mention the conversations with Mom until just now."

Vida blinked a couple of times behind her big glasses. "I know."

Of course Vida had eavesdropped. She'd probably been in the hallway all along, but had quietly retraced her steps to make it sound as if she'd just arrived. My House & Home editor was a wizard when it came to learning secrets.

She spoke gently to Beth. "You knew your mother had gotten out of the nursing home that night, didn't you?"

Beth nodded. "I'd gotten a call around ten. She'd gone to bed, but she wasn't there when someone checked on her. She could get around quite well without the wheelchair, of course. She used it only because I guess she thought she was supposed to. And she had had several falls, even while she was still living here at home with me. Anyway, I got another call just before I heard about the fire—and Tim. Mom was back in bed. They didn't know if she'd actually left the nursing home or had just been wandering around."

Vida nodded. "She set the house on fire, I suppose."

Beth sighed. "Yes. She must have. And the fire in the linen closet tonight. She was obsessed by fire. Her brother had been burned to death in a tank in Italy during the Second World War."

"Ah. Of course," Vida said. "She mentioned something about that when Emma and I visited her. His name was Tim. He's listed on the Alpine war memorial. I'd forgotten. Of course, I was quite young at the time."

We were silent for a couple of minutes. Beth was the first to speak again. "I suppose she'll have to be put in another, more secure facility."

"Yes," Vida agreed. "You'll have to tell Milo. Your mother certainly isn't competent to stand trial."

Beth shook her head. "No. She's not."

"You could wait until morning," I said. "It won't hurt

Wayne to spend another night in jail. It's already after eleven o'clock."

But Beth balked. "I can't let him do that. I'm calling the sheriff now. I want to do something right. I still blame myself for Tim's death."

"You mustn't," Vida asserted. "That's foolish. You had no idea what your words would lead to."

Beth didn't look convinced. Maybe she never would be. As she reached for the phone on the end table, she glanced at me. "Would you mind checking on Mom?"

"I can do it," Vida said, starting to get up.

"You've spent over an hour with her," Beth said as she started to punch in the sheriff's number. "You must be tired, too."

"I'll go," I insisted. The truth was, I didn't want to hear Beth's painful admission to the sheriff.

The bedroom door was ajar. I opened it quietly and stepped over the threshold. A night-light was plugged into an outlet near the bed. I could see Delia's small form under the covers, which moved ever so slightly with her regular breathing. I stepped closer. She was smiling in her sleep. Sitting next to her on an extra pillow was Vida's bird's nest hat. The eggs were safe.

After his release from the county jail, Wayne Eriks had vowed to sue for false arrest. Milo managed to forestall him by threatening to charge him with impeding justice. The ploy worked, and Wayne finally told the truth. He hadn't come home from work Monday night. Cookie was worried about him and called her parents. Dot and Durwood had rushed over to be with her, leaving Vida in the lurch.

Wayne explained that for most of the evening, he'd been drinking heavily at Mugs Ahoy, upset about the situation with Tiffany and Tim. The dinner at the ski lodge had not gone well between the in-laws. Wayne refused to believe Tim's insistence that Tiffany was behaving in an abusive manner. Intending to take out his drunken frustration on Tim, Wayne discovered that the house was on fire. Sobering up in a hurry, he tried to get inside, and was burned in his efforts. Realizing it was hopeless, he left in a panic. When he got home and learned that Tim had been killed, Wayne suspected his daughter. Maybe Tim had been right after all. At least, that was his rationale for his phony report about seeing Old Nick by the football field. He wanted to shield Tiffany. Wayne and Cookie Eriks had had plenty of practice doing that over the years.

On Monday, we didn't lack for news to fill the upcoming edition of the *Advocate*. The Rafferty story was a delicate matter, so I wrote it myself. There was no way to cover up Milo's error in judgment in arresting Wayne. Nor could I do much about the terrible part that Delia had played except to be compassionate and explain the ravages of Alzheimer's disease. Scott promised to do a series on early detection and ongoing research. Vida was going to write about support groups for family members and how to seek outside help.

There was other news, too, including an overturned double-wide trailer home near Deception Falls bridge, broken windows in the middle school, and a break-in at Donna Wickstrom's art gallery Sunday night or early Monday morning. As usual, I let Scott handle those items, along with other, more minor police reports that had come in during the weekend. I'd call Donna later about the break-in, but assumed she kept no cash on hand after she closed up on the weekends.

I didn't finish work until going on six. Clouds had gathered over the mountains, but the air remained heavy and oppressively warm. I'd had no word from Rolf Fisher. Still limping and very tired, I headed home to my empty log cabin. I'd left all the windows open to air the place out. No burglar in his right mind would break in anywhere during the heat of the day. I fretted that the hot weather could last into October. It had happened before. We used to call it Indian summer. Now the climate aberrations bore names such as the Pineapple Express. I called them Living in Hell.

I ate a ham and cheese sandwich and carrot sticks for dinner. It was still too hot to cook. There had been no messages on my answering machine. Around seven-thirty, I reached for the phone on the kitchen counter. I had to apologize to Rolf. I missed him. I liked him. I could even learn to love him. But love seemed to come with a high price tag these days. When love died, sometimes people did, too. Maybe that was the difference I sensed in the Eriks and the Rafferty houses. Beth still selflessly loved her mother. Wayne and Cookie had invested the wrong kind of love in their surviving daughter. Tiffany didn't know how to give it back. She knew only self-love. I wondered if she had any real love to give her baby.

Love suddenly seemed too complicated for my weary brain. My hand froze on the receiver. Maybe it was pride. Maybe it was stupidity. Maybe my emotional and physical resources had been completely sapped by the events of the last week. *My roots need to be watered,* I thought. *I'm withering like a fir in the forest.*

I wandered into the living room and sensed that something was different.

It took me a few moments to figure out what it was. Then I saw it.

On the wall where Monet's water lilies had hung was *Sky Autumn.* A small scrap of paper was taped to the frame.

I caught my breath as I limped across the room and detached the paper. There was writing on it, difficult to read, but I finally made it out.

"So you don't have to wait for autumn on the Sky. Craig."

I couldn't believe it. I stood there staring at the painting, awash in its beauty and power.

And when I finally turned around, I looked outside.

It was raining.

Read on for an exciting preview
of Mary Daheim's latest adventure
featuring the feisty Emma Lord.

THE ALPINE SCANDAL

Published by Ballantine Books
Available wherever books are sold

VIDA WAS SCOWLING at a single sheet of typewritten
paper. "This is bizarre," she declared. "There must
be some mistake."

"What?" I asked, perching on her desk.

"People get crazier by the day," she declared, handing
me the paper and the envelope in which it had arrived.
"Here. Read this for yourself. And check the postmark."

I looked at the postmark first. It was dated Saturday,
January 4, from Alpine. My eyes shifted to the typewritten sheet. There was no heading, only the date, which
was the same as the postmark. I read it aloud to let Vida
know I wasn't missing anything:

"Elmer Edward Nystrom, longtime Alpine resident,
died Monday, January sixth. Elmer, sixty-one, was born
in Williston, North Dakota, the son of Oscar and Alma
(née Engelman). He moved to Washington State in 1970
and worked as the service department manager at
Nordby Brothers General Motors dealership for the past
thirty-four years. Mr. Nystrom was a member of the Ro-
tary Club, the Kiwanis Club, the Alpine Chamber of
Commerce, the Elks Club, and Trinity Episcopal Church.
He is survived by his loving wife of thirty-six years, Eliza-

beth (Polly), and his son, Carter. Funeral arrangements are pending."

I stared at Vida. "Will we know when the funeral is by the time we go to press tomorrow?"

Vida's scowl deepened. "Emma! Didn't you pay attention to what you read?"

I looked again at the typewritten envelope with its canceled stamps and no return address. "Oh! Good God—this was mailed *before* Elmer died! It's got to be a mistake—or a joke."

"A nasty joke—and a stupid mistake," Vida said, retrieving the letter and the envelope from me. "I'm guessing that the son, Carter, wrote it and that he was rattled. From what I know of Polly, she's probably gone all to pieces. I'll call the house. Carter lives with his parents, you know."

I didn't know. But I was aware that Carter Nystrom had returned to Alpine two years earlier after having finished dental school and getting his orthodontist's degree at the University of Washington in Seattle. Our longtime dentist, Bob Starr, was glad to have a local orthodontist he could refer patients to instead of shipping them off to Monroe or even Everett. I knew all three of the Nystroms by sight but had never had any personal contact with the family. When Carter had returned to Alpine, Scott had interviewed him for a feature story. His office was in the Clemans Building on Front Street.

Vida had dialed the Nystrom number, but it was busy. "Not unexpected," she said, hanging up. "I think I'll drive over there. They live just this side of the college."

"I'll go with you," I offered. "That is, I'll follow you. I have to admit I'm curious about the obit, too, and I've scheduled an interview with May Hashimoto about a couple of new programs they want to introduce at Skykomish Community College."

Vida glanced at her watch. "What time?"

"Eleven," I replied. "It's ten-ten, so I might as well tag along."

Vida gazed at me through her big glasses. "Why?"

I grimaced. "Maybe I'm afraid Ed will come back. I'd rather not be here."

"Ed?" Leo had just hung up the phone. "What's he up to now?"

"You don't want to know," I said. "But I'll tell you when I get back. In fact, want to have lunch with me at the Venison Inn? I'll treat. I just decided it's Ad Manager Appreciation Day."

Leo grinned in his off-center manner. "Sure, why not? See you there around noon?"

"Right." I scurried into my cubbyhole to grab my jacket and purse. Vida was fastening the black galoshes that she hadn't bothered to take off. It had been raining all morning, steadily if not heavily.

Before we could make our exit, Ethel Pike limped into the newsroom. "Burl Creek Thimble Club Christmas pictures," she announced to Vida in her somewhat glum manner. "Got room?"

Vida looked as if she were trying to be patient. "Perhaps. You should have brought them last week."

"I couldn't," Ethel said. "Me and Pike were out of town for Christmas. Pike's sister invited us to Hoquiam for the holiday. I don't know why: She can't cook for sour owl's sweat, and Pike and her always get into it over some crazy thing that happened when they were knee-high to a gopher. But where else would we go, with our kids and grandkids all the way down to Orlando?"

Pike was her husband, Bickford, but he was known by his last name. Vida accepted the packet of photos. "I'll see what I can do," she said. "I noticed you were limping. Not bunions, I hope. Such a nuisance."

Ethel glared at Vida. "Not bunions. Circulation, 'specially in this damp weather."

"Ah." Vida nodded. She and I both knew that wasn't the whole story. Ethel suffered from diabetes but was too proud to let on. Even some Burl Creek Thimble Club members didn't know about her health problems.

Vida was smiling stiffly at the other woman. "If you'll excuse me, I was about to leave."

"So was I," Ethel retorted. "Pike's out and about on his errands, and I got to run him down so he can fix the electrical. The fuses all blew this morning. I won't touch electrical. Too risky. Pike don't even wear gloves when he does it."

"Very foolish," Vida murmured.

" 'Course it is," Ethel agreed. "He'll blow himself up one of these days. Serve him right, the crazy old fool." On that cheerless note, she stalked out of the newsroom.

We waited a few moments until we were sure Ethel was gone. Vida's Buick was parked two spaces down from my Honda. She carried a plaid umbrella; I simply put up the hood on my car coat. Like many Pacific Northwest natives—Vida notwithstanding—I didn't own an umbrella. They were a nuisance, especially in Alpine, where winds blew through the Skykomish River valley and down the mountainside from Tonga Ridge.

Skykomish Community College was a little over a mile from the newspaper office, nestled among tall cedar, fir, and hemlock trees. Between the college and the commercial area there were scattered homes, some old, some new, and some originally farmhouses or loggers' shacks. An occasional gnome or St. Francis sculpture stood forlorn in the rain. Several residents' idea of garden décor was an old tractor or a rusted pickup in the front yard. There were tree stumps and even a toilet that during the summer months served as a planter for perennials. But on a dark January morning, everything looked a little bleak.

Ahead of me, Vida turned into a gravel driveway. A

half-dozen mail and newspaper boxes stood slightly askew. I saw NYSTROM on one of them, a miniature red barn on top of a steel post. Pulling up behind the Buick, I studied the white one-story craftsman house set away from the road. It appeared well tended. The property probably once had been an orchard. A few bare fruit trees remained. Two of them sported large bird nests in their gnarled branches. A chain-link fence ran between the driveway and a newer, if faded blue house next door. There were fruit trees there, too. I suspected that the former orchard had been subdivided at one point.

But what struck me most as I got out of my car was the absence of activity. A death in the family—especially in Alpine, where everyone knows everybody else—usually brought visitors offering condolences along with casseroles and salads and an occasional dessert. There were no cars except Vida's and mine in the driveway or even alongside the road. The double garage's doors were closed. It almost looked as if the Nystrom house was deserted.

I said as much to Vida.

"Very odd," she agreed. "Odd, too, that I haven't heard about Elmer's passing. The Nystroms should be Lutheran with that Scandinavian surname, but they go to Trinity Episcopal."

I translated that to mean that Vida wouldn't have heard the sad news at Sunday's Presbyterian church service. But it also indicated that her grapevine somehow had withered. There'd be hell to pay for the slackers involved.

A dried huckleberry wreath hung on the front door, appropriate not just for the Christmas season but for the entire winter as well. Vida punched the doorbell. I could hear a soft chime inside. We looked at each other expectantly.

A few moments passed before the door was opened.

"Vida?" said the stout little woman I recognized as Polly Nystrom. "What a nice surprise! Come in out of the rain."

As usual, I felt like the caboose on Vida's train. But Polly collected herself as we entered a sunroom filled with bookcases. "You're the newspaper lady," she said to me. "I know you by sight." She put out a pudgy hand. "I'm happy to finally meet you. Let's go in the living room where we can be comfortable. I've just been putting the Christmas decorations away in the basement, and a cup of tea sounds good."

"Lovely," Vida said, her gray eyes swiftly appraising the tastefully appointed room with its whitewashed brick fireplace, framed French Impressionist prints, Oriental carpeting, and Duncan Phyfe–style furniture.

Vida sat down on a richly textured traditional sofa with coordinated throw pillows. I decided to join her. Polly smiled at us.

"I won't be a minute," she promised. "I'll put the kettle on."

"Polly," Vida said in a solemn voice, "before you do that, please tell us about Elmer. What happened?"

Polly looked mystified. "I'm sorry. What do you mean?"

Vida whipped off her glasses and began rubbing her eyes in a familiar gesture of frustration. "Ooooh! This is so . . . awkward!" She stopped beating up her eyeballs and sighed. "It must be a prank. I received Elmer's obituary in the mail this morning."

Polly's blue eyes grew enormous. "No!" She stared at Vida. "I don't understand."

"Neither do I," Vida admitted. "But Emma and I felt we should call on you. Obviously, an explanation is needed. If you have one."

"Oh, dear." Polly pressed her thick lips together. She was close to sixty, with short blond hair going gray, and probably had been a pretty girl, though her features had coarsened with age and weight. "I can't imagine." She twisted her hands as she stared into the carpet. "A prank. Who would do such a thing? Maybe Elmer knows. Shall I call him?"

Vida shook her head. "No, no. Don't bother him at work. He *is* at work?" she added.

"Yes, certainly," Polly replied, her composure returning. "He left at the usual time, right after he fed the chickens. We still keep chickens, you know. Would you care for some eggs? I'm watching my cholesterol and can't eat them very often, so we always have some extras."

"How nice," Vida replied. "Fresh eggs are such a treat."

"I'll put that kettle on now." Polly attempted a smile. "What a way to start the new year! Goodness, I hope it all isn't going to be so . . . strange." She bustled off through the dining room and into the kitchen.

I looked at my watch. "It's almost ten-thirty," I said to Vida. "Maybe I should leave. I don't want to be late for my appointment with May Hashimoto."

"Then let's skip the tea," Vida said, getting up. "Polly," she called out, "don't trouble yourself. Emma and I should be on our way. We both have work to do this morning."

Polly met Vida in the kitchen doorway. "Are you sure?"

"Yes," Vida asserted. "Tomorrow is our deadline. I'm just so glad this turned out to be a farce."

Polly's smile seemed genuine. "So am I! Elmer will be upset, of course. But Carter will make him laugh about it. Our son is so clever at always finding the funny side of things."

"Really." Vida sounded skeptical.

"My, yes," Polly declared, bristling ever so slightly.

"He has to be clever—and amusing—when he's dealing with teenagers who don't want braces, not even the new kind you hardly notice. They're so self-conscious at that age."

"Expensive, too," Vida said, never willing to give an inch. "Thank goodness my grandson, Roger, had his braces removed two years ago. His teeth are now perfect."

Roger's teeth. I considered them briefly. They were good, if not perfect. There were few positive things I could say about the spoiled-rotten kid, but maybe I could allow that his teeth weren't as bad as the rest of him.

"I'm going now," I said in case Vida and Polly had forgotten that I'd ever come.

Polly stepped forward. "Goodbye, Emma. It was nice to meet you."

I wasn't searching for sincerity, which was a good thing. The comment was perfunctory at best, even though Polly smiled politely.

Vida also announced her departure, wheeling around on her heel and heading toward the front door.

"Ninny," she remarked after we reached the driveway. "No wonder I've never enjoyed Polly's company. She constantly brags about Carter. So irksome."

I wouldn't have dared point out that Vida bragged a great deal about Roger, and with far less cause. Carter Nystrom was ten years older and had completed a rigorous education. Roger was still dawdling his way through community college.

Vida stopped just before reaching her Buick. "I wonder . . ." she murmured.

"What?" I said, taking the car keys out of my purse.

"Ohhh . . ." Vida made a face. "We didn't get any eggs."

"So?"

"I wanted to make an omelet for dinner tonight," Vida said. "My mouth is set for one. I'd only need three eggs. You run along. I'm going to the henhouse."

"Vida," I objected, "that's stealing."

Vida glowered at me. "Nonsense! Polly offered them to us. It'd be wrong *not* to take them. She said they'd go to waste."

"Then I'll go with you," I declared. "If Polly calls the sheriff, I want to be at your side when Milo Dodge comes to arrest you for egg burglary."

"Oh, for heaven's sake!" Vida gave me a reproachful look. "Very well. But you should take an egg or two for yourself. Do you know how to candle eggs?"

"You hold them up to a light and make sure the center is clear."

"Correct," Vida said, opening the wooden gate that led to the chicken coop behind the main house. "Or you can put them in a basin of cold water. If they sink, they're fine."

I hadn't known that, but I didn't admit it. I was too busy trying to keep to the intermittent brick path that led to the henhouse. I noticed a fishpond tucked in one corner of the garden. The lily pad–dotted pool was shaded by an apple tree in front and several azaleas and rhododendrons around the far rim. We had to pass through another gated fence before we reached our goal.

Chickens do know enough to stay out of the rain. But even though none of them were outside, their leavings were, causing an unpleasant smell and making it even more difficult to walk on the soggy ground.

The door was shut, and that made Vida frown. "Odd," she murmured. "Why does Elmer keep the henhouse closed up? Chickens should be free to roam."

"Maybe they have another way out," I suggested.

"Perhaps," Vida said, lifting the latch. "Oh, well. People don't use good sense."

There were at least a couple of dozen hens pecking around on the ground or sitting on nests. Two roosters perched on a rafter that ran the width of the henhouse. The chickens were all a handsome red-brown color. Despite being city-bred, I was able to identify them as Rhode Island Reds. The hen closest to the door seemed distressed. She was flapping her wings and moving from one foot to the other.

"Don't bother the ones sitting on their nests," Vida warned. "They may be broody, though this is not the time of year I would think they'd be hatching chicks."

"I know, I know," I said, stepping carefully toward a vacant nest on my right. A couple of the other hens clucked nervously at us. One of the roosters moved back and forth on his perch as if he might be preparing to attack. I eyed him warily. "Sometimes hens sit on their nests and sort of pretend they're hatching," I remarked. "Like women who want to have a baby but can't."

Vida was removing an egg from a nest just ahead of me. "Such a lovely light brown color. It may be nonsense, but I think the darker eggs have better flavor."

I collected two eggs and put them in a pocket inside my purse. Vida had confiscated her trio for the omelet. "I don't think Elmer collected eggs this morning."

"Let's go," I said as the rooster flapped his wings. "I think that one is at the top of the pecking order."

Vida had stopped almost at the far end of the aisle between the two sets of nests. She gasped. "Oh, dear!"

"What?" I asked, still keeping watch on the rooster.

"Elmer."

"Elmer? What about him?"

"He's here."

"What?" I was right behind Vida, trying to look around her.

"There." She moved aside a few inches. "You can see his shoes."

I saw them—black work shoes with the toes pointing straight up. The rest of Elmer was hidden under haphazard piles of golden straw.

"Holy Mother," I whispered.

"Call for help," Vida snapped, bending down. "I'll try to find his pulse. He may have had a stroke. Or a heart attack."

I rummaged in my purse for the cell phone. Of course I couldn't find it right away, and of course I broke both eggs in the process. Finally I retrieved the damned phone and was about to dial 911 when Vida spoke again.

"Tell them there's no rush." Vida paused, rubbing at her forehead. "I'm afraid that obituary was correct. I can't find a pulse or a heartbeat. Elmer's dead."